THE WORLD WEAVERS

By Kelley Grant

The World Weavers
The Obsidian Temple
Desert Rising

THE WORLD WEAVERS

A Desert Rising Novel

KELLEY GRANT

HARPER
VOYAGER
IMPULSE

An Imprint of HarperCollins Publishers

This is a work of fiction. Names, characters, places, and incidents are products of the author's imagination or are used fictitiously and are not to be construed as real. Any resemblance to actual events, locales, organizations, or persons, living or dead, is entirely coincidental.

EPub Edition APRIL 2016 ISBN: 9780062382535

Print Edition ISBN: 9780062382566

10 9 8 7 6 5 4 3 2 1

CHAPTER 1

Djinn lay in the middle of the dusty track where he'd been all morning, forcing warriors of the One and stable hands to veer around him. The great cat gazed northeast, as though expecting something or someone to arrive. Heat waves shimmered in the late morning air around the *feli* but he took no notice of the hot sun.

Sulis leaned lazily against Ashraf in the shade of a large *jetal* that housed the masters, watching Djinn's tail twitch. She anticipated the new arrivals just as impatiently as the great cat. She hoped that they had the answers to her fears, that they would carry with them the strength all of the Chosen needed to win the final battle.

Ava, sitting beside Sulis, drew patterns in the sand with a stick. She wore a blue scarf over her flaxen hair and around her neck and shoulders to protect her pale Northern skin from the brutal desert sun. Their teacher, the prophet Clay, had given them the morning off energy work. It was a rare moment of quiet time for their group.

"Why doesn't the One tell the *feli* to leave?" Ava asked Sulis. "Without the *feli*, the deities' acolytes can't channel their deities' powers, and the deities can't take over their human Voices. That would solve everything."

After the battle at the Obsidian Temple, they'd followed Clay's vision and traveled here, to the Hasifel warehouses at the edge of the deeper desert. They had arrived two days ago and were trying to settle in. It had only been two ten-days since warriors of the One had been *geased* to attack the Chosen. Seeing warriors all around the warehouses had frightened Ava into silence. Sulis was glad Ava felt comfortable enough in her and Ashraf's company that she had come outside instead of cowering in the *jetal*.

"Hey, Djinn!" Sulis called.

He glanced over his shoulder at Sulis's call.

"Come here, boy," Sulis said, holding out her hand. "Come into the shade with me. Here, boy."

Djinn gazed at her a moment, wondering if she had food, and then flopped down on his side, tail twitching in irritation when he realized she didn't. Sulis grinned at Ava.

"There's your answer," she said. "*Feli* don't listen to anyone."

"But the One is their creator," Ava said. "I thought they were companions to her."

Ashraf shook his head. "The One also created four

deities who plot to overthrow their creator. The *feli* have as much free will as they do."

Clay's voice interrupted them as he walked up to their group.

"The One promised he would not order the *feli* away from humans after he cast the deities down five hundred years ago. They protect us," he added, settling cross-legged beside them. "He would never go back on his promise."

Djinn sat up suddenly, looking north, and chirped the strange greeting call desert *feli* used. Dust rose in the distance—riders approached. Djinn rose and bounded off at a ground-eating pace. Sulis stood, admiring his speed. Her heart pounded in her chest. Sulis's twin, Kadar, was arriving, bringing with him two new Guardians to pair with the Chosen already here. Guardians Lasha and Dani were old friends of Sulis's from the Temple at Illian. Or at least, she hoped they were still friends. Sulis hadn't seen them in over a year, since the Pledging Ceremony where Luella, one of their pledge mates, had died.

Ashraf put an arm around her waist, feeling her distress through their bond. They'd been able to feel each other's moods more strongly since the Obsidian Temple attack. Sulis had fed energy to Ashraf, while he'd protected her with a shield, creating a deeper link between them.

Clay stepped up beside them. "The Weaver comes," he said, deep satisfaction in his voice.

"This will be the first time all the most important

people of the prophecy will come together," Ashraf said, his voice teasing. "You've done plenty of damage separately; I wonder what kind of havoc you will wreak as a whole."

Sulis elbowed him in the ribs and he chuckled.

Djinn raced back into town, another *feli* a black shadow close on his heels. Djinn spun and jumped on the newcomer, who was twice his size, biting the black cat's neck and attempting to wrestle it to the ground. Ava gasped as the new cat dumped Djinn to the ground and pinned him.

Sulis laughed in delight as she recognized Lasha's *feli*, Alta. Alta and Djinn used to wrestle like this when Sulis and Lasha were pledges together at the Temple at Illian. Both *feli* looked up as Ava's half-grown kitten, Nuisance, launched himself at Alta, squalling. Alta squashed the kitten under one big paw and washed his ears.

Sulis was relieved to hear Ava giggle. Ava's emotions were volatile since she had used forbidden blood energy during the attack at the Obsidian Temple. Her moods swung back and forth, and even the smallest things could unbalance her for the day. It was good to hear her laughing like a normal girl.

Sulis pulled her scarf over her nose and mouth as dust rose around the four horses and two pack mules trotting up to the main *jetal*. The riders and mounts were uniformly gray from desert riding. All wore scarves around their faces and hair. The slight form on the smaller pony must be the young Weaver, but the others were indistinguishable from one another.

They dismounted, knocking some of the dust off. Two of them wore golden robes. The third rider loosened his scarf and Sulis launched herself into his arms before he said a word. He staggered back.

She pressed her cheek briefly to her twin's. Kadar laughed as Djinn pushed his big head between them, shoving them apart so he could rub the length of his body against Kadar. Sulis searched his face, looking for some indication of his feelings. He'd lost the mother of his child over a ten-day ago, a woman of the Forsaken caste who died fighting for her people's freedom.

"I'm fine," Kadar said softly. At her skeptical look, he laughed shortly. "No, really, I am. I'm angry more than sad."

Sulis turned to the other three riders. Dani was helping the Weaver from her pony, his *feli*, Pax, beside him. Lasha smiled as she watched the twins reunite, her scarf pooling around her shoulders. Alta sat beside her, glossy black fur a contrast to Lasha's pale golden robes. Sulis felt awkward, uncertain if she should hug her old friend. She pointed to Lasha's cloak.

"When did that happen?" she asked in the Northern tongue. "I thought you'd be in healer's green."

Golden cloaks were reserved for Counselors of the One. Lasha had chosen to follow the deity Aryn in their Pledging Ceremony and had spent the past year training as a healer at an outpost of the Temple.

Lasha laughed. "That cat of Kadar's chose Dani and me," she answered in heavily accented *Sanisk*, the Southern desert language. "The little monster jumped up on a table, wanting to be petted. We reached out and wham—it felt like something had lighted me up on the inside. Suddenly I knew why Alannah wouldn't talk about what happened when she pledged directly to the One. I thought Dani was going to pass out. He barely tolerated channeling Voras and this was way bigger than a mere deity."

Lasha and Sulis grinned at each other and suddenly were hugging, Lasha pounding her on the back.

"Last I saw you, you were lying in a puddle of blood," Lasha said into her shoulder. "I didn't think I'd ever see you again."

"I'm really hard to kill," Sulis said. "Ask Voras, he's tried twice. How did you learn *Sanisk*?"

"Dani and I have been studying the past year. Aryn's healers showed me how to accelerate language learning by using healing techniques and it worked."

"You need to teach me that," Sulis said.

Sulis drew back first from the embrace, as Dani approached them, a big grin on his face.

A thin, high scream made Sulis jerk around. Ava stood behind them, pointing a trembling finger at Dani.

"You can't have me!" she cried shrilly, her face blanched white. "Get out of my head. I don't want you here."

Ava spun and ran. Master Anchee came around the corner and Ava ran into him. He scooped her up and looked questioningly at Sulis as he tried to hold her still.

"I don't know what happened," Sulis said. "She screamed and ran."

Anchee grimaced and Ashraf helped him get Ava into the *jetal*, presumably to look for the healer.

Dani stood, staring between Sulis and the door, a horrified look on his face.

"I didn't do nothing," he said in the Northern tongue. "I've never even seen her before. I'd never hurt a little girl."

"She must feel the connection between you and Voras," Sulis said, chagrined. "She was attacked by men *geased* by Voras, and you were once his soldier."

Sulis looked for Clay, hoping he could explain what to do next for Ava.

His weathered head was bent, listening to the Weaver, who was babbling incoherently. She was clutching a cream-colored housecat with orange points that Sulis assumed was Amber, the cat that irritated Kadar so much.

Kadar stepped beside Sulis.

"That's Sanuri," he said. "The one you call the Weaver."

Clay looked around at Kadar, Dani, and Lasha, his brow furrowed. "Is she ill?" he asked. "She is delirious. Should I fetch the healer?"

"This is Clay," Sulis said, introducing him to Kadar. "He's the teacher I told you about, the prophet."

"She's not sick, or not in a way that can be healed," Kadar told Clay. "She's always been like this, though she's been getting worse the past couple ten-days."

"But what is she saying?" Clay asked urgently. "She isn't speaking coherent prophecies. She isn't making any sense."

"We think she hears the deities," Lasha piped up. "But you have to really listen close because it's all a mishmash of different speakers and voices. Nothing you can understand."

Clay looked at them, hopelessness etched in the lines of his face.

"But the Weaver has to bring us all together," he whispered. "She has to make us all whole or we're doomed."

They all stared at Sanuri, who babbled softly to her cat. The cat looked around at all of them and purred.

"Why don't we get everyone inside?" Sulis's grandmother came up beside her. "This sun is hot enough to make anyone think it's the end of the world. There's cool juice, and water has been drawn so the travelers can wash the dust off. The hands will bring in your bags so you can change into lighter attire."

For once Sulis was glad to be startled by her grandmother. This was not the happy reunion Sulis had pictured in her mind. It was, in fact, a bit of a disaster.

"This way," Sulis said, wanting to seem in control as she led them to the *jetal*. She held open the curtained door.

Sulis smiled as she looked past the others filing in to see her tall, spare grandmother embracing Kadar, her white head close to his dark one.

"Ouch!" Sulis jerked her hand off the curtain as Amber reached out a claw from where she was nestled in Sanuri's arms, slashing at the dangling embroidered bracelet on Sulis's wrist. As Sulis followed everyone into the cool dimness, nursing her injury, she could hear the cat's purr.

Jonas's stomach roiled as he listened to the other Voices debate. There were only three Voices at this meeting, or Curia, but the table was crowded. The Herald of Aryn and the Templar of Voras were arguing across the table, the Herald coughing often into her hand. She was still recovering from a bout of lung sickness that had plagued her through the spring. Ivanha's Voice was absent. Ivanha had chosen a new Crone from a Northern Temple after the death of the aged Crone last month. The Mother Superior of Ivanha and an older maiden were representing Ivanha until she arrived. Parasu's Magistrate and an elderly scholar, who were serving as the Tribune for Parasu, flanked Jonas. They also served as Jonas's keepers because they deemed him too young and inexperienced to understand his deity's will.

Jonas had been shocked and horrified to feel something rummaging around in his thoughts when he awakened one morning in late winter. He'd slammed down his mental shields and called his *feli*, Pollux, to him to help fight what he'd thought was a mental attack. When he'd placed his hand on his *feli*'s head, he'd learned the invader was his own deity, Parasu. When Jonas and his pledge mates had sidestepped the traditional Pledging Ceremony and used an ancient ritual where they chose a specific deity and pledged only to that one, it was, apparently, taken as an invitation to his god to come and go as he pleased. Parasu could share Jonas's body at will, using that invitation, as long as Pollux was in the same room. When the old Tribune died, Parasu had chosen Jonas as his Voice.

"What does Parasu say about our motion to detain the Southerners?" the Herald asked, turning to Jonas and his keepers.

Jonas opened his mouth, but the Magistrate was already answering.

"Parasu believes that if the Southerners were involved in the uprising of the Forsaken, then we must reconsider their presence in Illian," he said. "The traitor Severin was killed when we hunted him down after the massacre of the children. But we captured the other conspirators, and they told us the identity of the Forsaken leader, who was killed when the Templar rescued the children. Her association with the Hasifel family raises suspicion. They should be brought in and questioned with a scholar present to record."

The Templar looked pleased as the Herald frowned. A spike of anxiety speared Jonas's stomach. *That's Sulis's family!* He wanted to cry. *Her brother Kadar, the aunt and uncle she adored. You can't arrest them!*

But Jonas had spoken those words to the Magistrate while channeling Parasu. It was Parasu's will. The Herald gave Jonas a sharp look, sensing his internal struggle.

"Is that true, Voice of Parasu?" she asked.

Jonas opened his mouth to protest, to say it wasn't his will.

"That is the will of Parasu," Parasu said, using Jonas's voice. Jonas bowed his head and looked down at his hands.

The Herald gave a heavy sigh. "I suppose Ivanha agrees with Voras, as always," she said.

"She does," the Mother Superior said.

"Then I am outnumbered," the Herald said. "I will bow to the will of the Curia. I want the transcripts from the interrogation of the Southerners on my desk as soon as you question the family. I see no reason to restrict travel for the other Southerners who were not involved with the Forsaken."

"A conspiracy exists. Arresting the Hasifels will alert other instigators. We need to lock down the city, Herald," the Templar said. Jonas looked up, surprised at the man's urgent tone.

"If we were going to lock down the city, it should have been done right after the Children's Home was attacked," the Herald protested. "Why are you insisting on this now? This is locking the gate after the cows have escaped!"

"Ivanha agrees with Voras," the Mother Superior interrupted. "Once one conspirator is arrested, the rest of the spies will flee. We need to stop them."

They looked at Jonas's side of the table. The Magistrate and scholar conferred in whispers across Jonas before addressing the table.

"We see no reason to doubt the Templar's information," the Magistrate said. "We do not feel it will harm relations with the Southern Territory to close the city for a short period while we obtain more information."

The frustration on the Herald's face matched Jonas's internal conflict.

"So be it, but I want it noted that I do not agree with these actions, and I consider detaining people of the Southern Territory a precursor to a war I will not condone." The Herald swept up her papers and left the room.

The Templar looked triumphant and walked over to speak with the Mother Superior. While they whispered, Jonas stood with the Magistrate and scholar and gathered his papers. As they left the room, Jonas turned toward the dormitories. The Magistrate put a hand on his arm to stop him. Jonas reluctantly turned.

"I know that bowing to the will of Parasu is difficult," the Magistrate said, his voice sympathetic. "You are young and cannot yet understand why we must make these decisions. As the Voice, you must trust in Parasu."

Jonas gave a short nod and turned away. He reversed direction, heading toward the Temple of the One instead, hoping to lose himself in the dark peacefulness of the domed building. He also hoped he might see Alannah, one of his pledge mates and a Counselor of the One who'd become his confidant the past few months. Talking to her refocused his thoughts. Talking to her made him feel like he was still completely human.

CHAPTER 2

Tori stared down at the faded epitaph carved into the granite grave—*Resting place of Vrishni Saria Agnew.*

Saria's name was still legible after hundreds of years. Tori's ancestors had carefully tended and recarved the letters as they faded.

Saria had been a Vrishni, a wandering prophet. She had traveled to the desert and given the Southerners the prophecy that the Chosen would weave the deities and the One into a whole once again. But Vrishni Saria had kept one final vision secret from the Southerners. She had returned to her home in the North and started a family, knowing that her bloodline was the key to completing the prophecy and keeping the deities from destroying mankind. The Descendants of the Prophet Saria created their own carefully concealed towns, trained their children to defend themselves and hid from the followers of the deities. Saria's Descendants revered her almost as a deity herself.

"All her Descendants except this one," Tori murmured, clutching a bundle of flowers in her hand. Tori's *feli*, Zara, bumped her white-and-black striped head against Tori's waist, sensing her mood. Tori knelt and placed the flowers beside the headstone.

Today was the Spring Festival of the Founding. Tori's temple, which was far north of Illian, and the Northern mountain temples like it, sent acolytes out to decorate the graves of important acolytes and Vrishni. But these flowers weren't in honor of Saria.

"I'm surprised to see you decorating her grave," a familiar male voice said from behind her. "I know you despise your role as Descendant."

"These flowers aren't for her," Tori said, glancing over her shoulder. "And I don't despise being a Descendant. I despise what it has cost my family."

Evan was dressed in travel leathers like her own and bore an uncanny resemblance to her, even though they were distant cousins. Each had thick black brows and hair, though Tori bobbed her hair and Evan pulled his long mane back with a leather cord.

"I forgot," Evan said, his stern features softening. "Your children . . . they were buried here as well?"

Tori gritted her teeth. "And my husband. You should not forget. They were murdered for the Descendants' cause. They're the reason I joined the Temple, to make myself a bridge between the Temple and the Descendants and prevent more needless deaths."

Evan tilted his head, looking at her. "Is that how you think of yourself?" he asked. "Some Descendants would say you are a heretic who recklessly risked all of us to get a *feli*."

Tori stood and dusted off her leathers. "And the Temple would say I'm a heretic for following Vrishni Saria and the prophecy. But the One believes in me and clearly the elders among the Descendants believe in me, or you would not be here answering my summons. Or did you come to tell me our people won't gather under my calling? I don't see an army behind you."

"I am the messenger. The Descendants are gathering, arming themselves. They will meet us on the road to Illian," Evan said. "Amon already travels south, answering a call of his own."

Tori grimaced. Amon had censured her translations of the Vrishni's scriptures and spoken against her decision to seek out the Temple and bond with a *feli*. She was happy he would be out of her way, but worried about the allies he might alienate in the desert.

"Are you ready to go?" Evan asked. "Your summons said you were called to immediate action. We must go meet our army. A large group of Descendants camped by the road, waiting for us, will attract dangerous attention."

Tori nodded. "I think my immediate plans will dismay you, though," she admitted. "The One calls me to become a Counselor for her as well as a Descendant. I had a vision. I must travel to the temples north of the mountains to create a bridge between the Descendants and the One."

"How so?" Evan asked, frowning.

"The One will choose Counselors from among the deities' acolytes at those temples. We will leave a few Descendants at each temple to teach the new Counselors how to shield their temple during the final battle."

"I didn't bring anyone with me to leave here," Evan said. "I thought the plan was to travel to Illian and use our shielding to support Amon's efforts from there."

Tori shook her head and brushed past Evan, walking down the stone path to the wooden backdoor of the temple. She knew the temple buzzed inside with acolytes decorating and setting up tables and chairs for the endless sermons that the townsfolk would attend later in the day. They were unaware that she was about to turn the order of this temple upside down.

"We will send some teachers back," Tori said.

Evan grabbed her arm, forcing her to stop before she could open the door. Zara snarled and he quickly released her and stepped back.

"Tori, we don't have time for these flights of fancy," he said. "Amon expects us in Illian to support him from afar when the final battle takes place."

"The reason the Descendants exist is to bring the One back to wholeness," Tori snarled. "Ignoring the One's actual needs because the Descendants have become tangled in dogma is stupidity. Close your eyes, reach out to the One, and tell me that I'm wrong. Go on."

Evan glared at her a moment, then closed his eyes.

He took a deep breath, letting it out slowly as his face and body relaxed. After a moment his brow furrowed and his eyes snapped open.

"You are not wrong," he said. "But I know we must be in Illian before the final battle, or Amon and the desert Chosen will fail."

Tori nodded and turned back to the door. "We will not let them fail," she said. She paused with her hand on the door, preparing to leave behind her life as an acolyte of Parasu. Zara leaned against her, comforting her.

Tori opened the door and stepped into her new role as a harbinger of change.

Kadar sat on a cushion in the back of an old warehouse the warriors of the One had turned into a meeting hall, and planned his escape in his head.

"All the important people are here, eh?" Ashraf said, settling in beside him. He gestured to the gathering. "Chosen on the right, warriors of the One in the center, and scholars from Kabandha on the left. The leaders of the South surround us. Are you not awed?"

Kadar snorted. "Terribly impressed. But focused on making myself small so they don't assign me any duties."

"Your friend Dani is trying to be small as well," Ashraf said, gesturing to the far wall.

"I think if he could turn invisible, he would," Kadar said sympathetically. "He traveled all this way and his Chosen screams and threatens to kill him every time they meet. Poor Dani."

"Poor Ava," Ashraf said.

"Yes, poor Ava," Kadar said, looking down at his hands. This meeting was already reminding him of the many Forsaken meetings he'd attended with Farrah. Seeing Farrah's sister, Ava, reminded him he wasn't the only person who had lost Farrah, who had loved Farrah.

"I failed her," Ashraf said softly. "Farrah, that is, not Ava. I left her when I promised to see her people's cause to the end. I loved her like a sister but I did not return to help her, and she thought I abandoned her. It is my fault she turned to the viceroy's son."

Kadar was silent, wanting to blame Ashraf. But he wasn't that unfair. Ashraf had known Farrah far longer than Kadar, had planned the Forsaken rebellion with her for years before Kadar had come along. He was hurting as well.

"Why did you leave?" Kadar asked.

"I had family business in the South, so I took it as an opportunity to scout at Kabandha, to see if the ruins were in good enough shape to begin sending Forsaken there when you came back at summer's end."

"And the warriors of the One never let you leave," Kadar said.

"Yes—the Kabandha warriors kept me there. And once Sulis arrived, it was clear I was meant to play a role in the prophecy, to be her Guardian. I could not go back after that."

Kadar glanced at Ashraf. Tears stood in the man's eyes. "Farrah chose her path. She chose someone who would bring her fast results with a disastrous price. I believe you have been given a more danger-ous and thankless task here. You have enough to worry about—don't take the blame for Farrah's fate upon yourself. The One is redirecting your energy to some-thing more worthy, not punishing you."

They were distracted by Master Anchee in the front of the room, calling the meeting to order.

"Lasha can't keep her eyes off Master Anchee," Kadar whispered to Ashraf.

Ashraf laughed softly. "It's a Guardian thing. You cannot keep away from your Chosen. Like moth to flame, we are drawn in."

"And here I thought it was because you were simple, the way you let Sulis abuse you and still follow her around."

Ashraf elbowed him in the ribs as Master Anchee introduced the Kabandha leader, Master Tull.

"We will need to coordinate between the Tigu nomads and our warriors of the One," Master Tull said. "The Tigu fighters will winnow down the army Voras sends before they come anywhere near the Ob-sidian Temple. We will be recruiting guards from the towns around this area."

Ashraf nudged Kadar again and whispered, "Your grandmother keeps looking back at you."

Kadar deliberately did not look over at her. "I know. She wants me to go with the Tigus—they need a *far-speaker* who can relay messages for them. My bags are already packed and I leave tomorrow to go to my daughter in Tsangia, or I would not have come to this meeting for fear of being volunteered."

A tattooed Tigu warrior stood up in front of the crowd, clad in an embroidered vest and loose, full trousers. He spoke rapidly in the Tigu tongue, pausing occasionally for Master Anchee to translate.

"Turo thanks Master Tull for her hospitality and for inviting him to this gathering," Anchee said, a moment after the warrior. "My people have joined together for the first time in centuries and are prepared to die for the benefit of the One who blesses us with water and health. We require supplies for our last stand: weapons, food for our warriors, and humpbacks to ride into battle. We need a *farspeaker* so we can direct our battle and know the will of this counsel. Praise to the One, the final battle is upon us!"

"Bloodthirsty, is he not?" Ashraf whispered. "The warriors of the One do not look quite as eager to die as he does."

Kadar shifted on his seat as his grandmother stood and walked to the front of the crowd.

He whispered to Ashraf. "If she volunteers me, I'm slipping out the back, getting on my horse and riding away tonight."

"I will cover for you. I can stand and start shouting the warrior's oath to confuse them."

Grandmother addressed the Tigu. "Great warrior Turo, we honor your people's sacrifice," she began.

Something climbed onto Kadar's lap and he looked down to see Amber arching her back against his chest.

He put his hands on her silky fur. Another *farspeaker* was calling for him. Kadar closed his eyes and reached with his senses, welcoming the sending of the other man.

Kadar, praise the One, Uncle Aaron sent. His voice was on the edge of Kadar's range. *I wasn't certain I would be able to reach you. Danger.*

Kadar felt his uncle's panic as the connection faded and broke.

"What is it?" Ashraf asked softly, drawn by the fear in his face.

"My uncle is trying to reach me," Kadar whispered to Ashraf. "I don't want to disrupt the meeting. Can you get Sulis? I need her energy."

The big man leapt lightly to his feet and ducked through the crowd, which was still focused on the speakers in the front of the room, to Sulis's side. Kadar closed his eyes, seeking Uncle Aaron. Sulis's hand touched his arm as she knelt beside him.

"What do you need?" she whispered.

"It's Uncle Aaron. There's an emergency. He's fading out and I need extra energy."

Sulis clasped his hand as he focused again, Djinn leaning against her. Her energy joined his. He caught the thread of his uncle's voice once again.

Sulis is boosting me, Kadar assured him. *What has happened?*

Tarik has been taken by Voras's men, Uncle Aaron sent. Sulis gasped—she could hear them speaking through their energy link. *The sales hall has been seized by Voras's soldiers. I don't know where they're holding Tarik. I was warned that Illian has been locked down. No Southerners can leave. The deities' troops are seizing entering caravans.*

Kadar gazed into Sulis's shocked eyes. *What of Simon?* he asked about his oldest cousin. *Did they take him, too?*

I don't know, Uncle Aaron said, his mindvoice worried. *I am traveling west of the city, staying out of sight of Voras's men.*

Sulis sent through him. *Why did they take Uncle Tarik? What do they want with him?*

They've taken several Southern men, ones with families in the caravan trade, supposedly to question them about their involvement in the Forsaken rebellion and the kidnappings at the Children's Home last month.

Voras is looking for trade route information, isn't he? Kadar sent. *The kidnappings gave him a reason to question Southerners without the people of Illian protesting.*

Sulis interrupted again. *Uncle Tarik would never give them information.*

Uncle Aaron's mindvoice was sad. *Voras is very powerful in the mind arts. You learned that yourself. Tarik has been trained in resisting, but his mind could be destroyed in the process.*

Kadar recoiled in horror. *What can we do?* he asked.

I'm sorry to leave it to you—but you must tell your grandmother and the elders. Someone must go tell Raella her husband has been taken. I will gather information and head to Stonycreek, where we have fighters who can help us free the Southerners from Illian. I must go now. It's not safe here.

Be careful, Uncle Aaron, Kadar sent. Sulis seconded the wish.

The sending cut off, and Sulis released his hand, her head bowed.

"I told Uncle Tarik he should come with me," Kadar whispered, guilt flooding him. "He refused. My love for Farrah brought this upon him. Our family would not have been involved in this if not for me."

"Kadar?" His grandmother's voice shook him out of his reverie.

Kadar looked up and realized the meeting had stopped and all eyes were on the twins in the back of the room. His grandmother took a step toward him, one hand out. There was fear on her face as she watched him and Sulis stand.

"Uncle Tarik has been taken prisoner by Voras," Kadar told Grandmother. She closed her eyes and her Guardian, Palou, put an arm around her. Kadar looked around the room. "Illian has been closed to trade; caravans are being seized by the Temple. Southerners are trapped in Illian. Several men were taken along with Uncle Tarik. I must go tell my aunt Raella and my cousins that Uncle Tarik is in Voras's hands."

Grandmother opened her eyes, looked into Kadar's. "I could feel Tarik was in distress, through our link, but I did not know why. I'll tell Raella that he has been captured. I want you to go with Turo as our voice with the Tigus. I need to go convince Raella's family, the Tasharas, to contribute metal and supplies for the Tigus."

Kadar shook his head as the Tigu warrior studied him with bright eyes. "No. I need to protect my family, my daughter. I've brought you your Guardians—my job is done. I leave in the morning."

Grandmother grabbed his arm in an iron grip as he turned away. "Don't be selfish, Kadar. Aaron's news means that war is at hand. We need every talented man and woman serving."

Kadar broke her hold. "War arrived months ago, while you were hiding in Kabandha. I couldn't protect my beloved from it—but I will protect my daughter, the aunt who raised me, my cousins. I'll serve while protecting them, or not at all."

Grandmother opened her mouth to retort. She was interrupted by a hoarse yell.

Kadar jerked around to see Dani on his knees, clutching his arm, which bled freely from shoulder to elbow. Ava stood over him, a bloody knife in her hand. A visible black haze shimmered between her and Dani. The crowd backed away, forming a clear space around the Loom and her Guardian.

"Ava, no!" Clay stepped forward, and Ava brandished her knife threateningly.

"He will not hurt me again," she declared. She muttered under her breath. Dani gasped and put a hand on the floor, his strength siphoned away.

Sulis stepped forward into the standing warrior pose. The dark haze flowed in her direction and Ava snarled. She raised her knife again to stab Dani, and Lasha darted in. She jerked the knife out of the younger girl's hands. The dark haze coated her hands and Lasha threw the knife away with a cry, trying to wipe the darkness off.

Ava slapped her hand on Dani's bloody wound.

"I own you now," she said. "Your will is mine. You cannot harm me again."

Dani looked up at her, bewildered. "I've never hurt you," he said. "I never would. I've a little sister like you. I'll protect you like I would her. I want to serve, like the One told me to."

Ava stared down at him, the rage on her face dimming as she really saw his face. She looked down at her bloody hands and backed away from Dani. Dani's *feli* came out of the crowd and bumped his head against Dani's side. Ava stared at the great cat and put her hands to her mouth, then realized they were coated with blood and jerked them away again, smearing blood on her face. The crowd was frozen, watching her.

Sanuri pushed her way through the crowd, humming to herself. She walked up to Ava, and grabbed her hands, turning them over to look at the blood. She shook her head, a frown on her pale face.

"No, no, no," she muttered. "Bad, bad."

She dropped Ava's left hand and reached and grasped Dani's bleeding arm. The dark haze thinned, then dissipated. He held still as Sanuri looked between him and Ava.

"Good now," Sanuri said, patting him on the back. "You come now," she told Ava, leading her by the hand. "Come, come now. We'll fix what's bad."

The crowd parted as the two girls walked out hand in hand, one fair haired and slender with bloody hands, one muttering and pale with strawberry curls.

"The fate of the world rests with those two broken girls," Palou said softly from beside Kadar. "One help us all."

"Shush," Grandmother said. "That doesn't help."

Kadar and the Chosen stepped forward to help Dani up. Master Tull stepped forward.

"Nothing more will get done today," she told the shocked crowd, shaking her head. "We will break while the Chosen regroup. And let's keep this incident to ourselves until the Chosen understand what has happened."

Kadar could see blisters forming on Lasha's hands where the black haze had touched her.

"What was that black stuff?" Lasha asked, wincing as Sulis examined her hands.

"Blood magic," Clay answered. "We think Ava learned it from Aryn, during the battle at the Obsidian Temple."

Master Anchee brushed past Kadar and pushed Sulis out of the way. He pressed his palms down onto Lasha's upturned ones. She sucked in her breath, but did not pull away.

"This is another convenient thing about the Guardian bond," Master Anchee said. "Large wounds require an expert healer, but Guardian and Chosen can keep each other alive by sending energy."

He removed his hands and the skin of Lasha's palms was healed smooth again.

"Thank you," Lasha said softly.

Kadar caught the Prophet Clay staring at him.

"You should go to your daughter," Clay said. "You will find your path at Tsangia. We will send a party of the Chosen with you. They will convince the Tashara family to contribute to the war effort."

"But what of Voras, and the war?" Kadar asked. "The Chosen don't have time to gad about the desert."

"There will be no war before the autumn winds set in," Clay said, his voice flat but loud. "Even Voras sees the folly in traveling to the heart of the Sands in the summer. He prepares, gathers information, and waits to strike. He will gather his army, and then come for us." Clay glanced over at Dani, who was looking pale and binding his wound with a bandage someone brought him. "We will send Dani with you to give Ava time to accept her bond with him."

"Did she hurt him with that magic?" Kadar asked.

Grandmother shook her head. "She did nothing other than tie the two of them more closely. She was interrupted before she could actually bind Dani's will."

"I can sense her," Dani said, shaking his head. "She feels scared, confused, angry, and guilty. How can one little girl feel so much?"

Lasha laughed and slugged him in the shoulder. "Just because your emotions center on eating and fighting, doesn't mean the rest of us are that simple."

"Very funny," Dani said. "But, why's a Northern girl like her even in the desert?"

"She was Forsaken," Sulis said. "She was the girl Kadar saved during our pledge year, after she was assaulted. We brought her to the desert to try to help, but she's gotten worse."

Dani looked horrified. "I remember that. Whiskers, no wonder she doesn't want me around. How am I supposed to protect her if she can't bear to have me beside her?"

"We have to give it time," Grandmother said. "She regretted her actions, even before the Weaver intervened. Hopefully that'll turn things around."

"Meanwhile, anyone who is leaving with me needs to start preparing," Kadar said. "I'm leaving in the morning, with or without an escort."

"I'm going," Sulis said. "I want to meet my niece."

Ashraf stepped up beside her and put an arm around her.

"I believe Anchee and I should stay," Clay said. "We can talk to Ava, get to know the Weaver a little better and start working her into our patterns."

Kadar glanced around. Lasha was staring determinedly at Master Anchee, so he assumed she would stay. Grandmother and Palou exchanged looks.

"I will go to speak with the Tasharas and take the brunt of Raella's anger when she finds out Tarik has been arrested," Grandmother said. "We don't want a big party imposing on them. Dani, Ashraf, and Palou can act as guards."

The Tigu warrior Turo stepped forward. "I will go, too," he said in heavily accented *Sanisk*. "Yes, I speak a little of your tongue," he said, at their surprised looks. "I will go to get the iron, see new places."

Kadar nodded to himself. He'd let the stables know to ready six horses besides his own and a string of mules for the supplies they'd bring back. It wasn't too large a group to travel quickly. In two and a half days he'd see his daughter again.

Jonas sat in the quiet of the Temple of the One, in the shadows at the edge of the round dome under the ledges the unpaired *feli* rested on. No visitor would see him sitting there. He knew it wasn't proper for the Voice of Parasu to meditate at a different altar. But Parasu's altar was not a peaceful place for him. He shared the private altar reserved for the Voice of Parasu with his keepers. Sitting in the One's Temple kept Parasu himself at bay, especially when Jonas left his *feli* behind, so Jonas's mind was free to think and feel and be human.

"And here you are again, brooding," came Alannah's voice. Jonas looked over at her as she settled beside him in the shadows. "What has disturbed you this time?"

Jonas weighed his words before speaking. The arrests were general knowledge, so he would not be giving away secrets of his altar if he confided in her.

"They've arrested Sulis's uncle," he said. "With Parasu's blessing. They will question him and other Southerners."

"You do not agree with this decision," Alannah said. It wasn't a question—she knew him too well. "You have doubts."

"Yes," Jonas burst out. "Yes, I have doubts." He stopped; worried that he might be overheard. Alannah gestured to the two doorways. Two large *feli* were blocking the entrances, signifying that the Counselor was in a private session.

A torrent burst from him. "I doubt my keepers are doing what's best for Illian," he said. "I doubt my deity cares for anything but worship. And I doubt that I can stay human, that I can stay myself, when he is always in my mind." Jonas looked into Alannah's sympathetic eyes. "I don't want to lose my humanity, Alannah. I feel like I'm losing me, like what makes me who I am is slipping away. How do I hold on to the things that matter most to me and still serve Parasu? Do I have to give up the things I value most? Do I lose compassion, caring, empathy, love?" Jonas stumbled over the last word as his voice cracked in distress.

"Do you remember when we were pledges and Sulis decided to cure your fear of horses by putting you on her favorite mare?" Alannah asked.

"How could I forget?" Jonas said. "It promptly jumped a fence, throwing me off into a straw pile. I had straw stuck everywhere and a huge rip in my pants. We had to tie a horse blanket around my waist so I could preserve my decency traveling back to the Temple."

They laughed together, the sound filling the room. Alannah put a hand on his arm.

"But you told me you were no longer afraid of horses, afterward," Alannah said, still smiling.

Jonas shook his head. "Strangely enough, I wasn't. The worst had happened and I survived. I'll never love the beasts, but they don't terrify me."

"That's why you need your friends and family. Turning to us is how you keep your humanity. We can help you face your fears in ways you can't by yourself. We are always there to remind you just how human you are. All you have to do is reach out," Alannah told him.

Jonas smiled. "I'll remember."

CHAPTER 3

The scrubby brush of the lowland desert opened before their delegation as they rode west on the mules Kadar had procured, heading for Tsangia.

Sulis snickered as Kadar rode up on her left side, putting her, Ashraf, and Dani neatly between him and Grandmother.

"What are you laughing at?" he asked.

"You know it won't work. She's going to have her say. Best get it over with rather than drawing it out by avoiding her," Sulis told him.

He flashed her a grin. "I like to make her work for it."

Ashraf shook his head. "You two realize most people beg your grandmother for her wisdom, don't you?"

"Well, *we've* never been known as wise," Sulis said.

"Reckless, perhaps," Kadar added.

"Wiley."

"Smart."

"Hot-tempered."

"Speak for yourself," Kadar protested. "I have a cool head."

They spoke together. "But not wise."

"And not getting any wiser," Grandmother said from behind Kadar. "I want to speak with you, grandson."

Kadar rolled his eyes at Sulis and pulled away to ride beside Grandmother. Ashraf chuckled and Sulis grinned, enjoying their old banter. The group had rode into Shpeth the day before, and stayed in Sulis's family home overnight. Aunt Janis had been cheerful for her guests, a smiling and gracious hostess. But Sulis had seen tears in her eyes when no one was looking; she was terrified for her brother-in-law Tarik and worried her husband, Aaron, was in danger trying to free his brother.

"How far do we ride today?" Ashraf asked.

"It's a half-day ride to the Tsang River," Sulis told him.

Dani frowned, looking over the scrubby brush. "I didn't know rivers flowed through the desert. Is the land around it green, like the oasis, or brown like this?"

"Green. The Tsang used to flow to the ocean, before the great battle turned all this to desert. Now it empties into a basin and seeps into marshland on each side."

"There is good iron there," Turo grunted on the other side of Dani. "Makes good axes."

Ashraf nodded. "The Tashara tribe mines iron and gemstones here. They're the most prominent family in this part of the North. Besides the Hasifels," he added quickly.

"Uncle Tarik met Aunt Raella when he went to propose that the two families combine forces and export their goods through our caravans," Sulis said.

"I don't remember seeing gems in your sales hall," Dani said to Sulis.

Ashraf chortled. "That's because the Tasharas rejected him. My father told me they wanted to keep their own caravans and not give anything to the Hasifels."

"Aunt Raella went with Uncle Tarik when he left, though," Sulis said. "She took the Hasifel name, too, which was a big scandal."

"Why?" Dani asked.

Sulis grinned. "By tradition, the couple takes the name of the more prominent family. So Aunt Raella gave the Hasifels precedence over her own family."

Ashraf nodded. "Your grandmother's status as a Chosen and priestess of the One gives the Hasifel clan higher social standing, even if they aren't as large or wealthy as the Tasharas."

"My own mother caused a scandal by taking my father's name," Sulis said. "She said it was because he was the last of his clan, but I think she wanted to tweak Grandmother."

"Your people are as bad as my own," Dani grumbled. "First circle, second circle, all that prominence stuff. Are you from Shpeth like Sulis is, Ashraf?"

Ashraf grinned. "No, I'm from Frubia, way down south."

"He's heir to a giant silk demesne there," Sulis said.

"Not anymore," Ashraf said quietly, his smile gone.

Sulis mentally kicked herself. Ashraf never mentioned his family now that he was a Guardian. She'd forgotten his sister had replaced him as heir.

"I was heir to my da's armory business before the *feli* took me for the Temple," Dani sympathized. "It was a kick in the gut to Da and me. I don't know . . . oh!"

They'd been steadily gaining elevation as they rode. The river valley came into view, and they paused at the top of the rise to take in the valley below them. The green trees, lush grasslands, and rushing river were a vivid contrast to the scrub surrounding them.

"There's the town," Sulis said, pointing. She moved her arm and pointed to a dark gash far in the distance, downriver. "And those are the mines. We'll arrive at the town by late afternoon."

Kadar barely glanced at Tsangia as they rode through the town. Dani and Ashraf gazed around in interest at the shops and corrals as they rode down the main square, but he and Sulis had often traveled here when they lived in Shpeth. It was the closest town to their childhood home, and both of their aunts had once lived by the river. Kadar was eager to ride to the outskirts where Aunt Raella's family lived. He wanted to see his daughter.

"We need to check with the River Inn if they have enough space for us," Grandmother said. "After we get settled in, we can make an appointment with the ironworkers and Raella's family."

Kadar shook his head. "I'll ride on ahead," he said. His daughter was the only reason he was here.

Grandmother conferred with Palou. "I'll go with you. Palou and the others will find spaces at the inn," she said.

"I'm going, too," Sulis said stubbornly. "Ashraf can take my pack to the inn. I'm finally going to meet my niece!"

"Fine," Grandmother snapped.

They paused, shuffling packs. Kadar kept his, hoping to room with his daughter. He would not be going with the Tigu tribes, as his grandmother had planned. He would stay here until Datura no longer needed a wet nurse. Then he had to decide if he wanted to move them to Shpeth. He'd made his contribution to the war when he brought Sanuri to the desert.

The Tasharas' merchant hall was heavily guarded. Kadar went past the actual sales hall, where the cut gems and jewelry were displayed, and on to the artisan and business side. Guards at the entrance stopped them, and a messenger was sent to Aunt Raella, announcing their presence.

"Kadar! It's good to see you. Come this way." Kadar's cousin Abram grinned at their surprise on seeing him. "Mother is in the office area. Good to see you, Grandmother Hasifel, Sulis."

He ducked as Sulis reached to ruffle his hair, and he gave Grandmother a hug.

"You're as tall as I am now," Sulis told him. "When did that happen? Are you apprenticed here?"

Abram nodded as he led them around tables of men and women sorting gemstones in various stages of being processed.

"I'm apprenticed to one of my uncles, with Kile. Yanis is here, too, acting as a runner between the buildings," Abram said. "I'm more of a salesman than a gemworker, but I can make friends anywhere."

"That's great," Kadar said. Abram had protested when his mother moved him and his brothers to Tsangia earlier in the spring. He had not wanted to abandon his childhood home in Illian.

Abram pushed open a door to reveal Aunt Raella bent over a desk in a smaller room, frowning at the tallies. It was a familiar sight to Kadar from his time with her in Illian, and he had to choke back a feeling of homesickness.

She looked up and smiled at Kadar. Her smile faltered as she took in Grandmother behind him. She respected Grandmother, but also feared her connection to the One.

"Kadar, Sulis, welcome!" Aunt Raella said. "Grandmother Hasifel, we are honored to have you here."

"I'm afraid we bear bad news," Grandmother said directly. Kadar sighed at her bluntness. He'd wanted to break the news more gently. Raella's smile faded, replaced by sick understanding.

"Tarik's been taken by Voras's soldiers," Grandmother said, and Aunt Raella sank onto a bench. "Aaron is scouting around the outskirts of Illian, staying far enough away that he doesn't get seized, trying to find out where he's been taken. We don't know if Simon is still in the city, or if he's escaped."

Abram put a hand on his mother's shoulder, his face tight with suppressed emotion. Raella's face went still, blank. She took a couple of deep breaths, then nodded.

"Then I was right to get the younger boys out," she said. "I'm glad I convinced Abram and Kile to apprentice here or they'd be in danger as well."

"If Aaron can't figure out a way to release Tarik on his own, he's going to travel to Stonycreek, the Forsaken city, gather our fighters, and find a way to free him," Grandmother said.

Aunt Raella shook her head. "That Forsaken city is the reason he's been taken," she said bitterly. Kadar's stomach churned with guilt. "Farrah used all of us, even Kadar, to get what she wanted. I don't think Aaron will get any help from the Forsaken."

"You know this is the beginning," Grandmother said. "The war is starting. We will need the Tasharas' help. We need iron, weapons for the Tigus."

Abram protested wordlessly, objecting to the timing of the request, but Raella just nodded and stood. "I'll speak to my parents, and they'll gather the elders. I manage the business operations for my parents, but they still make the major decisions."

A door at the back of the office opened, and a tall, golden-haired woman stepped through. She held an older baby girl on her hip and a small infant in a sling across her chest. Sulis choked and Kadar realized he'd never told her that her old nemesis from the Temple, Joaquil, was now Datura's *abda*. Joaquil smiled at Kadar, but he had eyes only for his baby girl.

"Datura," Kadar said.

Datura looked around at her name. "Da!" she cried, pointing at him.

Kadar was thrilled that his brilliant little girl still knew him. He reached for her.

"Da!" she said again, pointing at Grandmother. "Da!" She waved her fist in the air.

Sulis snickered at the disappointed look on Kadar's face and grabbed his daughter before he could. She spun the baby around and Datura chortled and pumped her fists. "Can you say Aunt Sulis?" she asked, holding Datura in front of her face. "Say auntie."

"Da!" Datura said, and then she belched milk down Sulis's front. Kadar howled with laughter at his sister's horror. He took Datura from her as Joaquil helped Sulis wipe milk off her shirt with a towel she had slung over her shoulder.

"I'm surprised to see you here," Sulis muttered to Joaquil in the Northern tongue as Kadar cradled his daughter, amazed by how much she'd grown in a few ten-days.

"I left the Temple after my son was born and my *feli* died," Joaquil said matter-of-factly. "Alannah placed me as Datura's wet nurse. Raella has me apprenticing with her—learning the language and helping around the office."

"And I could not have found a brighter apprentice,"

Aunt Raella said with forced cheer. "She's picking up *Sanisk* quickly and already knew her sums."

"I don't miss the backbiting of the Temple or the nastiness," Joaquil said. "Everyone here is a family. I like that my boy will be a part of this, instead of being lonely in the Children's Home."

Sulis seemed less disgruntled once Joaquil mentioned Alannah's name. "Dani is with us," she told Joaquil. "You should stop by the inn and visit him."

Kadar didn't hear her answer as Grandmother reached for Datura.

"Let me hold my first great-granddaughter," Grandmother said.

Kadar marveled as Grandmother's face softened, became younger as she gazed on Datura's face. Datura was just as awed and reached up to gently pat her wrinkled cheek.

"Where are you staying?" Aunt Raella asked.

"The River Inn," Kadar said. "But I was wondering if you'd have room here for me, by Datura."

Aunt Raella smiled. "Of course," she said. "I'll have a guest room made up. Datura spends most of the day here in the office with Joaquil and me."

Datura wriggled and Grandmother put her down. She scooted across the floor and pulled herself up using the bench. Raella laughed at Kadar's proud grin.

"Her newest trick. Won't be long before she's walking," she said. She nodded to Grandmother. "If you want to go get settled at the inn, I'll send word when the elders are ready to meet with you. Joaquil, why don't you go with Sulis and her grandmother and see where they are rooming. That way you can see your old Temple friend and know where to deliver messages to them."

"I'll see you later, little darling," Sulis cooed to Datura. She didn't try to pick her up again. She smacked Kadar on the arm. "Don't go signing any work contracts before we talk to the elders. You know it'd be a feather in their cap to get a Hasifel working for them, but we may still need you."

"Don't cause any riots in town," Kadar warned her. "And don't get poor Ashraf into trouble either."

"Oh, Mister Stodgy, no fun at all," Sulis shot over her shoulder as she shooed Grandmother out the door. Kadar turned to spend some time with his daughter, a smile on his face.

CHAPTER 4

Sulis stretched as the morning sun filtered in through the inn's window. Beside her, Ashraf just groaned and sank deeper under the covers.

Ashraf had mentioned to the innkeeper that his clan was the Nasirofs of Frubia, and their group had subsequently been given the best rooms in the inn. Ashraf had commandeered the only bedroom with a sitting room attached. When Sulis protested the cost, he laughed.

"Sulis, love, I could buy this entire inn if I wanted to," he said. "I am no longer heir, but my portion of the demesne has left me with deep pockets."

He'd also procured a bottle of the inn's finest liquor. They'd had a glorious evening. Having the privacy to release their passion made the trip worth the effort. Sulis hoped they hadn't been too noisy because Dani and Turo were sharing the room beside them.

Grandmother and Palou had opted for a room at the other end of the hallway, wanting some privacy of their own.

"Up, up. Grandmother wants a breakfast meeting," Sulis said, pulling the covers off Ashraf. He stretched and Sulis covetously admired his naked body.

"Ashraf, do you mind it much, not being heir?" she asked. "We've had so much going on, I never thought your heart might be somewhere else."

Ashraf sat up and put his breeches on. "I try not to think about it," he said, after a moment. "I felt betrayed when I got the letter from my parents letting me know my sister was heir. That hurt. I thought I would return to the demesne when this was all over. Now I try to appreciate each moment here, with you, and try not to think about the future."

"You've been comforting me, but you've been hurting as much," Sulis said, putting her arms around him. "I am such a selfish creature. When this is all over, we will create our own demesne, our own trading empire. Maybe we should start a new tradition—combine our names. We could be the Nasifels. Or the Hasirofs."

Ashraf chuckled and started to speak, but a knock interrupted them.

Palou's voice came from the other side. "You'll miss breakfast if you don't come down. We've word from the elders, and your grandmother wants everyone to gather."

Sulis sighed. "I guess we'd better get down to breakfast. Be thinking about what kind of Nasifel

Hasirof empire you want to build. The future will be ours, Ashraf."

Kadar was sitting at the end of the table, having joined them for this meeting. He was talking with Dani, and Ashraf scooted in beside him on the bench with Sulis, facing Grandmother and Palou. Turo was eating as though this would be his last meal, smacking his lips in appreciation of the fresh fruit and greens.

"The elders want to meet early evening, after the business day," Grandmother said. "At the pavilion beside the river. The Tasharas are business leaders. They need a compelling reason to give arms and supplies to the Tigus and warriors of the One."

Kadar nodded. "I think we need to focus on the caravans that were seized in Illian. I asked around yesterday. The Tasharas have a caravan in Illian now, which was probably taken by the deities' acolytes. The caravan masters could be compelled to give route specifics to the deities. The Tigus need to have better weapons to repel that threat."

Turo thumped a fist down on the table. "We already fight hard!" He grimaced and spoke rapidly in the Tigu tongue to Grandmother. She translated for the rest of them.

"The deities' army has a permanent station at the border, east of Illian, used for training. The Tigus have kept them from crossing the border into the Southern Territory for decades," Grandmother said. "It is the Tigus' mission to protect the Sands from Northerner invaders. But the deities' army has tripled in the past two years. The Tigus do not have the people to repel the army and check every caravan to see if the caravan masters are under a *geas*. The Tigus will be overrun if they do not have the humpbacks they need and are not armed properly."

Ashraf cleared his throat. "My family sent a large sum with the last caravan that came through the Sands," he said. "We should be able to buy much of the weaponry we need with that. We don't have to beg."

Grandmother frowned and tapped her fingers on the table, thinking. "That is generous, Ashraf. I will send you and Turo out before our meeting to secure as much as you can. Unfortunately, I think we'll need more weaponry than they will sell us. They keep close tabs on the iron worked in the city and feed out only as much as will keep the prices high. We need their reserves."

"Do the Tigus have anyone who can work the iron into steel if we do get the reserves?" Dani asked.

Grandmother spoke to Turo, who responded.

"He says yes, in their city. But it would be best to have as many ready-made weapons as possible. There is no time in war to make new weapons," Grandmother translated.

"I can tell quality weapons from bad," Dani offered. "Buying weapons was part of my job at home. I'd be glad to help."

"I'm not a weapons expert, but I can translate for Turo," Palou said.

"We'll go now," Ashraf said. "And report what we

were able to procure at late meal so we know going into the meeting how much more we'll need."

Grandmother nodded. "Good. Sulis and I will go over our energy forms and dances in the courtyard. Clay gave us some new patterns to think about. I want to remind the Tasharas that we Chosen wield power they do not have. Maybe that will make them more generous in their obligation to the One."

Sulis looked around for Djinn and found him and Pax sharing a giant length of sausage in the corner, much bigger than the one their table had been served. The innkeeper glowered at their table, a broom in his hand. Ashraf glanced at Sulis when she sighed.

"Let me settle up with the innkeeper," she said, gesturing to the *feli*. "It looks like Djinn found where the meats are kept. Find a butcher while you're out, would you? I don't want angry sheepherders running us out of town if the *feli* decide they want fresh meat."

"We bought out most of the weapons in town," Ashraf told Sulis later in the day. "Even the ones Dani thought were less than perfect. Your grandmother was right; it isn't enough for an army."

"She spent the afternoon showing off," Sulis said. "She lifted a huge rock, using just energy. And she made the energy visible, colorful; everyone could see it swirling around. Almost the entire town is made up of the Tashara family—so someone will have reported it to the elders. The innkeeper is regretting giving us his best rooms—no one will come to his tavern tonight with the scary priestess staying there."

Late meal sped by as they reported and devised a plan. Kadar joined them with Datura. Sulis asked what he'd done all day and he grinned.

"The Tasharas have been cosseting me," he said. "Showing me the splendid life in Tsangia. I've already had three job offers." He laughed at her dubious look, and Datura chortled with him. "Don't worry, I didn't accept any."

The group decked themselves in splendid Nasirof silks. Grandmother procured a knobby staff and led them down the main road, her white hair free and wild around her head, chin lifted. Djinn and Pax strode beside them, adding a dignified grace to their group.

They reached the river pavilion and were bowed in by a guard. Abram, looking solemn in his best robes, led them to a pavilion covered in colorful silks. A dozen men and women rose from their silken bolsters to bow and greet them each individually.

It took a long time. Even Sulis, used to the ways of a formal Southern gathering, could see that the Tasharas were not happy they'd been forced to meet with Grandmother's delegation. They were delaying to assess Grandmother and decide if they could refuse her demands without penalties. Aunt Raella was frowning and Abram looked glassy-eyed.

"Ooh, let me hold my little darling," a steely white-haired woman cooed, taking Datura from Kadar. "She's practically my own granddaughter, the way Raella has cared for her."

Sulis could see that neither Kadar nor Grandmother was happy with that statement.

"Shall we discuss our business?" Grandmother asked pleasantly. "This welcome has been gracious, but the shadows are deepening."

Sulis settled onto the cushion provided and watched the Tashara elders as Grandmother presented their case. Most were stoic, their faces showing little. Others frowned from time to time.

"It is not our fault if the caravans have been seized," a man from the metalworkers side of the family said. "We have lost much as well. If they have seized our caravan, then we cannot afford to give more."

Sulis scoffed to herself, looking around at the show of conspicuous wealth. Aunt Raella looked equally disgruntled.

"You cannot afford not to give," Grandmother said, standing to address the group. "The time has come. The Chosen have gathered. There will be war and it will spread even to Tsangia. Do you think you'll escape retribution if the deities regain their full powers? Do you think . . ."

"Yes, yes," an elderly woman interrupted, waving a dismissive hand at Grandmother. "We saw you showing off your Chosen powers in the courtyard. Very impressive." She didn't sound impressed. "But I worry the Tigus will turn against us if the deities offer them a bribe. One knows what they'd actually use the iron for—sell it or waste it, probably."

Turo leapt to his feet, yelling in the Tigu tongue. Palou stood, too, and tried to calm him. Grandmother turned away, bent to sit, and then straightened again, a hand on her chest. Abram, beside her, gasped and reached a hand toward her. As everyone else focused on Turo, Sulis watched her grandmother shrug off Abram's hand and take a couple of steps away from the group. She closed her eyes.

Grandmother shook her head and her face paled. Palou stopped translating and rushed to her, putting a hand on her arm. The room quieted as the Tasharas watched, puzzled by Palou's concern.

"You are in distress," Palou said. "What is wrong, Joisha? What has happened?"

"The link between me and my son. I felt a sharp pain, and then Tarik was gone. I need to find him," Grandmother said softly, urgently.

Grandmother looked up and over at Sulis, held out a trembling hand. She looked old, face lined and worn. "Help me," she said, her voice quavering with fear.

Sulis leapt up and joined hands with her grandmother, like they'd practiced in training, feeding her energy. Ashraf joined with her, and then Djinn boosted all of them.

For a moment Sulis was in her grandmother's mind. She saw all the energy links her grandmother had, not just to other Chosen, but also to her family and close friends. A link was missing, was a raw gaping hole, and

Grandmother searched anxiously, reaching far up to Illian. She connected with Uncle Aaron, who searched as well, anguished as he realized his brother was missing.

Kadar entered their link through his twin bond with Sulis.

Mother, Uncle Aaron sent to them through Kadar. *I tried to reach him. I tried to reach Tarik. We found Simon. The healers smuggled him out before the lockdown and he's with us now. But Tarik was in Voras's prison, being questioned. We couldn't find a way to get him out without being taken.*

He's gone, Grandmother sent, anguished. *There is a hole where he should be. His mind is gone. They destroyed him, trying to force answers from him. I should have told him to leave with Kadar. Oh, my beautiful little boy, my youngest. Dead.*

Grandmother collapsed to her knees, weeping into her hands. Sulis shuddered as the connection between them all was cut abruptly.

"Kadar," Aunt Raella said, stepped toward him. "What is it? What's happening?"

Kadar stepped forward, reaching toward Aunt Raella. "Aaron has Simon," he told her. "He's safe. But Uncle Tarik . . ." He trailed off as terrible comprehension dawned on her face. She threw her head back and howled. Abram joined her.

The elders took up the ululation. Datura screamed with them, and Kadar took his daughter, hiding his tears in her soft hair. Dani backed away from the gathering, eyes wide and horrified. Sulis went to him.

"My uncle Tarik is dead," she said softly, tears coursing down her face. "Grandmother felt him die. This is how we usher souls to the One, how we show our grief."

Sulis buried her head in Ashraf's shoulder as the cries went on into the deepening night. When they softened, Sulis looked to the weeping crowd. Aunt Raella stood in the center, her face calm. She addressed the elders.

"I am recognized as a daughter of the clan!" she stated.

They hesitated, looking at each other. Then the elderly woman who had interrupted Grandmother said firmly, "You are."

The rest of the clan took up the cry. "You are a daughter of the clan."

"I demand restitution for my husband's death."

Sulis gasped as she recognized the beginnings of the blood feud ritual. She couldn't imagine whom the Tasharas would feud with—the deities themselves? She watched as the clan responded.

"The clan stands ready to bring justice for our daughter. Who stands accused of this crime?"

"The murderers were the Northern deities," Aunt Raella declared, her voice shaking.

"We will avenge," her clan responded, but she shook her head.

"Our clan is merchants and miners, not warriors. I would not demand that we fight," Aunt Raella said. "But we will give our iron to those who do fight. We will support their war so that more of our clan does not die."

The elders looked around at each other. They bowed in acquiescence to Raella.

Aunt Raella turned to Kadar. "You brought this upon your family," she said. Sulis stepped forward to protest, but Ashraf held her back as Kadar bent his head. "You did so out of innocence, out of love. But your actions with the Forsaken brought this upon Tarik."

"Punish me as you will," Kadar said softly. "I accept my responsibility."

"You will go to the Tigus, be our eyes and ears," Aunt Raella said. "Make sure Tarik is avenged."

Kadar nodded, tears in his eyes. He held out his sobbing daughter. "Will you take my daughter as your own, until I return?" he asked. "If I do not return, will you raise her as a Tashara daughter, giving her every right?"

"Yes." Aunt Raella stepped forward, closing the gap between them. "Yes, of course."

"Ma?" Datura said, reaching for her. "Ma?"

Aunt Raella sank down, holding Datura, and wept.

"Come," Palou said from behind Sulis. "I want to get your grandmother back to the inn. We can do no more here."

Sulis tapped her brother on the shoulder, but he shook his head, indicating he would stay with Datura. Ashraf drew Sulis away and they trailed into the darkness.

"This is the beginning of the war, isn't it?" Sulis asked Ashraf. "Our first casualty. I wonder what we will be left with in the end."

Ashraf held her close. "We will protect each other. We won't leave another person alone to face the deities."

Sulis shook her head. "We can't protect everyone. Kadar will go to the Tigus; we'll follow Clay where he leads. Uncle Aaron travels through Illian. I'm scared, Ashraf."

"So am I," Ashraf said. "But we'll take care of each other."

Jonas wanted to vomit. He wanted to run away. But Parasu held him in the meeting, listened intently to the Templar's report on the death of the Southern man. The death of Sulis's uncle.

"You were supposed to have a scholar present when you questioned him," the Magistrate said, indignantly. "You know the rules, Templar."

"Your scholar didn't show," the Templar said.

"Because you gave him the wrong location!" the Magistrate protested. "Don't tell me that wasn't deliberate. A scholar would have warned you that you were pushing his mind too far. Now what will we tell the Southern Territory?"

"He was trained to resist," the Templar said, frustrated. "That proves he was important. Clearly he held secrets to have shields like that. He died before they were even broken."

The Herald coughed into her hand, looking as disgusted as Jonas felt. "And now the South has a good reason to go to war with us," she said. "To restrict trade, pull their people. We need to let the rest of the Southerners go, lift travel restrictions. If the Hasifels had anything to do with the kidnappings, they've paid for it with Tarik's life."

"There is no need to inform them. We will let them believe he is still imprisoned," the Templar said. "We cannot lift the restrictions. We've gained much from the caravan guides we brought in, but we need more. Trade routes, watering holes, ways to survive in the desert."

"You were not authorized to arrest the caravan guides," the Magistrate protested. "You were only to bring in those involved in the kidnapping. We did not give the approval for other arrests. And my people were not in on those interviews either. You have no grounds to bring in civilians, especially those from our allies to the south."

The Crone sat forward. "He did so because of news I brought from the North," she said silkily. "We felt it best to act quickly."

The new Crone had arrived from the North the day before the meeting and had cloistered herself in her altar with only the Templar attending. This Crone was much younger than the Crone who had passed, more the age of Jonas's mother than grandmother. She had a pale white face and used cosmetics to enhance her green eyes and generous mouth. She did not cover her long black hair as the last Crone had. Her voice was a low, husky croon.

"What news?" The Magistrate looked bewildered and glanced over at Jonas, asking Parasu for information. Parasu kept silent and Jonas shook his head.

"There is an uprising in the North," the Crone said. "That is why it took me longer to travel here—I had to put men on the problem. A group of anti-deity fighters who call themselves the 'Descendants of the Prophet' have risen up and are riding south, coming to overthrow the Temple system here in Illian. Voras believes they will seek the help of the other Forsaken and the Southerners."

The Herald protested. "I've never heard of this," she said. "Aryn has acolytes in the same temples as Ivanha, and Aryn has messengers all over the North. If a group of heretics had formed a resistance, we would have known about it."

"Ivanha herself did not know about them until about fifteen years ago, when she stumbled upon their secret city," the Crone said mildly. "They keep themselves apart from decent society. Ivanha has declared them Forsaken, but they are dangerous and have weapons and training. She thought she'd eradicated the enclave, but some survived."

"Eradicated?" Jonas choked out, before he could help himself.

The Crone gave him a contemptuous look. "They

are heretics, animals. I organized that first hunt, which is why Ivanha chose me as Crone. I understand the threat. These heretics will join with the Southerners."

The Herald sat forward, opened her mouth, and snapped it shut. Her expression was surprised. She glanced down at her lap, where her *feli* had placed his head. Jonas wondered if Aryn was telling her Voice through her *feli* not to speak. The only other *feli* in the room was Jonas's Pollux, who was always at his feet. Parasu stirred in the back of his mind, and Jonas began the meditation that allowed Parasu to take the lead in his own body.

The Herald took a breath. "You will send everything you know about this incursion to Aryn and Parasu," she said tightly. "The Tribune and I will go over it." She turned to the Templar. "We also want every interview you've had with the Southerners."

"I will personally come to your altar and collect them," the Magistrate said to the Templar, clearly still angry.

The Herald nodded. "We will call a Curia when we have reviewed those documents and are satisfied we know as much as you do. Do not make any more arrests and do not enact any plan that has not been approved by all four altars, or Aryn will decide you are plotting against her and take action." She turned to Jonas. "Voice, will you stay after?"

His body nodded, already in the control of Parasu. The Magistrate hesitated, and Jonas's hand lifted, waved him on. It was odd, when Parasu took over his body, like Jonas was having a vivid waking dream that was out of his control.

Hush, child, Parasu scolded as the Crone and the Templar filed out. Jonas was chagrined that his thoughts had escaped to bother Parasu and quieted them more firmly. That was one problem with Parasu sharing Jonas's body rather than taking it over. Parasu could overhear and be distracted by Jonas's thoughts.

When the door closed behind the other deities, the Herald's demeanor changed and Jonas saw Aryn staring out of her eyes.

"They are up to something," Aryn hissed. "They know something they are keeping from us!"

"I felt that as well," Parasu said.

It was a strange sensation, feeling his body move and form words without Jonas's volition.

"It has to do with the South, I know it! My spies say the Southern merchants are speaking about that ancient prophecy again. The one that says they have Chosen ones hiding something from us in the desert," Aryn said. She stood and paced.

"Yes. We must reconsider our original judgment that the prophecy was a fake . . . perhaps these Chosen really are protecting something," Parasu said. "And now we have a threat from the North as well. How is it your messengers had no knowledge of these Descendants? Have you been hiding something?"

Aryn hissed in frustration. "No. I'd think the hag was making it up, except . . ."

"The unrest in the North is evident." Parasu com-

pleted her sentence. "The One has taken our best acolytes and made them Counselors, both at the northern
Temples and at the southern outpost."

"I lost one up north," Aryn snarled. "And one in the
south."

"And I lost two in the North," Parasu said. "But
Ivanha lost one up north and Voras lost one in the
south."

"Your Magistrate was clearly shocked by everything he heard here today, so I'm guessing you know
no more than I do."

Parasu grimaced. "It is concerning. It is possible
that the new Counselors are due to the machinations
of these Descendants, but I believe the One is in fact
responding to whatever the Crone and the Templar
are up to."

"And what is that?" Aryn cried in frustration. "What
have they found that they would risk the wrath of the
One? It will change the balance between the deities, if
we don't find out. I feel this, Parasu. We must figure
out what they are up to."

"And do what? Stop them?" Parasu asked.

"Force them to include us. If they've found a way
to wrest control away from the One, to gain more
power—I want that power. I will not be left out, forced
to serve Ivanha and Voras. I want my due."

Parasu nodded. "I agree. We will review the documents they give us. We will also send our spies in the
household staff to find the information they are hiding
from us."

"Yes," Aryn hissed, sitting down at the table again. "Good. I will have my Herald meet with your group for the review. Your Tribune and my Herald will meet and we will speak again when we hear from our spies."

The Herald slumped to the table, her deity gone. Parasu disappeared from Jonas's mind, and he took a moment to take full control of his body again. He walked around the table to help the Herald sit up, and he gave her water.

"That's a good lad," the Herald said, as he helped her to the door. Her own people were waiting and took over the support of her. Jonas followed them into the corridor. He glanced around for the Magistrate, and not seeing him, ducked into the Temple of the One.

Alannah wasn't in the temple, but Counselor Elida was, speaking with a green-cloaked Vrishni. She beckoned with one hand before he could duck into the shadows, indicating she wanted to speak with him. He waited while the Counselor finished speaking to the Vrishni, and then approached the altar.

"Alannah is gone," the Counselor told him. She handed him a folded and sealed paper. "She has ridden south. She wrote you a letter before she left."

Jonas tried to swallow his disappointment. "When will she return?" he asked.

Counselor Elida hesitated, and then shook her head. "I don't know. A man came asking for help down south. It could be a long time before she returns."

"Is this about the Counselors the One selected at the Southern waystation?" Jonas asked.

The Counselor's hesitation and shifting eyes told him she was about to lie. "Yes," she said. "She has gone down to guide the new Counselors."

"I see," Jonas said, trying to puzzle things out. "Thank you. I will miss her company while she is gone."

The Counselor smiled and nodded, and Jonas turned away, heading to his own altar, his mind racing.

What was going on? he wondered. *The Templar was murdering Southerners, the Crone was murdering Northerners, and the One was stealing acolytes from all the altars.* He bowed to parishioners at Parasu's altar before going into his office. *And now Alannah, his only confidant, had gone south in the middle of all the intrigue. And Counselor Elida was lying about why Alannah had left.*

The Magistrate opened the office door, and Jonas slipped his letter underneath the stack of papers and put on a pleasant face. "Parasu and Aryn gave us much to do when they spoke," Jonas told him, putting his thoughts aside. "I will need your help. Let us begin."

CHAPTER 5

The sun had not yet risen when Kadar packed the last of the supplies onto the humpback he was loading and ordered it to rise. He nodded to the humpback tender, who led the beast to the string of loaded humpbacks heading into the Sands with Turo and Kadar.

"I wish they'd let me go with you," Abram said. He handed Kadar a sack of supplies to fasten to his humpback. "I want to fight Voras's men."

Abram had ridden back with them to train with the warriors of the One, ignoring his mother's protests.

"You're trained as a merchant, Abram, not a fighter," Kadar said harshly, irritated his cousin had choices he did not. Abram looked hurt, and he softened his tone. "As am I. The fight will come here, and sooner than we wish. But by the time it does, you'll be trained and ready."

They'd ridden back to the Hasifel family warehouses in only two days, pushing the mules and riding into the night. Kadar had kissed his daughter goodbye once again, leaving her in the safety of the river town. He'd avoided his Aunt Raella the last day in Tsangia. It hadn't been difficult with so many of the Tashara clan bustling around, loading mules up with supplies and iron ingots. She'd been more focused on Abram's mutiny than on Kadar.

Turo joined Kadar and Abram in the courtyard, gazing in satisfaction at the humpback train. The Hasifels were giving the Tigus a thousand humpbacks and the beasts were being strung together by ropes in their nose rings in groups of forty. Each of those groups would have a tender walking alongside.

"My people will meet us in the Sands," Turo said, clapping his hands together.

Kadar nodded. The Tigus would take the humpbacks and supplies, letting the tenders return to assist the warriors of the One. Kadar and Turo would distribute the supplies and beasts to Tigu tribes along the main caravan routes. Kadar would join the tribes in the east, along the boundary between the Northern and Southern Territories, scouting out Voras's troops and reporting to Sulis, who would relay his findings to the warriors of the One and the Chosen.

The sun was breaking over the dunes when they'd secured everything and were ready to leave.

"Be careful, brother of mine," Sulis said from behind Kadar as he did a final check on the lead line of his group of humpbacks.

Kadar turned and Sulis embraced him.

"I am so sorry," she whispered in his ear. "I wish you could have been spared."

Kadar hugged her. "You be careful as well," he told her. He looked over at Ashraf standing back from the farewells.

"Protect her," Kadar said. "Keep her from doing anything stupid, would you?"

"I will try," Ashraf promised.

Sulis pushed away. "I can protect myself. Who's going to protect you?" she asked.

"A thousand Tigu warriors?" Kadar guessed. "At least that's what Turo has told me. Apparently *farspeakers* are valued among the Tigus and don't fight. I have no idea how I'm going to communicate with these people. I've never studied a word of their language."

Sulis looked past Kadar and frowned, and he turned. Sanuri was attaching a large bag to the front of his humpback, which still knelt, waiting for Kadar to mount.

Sanuri turned her vague eyes on him. "You will need this," she said. "I was given it, but it is for you."

She wandered to the house and Kadar looked at Sulis.

"Cook must have given her more supplies," Sulis said with a shrug. "Sanuri was in the kitchens before I came out here."

Kadar nodded and mounted, ordering his humpback to rise. Turo joined him, leading his own string. As Kadar and Turo led the procession, Grandmother and the leaders of Kabandha met them at the front gate.

Grandmother put a hand on Kadar's foot in the stirrup.

"Go with the One, Kadar," she blessed him. "All our hopes go with you."

Kadar touched the back of his hand to his forehead in salute, and Turo did the same. They were saluted back. Sulis blew him a kiss, and they rode out into the scrubby desert, heading for the Sands.

They reached the Sands before Kadar's stomach rumbled for midmeal. The deep dunes swallowed them and it was not more than a sandglass before Tigu warriors rose out of the sand on each side of them. Turo stood in his stirrups and shouted at the cloaked figures who gathered around him and Kadar.

"Calim!" Turo said. He leapt from the saddle as another man dismounted. They embraced and slapped each other's backs. The humpback tenders were frightened as the nomads surrounded their caravan. Kadar signaled them to sit in the sand.

Turo conversed with the leader in the Tigu tongue. Calim frowned and pointed at Kadar, growling something. Turo shook his head, saying something insistent. The warrior shook his head again.

Kadar was distracted from the argument by Sanuri's bag, still attached to the saddle in front of him. It twitched as though it were coming alive.

"Muurrrp?" the bag said insistently, and Kadar sighed in frustration. It figured. He unfastened the ties, only now realizing the bag had air holes in it. An orange-tipped head popped out and looked around.

Kadar opened the bag wide and Amber burst out of the bag and leapt onto Kadar's shoulder. She gave a long, loud Frubian Flamepoint battle howl.

The Tigu warriors turned to stare at Kadar and his odd companion. Amber howled again, right in Kadar's ear, and the warriors flinched and whispered among each other.

"*Suma!*" Kadar heard over and over. Even Turo gazed wide-eyed at Kadar. He hurried over to Kadar.

"You're a *Suma*?" he asked.

Kadar shook his head. "I don't know what that means," he said.

Turo fumbled for words. "You have a suncat and can talk with the One, talk to hooved beasts?" he asked.

Kadar supposed that was one way of putting it. "The cat chose me," he said. "The One speaks through it. I can make hooved beasts do what I want."

By way of explanation, Kadar held out a hand and silently called over Calim's humpback. It wuffled his hand, then spit at Turo.

The rest of the Tigus stared at their leader.

Calim raised his spear. "*Suma!*" he shouted.

"*Suma!*" the tribe shouted, rattling their weapons.

Turo rubbed his hands together. "That is good. I did not know you were a *Suma*. That will make the other Tigus happy. This tribe wants us to overnight at their camp."

Kadar sighed in confusion as Amber settled into her

bag, purring. He needed to learn some of the language or it was going to be a long journey.

They headed east; off any trade route Kadar could see.

"How do you know where to go?" he asked Turo, seeing only unmarked undulating dunes into the distance.

Turo tapped his head, and then his heart. "We know in here. We feel the water."

Kadar closed his eyes, letting his humpback follow the others, and tried to reach out with his senses. He could sense other *farspeakers*, but not in this area. He wondered if the Tigus were sensing underground water, or knew a general direction to go in. They reached a decent-sized oasis around late meal. Calim's tribe of Tigus had large tents set around the water, and even tent-like shelters for the animals. Kadar was surprised to see horses this far into the Sands. They were staked directly next to their owners' tents, and in some cases in the owner's tent.

The Tigu men and women came out of the tents to stare at their procession of humpbacks.

"*Suma!*" the leader shouted, pointing to Kadar.

The crowd stared at Kadar, and erupted in shouting.

"*Suma!*" they cried, and gathered around his humpback, patting his boot and legs. Amber uncurled herself and leapt onto the ground as the humpback knelt and Kadar was ushered off and to a pillow by a large cook pot hung over a dung fire by the edge of the camp.

Calim, Turo, and the rest of the warriors settled in around the fire as well. Once the pale desert scarves, called shemaghs, that covered their hair, lower faces, and necks were removed, Kadar could see that their party was evenly men and women. A man of the camp served Kadar and the rest of the party on beaten tin plates. There were no children anywhere around the oasis.

The conversation between the Tigus seemed casual, and Kadar let the unknown language wash over him as he studied the horses the Tigus had tethered around the camp. They were a more refined version of his uncle Aaron's racing horses. They had wedge-shaped heads, broad foreheads, large eyes, large nostrils, and small muzzles. They were smaller than horses in Illian, built for endurance in the desert. He itched to ride one.

Turo noticed his interest and nudged him in the ribs. "You like the desert horses?"

Kadar nodded. "Yes, very much. They're beautiful."

"If you steal a horse, you will die," Turo said seriously. "Horses are important in this tribe, treated like babies by their owners."

Calim asked something, and Turo answered. Calim gestured and spoke rapidly. Turo's eyebrows climbed into his forehead. The crowd rose, and Kadar scrambled to rise with them.

"Follow Calim," Turo said excitedly. "He has a sun horse for *Suma!*"

Calim put a hand on Kadar's back and led him past the tents, to the far side of the oasis. There was a horse tethered in the shade between two palm trees.

The mare snorted nervously and pranced as they

approached. Kadar could see why she was called a sun horse—she was a palomino, her chestnut coat so pale she looked gold, with a flaxen mane and tale. She stomped her foreleg warningly and dug into the sand.

"She's beautiful," Kadar breathed. "Where is her owner?"

"Dead," Turo said cheerfully. "She threw him and stomped him to death."

Kadar looked sharply at the man, but he wasn't joking. Another Tigu came up and dumped a bridle and saddle at his feet. Kadar glanced behind and found the entire camp watching the scene. Calim gestured toward the mare. So this was a test to prove he really was a *Suma*. By the grins and nudges between the warriors in the crowd, it was a test the Tigus probably thought he'd fail. The mare was barely broken and dangerous. Kadar grinned. This was going to be fun. The gorgeous mare would be his.

Kadar moved toward the oasis beside the mare, not looking directly at her. All of his senses were extended, and he spoke nonsense in a soothing tone. She held her ground, and he knelt at the oasis a few feet from her. She stomped her hoof and he dipped his hands into the water and drank, ignoring her. He splashed water on his face as he focused his energy, sent soothing waves to the mare. He heard her wuffle in curiosity and he repeated the sound to her. They held a short conversation of snorts, until she approached him.

"Rowl." Amber startled Kadar, rubbing against him. The mare went still, and then snorted at the cat, who rubbed up against her, purring. Kadar slowly turned toward the mare and offered her his hand, letting his beast magic tickle her nose, tame her heart. She snuffled his offered hand, then snorted into his hair, lipping at it.

Kadar slowly rose and went to her side, rubbing behind her ears, down her neck, ruffling the pale mane. He pressed her back and gently put weight on it, making certain she was saddle broken. She gazed curiously at him, then lipped at the cat's tail. Kadar grasped her mane and flung himself up on her bare back.

She froze for a second, and Kadar held his hands on her neck, focusing his gift on calming her, making her accept him. She relaxed and Kadar nodded to Turo. Turo unfastened her tether, jumping away as she snapped her teeth at him. Kadar kneed her away from the crowd. She responded willingly, as he let her know with his legs and hands where he wanted her to go, nudging her mind with his talent so they understood each other. He let her walk, then canter into the desert. Keeping an eye on the tents, he allowed her to gallop, circling the camp and oasis.

They raced back to the crowd of people and slid to a halt. Kadar dismounted and took the mare by her halter; fastening the lead line Turo gave him.

"She moves like flowing water," he told the crowd. Turo translated.

He grinned as the Tigus went wild.

"*Suma!*" they shouted. Kadar had to calm the startled mare.

"Good riding!" Turo said, slapping him on the back. "Her name is Asfar. The horse and tent are yours now."

Kadar grinned at him. Maybe it wouldn't be as hard as he thought to fit in. His abilities with hooved animals had been appreciated in the caravan—but were always overshadowed by his twin's more revered abilities with the *feli*.

"Time to sleep. We rise early morning," Turo told him. "We will deliver the goods to Antajale."

"Antajale?" Kadar asked.

"Our city. *Antajale* means deep water. Few from the clans ever see its beauty."

Kadar tethered his mare, and then went to his new tent to unroll his mat. His head barely hit the pillow before he was asleep.

They were up again before dawn. They left many of the humpbacks, weapons, and supplies with Calim and his tribe. Calim would bring them the rest of the way south, to the other tribes.

The bulk of the beasts, most of the supplies, and all of the iron went with Kadar and Turo.

"We go east. Antajale is by the mountains," Turo said.

Kadar nodded. A group of Tigus rode with them. He tethered Asfar behind his humpback. He wasn't certain how far the next oasis was, and though they'd filled bags with water—he didn't want to put any more strain on the horse than necessary. She snapped and kicked at anyone who walked near her, calming only for Kadar and Amber.

The heat was oppressive, this close to summer. The Tigu riders seemed immune to it, not even wet with sweat when they stopped and ate and he watered Asfar. They camped under the stars that night. Kadar was bemused as his companions introduced him to an evening ceremony for the One, which involved bowing to the four directions and burning some sort of incense. Kadar had always muttered blessings to the One before bedtime and had watched his grandmother do her moving meditations in the mornings and evenings, but this was the first he'd seen of the Tigus' expression of worship. They put him in the center of the group as they made their prostrations, and he'd followed along the best he could, though he did not understand a word they said.

Late the next day, deep into unfamiliar territory for Kadar, they topped a rise of dunes. On the other side, blending in with the sand, were walls, opening into a city. The ridges of black mountains rose in sheer cliffs behind the city. Kadar's jaw dropped. Turo had said they were going to a city, but Kadar had pictured a small oasis town like Shpeth. This city was smaller than Illian, but still full of long low mud-brick houses and people. Guards at the gate shouted, and they stopped on a cobblestoned street and dismounted. Turo spoke with the guards as Kadar looked around in wonder. He did not see a river or even a large body of water—but somehow this place existed in the middle of what he'd thought was desolation.

"Kadar," Turo called to him, and Kadar stopped

staring, grabbed his saddlebags from the humpback, and settled Amber on his shoulder. Turo had been joined by a group of Tigus and was directing these Tigus to take the humpback strings. Kadar untethered Asfar and let them lead his string away, around the edge of the wall.

Turo was speaking with a younger woman whose dark features bore a resemblance to him. She had brown eyes, and her scarf was thrown back to show short, black hair. She turned her eyes on Kadar, assessing him.

"My daughter, Onyeka," Turo said proudly. "She will help you."

Kadar smothered a sigh, wondering how he would communicate with this new person, and smiled at her. Turo said something to her, she replied sharply, and then Turo headed after the humpbacks, leaving Kadar and the strange woman alone.

"Very nice to meet you," he said slowly and loudly.

She grinned. "You won't think so in a few days," she said in slightly accented *Sanisk*. "We've got a long ride ahead of us. I was expected back at camp three days ago. What took you so long? Where did you get a suncat?"

Kadar stared in astonishment. "We had to ride west to convince the Tasharas to give up their iron," he told her. "The cat became attached to me in Illian."

She clucked her tongue and reached out to pet Amber. "You came back with Tashara iron? The One must have pulled a miracle to pry iron out of their clenching hands."

Kadar sobered at the reminder. "My uncle paid for it with his death," he told her.

"Then we will honor him by waging glorious battle against the Northerners," Onyeka said briskly. "Come, let's get you and your horse settled and go through the lists to see what you brought and how to divide the supplies. I'm anxious to get to the Northern border and my tribe."

Onyeka grabbed one of his bags as he grabbed the other and they set off down a narrow lane between the houses. Kadar gawked as they walked through the streets. They were walking beside a very long, low house. A low wall connected it to other houses, and he could see a courtyard with a well in the center creating a compound of homes. Children were everywhere, playing in the streets and around the greenery surrounding the well.

"How is this possible?" he asked his companion. "Where do you get the water to support everyone?"

Onyeka smiled. "The One guided us to where the water was buried. It is water from before the Sundering, before the desert, before people even existed. It is *antajale*—deep pure water. We were able to dig down to bring it up to the surface. When it is gone, we will have to move to a new source of ancient water."

"Do you have to move often?" Kadar asked, picturing trying to move an entire city.

She shook her head. "No. Only once so far, a century ago. The reservoir under us is deep and pure here."

"This is the first I've seen children since I left Tsangia," Kadar said, watching two girls run past.

"Yes, we come here to have our children, where they will be safe and cared for by our elders while we fight," Onyeka said. "Each tribe has its own house here."

Kadar nodded as they came to another low-walled stone courtyard. A young boy met them and tried to take Asfar's reins. She snapped her teeth at him, barely missing his hand, and he backed away. Kadar put a hand on her neck and focused, letting her know it was safe to go with the boy. She stamped a hoof once and let the boy lead her off.

He turned to Onyeka, who was watching the scene and drinking from a thick pottery cup. A young girl presented Kadar with a second cup.

"She's a beautiful mare, though a bit wild. You seem to have a way with horses," Onyeka said.

"Yes," Kadar said. He said rather proudly, "Calim's tribe named me *Suma*."

Onyeka snorted into her water cup and choked.

"Oh dear," she gasped as she contained her coughing. "Do you know what that means?"

Kadar shook his head, confused by her reaction.

"Well, you'll find out in time," she said cryptically, but would not elaborate when he pressed her further. They walked into the coolness of the adobe building.

"This is the Sepacu tribalhouse. Let's get some food from the kitchen, then we can go over the lists and see the riches you have brought us, so I can translate the report to the elders who will divide it up."

Kadar nodded, and they settled at a long table. Amber leapt down from his shoulder and trotted off to investigate the kitchen. Kadar retrieved the supply lists from his pack and spread them on the table, pointing out what they'd given Calim's tribe, and what they'd brought to the city.

"I'm impressed you can read and write *Sanisk* as well as speak it," he said. "Do you speak the Northern tongue as well?"

She smiled. "I did not think you recognized me," she said. "I am too much older than you. You and your sister were still running wild while I was studying with your grandmother. You were just beginning to become civilized and notice the people around you when I left. I did not stay long enough to grasp more than a little of the Northern language."

Kadar thought back to his childhood, and remembered a shy, thin, dark-eyed girl, five years older than him, who'd spent most of her time cloistered with his grandmother, and the rest of the time practicing with the swordsmen. She was one of a series of girls from the tribes who were sent to Grandmother for extra training and finishing.

"You seldom had time for us children," he said. "And you could fight as well as any man in Shpeth. You left right after my mother died."

"You do remember," Onyeka said, delighted. "I came here to have my child. I was so impatient to be a warrior! I did not appreciate my time with your grandmother."

Kadar stuttered with surprise, "I had not heard, I mean, I did not realize you were sent away." He supposed his grandmother had hushed up that a Tigu girl under her became pregnant. He hadn't heard about the scandal. "Are you married then?"

Onyeka sputtered with laughter at his discomfort. "We do not marry, Kadar. It takes away from our commitment to the One. I was not sent away, I sent myself away. Tigu warriors cannot fight until they produce an heir because too many of us are killed in battle. I got pregnant to escape all the studying and tedium. Your grandmother was exasperated, but knew it was only a matter of time. I am a warrior, not a scholar, no matter what my father and the elders wanted of me."

"The father?" Kadar asked.

"A man I respected. A smart man who was brave and strong," Onyeka said, turning to the lists. "He gave me a good, strong son. He trains in a warrior camp, outside these walls."

Kadar wanted to ask if the man knew about his son, but he'd already asked too much. "I have a daughter," he offered. "Not quite a year old. I left her with her great-aunt, in Tsangia."

"That is good," Onyeka said, nodding as she made a note. "She will be safe by the great river, as safe as any of us as the second great war approaches. Where we travel to is no place for children."

Kadar did not want to cling too closely to Onyeka as she met the elders and did the night chores, but it was nice having someone speak his language. He played with the children in the courtyard, a game of tag that needed no words, until dusk. As the sun set, the courtyard filled with people facing the setting sun. Most of the people around Kadar were either very old or very young.

They bowed deeply to the west, and Kadar let the words wash over him. He could hear the same ceremony taking place in other courtyards around him.

"We bless the sunshine, giver of life and death, and thank our beloved, the One, for this gift." Onyeka whispered the translation in his ear. Kadar twitched. She'd silently crept up beside him.

They faced east.

"We bless the cool of the night, the glow of the moon which gives us the water and rain, and thank our beloved, the One, for this gift," Onyeka translated.

They bowed to the north.

"We bless the people of the north and know that the same light within our hearts glows within theirs, and thank our beloved, the One, for this gift."

They bowed to the south.

"We bless the life within ourselves and renew our vow to protect our people. We thank our beloved, the One, for the gift of life."

An elder at the center of the courtyard burned a pungent mixture, the smoke rising above the walls.

"What is that?" Kadar asked Onyeka.

"A bit of meat, herbs that are pleasing to the One, and incense spices," she answered. "You should turn in, now. We have had a messenger from the Northern border—the deities are moving their armies closer. All warriors must return immediately. We leave early; our mounts will ride light so we can make haste. Supplies will be sent to us as they are organized."

Kadar nodded. As much as he wanted to explore this strange city, he knew his duty lay to the north. He settled on his cot with a sigh, and smiled as Amber curled in a ball next to him.

He thought about checking in with Sulis before he fell asleep and decided against it. Although his world was changing quickly, he had nothing new to report.

CHAPTER 6

Tori looked down at the sea town of Caracas with dis-taste. It smelled like fish, even from this hill. She wrin-kled her nose at Evan, and glanced at the group behind her. Only about a hundred and fifty Descendants were riding with them, but more were gathering and train-ing in their small groups so as not to attract too much attention from acolytes of the deities.

"I don't see why this is necessary," Evan said. "Your duty is to the Descendants, yet we've stopped at four temples already in the North. We should be traveling to Illian. Why waste our time?"

Tori smiled as she thought of the disarray she trailed behind her. Over half of the acolytes at the small temples she'd stopped at had been transformed into Counselors. Luckily, each of the temples had a *far-speaker* among their ranks, so Counselor Elida could speak with the new Counselors directly and Tori did not need to linger and give them directions. She wasn't certain why the One was directing her to transform acolytes into Counselors, but she was enjoying the chaos it spread.

"I believe this is our last temple. The One has given me both tasks, and I will not fail her. Besides, we don't want to advance on Illian before Voras's troops head into the desert," she told Evan. "We may be stronger energy workers, but we cannot hold against an army. This temple contains the twins from my pledge group, Sandy and Shane. Alannah expects them to return to Illian with me."

"The larger group will stay in the wooded areas surrounding the town while you go to the temple," Evan said. "Do you want an escort?"

Tori shook her head, glancing at her *feli*, Zara, who was yawning at her horse's side. "I'll be fine. I'll return with the twins as soon as I can."

A voice from the side of the road startled both of them.

"But what if the twins don't want to come with you?" Sandy melted out of his surroundings in his green robe of Aryn as Evan drew his sword. "What if we're sick of being pushed around by the One like pawns and want to run off to the ocean and travel the far seas?"

"Put that down," Tori told Evan. "This is one of the men we were sent to find." She addressed Sandy. "Seems a little late for that now. You're as stuck as I am, *feli*-chosen and all. Where's your other half?"

"Right here," Shane said from behind Sandy. His cloak was still the blue of a Parasu acolyte.

"Where were you hiding?" Tori asked. "And how did you know I was coming?"

Sandy grinned and walked up to Tori. He ruffled Zara's striped neck and scratched under her chin until she leaned against him, her eyes half-glazed. "We've run wild in these parts since we could walk," he told Tori. "This was the most likely place you'd stop and regroup so we thought we'd meet you here and play escort."

"I saw in a vision you would be here today," Shane said quietly. "My connection to the One grows."

Sandy sighed. "I should have realized that with a mother who was a Vrishni, one of us would start having visions. Just glad it isn't me."

"I'll be glad of the escort," Tori told them. "Evan, find a place to camp. I don't know how long this will take. C'mon, boys, let's go shake up the temple."

Sulis watched Ava skirt around Dani, trying to pretend he wasn't beside the practice area. Ava was using her energy to draw patterns in the sand, creating a mandala for Clay. He'd asked Dani to attend as they focused on the task, but Dani flinched anytime Ava glared at him, and Ava kept smudging the design.

They were practicing behind the main buildings, working in an area of sand the Chosen had raked, cleared of thorn plants, and scattered with herbs to keep the scorpions out.

Sulis shook her head. If Ava didn't smudge the design trying to avoid Dani, Sanuri smudged it as she wandered around the ground they'd raked to practice in, muttering to herself. Ava giggled every time Sanuri stepped on a line, and Sanuri laughed back—the two had some sort of private connection and world they were sharing. It was baffling the way they had bonded without a word of sense between them.

They especially baffled Clay, who was desperate to draw the group together. Sulis worried that he was going to start tearing out clumps of hair, the way he clutched it when Sanuri did something particularly inexplicable. Like now, as she plunked her butt down right in the center of the mandala Ava was creating and sang tunelessly. Ava giggled and drew new patterns around the girl.

"No," Clay corrected. "That isn't the pattern for this mandala."

Ava shrugged. "I can't do it with her sitting in the center, so I have to create new patterns," she said. Clay clutched his hair and breathed deeply.

"This isn't going to work," Sulis told Ashraf. "I thought it was bad before, trying to tame a deity by dancing. But now we've added an insane Weaver, a newly unhinged Loom, and a frightened Guardian. How do we work with that?"

"You don't," a strange male voice said from behind them.

Sulis whirled with a gasp, hands up to send an energy blast, and Ashraf drew his curved sword and pushed Sulis behind him. Dani stepped to Sulis's other side, straight sword drawn.

A man with the pale skin of a Northerner stood at the edge of their clearing, looking amused. Sulis was astonished to see Alannah standing few paces behind him in her golden robes, arms crossed over her chest, looking irritated and rumpled.

"Who are you?" Clay asked. "How did you come here without being seen and challenged by our warriors of the One?"

As though a spell had been broken, a shout went up at the front of the building.

"Looks like they discovered our horses," the man drawled, looking at Alannah. She frowned at him as warriors of the One ran around the building, following their footsteps. Grandmother, Master Anchee, Palou, and Lasha followed the warriors as the man was surrounded. He held his hands out in a gesture of surrender.

"I am Amon, a Descendant of the Prophet!" he declared, unfortunately in the Northern tongue, so none of the warriors of the One understood him. "The Descendants have risen and the second Great War has begun."

Silence followed this announcement as the warriors of the One looked at the Chosen for translation and the Chosen looked at one another.

"Are we supposed to be impressed?" Sulis said into the silence.

Alannah snorted and Lasha hid a grin behind her hand. The man looked nonplussed.

"I mean, it was good delivery," Sulis continued. "Dramatic. But most of these people don't understand your language. And those of us who do, well, we're already Chosen by the One and have a prophecy of our own. We don't really need a new one."

Ashraf snickered, and Amon sighed and shook his head.

"It looks like you are as uninformed as we feared," he said arrogantly. "Come, we will go inside and I will relieve you of your ignorance." He turned and walked through the crowd, which parted before him. The Chosen stared at one another, and then Master Anchee shrugged and followed, cuing the others to do the same. Sulis came up to Alannah and embraced her.

"Arrogant little rooster, isn't he?" Sulis said. "But it's great to see you again, Alannah!"

"You have no idea. It feels like I've been traveling with him for years, not days," Alannah said, shaking her head. "I've wanted to set Yaslin on him at least a dozen times a day. Unfortunately, I really do believe the One sent him." She turned as Sanuri tugged at her robes. "Hello, little one. I've come, sooner than I expected."

"It is right that you are here," Sanuri said, grabbing her hand. "Come, come."

Amon insisted that the Chosen hear what he had to say, but not the other warriors of the One.

"I don't know all the people here," he insisted. "There are many spies for the deities—as you learned at the Obsidian Temple."

Clay choked on the sip of *tash* he'd just taken, obviously unhappy with this man knowing about the Obsidian Temple.

"Of course I know about the temple," Amon said. "I am a Descendant of the Prophet! We have long kept the secrets of the South."

Sulis could see her grandmother mustering her patience.

"Perhaps you could explain to us exactly what that means," Grandmother said. "Rather than chastising us because we do not know what your Northern secrets are."

"You believe you are the Chosen of a prophecy given hundreds of years ago," Amon told them. "But the prophecy was a fake, a distraction for the deities. The prophet who came to the desert gave her own children her true prophecy. We Descendants alone know the rituals to help the One become whole once again."

Clay laughed shortly. "So you are saying that my visions are fake because your great-grandmother had a vision. You believe that all the Looms and Shuttles and Guardians who have been called up through the ages were delusional."

Alannah leaned forward. "Amon isn't explaining this correctly," she said, with an irritated look at the man. "The Chosen are an important piece of the joining between the deities and the One. Their roles are not false, and the training you have gone through is necessary for the rejoining. But without the guidance of the Descendants, the prophecy will fail."

"Have you known about this since you became a Counselor?" Sulis demanded.

Alannah shook her head. "Elida knew about a group of people in the North who worshipped the One directly. They were considered heretics but had shielded themselves so well the deities never found them. Tori told me only a few months ago about their role in the prophecy."

Amon nodded. "Toriaran disobeyed our elders by seeking out a Temple *feli*. She felt that her translation of the scriptures passed down from our ancestors showed a *feli* was needed to follow the bidding of the One. It seems she was correct."

"You have your own scriptures?" Lasha asked.

"Yes. The blood of the prophet runs in our family," Amon said. "We have had many true seers, and they have recorded their visions through the centuries. Scholars like myself, Toriaran, and her cousin Evan have made it our life's work to study and interpret what our roles must be in creating this new world."

"So we really cannot just dance the deities into submission," Ashraf mused, looking over at Sulis. "There is another step."

"Why are you even listening to this madman?" Clay burst out. "He has no proof of who he is. Everything he says goes against centuries of learning and study at Kabandha!"

He gestured to Master Anchee and Palou, the two Kabandha scholars in the room, asking them to intercede.

Master Anchee was sitting on his cushion, looking thoughtful.

"I'm not certain what to think," he said. "I hope our new friend thought to bring some of these scriptures for us to study."

Amon nodded. "We have brought transcripts of the original scrolls and their translation into modern language as well as the pertinent prophecies that came after."

"Then we should look at them," Anchee told the Chosen. "Sulis is not the only person who was alarmed by our brush with failure when meeting only one deity at the Obsidian Temple."

Clay stood angrily. "I will go by no false prophets," he said. "I was already given a prophecy, and I will not dishonor the One by abandoning it to follow another." He brushed past Amon and stalked out the door.

Grandmother gave Amon her best glare. "We'll go over your documents," she said. "But we expect you to study ours as well, so you know how you fit in with the Chosen."

Amon bowed his head submissively, but he was smirking and Sulis thought that was what he had wanted. "Of course," he said. "Trust that the One knows what he is doing."

"I trust in the One," Lasha said. "I don't trust you."

"You will," Amon predicted. "Just wait until your scholars read what I have brought. You will believe then."

The Chosen met again the next day. Amon was in attendance but Clay had refused. There was a pile of papers and scrolls on the table in front of Palou and Master Anchee.

"It's real," Palou said, gesturing to the scrolls. "Their prophecies, the visions passed down through the ages don't contradict ours. They complete them and fill in several gaps. And ours fill in gaps in their histories as well."

"I see no gaps," Amon said with a frown.

"We'll get to that," Master Anchee said. "Their prophecies say the Descendants of the Prophet will go to Illian. They will put up some sort of shield to block the deities from sucking energy from their acolytes to feed their powers in the desert. I guess the Descendants have been trained in this, and most are powerful energy users."

Palou nodded. "And here in the desert, we are to prepare the statues, the empty stone shells of the deities captured in the Obsidian Temple. When the statues in the temple are empty of the deities, they have a kind of vacuum that wants to be refilled. Supposedly, we can weave patterns that will suck the deities into the shells they vacated five hundred years ago and trap them, so we can weave them and the One into a whole." Palou looked around expectantly as his words sank in.

"Whoa," Sulis protested. "Empty shells? What empty shells? The stone figures at the Obsidian Temple aren't empty. They still contain bits of the deities, specifically their ability to channel magic on their own. Does that matter?"

Master Anchee chuckled softly at the look of consternation on Amon's face. "That is where we see gaps in their histories. According to the Descendants, the statues are empty. They believe that when the battle was over, the One reabsorbed the deities' ability to channel without the *feli*. They don't realize that those abilities are instead trapped in those statues. Hence, no vacuum to suck the deities into. I believe that, as things stand, what the Descendants propose would make the deities more powerful because they would regain their lost abilities rather than being trapped."

Amon sputtered a moment. "What? You must be mistaken," he said. "Perhaps it feels like the deity is still in the statue. But it should be a void inside."

"Then why did Voras fight us to try to reclaim his powers?" Sulis asked. "You said you knew about that. Why would he bother, if they were empty and he couldn't reclaim his powers?"

"He must have been just trying to destroy the statues," Amon said. "You can't reclaim powers from an empty statue."

Ava spoke up for the first time. "Aryn showed me how to do blood magic, through her statue. I needed it to defeat Voras, and when I touched her statue, I knew how to do things with my blood. I heard her voice guiding me. If her statue was empty, how would I learn to do that?"

Amon was speechless as he gazed around at the Chosen, then at the scrolls in front of him.

"Your people did nothing to send those powers to the One?" he asked. "Why would you let the statues remain full, waiting for the deities to reclaim what they lost? Are you mad?"

Grandmother stared him down. "Because that is what the One asked us to do, youngster," she said. "Every prophecy we received was clear. You can read that in our scrolls, if you choose to quell your arrogance. Our vocation was hiding and protecting what the Obsidian Temple contains. We have fulfilled our duty to the One—your people misunderstood what the One needs."

Amon frowned at the scrolls.

"It is the time," Clay said from the doorway. His voice was flat, his eyes blank. He was having a vision. All four of the *feli* were standing behind him. "The Descendant of the Prophet will show the Chosen the patterns to prepare the trap. What is filled must be emptied. You must begin. The time is now."

Clay sagged against the frame and Ava hurried over and helped him to a cushion. His face was gray from the energy drawn out of him. Ava gave him a mug of water. The four *feli* sat like statues around the doorway, gazing in at the Chosen. Sulis shivered, feeling like the cats were guards, making certain none of the Chosen escaped before they understood what the One had in mind.

Amon stared at Clay, then at the Chosen, his arrogance gone. He looked panicked. "This isn't what I was sent for," he said. "I know the patterns to draw the deities in. I don't know how to release what's trapped in the statues. I thought that was already done!"

"Clearly the One believes you do know," Master Anchee said. "Or that we'll figure it out together."

"I'm more worried about the urgency," Grandmother said. "If we leave for the Obsidian Temple now, we will be traveling in the heat of summer. The spring that feeds the Obsidian Temple dries to a trickle in the summer months and can support few people, which is why most of the residents and warriors of the One leave for Kabandha before the summer heat sets in. I'm not certain the spring could support us."

"We will have to travel at night," Master Anchee said. "But that will make it easy to miss the waymarker of an oasis and die of thirst before we reach another."

"The Tigus stay in the Sands year round," Sulis reminded them.

"They have their own form of energy sensing that lets them find the closest source of water," Grandmother told her. "They are never lost in the desert."

"Then hire one," Sulis said, impatiently. "We gave them humpbacks and supplies. They can give us a guide."

Grandmother frowned. "Most have gone east to keep the army of the deities from moving south. I hope they have a guide in this area still."

"Does the Obsidian Temple have a *farspeaker*?" Alannah asked. "If we contact the temple master, the people at the temple can go to Kabandha, to make room for us."

Master Anchee nodded. "Yes, the temple master is a *farspeaker*. Unfortunately, we sent Kadar with the Tigus, so we lack a *farspeaker* here. We have to wait until he contacts Sulis."

Grandmother leaned forward. "We have a *farspeaker* here," she said. "The Hasifel blood ran true in Tarik's brood. Abram has been tested by the warriors of the One and shows slight *farspeaking* ability. With four *feli* amplifying his ability, he should be able to reach the Obsidian Temple."

Amon nodded. "We will find a Tigu nomad to guide us," he said to Grandmother. "And you will speak to the temple so they can prepare for us. I will ask the One for guidance."

"We've much to do," Palou said. "Sulis, prepare your Northern friends to travel in the desert heat, and get whatever supplies you need. I will speak with Master Tull. She will not be happy about being left behind. Pray to the One to guide us all."

"One help us all is more like it," Sulis muttered to Ashraf. "We're going to need it to get through the desert heat alive."

Abram sorted the inventory he'd brought from Tsangia and wondered if he'd made the right choice in joining the warriors. The warriors of the One didn't want to assign him to a cohort in case Grandmother needed him. But Grandmother seemed irritated he was there. He'd been making himself useful to the quartermaster until someone decided where he would fit in. He heard his grandmother's voice and looked up from his list. She was walking in his direction speaking to a warrior he hadn't met.

"Abram, I want your *farspeaking* talent amplified before the Chosen leave," Grandmother told him when she came abreast. "Tell Master Ursa it is a priority. Kirt will escort you to her office."

Kirt didn't look any happier than Abram about being ordered around, but no one disobeyed Grandmother. As they walked between warehouses they had to dodge a mini dust cyclone a weather mage had conjured and edge around warriors training in the courtyard. Abram plastered on a pleasant smile as he followed Kirt to the *jetal* housing the masters. They stopped in the doorway to the office, waiting for Master Ursa's attention.

"If I could nail Joisha's feet to the ground, I would've done it years ago, Tull," Master Ursa was saying to a woman with short-cropped gray hair.

"How can we protect the Chosen when they keep running off? We traveled here because the Chosen required it, and now they're leaving without us," Master Tull growled. "Joisha isn't letting us do our job."

"Have you told her this?" Master Ursa asked.

"Of course. You know what a silver tongue she has. Two words and suddenly I'm doing exactly what she wants. That woman will drive me . . ."

Abram's guide cleared his throat loudly, and the masters broke off and turned to them.

"Who do we have here, Kirt?" Master Ursa asked.

"Joisha's grandson," the warrior said.

"Ah," Master Tull said. "Thank you, Kirt, you may leave us."

Kirt turned and left, and Abram walked up to the masters, feeling their discomfort that he'd overheard their idle talk. There was another woman about his age sitting at a desk in the room, and she glanced up at him. He winked at her, and she grinned. He bowed to the masters.

"My mother says the only way not to be trapped by Grandmother's schemes is to play dumb or run like crazy," he offered. "I didn't run fast enough, so I'm here to be your *farspeaker*."

The women relaxed and Tull grinned at him.

"If you've learned that, you'll do well among us," she said. "I'll talk to you later, Ursa."

Master Ursa nodded as Master Tull left, but her attention was already on Abram. He shifted uneasily under her regard.

"Heavily shielded, like all of Joisha's brood," she said, stepping close to him. "May I?"

Abram nodded and she put her cool hands on his temples. He felt her in his mind and forced himself to relax.

"Excellent, yes," Ursa said softly. "Slight *farspeaking*—that rare talent runs in your family. Do you have any other abilities? Are you good with animals, does it rain when you're upset, things like that?"

"Besides a silver tongue like Grandmother?" Abram quipped, feeling uncomfortable. "I can often sense what other people are feeling, and . . ." He hesitated, then told her, "I felt my da die. I knew he was gone at the same time Grandmother did. I always know where my family is." He was embarrassed by the tears that welled up in his eyes.

"Ah, yes, there it is," Ursa said with satisfaction, then lowered her hands and stepped back.

He wiped his eyes on his sleeve and she squeezed his shoulder.

"Your father was a good man," she said. "I enjoyed training him when he was a boy. Now, you have slight *farspeaking*, which we will open more. That will not be pleasant. Once your *farspeaking* is opened, we will need to connect you to Kadar and to temple master Sari at the Obsidian Temple. You will need to stay close to Master Tull or myself so we can speak through you at any time."

"Master Tull needs an assistant," the other woman piped up. "Her last one asked to be reassigned."

"Excellent thought, Casia," Ursa said, eyeing him. "Casia is my apprentice and assistant. You will be Tull's runner. Casia, why don't you get him settled in your dorm while I talk to the Chosen about their journey."

Abram followed Casia into the bright sunlight, his mind whirling.

"She's intimidating, right?" Casia said cheerfully. "The strongest mind healer we will see in our lifetime. And Master Tull is the strongest warrior mage."

"What about you?" Abram asked, turning his full attention to her. He could feel her intelligence and good humor and smiled flirtatiously.

"I can sense weather, make little changes. I'm honored that I caught Ursa's eye," Casia said, blushing a little under his gaze.

"Working with weather is dangerous," Abram said. "You must be quite courageous."

"Stop using that charm of yours," Casia protested, stopping by a doorway and turning to him. "It's too attractive. I already have a companion."

"A shame. Do you have a sister?" he asked, his tone hopeful.

She shook her head.

"A brother?"

Her eyes widened and she laughed and smacked him on the shoulder. "Yes, and he'd love you. But he's in Frubia with our father. You are an absolute flirt."

Abram smiled. "I love people," he said. "All sorts."

"You would, with your talent," she said, holding the door flap open for him. "Let's hope you feel that way after being assigned to Master Tull. She went through four assistants this spring alone."

CHAPTER 7

Kadar gave a quick glance at Amber, who was curled in the box he'd rigged on the front of his humpback. He'd tried to leave her at the city for her own safety, but she'd howled and clawed the girl restraining her. He'd be grateful for the extra distance she gave his *farspeech*, but worried about keeping her safe. Kadar was more concerned about Asfar, tied in the string behind the humpback. They'd been traveling two days in the heat and he worried she would become over-tired. Only one of the other warriors traveling with them towed a horse—and he did not seem concerned for her wellbeing.

"She is a desert horse," Onyeka said from beside him. She was almost indistinguishable from Kadar and the other nomads with her shemagh covering her hair, neck and lower face. "She has been bred for this, and for war. She cannot travel as long without water as the humpbacks, but she can go far and this heat is no danger to her. She will endure far worse, willingly. Our best warriors and our fast strike teams use mares like her in battle."

Kadar nodded his thanks, but she was already distracted by another warrior and left him to ride alone. He smiled as he watched her joking with the other warrior, jostling him with her humpback. She'd organized this party, arranged weapons delivery, and led the warriors out into the desert in half a day. He admired her practicality and determination.

"You are looking at my daughter," Turo said gruffly from Kadar's other side, startling Kadar. "You are not Tigu."

Kadar looked over at him, irritated. The same kind of prejudices, the same kind of separation of clans and castes, here in the desert as in Illian. He'd left that behind months ago. Kadar shook his head and turned away.

"Ha, ha!" The man reached over and slugged him on the arm. "A joke. You and she would make beautiful babies. She likes you."

Kadar was certain something was missing in translation. "I thought Tigus didn't marry."

The nomad laughed loudly, doubling over in his saddle. "No, no," he gasped. "You would not be bound together, only making babies! The Tigus need new seed. You could give me strong grandbabies. Ha!"

Kadar shook his head. He knew that was the Tigu way, but he couldn't fathom having a child without marrying his partner and raising the child together, as he'd planned to do with Farrah. Onyeka seemed to have no problem leaving her child in the city, but Kadar hated leaving his daughter's care to other people.

"Ah, it is all funny now," Turo said, sadly. "War is coming. It is better not to have babies now."

Kadar tried to pull his mind away from Farrah, from his daughter, and from a newer interest in Onyeka and failed as they rode on into the dusk. They stopped at a tiny oasis, well into the night. Kadar dismounted wearily, tired of his own thoughts.

He watered Asfar at the hole, and when he turned to tether her with the rest of the beasts, Onyeka was beside him.

"We could share a bedroll, on this night," she offered as he tethered his mare.

Kadar tried not to show his surprise at her forwardness, but she sensed it.

"I am sorry," she said, taking a step back. "I thought you were interested. But I remember; you clans go more slowly than we do. Forgive me."

Kadar put out a hand to stop her, his own emotions turbulent. "No, it isn't that," he said. "I am interested in you. I am beginning to like you. But it's too soon . . ."

"Too soon because we just met?" she asked, cocking her head to one side.

Kadar paused, then decided to confide in her. "My daughter's mother died a few ten-days ago," he said.

"And you loved her, and don't want another in her place," she said, nodding.

Kadar pursed his lips. "I did love her, but . . . in the end, it wasn't enough. It's confusing to explain."

She shrugged. "We have time as we set up camp. It interests me to learn how the Northerners do love, if you do not mind talking about it."

Kadar helped her tend to the humpbacks. "She was a fighter, like you, but with words rather than weapons," Kadar explained unbuckling and handing Onyeka a saddle. "I fell in love with her when I first met her in Illian. When she became pregnant I wanted to marry her. Northern laws wouldn't allow us to, because she was a Forsaken."

"But having a child changed that love?" Onyeka asked, checking the tack for wear. "The mothers in the North are the main caretakers, right? A warrior is not a natural caretaker."

Kadar nodded. He ran his hand down a beast's back, checking for sores. "There were many things. But in the end, freeing the Forsaken was more important to her than her child and I were. She felt that harming children and killing *feli* were fine if done for her cause. I was torn between doing what was right and loving her. In the end, I lost that love. I did not even get to bury her, to return her body to the sand, because she'd bonded with another man. He took her to bury."

"Ah," Onyeka said softly. She turned to him. "Tigus do not make such commitments to each other. To do so forces us to choose between the love of a single person and doing what is good and right for the whole—which is what the One requires. You chose what was right, rather than your love for one person but still have doubts and pain because of that binding between you two. That is why the Tigu way is not to bind to one partner, is to let all raise the children. Then our minds are free to understand the way of the One."

She grabbed her bedroll and turned away, leaving Kadar to set up his own lonely roll with much to think about.

In the morning she approached him, as he was about to mount his humpback.

"It is not right that you did not get to mourn your love," Onyeka said. "We have a ceremony, releasing the dead. When we reach camp, we will honor her sacrifice and release her to the winds so your heart may be free."

She nodded firmly, and then turned to her own humpback. Kadar grinned. He seemed destined to be surrounded by determined women.

They reached a large encampment late that day. The warriors in the camp gave a desert war whoop when the newcomers arrived, and Kadar's group howled it back.

There was much confusion and bustle as they dismounted. Supplies were quickly and efficiently unloaded from humpbacks and carried off. Kadar helplessly stood behind Onyeka as she and Turo spoke to a group of warriors, not understanding a word they were saying.

A snarl and howl drew everyone's attention. A warrior had wakened Amber while unloading Kadar's humpback and she was annoyed to find herself surrounded by strangers. Kadar walked over, and she leapt from the humpback to his shoulder, arching her back against his ear and purring. She sat and let out a contented "murp."

Kadar turned to find all eyes on him.

"*Suma!*" Turo exclaimed.

"*Suma!*" the warriors roared, some brandishing weapons above their heads. Kadar was surrounded by warriors patting him on the back, as Amber hissed at the noise.

"They think you are good luck," Onyeka said from beside him, and he turned to her.

"Are you ever going to tell me what *Suma* means?" he complained.

She grinned and grabbed his saddlebags, leading him to a tent. "They are having a ceremony of release tonight for the warriors we lost this ten-day. We only recovered one of the bodies and will burn that one—but we will burn remembrance for the other two. Do you have something you would like to let go of for the mother of your child?"

Kadar hesitated and then nodded. He reached into a side pocket and pulled out a tattered sheet of parchment. He carefully unfolded it to show a color pencil drawing of a blond woman with startling blue eyes. Ava had created the drawing of her sister over a year ago. He'd tried to give it back to her, but she'd said she had others she preferred of Farrah.

Onyeka studied it a moment. "Northerners have

such strange eyes," she said. "When I first saw eyes of such blue color, I thought it was because the man was blind. Are you certain you wish to let go of this?"

Kadar nodded.

"I will let you know when it is time."

The ceremony was similar to the one held for his mother when he was a child, but less elaborate. A close friend or child of the deceased lighted the oil and wood and named the deceased. One large pyre burned for the one body recovered, but several small fires were lighted for consuming belongings rather than bodies.

Kadar looked down at the picture of Farrah, remembering the laughter they'd shared, remembering her fierce spirit. He sent a blessing out to her, wherever she was on the wheel of life and death and fed the picture to the fire. He joined the ululations as Farrah's beautiful features turned to flame and ash, and Onyeka sat silently beside him.

People placed meat and other food items into the flames of the surrounding fires.

"What are they doing?" he asked.

"They are making sacrifices to the One, giving her the best of their meals as a blessing," Onyeka said. She looked at him. "They call those sacrifices *suma*."

Her face seemed serious in the flickering firelight.

"*Suma* means sacrifice?" he asked. "They think I'm a bit of meat to throw on the sacrificial fire?"

"It means blessing of the One," she said. "They send blessings through sacrifice. You can communicate with the sacred suncat and the beasts of war, and you are used by the One. That's why you are such good luck—you are a living human sacrifice that the One uses as she pleases. It is hoped that the One will sacrifice fewer of us when she has you to beat around."

Kadar sighed and she put an arm around him. "Come, it is time to retire. We warriors must be at our sharpest in the morning."

Amber woke Kadar in the morning, and he realized guiltily that he had not contacted his sister the entire trip. He had no news for the warriors of the One, but he knew she would be waiting to hear from him.

He sat cross-legged and Amber curled up on his lap. He reached out with his mind, found his twin-bond and followed it to his sister.

Kadar? Sulis sent, somewhat sleepily. *It's about time! I was afraid we'd be gone before you finally called on us.*

Gone? Kadar asked.

Hang on, Sulis sent, irritably. *Can you contact me again in a candlemark? I need to gather some people.*

Kadar assented. He got up, washed himself in a basin of water left by his tent flap and dressed.

"Kadar?" Onyeka asked outside the flap. "Are you awake? Would you like breakfast?"

Kadar opened the flap. "Just contacted my sister. She said she needed more information and asked me to *farspeak* her again in a bit. I'll come eat after that."

"I'll bring you a bowl," Onyeka said. "When you

are done reporting we will ride to the front and see the army."

Kadar nodded his thanks and then settled down again. This time when he contacted Sulis, others were connected to her.

Kadar, I've got Grandmother and our cousin Abram here, Sulis said. *We Chosen have to go to the Obsidian Temple. The warriors of the One you report to are staying here. Abram has had his farspeech awakened so he will stay here and be your contact to the warriors of the One.*

Kadar sent a burst of puzzlement.

I'll tell you about it later, Sulis told him. *Grandmother said she can help create an energy link between you and Abram, so you and he can easily contact each other when needed.*

Why was it every time he spoke with his sister he ended up with more questions than answers? Grandmother's energy joined them, though she did not speak. Then another person's energy joined them. This person did speak.

Hello, Kadar, Abram sent. *I'm not used to this farspeaking, but I'm now the assistant to Master Tull, rather than a fighter.* His mindvoice sounded bitter.

So they roped you in as well, Kadar sent, hoping he sounded sympathetic. *I know your frustration.*

Kadar, Sulis interrupted. *Grandmother says you will feel a mental tug, and then a binding. Don't fight it.*

I'm not a very strong farspeaker, so they have to create this link, Abram admitted. *And I don't have a feli to en-*

hance me. They did something to make me much stronger and more open than I was.

Kadar winced, remembering Alannah opening his *farspeech* and the resulting headache. Kadar felt a tugging, a binding that made him want to break the connection. But he gritted his teeth, and let the binding settle in the back of his mind. It wasn't a smooth connection, like the one he had with Sulis.

Grandmother says it is set, Sulis sent. *If you have information for the warriors of the One, contact Abram, not me.*

Kadar directed his speech at Abram. *I will observe the army this afternoon,* he told his cousin. *I will report tonight to the warriors of the One.*

I will let Master Tull know, Abram said.

Abram dropped out of the meld, then Grandmother's presence faded away as well, leaving him with only Sulis.

Whew, that wasn't fun, he confided to her. *Not much to report here. Saw a Tigu city, traveled through a lot of desert, and got a new horse.*

It hasn't been a fun ten-day here, Sulis said grimly. *An arrogant Descendant of the Prophet is making life miserable, we had to bargain with a Tigu guide to lead us through the desert this late in the season, and we're leaving as soon as humanly possible.*

Descendant of the Prophet? Kadar asked.

He listened while she explained, until Onyeka's shadow fell on his door flap as she peered in. It must seem odd to her, this silent communication between the siblings.

Gotta go, Kadar said. *The Tigus await me. Careful travels, sis.*

You as well. I know you need to report to the warriors, but don't forget about me, Sulis sent plaintively.

You know I won't. Love and misses.

Love and misses.

Kadar ate quickly. He was pleased to see Onyeka and the other warriors on horseback rather than humpback. He calmed Asfar as he saddled her, then leapt onto her back.

Onyeka handed him a bow and a quiver of arrows.

"Do you know how to use these?" she asked.

Kadar tried the tension of the bowstring. "It's been a couple years since I practiced," he admitted. "And never on horseback. I was a good hunter when I was younger."

"You'll want to practice. We want you to stay back in battle. Give us cover as we fight. Observe for the warriors of the One and report to them."

"I don't mind fighting alongside your warriors," Kadar said.

Onyeka shook her head as they rode into the desert.

"No. *Farspeakers* are too important and rare to risk in battle. You must protect yourself," Onyeka said.

"I'm surprised the Tigus don't have *farspeakers*."

"Tigu children who can *farspeak* or work with energy are sent off to train with priestesses like your grandmother and take positions at Kabandha. Such abilities are protected and treasured. We are fighters and would not see such talents die in battle when the warriors of the One desperately need them."

Midday they were met by a sentry and directed to the scouts and to Jaiden, the sharp-eyed battle leader for the tribes. She and Onyeka spoke rapidly as directions were given.

"This outpost has been here over a century as a place for the army to gather and train their fighters. But the army of the deities has been quickly growing the past three years. In the past month those expanded numbers have doubled," Onyeka told Kadar. "The Tigus have allowed them to expand their encampment farther south than we normally would, in order to get a sense of their numbers. We've allowed them to believe that we have withdrawn farther into the desert after seeing their size."

"Wouldn't it be wiser to withdraw if they are that strong?" Kadar asked.

"We never confront them directly," Onyeka said. "All the warrior tribes of the Tigus are allied for the first time in centuries, but we cannot match their numbers. The warriors of the One will direct us, once the army begins to march on the desert." She grinned. "Turo brought orders from the warriors of the One that we should start harassing the army. The Tigus will send in spies to collapse the latrines, run off their horses. Men who venture far will disappear. Food will become spoiled or opened to rodents. This will turn a happy, sheltered army into an uncomfortable, hungry place where men go about in twos or threes and people spit over their shoulders expecting ghosts."

Another warrior held their horses as battle leader

Jaiden motioned them to follow her on foot. Kadar and the other warriors followed. The terrain here at the northern edge of the Sands was rocky and ridged, unlike the high dunes they'd been traversing deeper into the Sands. The ground rose as they hiked, the midday sun beating on their sand-colored scarves and light robes. Their feet were silent on the path—the soft soles of their leather boots were made for stealth. Jaiden motioned for them to crawl for the last portion, and they came out on a high ridge, looking down into a smaller, rocky plain. A small stream trickled through the valley, but only scrub brush and sage grew by the banks.

A vast field of tents, in groups of fifty or more, sprawled along the banks and receded into the distance. The plain was smoky from dung fires, and men milled around the tents, doing daily chores. Strings of horses were set far from the stream, so as not to contaminate the water source. Jaiden silently pointed to different places around the army, drawing Kadar's attention to the supplies, the latrines, training fields, and other strategic settings. They then crawled out of sight.

"How many?" Kadar breathed.

"The watchers estimate between eight and ten thousand," Onyeka told him. "They practice drills closer to the northern side of the encampment. We have tribes circling the entire camp. They are aware we are watching them, but our spies tell us they have no idea of our numbers."

"Spies?" Kadar asked. She flashed him a grin.

"Oh yes. We know the army's schedules, know which platoon is less organized or has recently gotten new members where we can slip in undetected. We have spent most of the past century keeping Voras's armies out of the Sands. It is the duty of every Tigu tribe to protect the Sands from invasion."

"Why doesn't Voras keep the army closer to Illian?" Kadar asked.

"This area is out of the way but has a good water source and plenty of land where they can train and drill thousands of men."

"There's no way Voras can bring ten thousand men through the Sands, not even in the winter when the oases are full of water," Kadar said thoughtfully.

"I don't know what they are planning," Onyeka said. "But we know Voras is looking for every known path through the desert. That is why they have captured caravan leaders in Illian. They don't realize only one route exists for larger parties. Have you seen enough?"

"Do the Tigus have charts, showing where the leaders are camped and what their movements are?" Kadar asked. "If so, that would be more useful than me trying to spy on the camp."

Onyeka nodded. "We will go back to camp. The Tigu elders are in charge and will gather the information for you. I've told Kai to expect you for training with the archers this afternoon. Then you will contact the Kabandha warriors and we will see what this nest of Voras's hornets looks like when we stir it up."

She sounded positively bloodthirsty. Kadar knew

that war was necessary, but he wasn't a fighter. He didn't want to kill other humans. Onyeka was a true warrior, and he wasn't sure he understood what made her so different than him, that killing and war were anticipated rather than dreaded.

Back in camp, Kadar was amused by the sight of Amber in front of the cook fire, scarfing down the remains of a warrior's food while three warriors looked on in apprehension.

"Did you steal that?" Kadar asked the feline. She arched her back and purred, not surrendering the plate.

"She's only a cat, you know," he told Onyeka. "Not some ghost from the desert. They don't have to give her their food."

"She's a suncat," Onyeka returned mildly. "A cat of legends, a cat of the One. Anytime a pale golden cat tipped with sunset orange appears, great changes happen to the tribes and the *Suma* she companions. The last one came to the tribes during the drought and led us to our new city. I'll tell you the legend of the suncat sometime."

"I'd enjoy that, after we steal some food from the cat and get to those charts. The Kabandha warriors are waiting for me to contact my cousin and give them a report," Kadar told her.

The room of commanders was quiet a moment after Abram relayed Kadar's information, then questions erupted from all sides of the room.

Master Tull raised her hand to silence her commanders. "Yes, the numbers are alarming. But we need answers, not hysterics."

Master Ursa tapped Abram on the shoulder.

"This will take some time and we don't need a record. We need the northern desert territory maps from my office. I want you and Casia to fetch midmeal and extra *tash* as well. Don't gossip. This information is for commanders' ears only. Abram, we'll use you to talk to Sari later this evening."

Abram nodded, and he and Casia slipped out.

"Why don't we just go attack the army, instead of sitting here letting the Tigus do the fighting?" Abram muttered to her as they fetched the maps from Ursa's office.

"Weren't you listening?" Casia asked, sifting through papers on a desk. "They have almost ten thousand fighters. How many do you think we have?"

Abram shrugged. There were more warriors here than he'd seen in one place, but he'd never counted them.

"Less than three thousand. The majority are also strong energy users, which tips our odds, but not enough. The Tigus number less than two thousand. But they're valuable. The Tigu magic can blend their warriors into the desert, so they can winnow the army down bit by bit to give us better odds."

Abram was aghast. "They outnumber us two to one? We're doomed. We can't win."

Casia shook her head. "Winning was never the

goal. We knew the numbers were bad, though not this bad. We exist only to give the Chosen time to weave the deities back into the One. Our job is to hold back an army double our size, get the Voices to the Obsidian Temple, and protect the rest of the desert."

"Easy, right?" Abram said weakly. "But why aren't the warriors fighting alongside the Tigus?"

"We don't have very many true fighters," Casia said. "The ones we have are already scouting closer to the western part of our border to make certain Voras doesn't slip spies in, while the Tigus focus on the army in the east. Our true strength is in our warrior mages. They raise energy and use it for protection. But that isn't fast or easy, and it is almost useless with the Tigus' strike-and-run style of fighting. When the deities' army comes, we'll need to raise a sandstorm to reduce their numbers further. It'll take months for us to pull together enough energy to suddenly change the winds and to cast protections around our people for the full-on battle with the army. Making over two thousand stubborn mages work together is impossible. I'm glad it's Master Ursa's job, not mine."

She rolled her eyes, then searched deeper in the pile. "Found them!" she said, pulling the maps from the pile.

She turned pale and leaned against the desk, and Abram quickly pushed a bench to her and helped her sit.

"Are you okay? Should I fetch Jarol?" he asked anxiously as she ducked her head and breathed deeply. Her lover had some skill at healing.

"Why, so you can flirt with him again?" she asked,

looking up. Her face had a little more color. "I'm fine. Master Ursa had me doing higher-level weather work and it rebounded on me. I'm just low on energy."

Abram grinned, relieved that she was recovering quickly. "Jarol *is* quite handsome. But you have no worries. Master Tull has already stolen my time and my adoration," he said, his tone joking.

"Isn't she a little old for you?" Casia asked, smoothing out the maps she'd wrinkled.

"Age does not matter to an empath," Abram declared. "It is what's in her heart."

Casia mock-gasped. "Master Tull has a heart?" she asked and stood. "I thought she was all iron. Come, we'd better go fetch food before your love starts eating her warriors for midmeal."

Jonas could feel the tension in the room as the other Voices waited for the Templar to arrive to this Curia. The Crone glanced uneasily at her *feli*, who was grooming himself beside her chair. The Herald straightened her cloak and caressed her *feli*'s head, coughing and clearing her throat. Pollux sat beside Jonas, twitching his tail and gazing at the pile of shortbread on the table. Jonas received a frown from the Magistrate, sitting beside him, as he slipped the great cat a cookie, but he felt Parasu's amusement in the back of his mind.

Alannah's note hadn't been the personal letter Jonas had hoped for. Instead she'd written "Remember who you are," and enclosed a second note. That note was addressed to Parasu rather than Jonas. A Descendant of the Prophet had written that note.

Parasu had asked Jonas not to share that note with the Magistrate. Instead he told Jonas to go to the Herald. Then Aryn had taken over the Herald and Parasu had spoken directly with her.

The Templar entered the room and waved away refreshments. He gave the Voices a transcript of the interviews from Southern caravan leaders. The Magistrate shuffled through the papers and Jonas felt a slight pressure in his skull. He slid out of Parasu's way, allowing his deity to the forefront of his mind. He felt his deity's approval.

"That is all I need you for, Magistrate," Parasu said.

The man stood and bowed to the other Voices before gathering his papers and fleeing out the door.

Parasu glanced around the table and one by one the deities possessed their Voices, who became something more than human. Jonas could feel Parasu's assessment of the Voices' strengths and failings; his concern at the advanced age of the Herald's body, and his appreciation for Jonas's adaptable body and mind.

Voras's eyes blazed red. "What do you want, Parasu?" he hissed. "You waste my time here. This is nothing my Templar could not have handled."

"What, you'd rather be out playing with your army by the desert?" Aryn growled. Voras shot a sharp look at her. "Yes, of course we know you've tripled its size. There isn't much about your activities we don't know," she said scornfully.

"We want to know what information you have on the Obsidian Temple," Parasu said calmly. "We are willing to share the information we have in exchange."

Voras's face twisted in rage, and Jonas felt a thrill run through Parasu as Voras took the bait so quickly. His assumptions of betrayal would be his and Ivanha's downfall. Voras glared over the table at Ivanha. "You idiot," he snarled. "You told them. You wasted our advantage."

She sneered. "It wasn't me, darling," she drawled, putting sarcasm into the endearment. "Probably one of your meatheaded advisors. They never could keep secrets."

"Or your Mother Superior," he shot back. "Sleeping her way through half the soldiers . . ."

"Enough," Aryn said. "What do you intend to do about the Obsidian Temple? Give us your information and we will give you ours."

Jonas's body tensed as Parasu waited. The note that the Descendant had left for Alannah to deliver had been cryptic, saying only that what Parasu truly wanted was in the desert, in a temple that had been built where the deities had been defeated—the Obsidian Temple. Neither Parasu's nor Aryn's spies had discovered more information. Parasu hoped that that by playing coy in this meeting, Voras would grandstand and volunteer the information they needed. They would prey on his belief that Ivanha had betrayed him, and he would squeal to them in his anger.

Voras looked between Parasu and Aryn, maybe

sensing the trap. But Aryn sneered at him, then smiled nicely at Ivanha, goading him.

"I intend to crush it and those miserable warriors of the One with my army," Voras said. "Do you see another way of getting our powers back? You can't tell me that you don't want your freedom and to be unchained from the *feli* and the One. For all your posturing and supposed goodness, you're exactly like the rest of us. You want that part of yourself they've trapped in that desert temple."

Jonas admired the way Aryn's face did not change. He hoped Parasu had good control over his own, because elation hit as Parasu understood what Voras meant. Voras was saying that the key to the deities' freedom lay in the desert temple. That their lost powers were trapped there. Neither Aryn nor Parasu had known that. His deity mulled over this information.

"And your army can get it for you?" Aryn said, still playing her part. "I don't think so."

Voras slammed his fist on the table and rose. "I almost had my powers returned! With only one soldier! If he'd been able to touch my statue I would already have been whole again. All we need to do is get past those cursed Tigu nomads, destroy the South's pathetic army and those Chosen witches, and we can push through the barrier to reclaim our true selves!"

"You thought to go in, only you and Ivanha," Parasu said coolly. "You'd thought to unbalance the system, make us subordinate. It won't work and would destroy us all. We must all join together to fight the desert menace, or we will all fail."

"Join together?" Ivanha asked, a slight smile on her face. "Apparently you knew about the Obsidian Temple as well, but you did not come to us. You would have let us become subordinate to you with half a chance."

"Unfortunately we are stuck with one another," Aryn said with a harsh laugh. "How do you suggest we proceed?"

"I had a letter," Parasu said evenly. "From the Descendants of the Prophet." He raised his hand as Voras and Ivanha protested. "No, I won't show it to you. They claim not to be a threat to us. They claim they wish to balance the power between the One and the deities. They feel that the only way to harmony is for us to regain our powers. They will help us, but only if we work as a whole to show we are willing to create harmony."

"They're infidels," Ivanha hissed. "I've been trying to eradicate them for years. They believe in the Southern prophecy."

Voras snorted. "Crazy fanatics. We don't want to be balanced with the One. We want to rule him."

Parasu remained calm, detached, and rational. "Ah, but the Descendants say the way to balance is by going to war with the South and traveling to the Obsidian Temple to reclaim what is ours," he said. "They don't have to know we don't want balance. We can use their fanatical beliefs and once we have what we need, nothing they can do will stop us."

This silenced the two deities. Aryn looked like a cat that had gotten into the cream. Parasu nodded to her.

"Because we are chained to the *feli*," Aryn said for Parasu, "we cannot simply order our humans into battle and control them as we like. Our Voices are not strong enough to *geas* an entire army. We must lay our plans carefully, feed our people information that will inflame their desire for war." She nodded to Voras, who had narrowed his eyes suspiciously at her. "You have laid a foundation, blaming the Southerners for the actions of the Forsaken. People trust my healers. I will have them spread more rumors about the Southerners. By the time we are finished, people will be begging us to destroy the South."

"I want to reclaim the Forsaken who left Illian and went north," Voras said. "They are murderers and kidnappers and should not be allowed their freedom."

"People will demand that you capture them by the time we're through," Aryn said.

Voras stared between the two of them and then abruptly sat. "I did not expect you to be reasonable about this."

"We want the same thing you do," Parasu said. "Our freedom. What we do after that freedom is gained is up to each deity. Until then, we will each contribute in our own way. I suggest meetings every five days, among only ourselves."

"Agreed," Voras said.

"I am willing," Ivanha said. "As long as you keep to the bargain."

"We are not the ones sneaking about." Aryn's temper flashed. "We will keep our end."

"Then it is settled. We gather our people and regain our freedom," Parasu said. "We meet again in a five-day."

As Jonas watched, the other three Voices slumped to the table, devoid of their deity. Jonas expected Parasu to recede, but his deity paused and examined Jonas from the inside.

You see now, my young Voice, why questioning the Southerners was necessary? Parasu said directly into his mind. *You serve me well, even with your doubts.*

Jonas was confused as his deity examined him, probing in his mind and examining his concerns. Jonas held himself still as his deity inserted his will into those doubts, smoothed over his concerns. Then a sense of purpose and satisfaction arose, as Parasu placed those feelings into his mind. Parasu allowed Jonas to see his pride in his Voice, and Jonas flushed with happiness.

Of course, Jonas said. *I am sorry. I was wrong to ever doubt you. You are always looking for the greater good. I am young and need guidance.*

Parasu enveloped his mind, sending him feelings of warmth. *You will serve me well. You will step into your place as Tribune, and the Magistrate will only guide you when asked. See how much stronger you are than these other human Voices?*

Jonas looked out over the collapsed Voices of the other deities and felt a wave of contempt. They were barely stirring and would need assistance to even stand. Jonas could walk out of the room and serve Parasu's will. These humans would need to rest and recover.

Exactly, Parasu said, his mindvoice filled with satisfaction. *With you as my Voice, I will be dominant. Together we will rule. Find the Magistrate, and we will tell him our desires.*

Jonas stood, in control of his body once again. He walked out the door and summoned a couple of acolytes. "Please return the Voices to their altars," he told them. His voice sounded flat, even to himself. "It is Parasu's will."

CHAPTER 8

Sulis shivered in the night air as her humpback followed closely behind Ashraf's. A line was strung between the humpbacks in their party, a precaution in the dim light of the half moon they were traveling by. If one of them fell asleep or their humpback fell behind due to injury or weakness, they would know right away. They would not become the bleached bones they'd run across in their trek.

The Chosen were approaching the Obsidian Temple, and exhaustion was setting in. Their taciturn Tigu guide Ramia thrived in this climate. But for the Chosen and Amon, sleep was hard to come by during the day, as temperatures climbed with the sun and made it hard to breathe, even in the scant shade they sheltered under. And dropping temperatures at night made for miserable travel, as wind whipped sand into their eyes and mouths. The scarcity of water hollowed out their faces and their skin split in the dryness.

Three of the supply humpbacks had succumbed to the harsh environment. Ramia had savored the fresh meat of the poor beasts, but Sulis could barely force herself to eat the tough, gamey, mostly raw steaks, and Ava had gagged and eaten her dried meat sticks instead.

Surprisingly, Northerners Dani and Lasha were the happiest among their group of travelers. Lasha spent most of her time questioning Master Anchee and gazing around as though the Sands were a beautiful discovery. Dani didn't mind the heat as much as the rest and developed a system of signals and small words to communicate with their guide. He and Ramia sparred before the heat of morning and in the evening when they woke. He'd decided his role with Ava was one of a big brother, and he tended her and Sanuri as they tumbled off their humpbacks in the morning, badgered them to eat and set up a sunshade so they could rest during the day. The two younger Chosen suffered the worst, their pale skin reddening even under their scarves and light robes. Clay helped them rub healing plant paste on their burns and around their chapped lips and hands every morning. Even Ava's *feli* kitten, Nuisance, was listless and ate little.

Dani and Lasha questioned Master Anchee about the system of elements they based their dances on and Sulis listened in.

"So why the five elements—metal, wood, fire, earth, and water—instead of earth, wind, water, and fire, the way we were taught?" Dani asked.

"The Southerners just like to be different," Lasha said with a grin. "And really, it's five elements for us as well, if you include the ether."

"No," Master Anchee reproved. "The deities in the North focus on what is material—air, water, earth, and fire. Tangible things. Southerners focus on energy—how those elements are in constant interaction with each other."

Dani frowned, concentrating. "So you mix earth and water elements and that creates wood energy?"

"It's more complex than that," Anchee said. "There are cycles of balance—creation and destruction. In creation, wood feeds fire, fire creates earth, earth bears metal, metal collects water, and water nourishes wood. In destruction, wood parts earth, earth absorbs water, water quenches fire, fire melts metal, and metal chops wood. There are many other cycles, but those are the most important because they cause the swirling energy around us."

Dani shook his head, baffled, but Lasha exchanged a grin with Alannah, enjoying this new view of life.

The dawn was breaking as they set up sun shelters and widened the small spring bubbling between the rocks so they could carry buckets to the humpbacks. It had been two days since their last water source, and the beasts drank greedily as the humans refilled their own flasks and waterskins. They were skirting the edges of the black mountains, approaching the Obsidian Temple by a route only the Tigus knew. The adult *feli* traveled with them by night, but they'd been disappearing by day, probably finding a cool cave closer to the mountains to rest in.

"Ramia says we should be at the waymarker the day after next," Grandmother told Sulis. "Has Kadar contacted you?"

Sulis thought a moment, trying to remember. The days blurred together with her exhaustion. "Not since we left the warehouses," she said. "The Tigus he's assigned to are harassing Voras's army and trying to winnow them down before the army goes to war with the South."

"Has he heard from Aaron?" Grandmother asked. Her expression was bleak, and Sulis knew she was thinking of her lost son, Tarik.

"Not that I know," Sulis said. "Should I ask him to search for Uncle Aaron when he contacts me again?"

Grandmother shook her head. "No, he shouldn't waste energy on the fears of an old, tired woman," she said, bitterly.

Sulis was alarmed by Grandmother's tone. Any other time Grandmother would swat Sulis for calling her old.

"Why don't you sit in the shade?" she said, pulling her grandmother to the canvas they'd set up. "I'll get you some water and dates. Let us youngsters tend the humpbacks."

Grandmother protested angrily, and Clay grabbed her arm.

"The girl is right, Joisha," he said, settling with a sigh. "We need our energy for the last push to the way-marker. One knows what challenges we will face at the temple itself. Let these youths treat us like revered an-cestors. I could use a little pampering."

Sulis bit her lip at this sign of weakness from their elder guides. She filled another bucket, coming along-side Ashraf as he watered his humpback.

"What was that?" he asked.

"I think Grandmother needs to rest more. She was asking about Kadar, and worrying about Uncle Aaron. I don't think she's recovered from Uncle Tarik's death. I'm worried about her, Ashraf." Her parched eyes burned, too dry for tears. "If she is this frail—how will she survive the trials to come?" *I don't want to lose my grandmother,* she thought.

Ashraf put an arm around her, pulling her close. "She is grieving for her son," he said. "She will have time to recover at the temple, before the final battle begins. You will see—she will be strong again."

"We won't all make it out alive, will we, Ashraf?" Sulis said into his chest.

"Probably not," he said seriously. "We must trea-sure the now."

The heat was making them sticky, so Sulis pulled away, splashed her face with a little of the water she was carrying. She looked around at the already blind-ing morning, the heat waves shimmering off the rocks.

"And what a moment to treasure," she said dryly.

"Uncle Aaron is probably cooler and happier wherever he is."

Tori stood in her stirrups, looking both ways at the intersection where they'd paused, and then at the mass of people who were following her. Her group was supposed to take the left-hand juncture and head straight to Illian. But something in her heart told her she should turn right to go west. Tori had to decide if the pull was something the One wanted or if it was her natural contrariness shoving her the wrong way.

"Where to, oh mighty leader?" Sandy asked, pulling his horse up beside her.

Once Tori and the twins had reached the altar in Caracas, the twins' conversion to Counselors had been very similar to her own experience at her temple—a glorious flash of white, cloaks turning gold. The twins and ten other acolytes had been converted to Counselors of the One, the most of any temple so far. Only the twins were called to go with Tori when she left, called to Illian. They'd been a welcome relief from Evan's frowns.

Shane was fine with leaving his seaside home, but Sandy was all fire and resisted. He was constantly asking questions. Tori wished she had some answers.

"We should head toward Illian," Tori said. "But it doesn't feel right."

Evan rode up beside them. "We go southeast, toward Illian," he said.

Shane cocked his head, listening to something. "Do we?" he asked.

"You feel it, too?" Tori asked, and he nodded. She breathed a sigh of relief, feeling less alone and responsible for all the decisions.

Evan frowned. "The plan was to go to Illian, take our places at the Temple of the One, and prepare for the great change. Amon has already traveled through the desert with your friend Alannah. We don't have time to run off on a side trip because you feel like it."

"That clearing back about a half mile looked like a good campsite for this many people. Let's stop for the night," Tori said. "I need to figure out what our next move is."

Evan glared at Tori. Tori gazed evenly back. Zara came and sat at Tori's side, her head touching Tori's foot in the stirrup. She yawned, showing her large white teeth.

Evan jerked his horse's head around and called out orders to the others milling about. They headed up the road, Tori and the twins trailing.

Sandy nodded toward Evan. "Thinks he's in charge, doesn't he?"

Tori nodded. "Until I went to the Temple and came back with Zara, he *was* in charge. He'd read all the ancient scrolls and was the authority on what the One wanted us to do."

"And you upstaged him with a *feli*," Shane said. "So he is resentful. Was that deliberate? Or did you feel a calling to pledge?"

"The Descendants of the Prophet serve the One directly and never pledge to the Temple," Tori said. "Mostly because a deity could seize our minds and find out what the second part of the prophecy says. I was confident that I could shield myself. I'd read the same texts Evan had. I'd translated the same ancient scrolls . . ." She paused, weighing her words. "I . . . was not convinced his interpretation was accurate. I wanted confirmation."

"And have you gotten it?" Sandy asked, glaring down at his *feli*. "Because I don't feel like having a *feli* has answered any questions for me."

Tori nodded. "I sometimes feel the One's will, if I quiet my mind enough and focus. That's why I want to stop for the night. I think the three of us should join together, try to understand what the One wants from us."

They set up camp far back in the clearing. Evan set a guard and looked on disapprovingly as Tori, Shane, and Sandy sat in a circle, their *feli* pressed against them. Tori held out her hands, and Shane readily took hers and held out his hand to his brother. Sandy grimaced at both their hands and gingerly took them.

"Let your breathing slow, deepen," Tori said softly. "Calm your mind. Allow the thoughts to start to spiral in and lessen, becoming one-pointed. Feeling the physical connection between us, reach out with your single-pointed energy and connect each to each."

Tori's palms became warm as she sent energy through that link. The heat became a tingling sensation as they connected as a group, the *feli* naturally joining them as energy enhancers and shields to distracting outside energy. Boosted by the twins, Tori let her senses range and felt her mind be gently guided. The One was pushing her toward another person. She could feel the energy of Vrishni traveling through the area, and in the seaport they'd recently left. There was no alarm in those minds, so she ranged farther, searching to understand the urgency she felt.

Far southeast of where they were camped, she sensed a disturbance: many bodies and energy in a place with no towns or cities. A mind that felt strongly like Voras came within her reach and the One guided her away from that connection.

Instead she was guided to another searching mind, a worried mind. Tori connected.

Who are you? the male mindvoice asked. *The One connected us, but you don't feel like a Vrishni, or even one of my Southern farspeakers.*

I'm a Counselor for the One, Tori told him. *Newly chosen and heading to Illian. I felt something was wrong and reached out. Who are you? What is happening that the One wants me to see?*

I am Aaron Hasifel, a merchant, the man said.

That was Sulis's clan, Tori realized.

Do you know Sulis? Tori asked. *I was a pledgemate of hers. A friend.*

Sulis is my niece, he answered, his mindvoice surprised.

Why are you here? Your home is in Shpeth, is it not?

I fled to the Forsaken city of Stonycreek when my clansman was taken by Voras and then killed. Now I'm trapped here.

By whom? Tori asked. She felt his hesitation. *The One guided me to help with your plight. You felt her connect us. You can trust me.*

I doubt anyone from the Temple is to be trusted, the Southerner said grimly. *Not after Voras went back on his word not to pursue the Forsaken of this town.*

Voras wants the Forsaken back, doesn't he? Tori asked, realizing why she might feel a Knight of Voras on the road. *He's trying to press them into his army.*

Yes. Voras has broken his promise to let the Forsaken go. He has sent troops to capture and claim the Forsaken for his army, Aaron said. *They will arrive in a matter of days.*

Tori nodded. The sense that the One wanted her to travel to Stonycreek, not Illian, heightened with his words. *How large a troop?* she asked. *How many men do you have?*

We have about fifty men and women who can fight. Several hundred Forsaken need protection. Voras has sent more than two hundred men to take us. I believe he will kill or capture us Southerners and conscript the Northerners.

We are coming, Tori said. *We can match their numbers. We are all fighters and energy users as well as three Counselors of the One. I believe we will arrive in three days. Can you hold them off?*

Yes, Aaron returned, relief brightening his mindvoice. *I believe we can. We have already set traps and collapsed bridges to slow them. I don't know who you are or why you are interceding, but One bless you.*

Bless the One instead, Tori sent. *She sends us to battle for you.*

Tori broke the sending and unclasped hands. Sandy shook his hands out to rid them of the tingling that still twitched her palms, too.

"How are we going to fight against two hundred of Voras's troops?" Sandy asked. "Is your group really that well trained?"

Tori nodded and rose to her feet. "It won't be much of a fight," she said. "You will see. Once we kill the leaders and the commander, who is probably Voras driven, the Forsaken troops will rally for the One. I doubt they're eager to attack their own people."

Sandy shook his head disbelievingly as Evan walked over.

"Well?" he asked.

"Our first battle for the One is ahead!" Tori said in a clear, ringing voice. The Descendants cheered in response and Zara roared. "We battle a cohort of fighters from Voras's army to save the Forsaken in three days!"

In a lower voice she addressed Evan, who was looking around with a sour expression. "We go east. The town of Stonycreek, a haven for the Forsaken, is under attack by Voras's troops. The One wants us to claim them. It will be a good place for us to wait and plan until the time is right to continue to Illian."

"We will serve," Evan said, adding sourly, "if that is truly what the One wants."

"Oh, it is," Tori assured him. "Three Counselors could not be mistaken."

No matter how much you wish them to be, Tori thought as he turned away.

Sulis had warned her friends about the fear they would feel as they approached the waymarker for the Obsidian Temple, but she could see the sweat on Dani's brow as he fought the urge to turn back. Ramia was not affected by the illusions.

When they reached the stones, Lasha stood behind Master Anchee with her hands on his back as he spoke the words to break the wards hiding the path to the Obsidian Temple.

"How does she know to send energy without the training Ashraf and I went through at Kabandha?" Sulis murmured to Alannah.

Alannah smiled. "Lasha is a fully trained healer now. Sending energy is what healers do. She has a strong connection with your teacher, which makes it easier."

"Guardians," Sulis said, glancing over at Ashraf on his humpback. "Do you feel your connection that strongly with Sanuri?"

"No. I don't believe any but the deities will feel an energetic connection with her," Alannah said. "She is not all of this world."

Sulis looked at her sharply, about to ask what she

meant, but the illusion came down and the path was revealed. Master Anchee smiled at Lasha in approval and they remounted.

"Guide Ramia has gotten us here early enough that we can make it to the bottom before dusk," Master Anchee told them.

"You aren't too weary?" Grandmother asked.

"Thanks to my Guardian, I feel full of energy," Master Anchee said.

Ramia refused to go farther with them. "My task is done," she said. "You know the way. I do not wish to walk in the valley of the One. I am returning to my people."

She left with their remaining supply humpbacks as payment, and they loaded their packs on the front of their saddles.

"The way is steep, and the footing is uncertain for your humpbacks," Sulis advised her Northern friends. "Don't tug at the nose leads and throw them off balance. They will place their feet carefully if you don't distract them."

Sulis watched her friends as they descended into the chasm. It was clear Dani did not like being at the edge of the chasm on the winding switchbacks down the side. He grasped his saddle convulsively. Lasha and Alannah gazed around themselves as much as possible, awe showing as the rock changed from shale to glossy black obsidian.

"Beautiful," Lasha breathed as the Obsidian Temple came into sight.

Unlike their last visit, where a crowd met them, only three people came out of the temple at their approach. Sulis recognized the temple master Sari, but not the other two. Sari greeted them with a bow.

"Your humpbacks will shelter here, behind the dormitories, for the night," Sari told them. "The first dormitory is open to you. We have a late meal set up for you in the dining hall."

"I am Amon, Descendant of the Prophet," Amon introduced himself. "I will need to access your archives and to view the site of the great Sundering."

"Yes, I was warned you were coming," Sari said. Sulis wondered what else she'd been warned about him. "Most of the archives are at Kabandha, but you can view any scrolls we have here. I will introduce you to the Obsidian Guards tomorrow, and they will judge your intent and decide whether to allow you access to the temple."

Amon frowned at her but seemed too tired to protest.

"We youngsters can stable the humpbacks," Sulis told her grandmother and Palou. "Why don't you grab the bags and settle us in the dorms, and we'll catch up at late meal."

It was a measure of how weary her grandmother was that she did not protest. She gathered Clay and Master Anchee, as Palou and Sari helped them carry the bags. Palou guided Ava and Sanuri, who were asleep on their feet, to the dining hall.

Sulis supervised the unharnessing and rubdown of

the humpbacks as they settled them in a rocky corral spread thickly with dried grasses. The small stream that usually trickled into a basin for the animals had dried and they had to carry buckets of water to fill it for the thirsty beasts. They dragged themselves to the dining hall and found the elders already settled in and apprising Sari of the most recent events.

"Where are the girls?" Sulis asked as she slid onto the bench beside Clay and began filling a plate with flatbread, bean spread, and cured meat.

"They were too tired to eat much, so we settled them in the dorm. Sanuri insisted on sleeping right beside Ava, and I left them and Nuisance snuggled in together."

"Good," Sulis said, sighing in relief. "I was afraid being back here would unsettle Ava."

Sulis glanced around and realized Djinn and the other *feli* weren't in the dining hall. She hadn't seen them all day. "I wonder where our *feli* are," she mused. "Hope they can find their way through the waymarker."

"*Feli* aren't affected by illusions," Alannah said mildly. "They're probably waiting until the day cools and will join us later."

"Djinn felt the fear illusion that usually repels travelers," Sulis told her.

"He was probably feeling the fear of everyone around him," Alannah said. "Elida told me that *feli* aren't tricked by the same things we are and can find their way through illusions. That's why they're so valuable as scouts and energy givers."

Master Anchee yawned and stood. "It was a long journey, so we will rest tomorrow and learn how we must adjust to living here in the summer. After so many nights traveling, we need to readjust our sleep schedules."

"I want to begin at the Obsidian Temple tomorrow, working with the energy," Amon said with a frown.

"You are very welcome to, if approved by the guards," Master Anchee said firmly. "That way you can understand what the temple truly contains. The rest of us will recover and join you when you have a plan of action."

Sulis hid a grin by stuffing some meat in her mouth. Amon was finding out that he was deep in Southern Territory now. Temple master Sari would not follow the arrogant man's orders if Master Anchee gainsaid him.

The dorms were built in the shadow of the cliffs rising on each side of the chasm, so Sulis had little idea of time when she rose the next morning. Half the beds were still occupied, and Sulis quietly dressed and made her way to the dining hall. She was surprised to find the sun directly overhead and a midmeal set out. Clay greeted her with a smile, pushing a carafe of *tash* her way.

"Ava and Sanuri are with Sari and Dani, exploring the chasm," he told her.

"Is Amon in the temple already?" Sulis asked.

"No, for all his eagerness, he has not yet awakened," Clay said, a twinkle in his eye. "I felt it would be good for his temperament if we let him sleep. Ashraf stumbled to the latrine a short time ago, but the remainder of our group are still resting."

Ashraf entered, and Sulis poured him a cup of *tash*. They sat in silence as they ate, still groggy.

"Ava and Sanuri are giggling and playing a game outside," Ashraf said after they'd finished eating. "They both seemed like normal girls."

"Sanuri is good for Ava," Clay said. "And Sanuri seems to stay present when Ava is around instead of becoming lost in the deities' thoughts. I don't know what to do with either of them. I can't *see* how to bring everyone together."

"Have you had any visions recently?" Sulis asked.

He shook his head. "Only the one telling us to come here. I feel that Amon has supplanted my role as teacher. You will have to look for guidance from him."

Sulis grimaced comically and Clay laughed. She patted him on the arm.

"He will never supplant you in our hearts. We still need you. I think you'll end up showing Amon a thing or two."

"Speak of a sand devil, and he comes," Ashraf muttered as Amon entered the hall, looking harassed. Clay winked and rose, and then sauntered off, whistling cheerfully as Amon came over to the table. Sulis quickly gulped down the last of her drink as he sat.

"You should have woken me," he said accusingly. "I have much to do."

Sulis piled her plate on Ashraf's and they stood. "Sorry, Amon, I just woke myself. I didn't realize you were still snoozing," she told him brightly. "Must go report to Sari."

She shoved Ashraf to get him moving and they deposited their trays and walked outside.

"Let's wake Lasha and Alannah and see what kind of trouble we can get into," Sulis suggested.

"How much trouble can there be in a hole in the ground?" Ashraf asked.

Sulis grinned. "Don't worry. The three of us can always find some excitement."

CHAPTER 9

Kadar focused his energy and will on the Tigu horses as the patrol of twenty fighters from Voras's army rode by the ambush point the Tigus had set up. The Tigu horses were lying in the desert sand, not ten feet from where the fighters passed. They were restive, but obeyed his silent command. He'd spent his first few ten-days working with the horses, teaching them to trust him, and it paid off in ambushes like these. He could feel other energy, the magic of the Tigu nomads mounted on those horses, swirling around him as well. His will kept their mounts lying down and quiet—the Tigus' will made the ambush invisible against the sand dunes around them. Desert magic.

Kadar and the ambush party were behind enemy lines, in the Northern Territory. Their party was only fifteen strong, but Voras's fighters rode with their swords sheathed, bows unstrung—unaware of their presence in what should have been safe territory. The shock of the nomads appearing behind them out of dunes would cost the fighters precious moments. The last of Voras's troops passed by the ambush.

"Hai!" Jaiden shrilled.

Kadar released his control and the horses heaved up out of the sand, riders screaming desert war whoops. The fighters in front of them froze as the desert came alive behind them with their bloodcurdling cries. Their mounts bucked and shied in surprise.

Kadar notched an arrow, staying to the rear, but his help wasn't needed. The troops barely had time to draw their swords before the Tigus were upon them. The battle was brief, but bloody. Kadar focused on summoning the now riderless horses, rather than on the Tigus dispatching wounded troops. He called the beasts to him, making encouraging noises. They were frightened and wanted a herd leader, and he convinced them that Asfar was their lead mare. He tried to ignore the blood on their saddles as they gathered around Asfar.

"Come," Onyeka called, wiping her sword off on a dead fighter. She swung up on her mount. "We are too close to their camp. They will be alerted by the noise. We must disappear."

They streamed back into the desert, the dead fighters' horses following Kadar like chicks follow a hen. He didn't hear anything behind them but knew it wouldn't be long before the bodies were discovered. This was the closest to the base camp they'd ever taken down a patrol.

They thundered into camp late in the day and Kadar leapt down from Asfar. Onyeka and Jaiden checked the saddlebags of the horses and Kadar murmured to the horses, keeping them still. A new warrior unsaddled Asfar for Kadar, rubbing her down as she lipped her grains.

"Hai," Jaiden said, flipping through some papers she pulled out of a bag. "Ard trinoka."

Here. Found the orders, Kadar translated. His grasp of the Tigu language was improving, though it was still hard for him to follow a full conversation unless the speakers slowed down for him.

Onyeka grinned and slapped Kadar on the back. One of their spies had told the elders that that cohort of Voras's troops would ride in today with special information they were delivering to the army. The Tigus had risked capture in the Northern Territory to ambush those troops and see if they could find out what the orders were. Kadar was relieved they'd ambushed the right group of Voras's fighters.

The Northern army would retaliate for the Tigu ambush today. They would send troops over the border to kill any Tigu nomad they could find.

The Tigus were stripping down their opponents' horses, piling the saddlebags and personal items off to one side. The horses themselves would be divided— the healthy, strong ones would be taken to the caravan routes and traded for more supplies for their people. The others, well, Kadar tried not to think about what went into his cookpot every evening. It was hard thinking that he'd lured these beasts into trusting him, only to send them to their deaths.

"We must survive, too," Onyeka said from beside him, interpreting his thoughts. "We would have captured them, or driven them away if we couldn't catch them. You saved them from a slow death in the desert. And your powers saved us—only one of our warriors got a wound, and that a minor cut." Her voice was full of satisfaction.

"Onyeka, Kadar." Jaiden motioned for them to follow her to the larger tent that housed their leaders. Onyeka and Kadar worked well together, translating Northern writing into the Tigu tongue. Kadar read the Northern tongue like it was his own. He would read the document out loud in *Sanisk* to Onyeka, and she would transcribe the *Sanisk* to the Tigu tongue for the leaders.

They had time to transcribe only two pages before evening fell and Jaiden told them to continue in the morning. The little they'd translated had been bad news, which Kadar had reported to the warriors of the One.

"This is exactly what Uncle Aaron feared would happen," Kadar said, shaking the tension out of his shoulders as they walked toward the cook fire and the warriors celebrating the day's victory. "The deities now know how to release the wards on the waymarkers at the oases. But the caravan leaders the Templar questioned didn't know the routes through the heart of the desert. Just the route from Illian to Tsangia. That puts my family in Shpeth and Tsangia, and anyone along the route, in danger if the deities decide to detour that direction."

"The caravan leaders were cowards to reveal so much," Onyeka said angrily. "Giving the Northerners the words of power to release the wards over the oases is treason."

"I'm not certain they had a choice," Kadar said. "Not to excuse them, but if Voras broke their minds, he could wring anything from them."

"You uncle died rather than reveal what he knew," Onyeka said.

Kadar shook his head grimly. "Because he was trained by my grandmother to create barriers in his mind that would resist a deity to the death. Most Southerners did not have such a formidable teacher."

Onyeka grinned at the understatement. They hushed as they approached the other warriors.

"*Suma!* Onyeka-sal!" their cohort roared as they caught sight of the pair. Grinning, they let themselves be pushed and patted along to the fire.

"*Suma.*" A warrior handed Kadar a plate and bowed to him. Kadar inclined his head, and a woman handed him a flask. He and Onyeka commanded a seat by the cook fire.

It was a new feeling, the warrior's respect for Kadar. He hated the fighting, hated the bloodshed. But he knew he was saving warriors' lives and protecting his family deeper in the desert. He was finally using his powers to their fullest—both his abilities with the hooved beasts and his *farspeaking*. Both abilities had grown tremendously with use. Kadar wasn't permitted to lift a sword in battle, but the warriors respected how his abilities made their warfare more effective and they had fewer injuries because of him. Even Onyeka looked at him with respect—and she was in training under Jaiden to become a battle leader.

Kadar listened to the other warriors talk and watched across the fire as Turo flirted with one of the men Kadar had ridden with. Though the Tigus did not marry, they did form attachments of a sort, and Turo had been sharing his tent with this warrior since he arrived. Onyeka hadn't shared hers with anyone. He wondered if she was worried about showing preference toward one warrior over another.

"You look so pensive," Onyeka laughed, gazing sideways at him. "What deep thoughts are going on in your head? Are you worrying about the caravans?"

"Nothing so serious," Kadar said. He gestured as Turo and his mate left the fire together. "I was noticing that your father has paired off." The beer in his flask made him daring, and he smiled at her. "I noticed that you haven't since we arrived. Are you trying to stay impartial with the other warriors, so they'll respect your leadership?"

Onyeka was silent a moment. "No. No, that is not why I haven't paired off," Onyeka said.

Kadar looked directly at her, looking in her eyes. "Yet many warriors would like to spend time in your tent."

Onyeka laughed softly, a sound Kadar found very attractive. "The one who I would have, felt it was too soon. So I wait."

"So it isn't true that Tigus do not form attachments," Kadar teased.

"It is not true. But we do not allow those attachments to get in the way of our duty to the One," Onyeka said. She stood and reached out, taking his plate from him, setting it down beside the fire. She grasped his hand and drew him up.

"Will you share my tent with me tonight, Kadar?" Onyeka asked him softly.

"Yes," Kadar said, letting her lead him away from the fire.

He'd seen the inside of her tent before, so he was not surprised by the riot of colors of the many pillows and rugs she had surrounded herself with. She had an artist's love for bold colors, and since as a warrior she could not wear them, she displayed them in her abode. Her friends loved to gift her with new ones.

"What would you do with all these, if we had to pack and run?" Kadar asked as he took off his boots before stepping inside.

She shrugged. "I will leave what doesn't fit in my saddlebags," she said. "They are beautiful but easily replaced. We have not had to move in a great while, so they gather like tumbleweeds before a sandstorm scatters them."

"They're very soft," Kadar said, sinking down on the cushions. She laughed as he grabbed her legs and pulled her down with him. "I should warn the rest of the warriors how hedonistic their leader is."

"Hedonistic?" Onyeka asked, brow puckered.

"Pleasure-seeking," Kadar said. She pummeled him with a pillow. "Soft."

She leapt on him, wrestling him into the rugs. Somehow, in their tussle, Kadar lost most of his clothes. Onyeka's robe was pulled off her shoulders to her waist and, as she triumphantly wrestled Kadar to the ground and her body pressed down the length of his, he admired the view. She pinned his arms over his head. He was enjoying his position, so he relaxed under her, letting her body mesh against his.

"Why don't you struggle? Can't you get away?" she taunted.

"Why would I struggle when I've got you exactly where I want you?" Kadar asked, grinning.

She shook her head in mock disgust. "You call this soft?" she asked, pressing her body against his.

Kadar gazed at her lean muscled body, up to her small well-formed breasts and then at her lips.

"Your lips do look rather soft," he ventured.

She bent down and kissed him fiercely, all lips and tongue. He kissed her deeply, until she came up for air, panting slightly.

"Not as soft as I expected," he judged. "But very, very tasty."

She grinned as she ran her hand down his thigh. "Your softness has hardened as well," she said. "But I know what to do about that."

She went on to prove that, with enthusiasm that Kadar returned.

Kadar woke in the morning before Onyeka did and discovered Amber between them, curled in a ball. She stretched her full length and purred when she realized he was awake.

Even in sleep, Onyeka was fierce, her brow set in a frown. He wanted to reach out and smooth the frown away, but knew she'd wake if he touched her. He wondered how the warriors in the neighboring tents had slept, as their lovemaking had been both fervent and noisy. But he couldn't feel bad—he'd had his own sleepless nights while others pleasured one another.

A pan clanged outside the tent, and Onyeka was awake and completely alert in an instant.

She gazed at him, and he reclined on the pillows. "I believe I may move into this comfortable space, now that you've spoiled me. It took you long enough to get the hint," he said.

Onyeka tilted her head and frowned at him. "If you wanted me before this, why did you not ask me? I was not going to ask."

Kadar laughed. "Because my tent is tiny and the bedroll hard. I thought it would be rude for me to invite myself to your tent rather than the other way around. So I had to wait for you to come to me."

"Hedonist," she teased. "Pleasure-seeker. Softy."

Amber yowled as Kadar pushed her aside and

pinned Onyeka to the mat, kissing her deeply. They heard Jaiden's voice and Onyeka sighed and shoved him aside.

"Tonight," she promised, as they dressed. "After we have done our duty."

She paused at the tent flap and looked at him, her eyes serious. "Nothing must change, out there," she said. "I must do my duty to the One, no matter what it costs me and you. And you must do the same. Do not let bed feelings skew your judgment and make you do something unwise."

Kadar nodded, though he wasn't certain he was made that way. But he understood that she had her position to maintain and would respect her need for distance. She was the One's during the day, poised and stoic—but he would enjoy seeing her wilder side at night. Amber rubbed against his ankles, purring, and he went to get his cat breakfast.

Master Tull cursed and shook her hand as the stone pillar she grasped exploded into a thousand shards. Abram grabbed a bandage and ran to her. There were a dozen small cuts all over her hand and fingers, and he dabbed at the blood welling up.

She growled and tried to push him away. He held her hand still and glared at her.

"I'm not what you're angry with," he said. "You will accept my help."

Her lips quirked up in amusement and she allowed

him to bind her hand. She turned to the other three masters. "It's no good. Our mages have been experimenting since spring and this is the best we can do. Spells alone won't change the waymarkers. The only thing that will change the stones at all is using blood energy. And that isn't strong enough to change the wards imbedded in them."

"Then we should send warriors to evacuate the villages in the path of Voras's army," Master Gursh, her second in command, said.

"Where will the villagers go?" Master Ursa said. "They have to stay near water sources, and the *geased* guides will lead the deities right to those. The deities will find and enslave our people. How can we ask our warriors to kill their own families, who will be attacking us once they are *geased*?"

"There must be something we haven't tried," Master Sandiv said.

"We've been experimenting for many ten-days. We've researched. We've found nothing on waystone magic."

"Except what Yaoni found in the archives. The scroll he's still deciphering," Master Tull said.

Master Ursa gestured, and the pieces of the stone pillar Tull had been experimenting on joined together again. "Yes. I have to agree with Tull. That scroll seems to be our only hope." She tapped the newly formed pillar, and it fell back into pieces. She shook her head. "The oases waystones' very natures have been changed by an energy we don't understand. Our spells can't do that. Our spells do not permanently change rock."

Abram looked over at Casia and she shook her head. Neither of them had heard of any scroll until now. The masters must have discussed it in private.

"Do you still insist on being the ones to go, if you try to follow its instructions?" Master Gursh asked.

"We must," Master Tull said firmly. "We are the only ones powerful enough. Mage Bento has volunteered as well."

Master Sandiv protested, "The scroll could be fake. You'd be risking everything for a tale we can barely read, or are mistranslating. Ursa is vital to controlling the winds and winning the fight in the desert. You cannot go."

"No one person is vital in this fight," Master Ursa reproved. "You and your warriors have the training. You will succeed if I'm gone."

"I wish the One would give us some sign that this is the right path," Master Gursh growled.

"We have time yet," Master Ursa said quietly. "The army is not moving. Maybe the One will present another solution before we need to act."

"Maybe," Master Tull said, her face bleak. "But I will protect our people, whatever it takes."

"What did Aaron say last time you contacted him?" Evan asked.

Tori and the Descendants had arrived at Stonycreek

behind the army of Voras, which surrounded two sides of the town. The other two sides were backed to the cliffs of the foothills. Only a mountain goat could approach from that direction.

Tori's group had abandoned the main road and disappeared into the thick forest when they realized they were getting close to the town. Moving as silently as possible, they'd reached the wide cleared space around the town. Tori, Evan, Sandy, and Shane were lying in thick brush at the edge of the forest, looking down the slight incline to the army below them. Aaron had *farspoken* with Tori several times as Voras's army approached the town and he was able to get a better count of the total fighters the Knight had under his command.

A high stone wall surrounded the town proper, probably built more to keep out wolves and other four-footed invaders than to hold off an army. Through her spyglass, Tori could see archers on it, guarding the town.

Voras's army was camped on the crops the villagers were growing, out of reach of the archers on the walls. The fighters were tearing down wooden fencing that would keep deer and livestock out of the tender plants, and they were stomping on the vegetables. The village was under siege, but not overrun yet, which matched what Aaron had told Tori the night before. The army had arrived last evening and the Knight had given the Forsaken in the village an ultimatum to surrender and join the army or be taken by force. The Knight didn't want to fight any more than the Forsaken did, and would wait for the townspeople to realize the hopelessness of their situation.

"Looks like we got here before he ran out of patience," Sandy said.

"They're destroying the crops and killing livestock to demoralize the Forsaken," Shane said. "The Forsaken know they will starve in the winter if they don't have food to salt and dry. They won't starve if they join the army."

"It might have worked, if they didn't know we were on the way," Evan said. "I doubt Aaron and the Forsaken leaders could keep the townspeople from surrendering with the food destroyed and an overwhelming force on their doorstep."

Sandy looked over at Tori. "What's the plan, oh glorious leader?" he asked.

Tori looked through her glass again.

"The Knight has five soldiers of Voras with him—which means six *feli* total. Only one soldier and *feli* per squad of fighters," she said. "The rest of the army are common fighters or pressed Forsaken."

"The Forsaken are *geased*," Shane said, and the others stared at him. "What, you don't feel it? It seems obvious to me."

"Show me," Tori said, holding out her hand.

He took it, and Sandy grabbed his other hand. Tori closed her eyes and focused on melding energy with him, the way she had the past few evenings when they'd checked in with Aaron Hasifel. It was becoming second nature to link with the twins. Usually she took the lead, but this time, he did. With his guidance, she could see a link between the Forsaken, who made up the bulk of the fighters. She followed the energy as it thickened, braided into a rope connecting to one person. She noted the distance from her, and the seeming location, and opened her eyes.

"The Knight holds the *geas*," Tori confirmed, looking at the fancy tent. "He's the one we need to take out. We take him out, and any compulsion they feel will disappear."

"That doesn't mean they'll stop fighting," Sandy said. "Some might be happier in the army. The *geas* is added insurance for the Knight."

"But it's Forsaken against Forsaken," Shane argued. "I think many will choose not to fight their fellows. They may not fight for us, but I think many will flee."

"Fellows? They don't even know each other," Sandy said with a snort. "How much fellowship could they have?"

Tori ignored their bickering, conferring with Evan.

"Tell everyone not to kill the soldiers' *feli*," Tori told Evan, "We don't want to anger the One. Probably best to take the soldiers captive, rather than kill them as well. But we have to take out the Knight."

"You can't take down the Knight if you don't kill or block his *feli*," Evan said. "Any Knight of Voras will be a very powerful mage. Even with your training as a Descendant, he's probably more powerful than you are."

Tori looked over at Zara, lying beside her, alertly

gazing out on the army. The great cat turned and looked directly into Tori's eyes and she felt an affirmation, a feeling that the cat understood what she wanted. She looked over at Shane, to see if he'd felt anything.

Shane nodded. "Our *feli* will take care of his," he told Evan.

"How?" Evan asked.

Shane shrugged. "He doesn't communicate in words. I just know our *feli* are going to block the Knight from channeling Voras through his *feli*."

Tori could feel that Evan was holding back, uncertain who was in charge. He'd trained his whole life to be the leader of this movement, and now he was shut out because he didn't have a *feli*. He didn't seem to realize they both had essential jobs in this battle. He was a part of the team and she needed him to take action.

She looked directly at him. "Evan, how do you want to attack? Have you organized your fighters yet? I've my own job to do here working the energy. I need you to focus and plan the battle itself."

Evan looked surprised, then gazed narrowly out on the field. She could see him forming a plan. "I need you to contact Aaron and ask him what fighters they have. You told me Aaron has several experienced Southern fighters under his command as well as some Forsaken guards. His fighters are closest to the Knight's tent, by the walls. Can you tell me when the Knight moves, and where?"

Tori nodded and Evan continued, "There will be some chaos when we attack from the rear. At the same time we attack, a small force from the town should be able to move quickly, killing the Knight while he is still close to or in his tent. They won't expect us to coordinate with the townspeople."

He pointed to the larger tent. "The biggest obstacle is the Knight linking with his *feli* and blasting the fighters who come after him. Your *feli* are a bit large to slip in unnoticed from the back and kill or disable his before we attack."

"They can climb in those cliffs behind the town," Sandy said. "And slip into the town. Once they're in the town, they can attack when the villagers do."

"You can direct them?" Evan asked. "Impose your will on them?"

Sandy snorted. "We can very nicely nudge them with our minds, show what we want and promise them a tasty sheep if they do it," he said. "But the choice is theirs."

"I feel that they will act in accordance to our will, this one time," Shane said.

Evan nodded. "Then we fight at dusk, when the army is settling in for late meal. You three will stay behind the troops. Can you contain the soldiers who lead the squads? While most of us are magically shielded against hostile energy, we have some Descendants who are only fighters."

"We can protect them," Shane said. "I have already sought out the energy of the soldiers and will know if they try to use their *feli*. They are not as strong as the three of us linked together."

"Good. Contact Aaron; get the townsfolk ready. I'll organize our fighters into smaller strike groups and move them into position around the forest. We will hit many locations on their flank, distracting and disorienting them so that the smaller group from the town has a chance to kill the Knight."

Several hours later, Tori stood behind the Descendants, on foot with Sandy and Shane. Evan was at the head of his fighters, giving final orders in a quiet, terse voice. Tori had spoken with Aaron several times, relaying information and affirming that the *feli* had arrived in the town.

Tori could feel Zara's tension as she waited for the gates of the town to open and let the *feli* and village troops out. It was strange not having Zara beside her as she prepared for battle, but her role wasn't one of fighter. She and the twins had practiced joining together and blocking. She was confident they could block any magical attacks by the soldiers, but only if they stayed away from the battle and focused.

Voras's troops were wary, ready for any attack from the town. The Descendants had been able to cloak their presence from the sentries and patrols that passed by, so Voras's troops wouldn't be expecting their attack. But Tori was nervous. Anything could go wrong in battle.

Shane reached over and grasped her hand. He gave it a squeeze before taking Sandy's hand. They linked their energy together. As Evan gave the signal and his strike team rode into the back of Voras's army, Tori closed her eyes and mentally searched for the soldiers of Voras, finding their *feli* links. Shane turned his focus to two of the soldiers on the west side, Sandy turned his to the soldier in the middle and the Knight, and Tori took the two on the right side.

A rush of euphoria came from their three *feli* as the great cats streamed out the village gates. As the Descendants attacked the shocked troops from the rear, all attention was turned to the back of the army. The *feli* slipped unnoticed through the tents, tracking the Knight and his *feli*.

"There," Sandy said. Tori followed his link, seeing the energy shift as a soldier tried an energy strike. They threw up a wall between the energy and the Descendant he was throwing it at. The energy flared briefly against their shields, and Tori winced. It was like getting slapped on the inside of the head.

"Wait," Shane muttered. Tori was lightheaded as he sucked energy from her, and then he blocked the soldier's link to his *feli*. When the soldier tried again, he couldn't reach the energy.

"Nice shielding," Tori said. "I thought only a Descendant could do that."

He didn't have time to answer as another soldier, on the west side, attempted to use his magic, and they blocked it. Again, energy drained from her as Shane blocked the soldier's connection to the *feli*.

A burst of shared pain, not her own. She looked for the source. Their *feli* were fighting the Knight's *feli* and one of them was injured. The battle became a blur as the three Counselors reacted to a multitude of attacks, blocking the soldiers' energy flows or shielding Descendants from blasts. Tori's legs gave out and she sat hard on the ground. The twins settled beside her.

"I didn't realize how much this would take out of us," Tori gasped, sweat turning cold on her brow. A wave of satisfaction rose from their *feli*. They must have killed the Knight's *feli*.

"It's being without our *feli*," Sandy said, sounding as exhausted as she did. "They feed us energy from the One. Without them, we're draining our own energy."

"Another one," Shane warned.

Before they could turn their attention to the soldier, energy flared, closer to the town walls.

"The Knight," Shane said, "He must have some natural ability, even without his *feli* to feed it to him."

"Got him," Sandy said, through gritted teeth. "I feel what he is doing. Give me energy."

Tori fed him all she had, and Shane bolstered them. Sandy wove a net around the Knight, holding his energy in. Tori flinched as the man hammered the net with his energy, feeling her skull reverberate with every blow. He was more powerful than any of the three of them alone, but he was also distracted by the physical fight for his life against the Forsaken from the town.

Tori felt the now-dying Knight reach desperately out to the energy around him. Tori found herself caught, spiraling to death with him. Shane and Sandy fought with her against the Knight. Then suddenly she felt Zara in her mind, the *feli*'s energy slicing through the Knight's as though she'd slashed it with her claws. Tori slumped to the ground, exhausted.

A great roar echoed over the battlefield. Tori opened her eyes to see a chaotic scene unfolding before her. Evan screamed orders, and the Descendants broke off, retreating toward the woods. The energy of the remaining soldiers flared and then disappeared as furious Forsaken troops, no longer bound by their *geas*, turned against their commanders. Other fighters simply dropped their weapons and fled. A man on the battlefield bellowed for the troops to surrender.

A scrabbling behind their rocks made Tori reach for her knife, but it was Zara who appeared around the side, looking pleased. She was followed by Sandy's spotted Shiv. Shane's Ruta limped in behind, her flank bleeding sluggishly from four deep claw marks.

Zara flopped down beside Tori, and her energy began to return as soon as she threw her arms around the great cat. Shane exclaimed over Ruta's wounds, and Sandy pushed his hands aside to send healing energy to the wounded cat. The claw marks stopped bleeding.

"That's a new trick," Tori said.

"I spent a year with Aryn," Sandy said. "I have a very slight healing gift, but *feli* are easy. The One always grants healing for them."

Tori peered around the rock as horses galloped toward them. Evan swung down from his mount.

"Are you well?" he asked. "Cleo said you collapsed."

"Unharmed, but drained of energy. We'll be fine as

long as we don't have to go anywhere very quickly," Tori told him.

"What's happening on the battlefield?" Sandy asked.

"The troops surrendered, but not before the Forsaken killed Voras's soldiers," Evan said. "The Forsaken leaders and Aaron Hasifel are waiting to greet us at Stonycreek."

Tori tried to lever her body up against the rock and failed. Shane grimaced and managed to stand, but sat heavily against the rock. Sandy didn't even try.

"Well, this is embarrassing," Tori said. "But it looks like we'll need a chariot to cart our triumphant butts to the town, if they've got one."

Evan frowned, but Tori sensed he was more amused than irritated.

"I think the army had some supply carts," he said. "Not exactly a chariot but it'll have to do. Wait here."

"Don't know where else he thinks we're going," Sandy muttered as he rode off.

"Not exactly how I'd planned to meet Aaron Hasifel," Tori said. "Fainting and carried around."

"If he's Sulis's uncle, he's probably used to it," Sandy said. "Try cursing and protesting that you don't need help like Sulis would and he'll feel right at home."

CHAPTER 10

"I don't need help," Sulis growled at Ashraf as he put a steadying hand on her elbow when she tripped over her own feet. They were walking into the Obsidian Temple and she was already off balance, both physically and mentally.

He gave her a wounded look and she sighed.

"Sorry," she said. "You're not the one I'm irritated with."

He frowned, looking toward the center of the temple. "I know. An uncertain Amon is even worse than an arrogant Amon. I'm getting tired of being accused of hiding information from him. Not my fault he doesn't know things a Southern child learns in his small clothes."

"Are you going to dawdle all day?" Amon called sharply to them. "We're wasting precious time."

Sulis growled under her breath. Ava was already

drawing her mandala on the stone floor with her energy and chalk. Clay was supervising her. But Grandmother and Master Anchee had not arrived yet with their Guardians. Sulis couldn't dance alone.

Sanuri played her own little game with the statues of the deities, humming. The Obsidian Temple seemed to shield her from hearing the deities and she was happiest wandering around the statues. Alannah and Dani leaned against the wall their *feli* were sleeping by. Alannah was glaring at Amon and would occasionally mutter something to Dani. He looked both amused and apprehensive about what she was saying.

They'd been at the temple a ten-day and Amon still hadn't figured out how to empty the statues of the deities' will and energy. He'd been making Ava chalk every mandala she knew, and some that Clay taught her as they went. Then he made the Shuttles—Sulis, Master Anchee and Grandmother—dance them, raising as much energy as they could in a place devoid of green life force. He was able to channel that energy and send it. But where he sent it, Sulis didn't know. Amon had been growing angrier as his attempts failed, and he directed the blame at whichever Chosen caught his eye. Alannah believed that the same ritual Amon knew to trap the deities and then combine them back into the One's energy could be modified and used to empty the statues of the deities' essence. Amon had coldly told her she knew nothing of the ritual—it was sacred, and to play around with it would be sacrilege.

Grandmother, Master Anchee, and their Guardians

arrived, tailed by temple master Sari, as Sulis was beginning to study the lines of energy in the mandala. This circle was directing energy to the One's statue, rather than any of the deities, and used heart energy. Sulis's back ached thinking of the heart-opening poses she'd have to move through in this form.

"It's about time you showed up," Amon snapped as Master Anchee came abreast of Sulis.

Master Anchee raised his eyebrows, but Grandmother bristled and growled low in her throat. To Sulis's disappointment, Palou touched her arm and she subsided. Watching Grandmother take down the arrogant Northerner would have been fun.

Ava connected her last line and stood, swaying slightly. Dani stepped forward and steadied her, helping her over to a cushion he'd brought for her. Nuisance pounced on her feet and she pulled him onto her lap, giggling as he batted her hair and purred. He was almost full-grown now and his legs spilled off each side of her lap. Sulis smiled to see Ava looking happier, less tense than she had been.

"We've had some bad news," Sari announced to the group. "Master Tull contacted me this morning. The Tigus intercepted messages being sent to the troops along the border. The caravan leaders Voras captured in Illian were forced to reveal the locations of the oases. They told Voras everything—where the waymarker is, the words of power, and the mudras to use to release the wards."

"Then my Tarik died for nothing," Grandmother

said, anguished. "They will find us before we are ready for them."

"No," Sari said. "The caravan they captured was one of the Tasharas'. The leader was new and had been permitted travel only to and from Tsangia. They don't yet know the way to the oases deeper in the desert."

Sulis stared at her in horror. "But they'll go after the towns on the path to Tsangia," she said. "My family lives in Shpeth, Aunt Janis and my cousins. You have to send the warriors of the One to protect them."

Sari shook her head. "We are counting on the Tigus to winnow down Voras's army as they move through the desert," she said. "There aren't enough warriors of the One to stop Voras's army all at once."

"Then change the words of power that reveal the oases," Sulis said, turning to her grandmother. "Or hide the waymarkers so they can't find them."

Sari spread her hands. "The spells that set the waymarkers into the ground also prevent them from being hidden," she said. "So that if desert tribes went to war, they could not damage or destroy access to the oases."

"We don't know how the ancients did it. How they created words of such power that have lasted five hundred years," Master Anchee said. "It must have taken five or six energy users, more powerful than we are, to set such illusions."

"Do the Descendants have records of how it was done?" Sari asked Amon. He shook his head.

"It was only one person," Ava said.

They turned to look at her, and she ducked her head into her *feli's* fur.

Alannah knelt beside her and put a hand on her shoulder.

"Why do you say that?" she asked, her voice warm, confiding. Sulis wasn't certain if she was using magic, but even Sulis wanted to respond to that voice. "Did you read something on it that could help us?"

Ava raised her head. "Aryn told me," she said.

They all glanced at Aryn's statue and Sulis shivered.

"Blood magic?" Master Anchee asked.

"No," Ava said softly. "Worse than that. Death magic."

They stared at her in horror and she nodded solemnly. "Aryn put a lot of things in my mind. It's unhealing, so she knows how to do it."

"Knows how to do what?" Alannah asked.

"Make the waymarkers. They're planted in the body of a powerful energy user," Ava said. "Blood of the energy user anchors the illusion and the ward over the oases. The waystone is planted into their bodies as they kill themselves: a death offering."

Dani looked horrified, but the elder Southerners nodded.

"Such a sacrifice," Sari murmured. She put her hands together and touched them to her forehead, lips, and breastbone in tribute.

Sulis blew her breath out. "Well, then we can't change the markers," she said. "We can't ask someone to make that sacrifice. We need all our energy users."

"They wouldn't have to change all the markers," Lasha said thoughtfully. "Miss one or two oases, and horses and people would die before reaching the others. They'd have to turn back."

Sulis turned to her. "Don't even think about it," she exclaimed.

Lasha smiled ruefully. "I don't have that kind of power, anyway. Just thinking out loud."

"I'll discuss this with Master Tull," Sari said, looking troubled. "We'll see what she has to say."

"If that's all, we have work to do," Amon said, dismissing the temple master.

Sari pursed her lips, but nodded to the others and left them.

"That woman is the most powerful channeler of the One's powers I have ever encountered," Master Anchee told Amon coldly. "You will treat her with respect."

"Enough talking," Amon ordered harshly. "Shuttles, do your dance."

Sulis conferred with Master Anchee as they decided which lines to start and end with and which forms they would move through to raise the highest energy. Grandmother listened in. Her dance was outside the circle, but she would echo their energy. She'd tried sending energy to Sanuri to weave and ground it, but had been unable to connect to the girl. Sanuri had been completely uninterested in the energy they raised, and Clay had clutched his hair even harder as he tried to talk to her about it. Grandmother was sending the energy to Amon instead.

Sulis took mountain form, hands at heart center, as Master Anchee faced off across from her. She flowed to the next form, stepping over the line of energy of the mandala and filling that space with heart energy. Alannah had told her the entire quadrant of the mandala glowed with the color of the energy she raised, and at the end the mandala was as brilliant as a rainbow. But Sulis could not see energy. She felt it, created it. She reached her senses out to Anchee as he flowed with her. He took the energy she raised and echoed it into the quadrant of the mandala he stepped through, expanding her energy. She adjusted her pace to his, making certain that their steps matched and their motions were synchronized. She was barely aware of Grandmother swirling around them, sucking in the raised energy. She shut out the people watching and focused on the mandala and the dance.

She was panting when she and Master Anchee finished together. He was drenched with sweat, and Sulis realized she was as well. He smiled approvingly at her and she flushed with pride. She hadn't missed a step, hadn't faltered or forgotten what the next move was.

They bowed to each other and slowly released the circle. Ashraf was standing outside the mandala, ready to support her if she needed his energy. This time she did not, though she was weary.

All eyes turned to Amon, who stood like a statue by the Altar of the One. His face was drawn in a scowl as he tried to contain the energy Grandmother had thrown him. His hands and body shook. Sulis wasn't certain if they'd raised a different type of energy or they'd raised more than he was capable of holding, but he was clearly struggling to contain and channel it.

Alannah made an inarticulate sound and hurried over to Amon and the altar, Yaslin by her side. Sulis didn't know what Alannah would do if he lost control, but she and Lasha stepped up beside Alannah in case she needed help.

Amon opened his eyes and turned, barely able to control his body enough to take the two steps to the altar.

"Stay out of the way, you fools," he rasped, though they were out of his reach.

He placed both hands on the round stone of the altar and light flared around him, so bright Sulis had to look away, her eyes watering.

The light dimmed and Sulis looked back. Amon was sitting on the floor beside the altar, his head in his hands. The altar's orb glowed, suffused on the inside with light and energy. It occasionally sent small sparks off.

"Very pretty," Alannah said dryly. "What were you trying to do?"

Amon looked up at the altar. "Give the One enough power to take the deities' power by himself," he said, standing again. He swayed slightly, but none of the Chosen gathered around tried to support him.

"I don't think it worked," Ava said, her hand on Parasu's statue. "I can still feel them here."

Amon turned on Ava, furious, and she cringed against the statue.

"And where was your focus, when you messed up the mandala? It would have worked if the lines were correct!" he shouted at her. "You were playing with that stupid kitten of yours, weren't you? I should have that beast killed! You're a useless little bastard, and crazy besides . . ." He advanced on her, arm raised to strike her.

Sulis stepped forward, afraid that he'd either harm Ava or that the girl would draw something ugly from Parasu to defend herself as she had from Aryn. She stopped and turned as Yaslin snarled. At Yaslin's squall, everyone turned toward the Altar of the One.

Alannah had slapped her hands on the glowing orb and now glowed with energy herself. Unlike Amon, she was taller and radiant with it, her pale hair crackling in an aura around her head. It took no effort for her to control the energy. Sanuri giggled. Amon stared at her, mouth open, attack on Ava forgotten.

"This is how you control energy," Alannah said, her voice otherworldly. "With acceptance, not force. You seek wisdom inside yourself, my son. But you ignore my wisdom. Who do you truly serve?"

She became radiant, too beautiful to look at. A being of light. An embodiment of the One. Amon fell to his knees.

"I don't know what to do. You have given me an impossible task," Amon cried. "How can I do this alone?"

Grandmother stepped forward. "You aren't alone, you young idiot. The One chose us as much as she chose you."

Alannah smiled. "My Chosen speak wisely. Be guided by them. This Counselor will share the burden. I will be whole again."

The altar and the being beside it flared with light, and Sulis looked away. When she looked back, Alannah was standing in front of the altar, her brow furrowed.

"Well, that was something," Dani said. "Didn't know you had it in you, Alannah."

"Had what in me?" Alannah asked. "Why is everyone staring at me?"

"You know, becoming a being of light, channeling the One," Lasha said, walking over to her. Alannah stared at her, baffled. "Well, maybe you don't know. Don't you feel any different? Tired perhaps?"

"We will use the ritual, as you requested," Amon declared, bowing to Alannah. "I will train you in the final words of power. We will start tomorrow. We will move forward together as the One directed."

He turned and walked out of the temple. As he passed Sulis, she saw he was trembling. Whether from fear or excitement, she couldn't tell.

"What beat sense into his thick head?" Alannah asked. Lasha and Sulis exchanged glances, bemused. "Is someone going to tell me what's going on? I walk over to the altar and everyone acts like I've grown a second head."

Lasha slung an arm around her shoulders. "I'll explain on the way to late meal. Somehow, I don't think Amon will be there."

"You were right," Ashraf told Sulis as they walked to the meal hall. "With you three troublemakers around, things are always interesting."

Abram felt Sari nudge their mind connection to get his attention. He had just fetched breakfast for himself and Master Tull and was pouring *tash* for her in her office. He put the carafe down and sat on a bench, opening to Sari's *farspeech*.

Master Tull looked up from her papers, eyebrows raised.

"Sari is contacting me," Abram said, and closed his eyes, focusing inward.

Sari's mindvoice was impassive, but Abram listened in growing horror to Ava's revelations about how the waymarkers were set. Abram hesitated, opening his eyes to stare at Master Tull.

"Well?" she asked.

Abram's silver tongue stumbled as he repeated Sari's gruesome description of how the ancients created the waymarkers.

"Tell her this confirms the information we found in an old scroll. We'd deciphered its instructions, but were worried it was a fake. Thank her. I will speak with the other masters and decide a course of action," Master Tull told him.

Abram relayed her words and broke the connection between Sari and himself. Silence fell over the room as Master Tull stared into space, her expression brooding.

"You . . . you can't," Abram said. She looked bleakly at him and he held out a hand. "You can't want to do this."

Her expression softened. "Sacrifices in war are bitter, Abram," she said. "I find it less bitter that the sacrifice is mine, rather than others'. Please go summon Ursa, Gursh, Bento, and Sandiv. Ask them to come without their assistants."

Abram shook his head and she put her hands on his shoulders. She squeezed gently, almost a hug, then turned him and pushed him toward the door.

"Go, Abram. Tell no one, not even Casia. I'm sorry. It will be a hard burden to bear in silence."

Abram walked out, then leaned against the building a moment to compose himself. "Not half the burden you willingly carry," he said softly. "May I someday be worthy of your sacrifice."

CHAPTER 11

Kadar loosed another arrow from his position up on the ridge, but the fighter turned and it bounced harmlessly off his armor. It distracted the man enough that the Tigu he was fighting found his footing again.

Kadar notched another arrow, but he could see that the Tigu warriors needed to retreat. The Sepacu tribe was buying time for the Zanta tribe to gather their belongings and move deeper into the desert, but this cohort of Voras's fighters was too strong to engage for long.

Voras had taken the loss of his troops poorly. The information the Tigus had stolen was essential, but the retaliation had cost them dearly. They'd lost over a hundred warriors to a surprise attack on the closest tribe to the army encampment. Voras's army had pushed the Tigus farther into the desert. Soldiers had arrived from Illian with their *feli* and they directed the great cats to scout out the surrounding hills for the nomads. Desert magic did not affect the *feli*, who could see through illusions. So the Tigus were forced to retreat and regroup. True to her words, Onyeka had abandoned her colorful tapestries and pillows without a second glance, moving to a single bedroll with Kadar, which they could pack quickly onto one horse.

Jaiden whooped her signal and the Tigu nomads disengaged, fading into the desert at random, having done their job of slowing the army. They would regroup farther up the ridge. Kadar swung up on Asfar and glanced behind once, surveying the retreating Tigus. He recognized Onyeka's mare galloping toward the ridge closest to him, trailing two others. He looked ahead in time to see an army archer stand and take aim, but wasn't fast enough with his own bow to stop him from making the shot. Onyeka's mare went down, shot in the chest, as Kadar drew his bow. Kadar planted an arrow in the archer's neck, and then galloped down the rise to where the mare lay. The horse's body hid Onyeka; he couldn't tell if she was injured. He drew his sword, ready for battle, but they were at the edge of the battlefield and Voras's fighters were regrouping.

Onyeka struggled to get her foot free from under the mare's body. Kadar cast out a wave of fear that would keep their opponents' horses from approaching them and leapt down, keeping her dying horse between him and any archers.

"Kadar, get away," Onyeka ordered harshly, still struggling. "You need to protect yourself."

Kadar ignored her and helped lift the saddle enough that she could free her foot. He flung himself onto Asfar's saddle, feeling Onyeka scramble up behind him. Her arms wrapped around his waist and he signaled Asfar to leap into a gallop.

"Are you hurt?" Kadar asked Onyeka.

"No," she said, voice clipped. "Keep riding."

They slowed to a trot when Kadar realized they weren't being followed, and circled around to the meeting point. As other warriors straggled in, Kadar realized he and Onyeka weren't the only ones riding pillion. Voras's archers had targeted their mounts. They were probably hoping to demoralize the Tigus, since their love for their horses was legendary. Kadar smiled slightly. The Tigus loved their horses but were terrifyingly blasé about death. If they had to switch to humpbacks, they'd treat them with the same meticulous care as their horses, and their weapons.

Jaiden signaled for everyone to move on to camp. As they rode out, she reined in beside Kadar to speak with Onyeka. He could understand most of what was said now, having been immersed in the language for months now. He couldn't hear thoughts with his *farspeech*, but if he focused, he could hear the intent behind the words spoken. That helped his mind translate the words, so he had learned the Tigu language with surprising speed.

"We lost Duran, Jase, and Sella," she told Onyeka. "I thought you were gone as well when your mount collapsed. Are you injured?"

"Bruise or sprain to the ankle," Onyeka said. "Nothing major."

"Good," Jaiden said. "I need you to take over for Duran. We will meet the others at the spring and camp for the evening."

"What then?" Kadar asked.

"That's for the elders to decide," Jaiden said. "But I'm guessing we'll stay on the move, teasing the troops, not letting them feel safe."

They traveled on into the dusk, others coming to ride beside and confer with Onyeka and tease Kadar about rescuing his bedmate. Onyeka become more and more tense with the teasing.

They reached the camp a little after dark, guided by the Tigus' water sense. The camp was well hidden, and they were upon it before Kadar realized. Onyeka slid down immediately, and Kadar dismounted. He handed Asfar's reins to a waiting helper, and then was suddenly busy untangling Amber from his breeches as she tried to climb up him. The cat had an uncanny sense for when he entered camp, demanding attention and treats. He settled her on his shoulder and turned to find that Onyeka was limping off.

He ran up beside her. "Any idea where they've pitched our tent?" he asked.

"My tent," Onyeka said, turning to him. Her face was tight and angry. "Not ours. I think you need to find your own tent, Kadar."

"Why are you so angry?" he asked, though he suspected what she'd say.

"You risked yourself in battle because you were too attached to me," she said. "I can't trust you to be dispassionate. I can't trust you to do what the One needs for you to do in battle. You broke the one rule I set for us. We're done."

She turned away, and he stepped in front of her again, forcing her to look at him. They were getting looks from the other warriors, but Kadar didn't care. Amber growled low in her throat at Kadar's abrupt movements.

"I rescued Dono in the last battle," he told her, letting his own anger show. "It is part of my job as a lookout to see where I can assist the warriors on the field."

"You are more important than I," Onyeka said, her voice harsh. "If you had been killed, we would have no way to communicate with the warriors of the One. We would be cut off. Your attachment to me made you forget that and run into danger."

"I forgot nothing," Kadar said. "I killed the archer who felled your horse. There were no troops around you, and none except the archer saw you fall. I assessed the danger to myself against the danger to another comrade, as I did with Dono. I had already mounted Asfar, so it was easy and quick."

She looked down at her feet, too furious to listen to him, and he reached out and lifted her chin. He directly looked into her angry eyes.

"I think you're the one who is too attached to think straight. You're so attached to your own independence, to your view of what you think the One wants that nothing anyone else does can penetrate your thick skull. I will not let a comrade fall in battle if I can safely get her out—that's how the One made me. If you can't let me be as the One wills, then you are right, we are done. But you will never be a good leader until you recognize the One in everyone around you, not only in yourself."

Kadar turned on his heel and walked to the heap of supplies and extra tents by the packhorses. Jaiden fell in beside him as he sorted through the pile.

"You are good for her," she said slowly, so he could understand every word. She slapped him on the back and Amber hissed at her. She chuckled at the cat's ire. "You will make a leader of her yet. You did the right thing. Others saw you. It was a clean rescue. I will tell her. She will learn from this."

Kadar wasn't certain what to make of this encouragement, so he set up his tent.

His sleep was restless and he woke with first light before the rest of the camp stirred. Amber settled on his lap, a cream-colored ball. Kadar allowed his mind to wander. He could feel that several of the soldiers in Voras's camp had *farspeech* and shielded his mind from them. He let it wander down the twin-bond, but Sulis was still fast asleep and he did not have a good reason to wake her.

His cousin, with the warriors of the One, was also sleeping. Kadar thought of the woman he'd spoken with several times in the past year, Sulis's pledge mate Tori, and let his mind wander in that direction, hoping that perhaps she could tell him what was happening in the North.

He cast about, looking for that link he'd formed with her. He followed it and found another mind active, searching as he was. One as familiar as his own heartbeat.

Uncle Aaron? Kadar queried.

Kadar? Do you have a message from Mother? Uncle Aaron asked.

No, I'm with the Tigu warriors, at the edge of the desert, by Voras's army. Where are you? Sulis said Grandmother has been worrying about you, Kadar sent.

At Stonycreek, Aaron said. *I was almost trapped in Illian trying to get some of our Southern families out. I knew we'd left guards in Stonycreek, so we regrouped here.* Aaron's mindvoice became rueful. *But Voras's army was on our heels, hoping to recapture the Forsaken here.*

Are you besieged? Kadar asked anxiously.

No, Aaron sent. *Oddly enough, we were rescued by one of Sulis's old friends—Tori, and a whole group of fighters calling themselves Descendants of the Prophet. They defeated Voras's army, helped free the geased fighters.*

Tori? I thought she served Parasu, Kadar sent. *Sulis has been working with one of those Descendants at the Obsidian Temple as well.*

She's a Counselor now. There's a whole wave of acolytes becoming Counselors, all across the North, Aaron responded. *And she's a Descendant.*

And the geased fighters? Kadar asked. *How did she free them? Are all the army fighters geased?*

Kadar thought back to his own battles against the army. He hadn't felt any sort of compulsion on the fighters, but he was only a *farspeaker*, not an energy channeler.

Tell your battle leaders, Aaron said. *The Forsaken who fight for Voras are under a compulsion to fight. Tori and her companions were able to feel it. They broke that geas, and most of the army either fled or fought against their commanders. Many of them have joined us now.*

Break it how? Kadar asked.

We killed the Knight. He had bound the will of all the Forsaken to him. Kill the Knight and you free every Forsaken. Not all the fighters are geased.

That is huge news for us, Kadar told him. *Did you know the Tasharas' caravan leaders were forced to tell the deities the location of the waymarkers and the words of power? They know the route from Illian to Tsangia.*

Has anyone warned the villages along that route? Uncle Aaron asked, and Kadar knew he was worrying about his wife, Kadar's aunt Janis, and their friends in Shpeth.

I think so, Kadar said. *We passed all the information to the warriors of the One. It's up to them to protect the border towns.*

I must go, Aaron sent. *Protect yourself, son of my heart. Contact me if you hear anything that might help our march on Illian.*

I will. Take care of yourself, Kadar said. *I could not bear to lose another loved one. Let me know when the march on Illian begins. We begin one of our own here, retreating from Voras's army.*

Aaron broke contact and Kadar opened his eyes. Onyeka sat cross-legged in front of him, watching him intently. Amber stood and arched her back in a stretch before sauntering over and walking across Onyeka's lap, her tail waving in the woman's face.

"It looks strange when you do that," Onyeka said in his own tongue. "Your face is exactly like when you talk to someone in person. I can almost guess what you are saying, mind to mind, by what your face shows. But you don't speak out loud."

Kadar stretched and stood, putting on his cloak.

"It is odd, not being able to see the faces of the people I'm talking to," he told her. "Have the elders sent you to fetch me? I have some information for them from Aaron."

Onyeka shook her head, looking uncertain. Kadar didn't like that look on her.

"Many warriors have told me that you were in no danger, rescuing me," she admitted. "I did not sleep last night, thinking about it. I believe you are right. I become so worried about being too attached that I forget others can judge for themselves, know what is right. My mother was a battle leader. But she died because she became too attached and rode back when it was clear that the only thing she could do was perish with her companion. I feel . . . judged by her actions. I want the camp to respect me."

"You are respected," Kadar said. "Everyone reveres your battle skill. If anyone used to judge you by your mother, they don't anymore." He grinned at her. "You are right though, I would risk a good deal to rescue you. Not because we share a bed, but because you are more essential to your tribe, as a leader, than you realize. Luckily, all the warriors who ride with you feel the same way, so they rescue you before I do something stupid."

Onyeka smiled. "I guess I am lucky," she said. "The One wants you safe and protected, so I do not have to choose between my duty and my heart."

It was the closest she would ever come to saying she cared about him, Kadar realized. Even admitting that much was hard for her. He wouldn't ask for more.

"So can I move back in?" Kadar asked plaintively. He kicked the bedroll beside him. "These leftover bedrolls feel made of brick, and a man gets used to a little softness in his life." He did his best leer, looking at her chest.

She laughed and swatted him on the arm. "If you want softness, you should share Remy's bed," she said, naming the camp's cook, a man with a soft, round belly. "You won't find much here."

He grabbed her in a hug and kissed her. "More than enough for me," he said.

"The people of Stonycreek have formed an army, along with the Forsaken fighters we just freed," Aaron told Tori. "They have no food for winter because of Voras's attack on the town and cannot stay here. They are arming themselves to fight."

Tori stared at him in shock. "Do they plan on raiding other towns?" she asked. "We can't let them kill innocent townspeople."

"No, they plan on attacking Illian when the Voices of deities and Voras's army leave it unprotected. They are angry and want the riches the temple hides. They say they want to help with the Descendants' plan."

Tori looked around at their group. "How do they know the plan? Who told them the deities were leaving Illian?"

The twins shook their heads, mystified, but Evan stared her down.

"I told them," he said.

"Why would you do that?" Tori asked, furious.

"You chose to involve them in this fight. We helped them, now they can support us. With the deities gone, they will soon be free to go wherever they wish. If they choose to fight to make that happen, it is to the glory of the One," Evan said.

"Voras won't leave Illian unprotected," Tori said. "We'd planned to trickle the Descendants into Illian in small groups, to avoid alarming the guards. We can't do that with a Forsaken army on our heels. You have destroyed the chance of a quiet revolution. Now blood will be shed."

"Unless the Forsaken army doesn't march on Illian until you are ready for them," Aaron suggested.

Shane grinned. "I like the way you think," he said, quicker than Tori to grasp Aaron's meaning.

"You're suggesting we use them as a distraction," Sandy said.

Aaron nodded. "My men can join their army. We will delay marching on the city until your people are inside the walls."

"The soldiers will be so focused on an army approaching Illian, that a trickle of us fleeing before that army to the safety of the city will seem normal," Tori said. "Sandy, Shane, and I arriving as new Counselors of the One to take our place at the Temple will be another distraction. This could work."

Aaron nodded. "When the final battle comes, you can *farspeak* me and our army will attack the gates, pulling Voras's soldiers out of the city."

"We won't have to stave off Voras's soldiers while shielding the city from the deities," Sandy said. "This distraction could save us."

"How do we convince the townspeople to agree to our plan?" Aaron asked. "We want them to attack, but with no promise of a reward. They want revenge."

"By promising them food and livestock to replace what they lost," Evan said. "I can speak for the Descendants. We have large herds and can share our resources."

Tori nodded in approval. "I cannot promise the Temple's resources, but I believe once the war is won, Counselor Elida will be generous to the people who fought for us."

"Good. Evan will speak to the leaders. We'll start

dividing up the Descendants to send through the forest so they can join parties on the road," Shane said.

"This is the time of year when scholars and craftsmen tithe to Parasu and Aryn," Sandy offered. "There are several crafts gatherings in Illian before the harvest brings in the farmers."

Tori nodded. "Excellent."

"Only the men should carry weapons if you don't want suspicion raised," Shane reminded her. "Have them take residence at different inns around the Temple. We three Counselors and a retinue of Descendants will ride in midmonth."

"And by that time, our army will already be inside," Tori said with approval. "Sneaky. I love the way you boys think."

The twins grinned at each other as Aaron nodded in satisfaction. As Zara bumped her head against Tori's waist looking pleased with herself, Tori was satisfied she had the right people on her side.

CHAPTER 12

The Chosen and their Guardians were gathered in the Obsidian Temple. All the *feli* had chosen to join them, including a wild *feli* who had shown up and attached himself to Palou.

"The *feli* augment our power, but they also shield us from excess energy that might backlash," Alannah told Sulis. "I'm guessing that's why every pair of Guardian and Chosen have a *feli*."

Amon had called them to the temple today and stated that Alannah had learned enough and it was time to actually try joining the deities with the One.

"I know you've been teaching Alannah the final words of power in the joining ceremony," Clay said to Amon. "But what mandala does Ava use? It would make her feel better if she could practice it before we do the actual ceremony."

"The mandala for the joining is fluid," Amon said.

"It is expected that the Loom and the Weaver will know how to set the pattern." He looked doubtfully over at Ava, who had Nuisance on her lap and looked terrified at the thought, and then over at Sanuri, who was wandering around, touching the statues of the deities. "The words Alannah and I speak are specific, as is the power needed to invoke the One and allow the joining to happen. I have been training Alannah in the ritual. But the pattern set by the Loom matches the energy of the deities. Ava should know in her heart how to chalk the lines."

Sulis glanced over at Alannah, who looked a little smug. Amon was still a haughty jerk, but less offensive and more reverential to Alannah.

"I don't know what to do," Ava said, looking panicked. "Clay teaches me set patterns. I can't come up with them on my own!"

"Nonsense," Clay said soothingly. He knelt down beside her. "I'm the one who has been holding you back! When Sanuri sits down in your patterns, you improvise and draw a new pattern around her. When a crack or rock gets in your way, you find a way to create around it." He lifted her chin when she looked down. "You are more talented than I, my young friend, and I'm not ashamed to admit it. Let the student outstrip the teacher."

Ava smiled up at him as he held out his hand. She let him lift her to her feet. They walked over to the statues, and Clay put an arm around her shoulders.

"So, what do we do first?" Clay asked.

Sanuri wandered over and placed her hand on Parasu's figure. "This," she said.

They looked over at Amon, who shrugged. "Seems as good a place to start as any," he said.

They stared at the statue. Parasu was a thin, long figure with a painfully resigned expression.

Ava gulped and stepped up, looking at the figure and then at the Altar of the One.

"So," she said hesitantly. "Am I supposed to include only Parasu and the Altar of the One in my mandala if we are focusing on Parasu?"

Amon looked puzzled. "In the main joining ritual, all the deities are woven together at once," he said. "So the mandala encompasses all of them."

"So should we try joining them all at once?" Sulis asked. "Will the ritual only work if all are woven into the One at the same time?"

"No!" Sanuri said, her face drawn in a scowl. "This!"

Sulis looked at Alannah, who was focused on the girl.

"Is she channeling the One?" Sulis asked.

Alannah nodded slowly. "I think so," she said. "I feel something connecting to her, similar to what I feel when Yaslin connects to me and the One."

Clay heaved a sigh. "So, one at a time it is," he said. "To be honest, that is easier. We can practice handling more energy before we have the full energy of the deities here and have to weave four at once."

"I do wish this would have been done before I came," Amon said, fretfully.

"How could we know the ritual," Grandmother said acerbically, "since the Descendants have been keeping it from us all these years?"

He didn't answer and they all turned to watch Ava circle the statues. She glanced over at the group, looking lost.

"Come, come," Sanuri sang. She grabbed Ava's hand and sat. Ava sat with her and Sanuri grabbed her other hand. They closed their eyes. Sanuri hummed a tune that seemed familiar, but Sulis couldn't place it.

"Oh my," Alannah breathed softly.

"That's interesting," Lasha whispered.

Sulis closed her eyes, looking for what they were sensing. She could feel energy swirling, but not as obviously as they saw it.

"What?" she whispered.

"There's all kinds of energy being exchanged," Alannah said softly. "It's like the two are connecting more deeply. I see many colors. I think Sanuri is weaving their energy together, so the One can direct Ava through her. Or maybe so Ava can sense the deity's connection to the One better? I don't know exactly what is happening."

They stayed like that for a half sandglass, motionless, eyes closed.

Then Ava opened her eyes. She looked dazed.

Sanuri giggled and Ava looked at her and grinned, then stood. She grabbed her box of colored chalks and knelt on the black floor, at the midpoint between the Altar of the One and Parasu's statue. She chalked lines, intently. Sulis could feel energy corresponding with the colors she chalked and wondered if she was chalking a visual cue for Sulis, who could not see energy colors, or if it helped her focus.

"Unusual," Clay whispered to Sulis. "She always starts from the outside and works her way in, so the lines are even. This time it is reversed."

"Does this mean I have to dance from the inside out?" Sulis asked.

"I don't know," Clay said. "Everything we've done before was theoretical, practice. This is real. We are breaking new ground. You'll have to see how it feels when she is finished, and decide with Master Anchee on a starting point."

"The colors are incredible," Lasha said.

"So you can see them, too," Sulis said sourly. "All I see are pale chalk lines."

"Extend your senses," Grandmother chided her. "Then you will understand."

Sulis closed her eyes, and the sensation of the energy nearly knocked her over. Each chakra felt strong. Alannah put a hand on her arm, and she could see the vibrant colors as well. And in the center of each line of energy a link, leading to . . .

"She's tying Sanuri into the mandala," Sulis whispered.

Alannah nodded. "Do you see what Sanuri is doing?" she asked.

Sanuri was standing beside the Altar of the One, her hands and cheek resting against the orb in the center.

She looked restful, happy. Sulis closed her eyes and Sanuri glowed white, pulsing with the same energy as the orb.

"She connects with the One," Clay said. "And Ava lays a path from the deity to her and the orb."

The mandala was oblong, not the perfect circle Sulis was used to dancing. The altar was on one end and Parasu on the other. She paced along the outer edge, feeling the energy and trying to figure out how to dance it. She found Anchee doing the same thing.

"Do we even need to dance it?" she asked him. "It feels powerful without us adding to it."

Anchee nodded. He pointed to the outer edge, which Ava was still chalking. "If this is similar to other wards of power, she'll need to add a layer on the outside of Parasu to enclose him in the mandala, so we can collect his energy and dance around him. You will dance the lines of the mandala and enhance the energy, drawing Parasu's power from the statue. You will direct his power to me and I will expand it. I will give the energy to your grandmother and she will capture all that energy and spin it to the Weaver, who will weave it together with the One's energy. Alannah will speak the words of invocation, and the One will draw that energy into himself."

"And that will empty the statue?" Sulis asked. "What will be left?"

"I don't know," Anchee said. He looked past Sulis and sucked in a worried breath. Sulis turned. Ava was standing, chalk in hand, but swaying on her feet.

Dani supported her, his arms around her, steadying her. Sulis could feel him sending the girl energy. Ava smiled up at her Guardian, and then her eyes fell on the knife in the sleeve by his side. She grabbed his knife and drew it, and Sulis groaned.

But Ava turned to her drawing, walking to the Altar of the One. Sanuri smiled and held her palm up. Ava pricked her palm gently, and then slashed her own. She clasped her hand to Sanuri's, smearing their palms together, and then pressed her palm against the altar. There was a hint of dark energy where she pressed it. Then she dragged her hand along a line she'd drawn from the altar to Parasu. Sulis winced in sympathy as the girl dragged her wound on the stone of the floor. There were only trace amounts of blood, but Sulis could feel the dark energy rolling off the line, linking the altar, Parasu's statue and Sanuri even more deeply. She went to the line on the other side of the mandala, and did the same, enclosing the center with blood magic.

Clay leaned in to say in Sulis's ear, "So, learning blood magic from Aryn was part of the One's plan," he said. "When will I learn to have faith in his guiding hand?"

When Ava finished the line, she handed the dagger back to Dani, and then turned and chalked more lines, this time fully around the altar and Parasu, as Master Anchee had predicted.

When she was done, Ava closed her eyes, checking the design's energy. She opened her eyes and rechalked two lines more deeply. She stepped back again, and then went to her pillow and sat, closing her eyes. Her face was weary as Nuisance bumped his head under her chin and lay across her lap.

"Good!" Sanuri chortled. She carefully stepped over the lines, going to Grandmother. She pressed her bloody hand to Grandmother's lips and Grandmother jerked away, startled. She grimaced, licked her lips, and swallowed, creating a blood connection to Sanuri.

"I would rather have cut my palm than swallowed blood," Grandmother complained, and Sanuri doubled over with laughter.

"This is where we begin," Master Anchee said. "Joisha, are you ready?"

Grandmother took a final lap around, examining the mandala, and nodded.

"Alannah?" Master Anchee asked.

Alannah positioned herself outside of the Altar of the One, Yaslin beside her. She nodded, her face serene.

Sulis took a deep breath.

"Do we need to exchange blood?" she asked Master Anchee nervously.

"I don't think so," he said. "All we need is an energetic connection to each other, which we've already formed through practice." He grinned. "That is the theory. But most of my theories have been turned upside down today. Sanuri is not cutting us and pressing our bloody hands together, so I think we are safe."

Master Anchee pointed to an energetic line. "I believe that is our start point. We will wind around the circle, like it is a labyrinth. The end point will put you behind the Altar of the One and me behind Parasu."

As Master Anchee walked her though the pose changes on each flow of energy, Sulis's confidence waned.

She stood outside the mandala as Master Anchee circled around and Grandmother took her position outside. Sulis was worried that Sanuri would get in the way, but the girl climbed onto the altar and sat on the orb as the Guardians gathered outside the circle—close enough to give energy but not be in the way. Sulis glanced at the doorway, wondering if a girl sitting on their sacred altar would scandalize the guards, but they faced away, guarding the door against intruders. Sulis had a sudden fear that they should be guarding the altars against the Chosen. None of them knew what would happen in this ceremony, especially if one of them made a mistake.

"I can't do this," Sulis whispered, unable to bring herself to step into the mandala. "I always mess it up. I'll smear a chalk line, and that'll be it."

"Nonsense," Ashraf said, kissing the top of her head. "Take a deep breath in. It has been many ten-days since you smeared a single line. Our Nasifel clan will tell tales of your magnificence. Focus on your breath. That will calm you, guide you."

Sulis took emotional as well as physical strength from his embrace, and then looked across the oblong space at Master Anchee. He was speaking with Lasha, who nodded earnestly. They clasped hands once, and then broke apart. Lasha took a few steps back, and

Ashraf did the same. Alta stalked over to Lasha and nudged her hand, sitting at her side. Sulis glanced back and found that Djinn was seated beside Ashraf, staring unblinkingly at her. She looked around the circle. Yaslin stood with Alannah, well behind Sanuri, outside the circle. Clay stood at the edge, by Parasu's statue, watching with interest.

Sulis stepped carefully over the chalk lines into the center and stood facing the Altar of the One. Master Anchee stood at her back, facing Parasu. This would be the only time he would face away from her. His focus would be on mirroring her movements. Though they had discussed what to flow to, it was up to Sulis to keep the energy rising out of the pattern.

"Calming ritual," Master Anchee said softly.

Sulis closed her eyes. As they breathed and moved their arms in the calming ritual, energy stirred around her—more than she'd ever felt in this place with so little green life energy to draw on. This ritual was drawing energy not only from what was around them, but also out of the Altar of the One. There was resistance, the essence of Parasu resisting the pull to join with the One's energy.

Sulis noticed her thoughts drawing her away from the breath, from the ritual, and acknowledged them, releasing them. She opened her eyes to begin the dance, but everything distracted her. The feel of the energy was more intense if she closed her eyes. Sulis made the choice to dance with her eyes closed, moving by the feel of the energy. It didn't matter if she could not see the chalk lines—she felt where they were. Master Anchee would have to see to mirror her, but she could close her eyes.

Sulis was moving before she realized it, flowing with precision. It felt right to start with a slant fly position and dance to sparrow's tail. The energy line flared as she did, and she watched it flare more as Master Anchee followed a second behind. Moving from sparrow to warrior pose, she stepped into a third chakra space and she exalted the warrior, pointing her hand at the sky as the energy channeled through her core, through her heart. Each step was placed with precision, yet the energy flowed from her arms, her heart. The energy around her grew more and more intense as she flowed. Several times the energy was not correct to fill the space with the pose they'd decided on, and Sulis struck the correct pose instead. Master Anchee did not hesitate, trusting her intuition and following her so quickly she could feel the crackle of energy between them.

The air became thick inside the mandala. Sulis could feel herself drawing energy from Ashraf to help her body keep moving. Sulis and Anchee danced farther away from each other as they spiraled to the outer edges. The energy was so raw that it was pushing them apart. Now they were skirting the black blood line, which pulsed with energy like a beating heart.

Sulis was gasping as she entered the final pose, kneeling behind the Altar of the One, her forehead on the earth in a bow and prostration.

Sulis opened her eyes and looked up as she heard giggling. Sanuri was seated on the Altar of the One, above Sulis, her face alight with joy. She made intricate motions with her hands as though drawing rope in and knotting it. Grandmother still spiraled around the mandala and her whirlwind siphoned in the masses of energy raised by Sulis and Anchee. She spun it, twisting it like fibers of silk, and gave it to Sanuri, who somehow knotted the fibers of energy together into a continuous whole.

Sulis was afraid to move, to disturb that fragile weave, so she knelt as Sanuri completed the knot and tied it to the blood line with a flare of light and heat that was seen and felt.

As Sulis blinked, Alannah stepped into the mandala beside Sulis and placed her hands on the orb.

She chanted, low and deep. Sulis did not recognize the language, but the orb glowed brighter, and Sulis could feel the knotted energy being drawn in by the One. It felt like a tug-of-war—the One pulling, the deity resisting.

"Ahmatora!" Alannah cried.

The orb flared, and the One's presence reached out through the woven link. The deity tried to pull away, but the knots were too tight—it and the One were woven together. When the One's essence touched Parasu, a feeling of relief, of release occurred. A sense of wonder and adoration rose in Sulis as the trapped core of the deity reached for the One, longing for reunion. Sulis reached for that reunion as well, feeling that longing.

Clay gave a great shout, clapping his hands and startling her away from the energy.

"Do not follow the energy to the One," he shouted at the Chosen. "It will kill you!"

The orb flared again as deity and the One reunited. Then everything went still.

Sulis collapsed on the floor, breathing hard. She was shocked that she'd come so close to following the weaving to the One, to killing herself. She pushed herself up to her knees, and then staggered to her feet, looking around.

Most of the Chosen were sitting, stunned, around the mandala, barely stirring. Palou knelt by Grandmother, tending to her. Only Clay, Amon, and Alannah looked untouched by the ritual. Clay was studying Parasu's statue, a frown on his face.

Amon stared openmouthed at Sanuri, who giggled and put her arms around Alannah's neck as Alannah picked her up and carried her out of the pattern.

Master Anchee levered himself to one knee, looking unsteady and exhausted. He tried to stand and swayed toward Parasu's statue.

"Careful," Clay warned, jerking forward. "Don't touch . . . No!"

Master Anchee put a hand out to keep himself from falling, reaching toward Parasu's statue. Clay knocked him aside before he could touch the deity, putting his body between the master and the statue. Master Anchee was knocked out of the pattern, but Clay's shoulder hit the statue. He cried out once, an agonized sound. His body fell heavily to the ground.

"Clay!" Ava screamed. She flew over to him, tried to turn his body over. Dani helped her, and she patted at Clay's cheeks. Dani put his head to Clay's chest.

"His heart isn't beating," he told Lasha as she knelt beside him.

As Sulis staggered over, supported by Ashraf, Lasha's hands glowed, and she pushed them against Clay's body, once, twice, making the body jump.

"Stop," Amon ordered. Lasha ignored him, pressing down on Clay's chest, and then breathing into his mouth.

"It will do no good," Amon said, pulling her away. "His being, his essence, is in the statue now."

They all stared at him and then at Parasu's statue.

"It killed him?" Ava shrilled. "My mandala killed him?"

"He is not fully dead," Amon said gently. "Though his body is. That is what we are creating, traps."

"Why didn't you warn us not to touch the statue?" Sulis asked, tears running down her face as Ava slowly approached the statue.

"I thought only Parasu's energy could be sucked in by the trap in Parasu's statue," Amon said helplessly. "I did not know it could take us instead."

"Clay realized it," Master Anchee said, his voice full

of sorrow. "He tried to warn me. I was too weak. He saved me."

Lasha stepped up beside him, "Too proud to take my energy," she said softly, anger in her voice.

Ava reached a hand out to the statue, and then hesitated.

"Will it suck me in, if I touch it?" she asked.

Amon shook his head. "It is full of energy now. In order to set the trap, we will have to empty it again."

Ava looked horrified at the idea of emptying Clay out of the statue. She touched it and her eyes unfocused.

"He's here," she told the group. "He's still alive in here. We have to get him out."

Sulis looked over at Amon, who shook his head, and then down at Clay's body. She didn't know how they were going to break it to Ava that Clay could not return to a corpse. Nor could he stay in the statue, which needed to contain Parasu. Sulis realized with horror that Ava's next mandala would be chalked to drag Clay out of the statue—and Sulis's next dance would be to finish Clay's death and send him on.

Jonas gasped and clutched his chest, feeling a sharp pain and then a sense of emptiness. He could not feel Parasu inside himself for the first time since winter.

"Tribune?" The Magistrate put a hand on Jonas's arm, his voice full of concern. "Are you ill?"

He guided Jonas away from prying eyes at the altar, to a chair in the office area. "I will fetch water and a healer," he said.

"Water, but the healer is unnecessary," Jonas said. The pain was gone, but the sense of emptiness remained. "I think the pain was Parasu's. I must meditate to open myself and communicate with him."

The Magistrate fetched water, and Jonas motioned him to leave, to close the door.

"I will check on you in a half sandglass," the Magistrate said, clearly still worried.

"That would be wise," Jonas said. "I do not believe this is a physical pain, but I appreciate the intercession if I am incorrect."

Left alone in his office, Jonas knelt on a bench beside his deity's altar. He poured some of the water into a copper bowl on a stand, and added a few drops of scented oil, then lighted a candle under the bowl. As the water steamed, he relaxed enough to search in his mind for Parasu.

Parasu's presence trickled into Jonas's body, but he could feel that Parasu's attention was focused elsewhere. Time passed as Jonas kept his mind open for his deity, waiting for him to help Jonas understand what was happening. Magistrate came to check on him twice, but he knelt and waited.

Jonas jerked fully awake suddenly, his deity within him. He hadn't realized he'd been nodding off in his vigil.

You have been faithful, Parasu said approvingly. *You felt trouble, and kept yourself ready for my needs.*

His weariness melted away, the pins and needles in his numb feet disappearing as Parasu fed him a wave of energy.

Thank you, Jonas sent. *You were in pain. How may I serve you?*

I don't know, Parasu said, confused. *It came upon me suddenly. I do not usually feel overwhelming human emotions, but I felt fear. I was struggling against something mighty that would consume me. But the fear passed. Then joy arose, and I was suddenly more alive and complete than I ever had been before.*

The longing in Parasu's mindvoice brought tears to Jonas's eyes.

Then it all disappeared, Parasu said. *My being does not feel different. I do not know what happened.*

Did you sense a direction? Jonas asked. *Was it something being done in the desert, at this temple we will travel to?*

Jonas felt a wave of negation. *It was in the ether,* Parasu told him. *That plane of existence that deities and the One occupy, outside of human experience. I felt no physical presence on the earth for this battle.*

Should we go to the Herald? Jonas asked. *See if Aryn felt the same?*

Parasu sent a wave of negation and resentment. *No. We must show no weakness to the other deities. I cannot have them take advantage of us if somehow I have become weakened in the ethereal plane.*

Who would attack you there? Was it the One? Jonas asked.

Parasu hesitated for so long Jonas feared he'd left again.

I do not believe so, Parasu said. *I feel exactly as I always have since the Sundering. I do not believe I am damaged.*

Could it have been a premonition? Jonas asked, wondering if deities had such things.

Parasu considered it. *We do not have visions as you humans do. But sometimes our consciousness escapes the boundaries of time and we are able to gain a view of the future. It has not happened to me since the Sundering, but sharing your body has made me stronger.* Parasu's presence became stronger, more confident. *That is the only explanation that makes sense though. I am truly fortunate to have such a wise servant in these uncertain times.*

Parasu's warm regard made Jonas flush with pleasure.

Yes, Parasu said. *What I was seeing was the future. We will have a difficult, painful battle to regain what we were before the Sundering. But when we are complete once again, when we have regained our lost selves, we will have great joy in our victory.*

Jonas smiled with relief.

I felt urgency, though, Parasu said. *We will march as soon as possible. You will convey this to Voras, without telling him of my vision. Tell him our sources say it must be soon. We will not allow him to delay us with his vendetta against the Northern Forsaken.*

Your will is my own, Jonas told him. *It will be as you asked.*

Parasu was satisfied as Jonas levered himself off the

kneeling bench. His body was energized from Parasu's touch—a little too much so, and Jonas thought of cold water and nonarousing things as he wrote a summons for the Templar and the other Voices. Once his body calmed a little, he would explain what was needed to the Magistrate and set forth what his deity wanted from him.

"How can we do it?" Sulis whispered to Alannah. "How can we force Clay out of the statue—kill him?"

The group of Chosen and Guardians were half-heartedly eating late meal. Sari had greeted them when they left the temple. It had been painful, telling her about her old friend's sacrifice for the Chosen.

Alannah shook her head. "It will not be difficult," she said softly, and Sulis looked at her. "I put my hand on the statue; I spoke with Clay while everyone was filing out of the temple. He does not fear death. He is happy to rejoin the One. All I will need to do is connect him to the Altar of the One, and he will go of his own free will."

Tears filled Sulis's eyes. "I don't want him to go on," she said.

"Which is why he stays," Alannah said gently. "He needs to convince Ava it is okay for him to leave; otherwise, it could destroy her."

"But we do not have time," Amon said. "I know it is cruel of me to say so. I believe Parasu knew when we emptied his statue. The deities will be alert. They will be coming as soon as they can. We must empty the other shells and prepare for their arrival."

Lasha shook her head. "There's no way the Chosen could repeat that ceremony tomorrow, or the next day. Look at them—they're exhausted."

Alannah looked directly at Lasha. "What happened with Anchee?" she asked.

Lasha shook her head, frustrated. "He thinks I'm too young. He has not opened himself fully to me. Even now he resists my energy."

Palou overheard and looked sharply at her. "I will speak with him," he said. "You need that connection if he is to survive."

Sari looked over at their group and cleared her throat to get their attention. "We will need to take Clay's body out of the chasm in the morning for the burning ceremony," she said. "Will you want to go with it, to send him on?"

They looked around at each other. Then Grandmother shook her head.

"There is nothing to send on in that body, so it would be a waste of energy we are already lacking," she said. "We will have our own ceremony when we have truly sent him to the One. We will rest tomorrow."

In the morning, Sulis and Alannah tried to convince Ava to let the guards take Clay's body, while Ashraf and Dani fed Nuisance and talked quietly.

"Ava, we cannot put Clay into a corpse," Alannah said. "His body is dead. If his spirit were not trapped by the ancient spell, he would be with the One now."

Ava shook her head stubbornly. "We can't do this without him. We need him. You have to find a way to bring him back. He's still alive."

She'd refused to leave the statue and Clay's body when the rest of the Chosen left the Obsidian Temple. She'd spent the entire night resting against the stone as the guards wrapped his body.

"He needs it," Ava said. "If they burn his body, where will he live?"

Sulis put her hand on Parasu's statue for the first time since the ceremony. Clay's warm presence was inside.

You must convince her to allow this, Sulis told him.

His voice filled her mind, but not her ears. *I have been trying. She is a stubborn one, our Ava. Since I told her to let me go, she has refused to touch the statue again, to communicate with me. Tell her I do not wish to go back to that empty shell. Even if you could put me in that body, it has been dead too long. I would be crippled in mind and body.*

Sulis relayed that information and Ava burst into tears and turned away from the body. Dani hugged her as Sari motioned for the guards to carry Clay's body out.

"You cannot force me to draw the pattern to chase him out," Ava said stubbornly. "I will not kill Clay. He's my best friend."

Alannah glanced quickly over at Sulis. "You won't have to draw that pattern," she promised.

Amon approached them and Sulis braced herself for a nasty comment from him. If he upset Ava, Sulis wouldn't wait for the One to knock him off balance. A fist to the chin would work as well.

He looked at Ava and knelt beside her, taking her hand. "I am so terribly sorry," he told her. "I did not know what would happen. I know now why the Southerners did not empty the statues. The empty statues are a deadly trap for energy users. I am so sorry that a wise advisor died because of my ignorance."

"He isn't dead," Ava said. "He's still alive in the statue."

Amon opened his mouth, caught Alannah's glare and wisely closed it again. He patted Ava on the back. "Yes, well," he said awkwardly, and walked away to study the stone around the Altar of the One.

"No chalk lines," he pointed out to Sulis and Ashraf. "They were absorbed with the energy. The stones are swept clean. Ava's hand is completely healed as well."

Sulis came closer to study the rock. He was right. Her memory of the previous day was jumbled, so she could not say if the lines disappeared after the ceremony, or overnight.

"What do we do about Ava?" Amon whispered to Sulis. "We need her whole, so I don't want to force her to send Clay to the One. But we also need to empty the statue to trap Parasu. And we need to empty the other three before the deities come."

"Alannah says Ava won't be necessary to connect Clay to the One," Sulis said. "He is willing to move on."

Amon looked relieved.

"But he won't move on until Ava is ready," she

warned, and he frowned. "He thinks forcing her to accept his death before she is ready will make her more unstable. He will convince her; give him time." Sulis tried to sound certain. Sulis wasn't certain she herself would ever be ready to let Clay go. Ava would have an even harder time.

"Sari told me the army is on the move," Amon said quietly. "I know the Chosen need to rest, but it is urgent that we finish emptying the statues and prepare for the deities."

Ashraf said from behind Sulis, "Do we have to empty Parasu's vessel before we perform the ceremony on the other statues?" he asked. "Sending Clay to the One could be the last thing we do, after all the other vessels are empty."

Amon frowned, not liking that option, but he nodded reluctantly.

Giggling made them turn. Sanuri had her hands pressed against Parasu's statue and was whispering loudly to it. She giggled again.

"You leave him alone," Ava shouted, standing to grasp Sanuri's arm roughly.

Dani stepped forward, alarmed, but Sanuri grabbed Ava's other arm. She leaned forward and kissed Ava on the cheek, and then placed her hands against the statue.

"You talk," she said. "We all talk."

Ava sank down, leaning her cheek against the statue. She closed her eyes and tears streamed down her face. She nodded a couple of times, as though responding to Clay. Sanuri sat beside her, reached over, and wiped tears from Ava's face.

"Not sad," Sanuri whispered. "Happy. Love."

Sulis turned away, into Ashraf's chest, choked up from Ava's grief. Ashraf put his arms around her and she cried onto his chest.

"You need to rest some more," he told her softly. "Away from this place. You are still exhausted from yesterday. We don't have to make any decisions today. Just let everything go."

Sulis let him lead her out of the temple, his arm around her waist. She didn't look at anyone, hoping they wouldn't judge her for her weakness.

They exited the temple and nearly ran into Master Anchee and Lasha, who were arguing in the courtyard.

"Why can't you take my energy?" Lasha was protesting. "Why do you shut me out?"

"I take as much as I can without . . ." He trailed off, seeing Ashraf and Sulis.

"Without what?" Lasha persisted, unconcerned with witnesses. "Ava takes fully from Dani, even though she tried to kill him once. Why can you not connect with me?"

"You are so young," Master Anchee said.

"So you don't trust me to give you energy?" Lasha asked.

"No," Anchee said, shaking his head. "It just feels wrong, stealing energy, stealing life force from a girl who could be my daughter."

Sulis felt fury rising in her. She rounded on Master Anchee.

"Are you stupid? Are you so ungrateful?" she growled, unleashing her anger.

"Sulis," Ashraf warned.

She shrugged it off. "Her energy is a gift she is giving you. It is precious and beautiful and you scorn it. You endanger the rest of us with your idiocy."

Master Anchee was staring at her, his eyebrows high in his forehead. Lasha had her hand clamped over her mouth to stifle a giggle, her eyes dancing. Sulis pushed past them both and stormed off.

Her angry energy didn't last long, and she slumped against the food hall building when they were out of sight, feeling drained.

"Perhaps we should find a bed we can slump into?" Ashraf suggested, grinning.

Sulis pushed off the wall wearily. "No offense, love, but I lack the energy for romping."

"Then I'll simply hold you until you sleep," he said quietly. "I'll tell you stories about our Hasirof clan and the empire we'll build after this is all over."

Sulis's eyes filled with tears again. "I would like that," she said. "Very much."

CHAPTER 13

"There's another troop of Forsaken." Onyeka pointed toward the encampment as they hid on the ridge. "That group is *geased* as well."

"Why do you say that?" Kadar asked. He couldn't see much difference between the cohorts of the army.

"It's a huge group, three times larger than the rest. But in spite of that, the fighters are doing exactly what a model fighter should do—no pranks, no joking around. When they're done with the tasks assigned, they simply sit. One of our spies had reported seeing a cohort like this. He and the other troops were told the men in it were criminals, so they would not befriend the *geased* men. We'd never put two and two together before. Look, see, their commanders are with them all the time."

"Commanders?" Kadar peered through his eyeglass

to confirm that several of Voras's men were with the group. "There's more than one. Aaron said that only one person controlled the *geased* fighters."

Onyeka shrugged. "They would have learned from their mistake up north. They will spread the command to make it harder to free the Forsaken. We have seen many more Knights and soldiers come into camp the past ten-day."

"They're getting ready to move the army, aren't they?" Kadar asked.

There was more activity in the camp beside the endless drills they'd observed. When not drilling, fighters were taking down clotheslines, grooming horses, and sharpening weapons.

"Yes," Onyeka said. "It begins."

She squinted, and then put the glass to her eye, scanning the far side of the ridge they were on as she saw movement. "Time to go. I see a *feli* patrol scouting the ridge."

She and Kadar slipped down the steep trail on the ridge to where another warrior guarded their horses. They silently mounted. The veil of desert magic slipped over them, hiding them as they rode into the dunes.

Gone were the days when they could spy on the army at will. Soldiers now regularly patrolled the cliffs with their *feli*. The Tigus still snuck up to the ridge to assess the camp, but they were far more wary and could not stay long. It was now a longer ride to their main camp to report to the elders and warriors of the One.

Abram felt self-conscious as he *farspoke* with his cousin. Kadar had interrupted Master Tull's meeting with her commanders and all eyes were upon Abram as he relayed the information from the Tigu elders.

We have located the geased fighters in the camp. We wish to know when we should attack their controllers to release the spell, Kadar sent to Abram.

Abram waited for Master Tull's response to the elder's request, and then relayed it to Kadar.

Our commanders believe the army will move to the waystation south of Illian to await the Voices of the deities, Abram sent. *We wish you to attack the army and free the Forsaken once the troops reach the waystation.*

Master Tull paced while they waited for the elder's reaction. Master Gursh drummed his fingernails on the table. They knew this would put the Tigus in greater danger. The Tigus' desert magic would not conceal them as readily outside of the Sands. If the Tigus refused, the masters would have to send most of the warriors of the One north, at a time when they needed to be southbound, preparing for the weather working and battle.

Why not free the slaves earlier, before they leave here? Kadar sent after a moment.

If the Forsaken are released too far into the desert, they will not revolt because they'll fear dying in the desert. If they are closer to home, we expect them to run away from the camp and toward their former homes. Abram relayed Master Tull's answer.

A tense moment, then Abram was able to announce, "The Tigus agree. They will travel ahead to the waystation and free the Forsaken there!"

The commanders sighed with relief, and Master Tull produced one of her rare smiles and sat down.

Have you heard anything from Tsangia? Kadar sent, hesitantly. *I was wondering how Datura was doing.*

Sorry, Kadar, Abram said, sympathetically. *All the farspeakers are here, and no caravans are running so we haven't gotten mail.*

I'm not surprised. Blessings, Abram, I must go see what the elders want.

Keep safe, Kadar, Abram sent before he cut their connection.

The other commanders began to file out of the office, but Master Tull held up a hand to stop them.

"The army is on the move. It is time for Ursa, Bento, and I to leave for the northern desert oases in their path. We will take a cohort, who will then meet the Tigus at the waystation to render any aid necessary. Gursh and Sandiv will take charge here. Tell your warriors that we go to protect the cities in the path of Voras's army. We will stop by and personally speak to each of you before we leave."

This sobered the group, and they filed out silently, leaving just Masters Tull and Ursa.

"Why don't you and Casia take a break?" Master Tull said to Abram.

Casia brightened, but Abram knew why they were dismissed. Casia still did not know how the masters would reset the waymarkers. The masters wanted to talk without her learning the plan.

As they walked toward the meal hall, Casia bumped his shoulder. "You look like you bit a lemon," she said. "Did breakfast disagree with you?"

"Actually, yes," Abram said, stopping and looking back. "I'm not feeling well. You go ahead. I'm going to duck back into the office to let the masters know, then sleep it off."

Abram rushed back to the office, and both masters looked at him. For a moment he couldn't say anything and his eyes filled with tears.

"Abram . . ." Master Tull began, her tone exasperated.

Abram interrupted her. "I wanted to let you know it's been an honor to serve under you," he told her. "Both of you. My children and their children will sing songs of your bravery and generosity. You will not be forgotten."

He touched the back of his hand to his forehead, then bowed himself out of the room, unwilling to see their faces. He dashed tears out of his eyes and went to find a quiet corner in which to grieve.

The Sepacu tribe was not among the tribes the elders sent ahead to scout out the lands around the waystation. The Sepacus would scout and report what the army's movements were, shadowing the troops as they organized their march. Even the elders packed their camp to move.

"You are to go with the elders while we track the troops," Onyeka said, sitting down at late meal beside him. "We will send a rider if they do anything unusual, but your place is with the tribes as they prepare to liberate the Forsaken."

Kadar glanced over at her. "And I suppose you'll be here, having all the fun playing with the army while the rest of us work," he joked, trying to hide his regret at being parted from her.

"It's too bad you'll have to sleep on a rock-hard mat, with just a cat for company," Onyeka teased.

"Ha, that's what you think," Kadar said. "I grabbed one of the softer mats before Desial could send it to the city on the pack horses. And I'll be able to keep it all to myself rather than being pushed off in the middle of the night when some warrior has bad dreams."

She opened her mouth, but looked around as her name was called. "One more night before the elders move, and they are being needy." She sighed, getting up.

"That means I have a night to make certain you don't forget me when I ride off," Kadar said.

Onyeka shot him a smoldering look. "I look forward to your efforts."

In the morning, Onyeka helped him pack his humpback as he tied Asfar in line behind the beast. They were silent as the rest of the camp shouted and cursed, packing the last of the tents onto some of the supply humpbacks. Most of the horses were staying on the front, closest to the army for faster battles and nearer the sources of water the Tigus could sense. Humpbacks were better pack animals for the region they would be traveling, which had fewer water sources. Asfar was useless for other riders, permitting only Kadar on her back, so he would lead her. She would be useful if he needed to make quick scouting trips closer to the way-station.

Kadar's humpback knelt and he turned to Onyeka, wanting to say many things, but resisting an emotional farewell that would make her uncomfortable.

Her face was solemn. "Go, warrior, protected by the One. If we do not meet again in this life, we will meet in the embrace of the One." She intoned the formal blessing spoken by parting Tigus.

Kadar grabbed her shoulders and pulled her in. She melted into his passionate kiss, giving as much as he gave. They pulled away to the appreciative hoots of the other warriors. She gave him a quick hug.

"I will miss you sorely," she whispered into his ear and then pushed him away and walked off.

"And I, you," Kadar whispered to her back, as she dodged a humpback and disappeared into the chaos of a camp being packed. He mounted the humpback and prepared to ride.

"I told you my daughter would break your heart," Turo said, riding up beside him.

"You told me we should get together, make babies," Kadar said, mock-frowning at him. "There was no mention of broken hearts."

Turo shrugged. "Perhaps I forgot to mention her independent nature?" he mused. "You will never tame that wild heart of hers. Ah well, she likes you very much—that is something."

"Why are you traveling with us and not staying with the Sepacu tribe?" Kadar asked.

"Too slow, too old." His voice sounded mournful, but Kadar thought he looked pleased. "They are assigning me to the elders. I will be their messenger."

No wonder he looked pleased. Being assigned to the elders meant he was a revered warrior, apprenticed to them. He would join their counsels soon, once they were certain he'd learned their laws.

They rode for three days, traveling far south of the road that marked the line between the Northern and Southern Territories. They stopped only once, at a watering hole so the humpbacks could drink and rest. Kadar filled the large skins of water tied to each side of his humpback for Asfar to drink on the days they did not find water.

They reached an encampment of the Duradin tribe on the fourth day and the elders took it over, setting up their large command tent and widening the basin their spring fed into. The summer was cooler now, not the intense blasting heat of midsummer.

"We are about a day's ride south of the final waystation of the Northern Territory," Turo said. "It is where our spies say the deities will ride to join the greater army."

The elders summoned Kadar that evening. Amber demanded that she be picked up, so he arrived with his suncat perched on his shoulder.

"The troops should be here in less than a ten-day," Elder Turin told Kadar. "We will slip some warriors in to kill the Knights holding the Forsaken captive after the army arrives, but before the Voices of the deities come. We would like you to contact the warriors of the One so we can discuss strategy with them."

Kadar made contact with Abram, who spoke with his leaders. It was strange being the go-between as the two groups discussed numbers and tactics. But in the end, they'd decided upon a plan.

"Almost half of Voras's army is *geased*," Turin concluded. "If our assassins can free even a quarter of those Forsaken troops, the Tigus and warriors of the One will be better matched to the army in numbers. We will have a better chance of winnowing down the army as they march across the desert."

Jesah nodded. "We will ask the tribes to send their most skilled fighters to assassinate the Knights."

"But how do we know the deities won't simply turn and return to Illian if their army's numbers are decimated?" one of the elders asked.

"The warriors of the One believe they are too invested at this point," Kadar said, relaying the message. "To turn back would be to lose the war and the deities' chance at regaining what they lost. The warriors of the One believe the deities will push on to get to the temple and regain their power. If that happens, they will be able to take energy from any human, not just their acolytes."

"What happens if the deities do push through and

the Chosen cannot contain them?" someone asked. "What if they regain their full powers?"

"It is not for us to question," Turin said. "We are warriors and we will fight!"

The other elders nodded and rose, the meeting breaking up.

the Chosen cannot commit them," someone asked.
"What is they regain their full power?"

"It is not for us to consider," Amun said. "We are
warriors, and we will fight."

The other elders nodded and rose. He meeting,
breaking up.

CHAPTER 14

The Chosen met at the temple again a few days later
to empty another deity statue. Sanuri chose Aryn's
statue as the next focus. Ava communed with Clay, in
the statue of Parasu, before starting her mandala, and
what he told her made her eyes shine with pleasure.

"You were right," Amon whispered to Sulis and
Ashraf. "Having Clay still here stabilizes her, gives her
confidence."

Master Anchee and Lasha clasped hands while they
watched Ava chalk this mandala. Sulis could feel the
energy exchange between them. It had taken a couple
of practice sessions after Sulis's rebuke for Master
Anchee to start treating Lasha like an equal, but she
could feel the energy link between the two. Lasha and
Anchee working together was much better energy for
the entire group.

Aryn's mandala had different energy than Parasu's.

Sulis closed her eyes, feeling Aryn's higher chakra energy. Ava once again slashed her hand and created a blood line on the outside, linking Aryn, the One, and Sanuri.

Ava wasn't as exhausted this time, and Sulis hoped that would be true of all of them.

The dance was less physically taxing than Parasu's had been, focusing on intuition and creativity. The amount of energy raised was the same—the air inside the mandala was thick and hard to breathe—but Sulis was less exhausted at the end. As she watched Sanuri weave Aryn's energy and the One's energy together, she hoped Master Anchee felt the same.

Alannah spoke the words of power, and Sulis drew back from feeling the energy, not wanting to be drawn into the One along with Aryn, as she'd almost been last time.

A clap of energy, and everything was still. This time, as Sulis climbed to her feet, she saw the chalk lines were gone. Lasha was by Master Anchee's side in an instant, but he did not need her assistance to rise. They stayed far away from the now-empty statue.

They stood around Aryn's statue, staring at it.

"I can feel it," Grandmother said. "I can feel the trap inside, calling to me."

"A seductive prison," Amon said. "Hopefully it will call the deity it was built for even more strongly, so the call cannot be resisted. I will have Sari cordon the statue off, so we cannot accidentally be trapped. You must go rest. I would like to do both Ivanha's and Voras's ceremony together, if Sanuri is willing."

She giggled, which Sulis took for a yes.

"We need to practice containing more than one energy source, and Sanuri needs to practice weaving three energies together," Amon said. "We will need to weave all four at once to the One when we have the full essence of the deities trapped here. Shuttles—practice drawing energy every day with your Guardian."

He glanced around Sulis, grimaced, and turned away. Sulis looked back to see Ava standing with her hands against Parasu's statue, speaking with Clay.

"Convincing Ava to let Clay go may be our hardest task," Alannah said.

"We can release Voras and Ivanha before it becomes urgent to send Clay on," Sulis said grimly. "We should go eat."

They practiced several days at the Obsidian Temple. Ava ate her meals with the Chosen, though she still insisted on staying with Clay overnight and most of her waking hours.

"He's closing off," she told Sulis unhappily at midmeal.

"What do you mean?" Sulis asked.

"He says it's too hard stay in the present without a body. So his mind drifts away and he can't draw it back to talk with me."

Alannah shook her head. "This is a half state for him, neither in a living body nor returned to the One. It is painful for him."

Ava ducked her head and focused on her food, her

face set. They finished eating and cleaned their plates. Alannah, Lasha, and Sulis turned to walk to the dorms, and Ava paused.

"He shouldn't have to die," she said. "It isn't fair. We have lots of magic. We need to find a way to get him a new body."

"Ava, it isn't possible," Sulis said. "We can't bring the dead back."

"You just won't try," Ava cried, and she ran to the Obsidian Temple.

That evening Sulis left Ashraf and her friends talking in the dormitories and crept into the Obsidian Temple. The orb in the Altar of the One softly illuminated the darkness. It had been glowing since they'd begun filtering energy through it. It illuminated Ava, hunched against Parasu's statue, head on her knees with her arms wrapped over her head. Sulis sighed, looking at the sad figure. She walked over and sat beside Ava, leaning against the statue. She put her arm around Ava, who didn't move.

"It isn't fair, is it?" Sulis said. "I lost my parents when I was a little younger than you and I remember how it felt."

Ava raised her head. "Don't tell me everything will be fine and that I'll get over him. I won't. I've never forgotten my mother and father, my sister. I'll never forget them."

"I've never forgotten my mother and father either," Sulis said. "It simply hurts less with time. You think about it less."

"I don't want to think about it less," Ava sobbed. "I don't want to forget anything. That's like betraying them, to forget anything about them. Not feeling the pain of their death is like erasing them."

"I've thought that, too," Sulis said. "But we can't live with such grief every day. It destroys us. And I know the ones who left me loved me and wanted happiness for me, more than anything else. Do you think your parents, Farrah, and Clay want you to be happy? That they loved you?"

Ava nodded.

"And are you happy holding on like this, causing yourself pain by feeling them die over and over? Is that what they would want for you?"

Ava shook her head, gulping air. "Farrah would swat me upside the head and say, 'Momma didn't raise an idiot—stop moping about. Go live your life.'"

Sulis smiled. "I can hear her saying that. She wanted to create a better life for all the people of the North. She would hate for you to have a worse life, because of her death."

Ava nodded, her tears drying on her cheeks. She looked over and rested her shoulder against Sulis's.

"Do you think it hurts, dying?" she asked. "It scares me, thinking that it'll hurt and then nothingness will take over. That I'll be in darkness, forever."

No, Clay said in their minds. Sulis had felt him listening, but this was the first he'd spoken. *It isn't like that. It is a union.*

Ava shook her head. "I don't understand what that means," she said.

The warmth of Clay's love washed over them. *My dear girl, it is like the biggest, best family gathering ever,* he said. *Like rejoining someone you adore after a long absence. But even greater. We humans are always looking for something to complete us. We study, work, play—always knowing that something is missing in our lives. It's only when we return to the One that we find true completion, true love.*

"Then why don't humans kill themselves to get that completion?" Sulis asked.

We must be worthy of union, Clay said. *We must create a better world for those around us and better ourselves. If we do not, the One then sends us back to another circle of life. Through life, we learn compassion, love, and generosity. There is much to be learned in this physical world.*

"Are you worthy?" Ava wanted to know. "Will you go to the One or be sent back? How do you know if you are?"

Most don't know, Clay said. *But I have communed with the One and I know. He waits for me. So close. I long so much for reunion with my beloved, the One, and he is so close.*

"You want to leave me!" Ava cried, turning and placing her hands on the statue. "I can't do this without you!"

But I will be with the One, Clay said. *And the One is always with you. The energy that is within me is the One's and it is the same energy that is in you.*

"The One won't find me worthy," Ava said. "She won't want me and I'll never join you."

The One has already found you worthy—he chose you to make him whole. What could be a greater task? The One has recognized that splitting himself into the deities was a mistake and created dissonance instead of harmony. The union of deities with the One is a monumental undertaking that will bring lasting wholeness to all. You, Ava, were judged worthy and were called to this task. The One will welcome you when your time on earth has passed.

Ava was silent for some time, her chin on her knees, which were drawn up to her chest. Sulis didn't blame her—Clay had given them both much to think about. As the dusk deepened to night, she stirred.

"I'm keeping you from bliss, aren't I?" Ava said. Clay was silent. Ava looked over at Sulis. "It is selfish of me. But I'm afraid without him. Clay made me feel whole, undamaged. Who will do that if he goes away?"

Trust in the One as you always have me. I will be in the One's energy.

Ava nodded and stood, putting her hand on the statue. She was crying, but determined. Sulis stood as well. She sent out a mental call to the other Chosen, a summons for them to come to the temple.

"I don't know what to do," Ava told Clay.

You must connect my energy to the One's, Clay said. *The One will draw me out of this trap.*

"So I should draw a line of energy from you to the Altar of the One?" Ava asked. "Why do we have to do all those crazy dances with the deities if it's that simple?"

They have forgotten they were once a part of the One, Clay said. *They are afraid, and do not wish to be reunited. We hold them and weave their energy with the One until they realize that union is what they truly long for.*

Ava startled and turned as the door to the temple opened and the crowd of Chosen and Guardians rushed in, most in night robes. Even Sari trailed in their wake, alarmed by their rush to the temple. Sulis thought in chagrin that maybe her sending shouldn't have been so urgent.

"They have the right to say goodbye," Sulis told Ava. Sulis turned to the group. "Ava is ready to help Clay reunite with the One. I thought he might wish to say goodbye before leaving us, and each of you might want to speak with him."

Relief and understanding shone on most faces. Sari stepped up.

"Thank you, yes," she said. "I would like to speak once more with my old friend."

The crowd was solemn as they waited their turn. Sari left after she'd spoken with Clay, a sad smile on her face, but most lingered. Grandmother and Palou both spoke to Clay at once, and Palou laughed and glanced over at Grandmother, eyes shining. Even Alannah spoke with him, stepping back to Sulis after, smiling.

"Oh, how I envy him," Alannah whispered at Sulis's inquiring gaze. "The glory that he will know." She shook her head and looked down.

Sulis went next to last. She had no words—only sent a burst of emotion to Clay about how much he meant to her and how much she was going to miss him. He sent a burst of energy, of love and joy and celebration. She couldn't help but laugh at his giddiness.

Ava was last. She stood still for a long time, eyes closed, nodding or shaking her head to things Clay said. Then she turned away, her face dry of tears. Ava gathered her energy, and then pricked her finger with her dagger. She touched Clay, and connected a line to him. She did not drag her hand on the ground this time—instead she drew an invisible line of energy to the Altar of the One. She touched her bloody palm to the orb, then walked to the group of Chosen and stood with them as Dani put his arms around her.

The line between Clay and the One flared, became visible as Clay reached for the One. The orb shone bright for only a moment, and then there was a flash of light. A burst of intense joy washed over them, and then all was silent again, the orb glowing faintly.

"Did you feel that?" Ava asked. "That was him, wasn't it? He was so happy." She turned away and cried into Dani's chest.

"I think we can rest tomorrow," Amon said heavily. His face had been drawn since he took his turn speaking with Clay. "It will be a day of mourning."

"It will be a day of celebration," Grandmother corrected. Ava raised her head and looked at Grandmother, who smiled and tapped her on the cheek. "Clay is with the One. We will celebrate that, even as we miss his physical presence among us. Thank you for giving him joy, dear one."

Ava nodded, not smiling but seeming wearily content. "I will never forget him," she said.

"But you will be happy," Sulis reminded her. "It is what he wanted."

"I will be happy again," Ava promised.

When they met again in two days to empty the final two statues, Amon had different orders for them.

"Ava will draw her mandala only with energy," Amon said. "Sulis has been dancing with her eyes closed, so she does not need to physically chalk the lines. When we set the final mandala, the actual trap for the deities, we don't want the deities to see the lines connecting the statues together and realize it is a trap."

"But they'll see the energy lines if we create the mandala before they are trapped in the statues, whether we chalk them or not," Master Anchee protested. "They exist in the ether, where that energy is."

Amon shook his head. "I have a masking spell. It will look like a misty fog inside the mandala to the deities."

"Wait, so Ava has to create the mandala before the deities are trapped?" Sulis asked. "I thought they would get stuck in the statues, and then we would create the mandala and dance them to the One. For that matter, I don't understand why we have to do all of them at once. They'll be so much more powerful in person than the echo of them we emptied out of the statues—we should do them singly to make sure we can."

Alannah answered, "Just having the empty statues won't call the deities strongly enough. Ava will use the mandala to connect each statue with the element the deity is affiliated with—Voras to fire, Ivanha to earth, Parasu to water, Aryn to wind. That should make the trap stronger and irresistible to each deity, drawing them out of their Voices' bodies."

"As for why all at once," Amon said, "the final spells are ones of destruction—destroying the shells so the deities are reabsorbed. All have to be destroyed with one spell. When the last of the deities' energy is pulled into the One, the Altar of the One will be destroyed."

Lasha looked between him and Alannah. "Who will recite the destruction spells?" she asked.

"Alannah will recite the words of power to draw the deities to the One, and then I will speak the destructive spells," Amon said.

Ava was staring at Parasu's cordoned-off statue, looking lost. Dani put an arm around her and whispered something and she smiled up at him.

"Dani does well with her now," Lasha murmured to Sulis.

Sulis nodded and watched as Sanuri took Ava's hand and led her to the center of the circle, by the Altar of the One. The girls sat beside the altar, holding hands and connecting energetically. The statue of Ivanha and the statue of Voras were at opposite ends, so the altar would be in the center of whatever mandala Ava created with the energy lines. It would be a very long oblong, danced between two statues of Parasu and

Aryn that were cordoned off because they were traps. Sulis shivered, and Grandmother looked over at her.

"It scares me a little, dancing between the trapped statues," Sulis told her. "How are you going to weave your way among them?"

"I won't. I'll dance around the whole circle, as I would if we were doing all four." Grandmother gestured to the circle. "I'm worried about you and Anchee. Be careful, my girl. I don't want to send you on with Clay."

"I will," Sulis promised as Ava stood and circled the altar.

Sulis could feel the colors of energy being drawn. Red earth energy as well as green heart energy for Ivanha. Yellow power energy, mingled with orange and red for Voras. Sulis found it interesting that the chakras were all the lower ones—all very close to humanity and far away from the energy of spirituality, intuition, and mind arts. She wondered if that was why Ivanha and Voras rejected the One so strongly—they were very much tied to humanity and the earth. As Ava drew, both were tied together in as intricate a mandala as Sulis had ever danced.

Master Anchee came up beside her and they talked through the poses of the mandala while it was being drawn with Ava's energy.

"Lasha and I will be on alert," Ashraf told Sulis. "If it looks like one of you is about to get too close to the empty statues, we will intervene."

Sulis was startled. "I don't think you should break the mandala once we are dancing it," she said.

Amon piped up. "They should. There could be a slight backlash of energy, but you are more important than completing the dance. We can always try again another day. But if we lose one of you, the battle is already lost. Clay knew that, which is why he sacrificed himself."

Sulis eyed Ashraf. "Don't you sacrifice yourself," she muttered to him. "Amon may think you're expendable, but I can't continue without you."

Ashraf simply looked at her, not saying anything. Sulis knew he'd sacrifice himself in an instant for her, as she would for him. She would be very careful while dancing.

Sulis was a bundle of nerves as she stepped over the energy lines, trying not to blur them. Anchee made them do a calming ritual, and then it was time to dance. Sulis danced more slowly this time, which taxed her energy, but was more precise. She thought the dance would seem endless, because twice as many energy lines needed to be filled, but soon she was prostrated by Ivanha's statue, panting and sweating as though she'd run a race.

She could feel the energy around her, and it resisted being woven in a way Aryn's and Parasu's had not. Grandmother danced, smoothing the energy to feed to Sanuri, who knotted and reknitted it as it resisted being woven. There was a pulling, a tearing apart when Alannah spoke the words of power. But both Ivanha's and Voras's energies were finally pulled into the Altar of the One, reabsorbed by the One.

Sulis sat still, uncertain she could get up and terrified she'd fall into Ivanha's statue and be sucked in. She could feel it calling to her and wanted to reach out.

Djinn blocked her reach and flopped down on her lap with a sigh. She sank her hands into his fur and buried her head in his ruff, absorbing energy from him. Ashraf's hands on her shoulders sent her even more energy and he massaged her stiff neck until she was revived enough to stand. Master Anchee received a similar treatment with Lasha's Alta on his lap.

Alannah and Palou bent over Grandmother, who had her head between her knees, her skin ashen. Sulis stumbled forward in alarm.

"She will be fine," Alannah said quietly. "This was a very difficult weaving."

"But next time we will have the full powers of the deities fighting us, and all four at once," Sulis said.

Grandmother lifted her head. "I must practice more, then. I have not had to move so much energy since I was young. I will need to find more sources to draw on besides poor Palou."

Sulis glanced sharply at Palou, who looked as exhausted as Grandmother. Age was making them wearier, she realized. Palou didn't have the resilience the other Guardians did. Master Anchee was of age with them, but Lasha was much younger than her Chosen.

"I wonder if we Shuttles can share energy," Sulis mused. "Once Master Anchee and I are finished, we might be able to send you energy from our Guardians and *feli* to help you complete your dance."

Grandmother nodded, considering the idea.

Amon spoke from beside Sulis. "This is why we needed to do both vessels at once. Having four deities, with full power, will stretch us to the limits of our strength. The time until the war comes to us must be spent practicing."

Ava nodded. "I will need to draw the final mandala with energy and ground it in the stone," she said. "I have to create something for each deity, and Sanuri will be able to tell me if it is enough to trap them. And then I'll need to weave it all together in the center, with the One. I hope I can do it. It's really complicated."

"The One will guide us," Alannah said quietly. "She longs for completion."

Jonas waited beside his horse for the other Voices to arrive, the Magistrate fidgeting beside him, fussing with saddlebags. Jonas wasn't fond of horses, so he was staying off his as long as possible awaiting the rest of their party. He gazed at the Temple, wondering if he would ever see it and Illian again.

They were riding off to war. Jonas was a scholar, a man of laws and books, and preferred the cool indoors of stone corridors to being outside in the dust and heat. He was not a great rider, not a great swordsman.

You will have protectors riding with you, Parasu said. *They are swordsmen. Your skills are far more valuable than those of a sword-for-hire.*

Jonas wished that comforted him as the Herald

and her Ranger rode up, looking as at home on their mounts as they did striding around the courtyard. They had bows slung on their backs and slender swords hung across the pommels of their saddles.

Jonas climbed awkwardly onto his mount, blessing the stableman for picking a placid older beast. He hadn't been near a horse in over a year, since his lessons as an acolyte ended and he'd been assigned to Illian. He knew he sat like a sack on the animal's back, but he'd never felt graceful in the saddle.

"Sit a little farther forward," the Ranger advised quietly, seeing Jonas's discomfort. "Tilt your tailbone up more so your body doesn't slouch. Those stirrups are a little long."

Jonas gratefully smiled at the aide who adjusted his stirrups. He was sitting more naturally, feeling more comfortable when the Templar and his Knight galloped up, dramatically pulling their big-boned horses to a sliding stop. The Crone rode in after him, on a dainty mare that stamped restlessly when reined in. Her Mother Superior rode a calmer horse, similar to Jonas's, and looked as uncomfortable as he felt.

"Are we ready?" the Crone asked.

Jonas looked around. It was a large crowd. The Herald and Aryn supplied the largest party, with close to a hundred healers riding out to boost those already stationed with the army. Besides the healers, each Voice, and his or her second, each party had five to ten men at arms guarding them. *Feli* wove between the mounts and hissed at each other restlessly, following their acolytes to war. In the center of this chaos were three dark faces—Southern caravan leaders who had been forced into the service of Voras. Jonas didn't ask if they'd been *geased* or if Voras had broken their minds somehow. They stared dully off into the distance, guarded by the soldiers the Templar was bringing. They would lead the army to the western desert town of Shpeth, which the army would conquer to find guides for the journey into the Sands.

"I have left five hundred men in the city at the viceroy's request, to protect it against the Descendants," the Templar said. "They say they are friends, but I don't fully trust them. We will head south, camp this evening and reach the outpost where the army has been stationed the next day." He glanced over at Jonas. "We also have wagons loaded with supplies and medicines. Anyone who tires of being on horseback can ride in the wagons."

Jonas inclined his head graciously, seething that the Templar would single him out.

He does not matter, Parasu consoled Jonas. *He is nothing compared to you. A flawed vessel for his deity. Your worth is beyond measure and has nothing to do with pathetic things like riding horses or swinging weapons as any commoner can do.*

Pride surged through Jonas and he held his head high. His was a regal figure as they wove their way through the crowds to exit the city. And he kept his head high when he chose to ride in the wagon after a half day in the saddle rubbed his thighs raw. The Templar could posture all he wanted. Only Jonas could share himself with his deity. Only Jonas was truly beloved by his deity, as more than a vessel to be used and tossed away.

Abram gasped and sat down suddenly, his hand on his chest. He closed his eyes as he recognized the feeling from his father's death. A connection severed. Master Tull was gone.

"Abram? What's wrong?" Casia asked. She poured a glass of water and handed it to him. Abram looked up to find Master Gursh gazing intently at him. Abram slowly nodded to him, and the man closed his eyes and looked away. Abram drank the water and stood.

"Sorry," he told Casia. "Must be the heat. Where were we again?"

CHAPTER 15

Kadar huddled with Onyeka and their band of warriors at the northern edge of the army encampment, two hours before dawn.

Kadar was controlling twenty-five horses with his talent—forcing them to lie in the desert sand and keeping them unnaturally still and quiet. Onyeka and one of the other Tigus focused on the desert magic, creating the illusion that they were a part of the sand and life around them. There were four other teams like theirs spread along the south side of the camp, helping the sixty assassins from the tribes sneak into camp to kill the Knights controlling the Forsaken. Those other groups did not have horses to control and keep quiet. The returning assassins from those teams would simply melt back into the desert when they finished their tasks and meet at a set point where their mounts would be waiting to carry them south, to the Sands.

Kadar and Onyeka's group was on the northern side of the camp and would need the extra speed a horse could give to escape the fighters and retribution.

They watched as two assassins crept behind the idling guards. Kadar flinched as the Tigus knifed the men and dragged their bodies farther out into the desert, behind a large cactus. The two assassins scouted the area, making certain no guards remained, and then motioned for the others to enter the camp.

Onyeka's tribe had stolen enough uniforms for all the assassins entering the camp. In the predawn dark, they would hopefully not be noticed as they walked the edges of the camp with army-issued hats and scarves covering most of their faces.

Kadar unslung his bow off his back to prepare for any trouble that might block the assassins' fast escape after they'd killed the Knights.

Onyeka took his bow from him. "You will not linger to fight. You promised the elders. At the first commotion, you release the spell on the horses and race to the camp. Leave the fighting to us."

Kadar frowned but let her have the bow. There'd been a fight about Kadar's involvement. He was the only one who could keep the horses lying down and quiet, but they did not want to risk him getting injured this close to the army. Onyeka had come to his defense and vowed to guard him. Kadar suspected it was because Onyeka wanted action. She'd been disappointed that she would not be one of assassins. This way she could direct the action and be useful protecting Kadar.

"No noise so far," Kadar said. "Do you think that means the other teams made it in without being discovered?"

Onyeka nodded without moving her gaze from where the Tigu assassins had entered the camp. It was maddening not having a way of communicating between the groups. The elders had considered using hoots or other animal noises, but in the end they decided such noises would attract too much notice. Instead, the cue for the assassins to kill the Knights was the complete set of the moon, when the cat star was directly overhead. It seemed too imprecise to Kadar.

There was no convenient hill or ledge from which to watch the progress of the assassins. Kadar had no way of telling where the twenty Tigus of their team were as they split again into groups of four and sought out the Forsaken cohorts they'd been assigned to. The warriors of the One had assured Kadar that when the Knights were killed, the Forsaken would wake immediately with the freeing of their *geas*. Kadar hoped they would have enough sense to recognize their chance to flee and take it.

Kadar glanced at the moon, which was now only a sliver above the horizon.

"Did we give them enough time to get in place?" he asked.

She looked over at him, a small smile on her lips. "Shhh." She put a hand on his arm, and he realized he'd been fidgeting. He hated waiting.

The moon disappeared and Kadar held his breath,

knowing it was the moment. The warriors who had taken out the army sentinels returned. Minutes passed, and no uproar came from the camp.

"How long should we wait?" one of the other Tigus asked Onyeka.

"Until the camp rouses and we know something of our comrades' fate," she said grimly.

"Do we attempt rescue?" a warrior wanted to know.

"No. They knew the risks. They have been given poison capsules. We would only be recovering bodies."

Their first hint of success was when men trickled quietly out of the camp, fleeing north. At first Kadar thought it was their assassins returning, and allowed the horses to rise to their feet. But these men looked bemused, shocked as they stumbled out. Once they reached the edge of the encampment, where the Tigus were, they realized they were clear of the army and ran north. One tried to grab a horse, but Kadar stopped him. The Forsaken man jerked back with a gasp as Kadar materialized in front of him.

"These go south, with the men who freed you," he said gently, pushing the man away. "Go north, blessed by the One."

The Forsaken man stumbled, and then ran north with his fellows. It was a strangely quiet exodus from the camp. Kadar was shocked an alarm had not yet sounded and said so to Onyeka.

"Our assassins killed as many guards as they could, going through camp," Onyeka said. "I thought the Forsaken themselves would be noisy, like Northerners usually are, but I guess they have learned quiet in their captivity. This cannot hold."

Onyeka was correct. A great shout went up in camp. As they watched, smoke rose over the camp. It was clear that tents had been set on fire and the fire was spreading through the camp. Kadar slung himself up on Asfar's back as the camp was suddenly boiling with fighters roused from their sleep, coughing in the smoke and wanting to know what the commotion was about.

The other Tigu guards mounted as well, bows at the ready, but all attention was focused inside the camp at the choking smoke that now covered the area and masked the torches.

"There's Jein," Onyeka said, as one of their Tigu assassins sped out of camp in the middle of fleeing Forsaken. Other assassins quickly followed her and flung themselves up on the horses.

"Move out. The rest are lost," Jein shouted.

Onyeka covered their fleeing group with arrows as fighters pursued the escaping Forsaken.

"Go," she yelled.

Kadar urged Asfar to a gallop, leading their team. The army troops were not organized enough to follow.

When they were well out of range, Kadar circled their group around to the south and their meeting point with the other Tigu teams.

Onyeka caught up with them quickly.

"They were too busy trying to keep Forsaken in and too worried about the fires spreading to pursue us," she said. "I think we've caused chaos in the group. How many assassins returned to us?"

Jein reined in beside Onyeka. "We lost three in one group," she reported. "A soldier caught them escaping after their strike. Kana and Dray each lost two to guards, but the rest were able to kill the Knights to finish their missions. All succeeded in killing their targets. All killed or died by their own hands. No captives."

Onyeka nodded approvingly. "You have honored the Sepacu tribe," she said, and Jein beamed with pride. "You all have served the One well and will be rewarded."

The sun was rising when they met up with three of the other groups. Battle leader Jaiden was speaking with the returning groups.

Kadar watched the other Tigus as Onyeka reported. The assassins were stripping off the army gear, changing to robes, and laughing among themselves. None seemed disturbed that they'd killed men who were sleeping in their beds.

"Who set the fires?" Onyeka asked.

"When the camp roused, several Forsaken men used torches to set fire to the canvas tents. The smoke masked their exit and the fires, rather than the fleeing Forsaken, got the attention of the fighters. When we fled south, the Forsaken were lighting up every tent as they ran."

They rode well east of the army before finding and digging up a small spring to water themselves and the horses and stop for a quick rest. Jaiden sent a messenger ahead to the elders. It would be a two-day ride to the camp, which had moved south into the Sands in anticipation of army retaliation.

Onyeka was ebullient about the battle but saw Kadar's reticence.

"Why do you not celebrate?" she asked. "We freed thousands of slaves in one blow."

"But how many will actually stay free?" he asked. He'd wanted to escort the Forsaken to a safer location, but the elders had overruled him. There weren't enough Tigus to protect the Forsaken they had freed. "And how will they be punished if they're retaken?"

"Jaiden said most of the Forsaken were smart and took their weapons when they escaped. If Voras wants to recover them he will have a fight on his hands. We will know for certain how many stayed and how many the deities recovered when our scouts report back. Jaiden says we were very fortunate. The Voices will arrive late today. Tomorrow night the camp will be more closely guarded. Their presence could have meant total failure."

He and Onyeka slept side by side in the chilly night. He knew they'd probably be separated again soon if her tribe was assigned to follow the army and he stayed with the elders. He treasured the feel of her in his arms under the starry sky.

When they rode into camp, Amber was waiting to climb onto his shoulder.

"We knew you'd be returning soon thanks to

that little one," Turo told him. "She is better than a watchdog."

The elders wanted Kadar to report the assassins' success to the warriors of the One, so he settled on his mat and reached out for his cousin.

Abram's sending was shaky and he seemed upset. Kadar relayed his messages from the elder, and then asked, *What is it Abram? Has something gone wrong?*

Abram hesitated, speaking with someone on his side. *They say I can tell you. Kadar, they're dead.*

Who is dead? Kadar asked, alarmed, thinking of his family in Shpeth and his daughter in Tsangia. Had the deities reached them already?

Master Tull, Master Ursa, and the rest of their party, Abram sent. *They said they were going on a mission to protect Shpeth and the towns in the path of the army, but . . . they never intended to come back.*

"By the One!" Kadar exclaimed, and then he realized he'd spoken out loud. "Abram says Masters Tull and Ursa dead," he told the surprised elders.

Were they attacked? Kadar asked.

No, Abram said. *They sacrificed themselves. They learned how to change the waymarkers at the oases, but they had to kill themselves to do so. They changed three of the markers leading to Shpeth. They were my mentors, my friends. But they died to protect our families.*

"They sacrificed themselves," Kadar told the elders. "They changed the waymarkers with blood magic so the deities will not be able to attack Shpeth."

The elders murmured among themselves.

"We will honor them, along with our fallen warriors," Talin said gravely. "Who has the new words of power for the waymarkers at those oases?"

Three warriors of the One, Abram told Kadar, after he'd relayed Talin's query. *It will take some time for the new words to be shared among all our people. The warriors of the One travel to the caravan route that enters the Sands on the west side. Have the Tigu army meet us so we can plan the next step together.*

"But how will the army of the deities proceed through the desert?" Talin asked. "Without a guide through the Sands, they will be forced to turn back. The Chosen still need them to arrive at the Obsidian Temple—who will lead them there?"

Abram said, *The warriors of the One will choose someone who knows the route and let the deities "capture" him or her.*

The elders nodded in resignation as Kadar relayed this.

"Tell them we will meet them on the western edge of the Sands," Talin said.

Be safe, Kadar, Abram said. *Have you spoken to cousin Sulis recently? She is worse than a mother, nagging to learn more about you. Please talk to her. The Chosen at the temple have been through a great deal. She asked me to tell you to contact her when you can.*

I will, thank you, Kadar sent. *You stay safe as well.*

Kadar was too exhausted from the ride and his *far-speaking* to get in touch with Sulis, so he and Amber found the Sepacu cook fire instead.

Onyeka met him with a plate of sliced meat and a mug of ale. "We will honor our fallen this evening," she told him. "Jaiden just told me the Sepacus will shadow the army and report their position and numbers while the rest of the tribes travel to meet up with the warriors of the One. So it looks like we will part again."

"We honor more than only our warriors," Kadar said, and he filled her in on the masters' sacrifices.

She was silent as Kadar ate, lost in her own thoughts. When he'd finished and set his plate down, she took his hands.

"There's something else bothering you, isn't there?" she asked.

"The warriors of the One will need someone to guide the deities to the Obsidian Temple now that the path to Shpeth is closed to them and they cannot find a guide there. They will need someone who knows the caravan routes, the Northern language, and the words for the waymarkers."

Onyeka gazed into his eyes a moment. "You will volunteer," she said.

Kadar nodded. "I will no longer be necessary as the go-between because the elders will be with the warriors of the One. My cousin can continue to speak with the Chosen. I know the routes. I even know one of the Voices, the Voice of Parasu, and have taken classes with him. I have a plan that differs from that of the warriors of the One. Rather than having the deities capture me, I believe that with some mind blocks I can convince the deities that I have defected and get them to trust me."

"Why would the deities believe this?" Onyeka asked. "If this Voice of Parasu knows you at all, he will know your loyalty to the South."

"But he also knows my bond with my sister. If I could convince them that the warriors of the One sacrificed my sister . . ."

"Then they would think you were out of your mind with grief," Onyeka said, nodding. "You would do anything for revenge if Sulis was murdered."

"I need a more detailed plan," Kadar said. "But yes, that is the essence."

Onyeka nodded and looked down, clasping his hands between hers. She looked up, determination in her eyes. "You make me proud," she said. "Such glory you ride to! We will think of a plan to tell them, between us. One that will allow you to do honor to your tribe and still return to me whole."

Kadar laughed softly and leaned forward to kiss her. "I should have realized you'd understand," he said. "I know I am not a fighter like you. But I know when the tribes need me and I would like to make you proud. But I need you to make me a promise," he said, and she turned to him, her face serious. "If I die, I want you to visit Datura, when she is old enough to understand. I want you to tell her what I did and why I had to leave her. Make her understand that I left because I loved her and wanted to protect her. I did not abandon her without a thought."

Onyeka nodded. "You are always thinking of her and speaking of her. If you do not return, she will know this. I will tell her what glory you gave her name."

They almost missed saying goodbye in the flurry of packing the next day, as he helped the elders and she organized her fighters. He had mounted and was looking around frantically for her when Asfar snorted. He glanced behind to find her galloping up.

They leaned over their saddles and kissed breathlessly, and then were pulled apart by their restive mounts.

"Here," she said, pressing something into his hand. Before he could respond, she'd turned and galloped to her tribe.

Kadar opened his hand to find a bracelet, woven of beads and hair. He suspected she'd mingled her short black hair with the lighter, longer hairs from her horse's tail, to create something long enough to fit around his wrist.

"I see I was wrong," Turo said as Kadar fumbled to tie the bracelet on his wrist. "You have captured my daughter's heart." He looked more closely. "And you have captured her horse's heart as well, it seems."

Kadar laughed with him as they rode into the Sands, leaving the shifting dunes to sweep over the flat impressions of the camp.

Tori, Sandy, and Shane swept into Illian on the heels of the Voices exiting the city, with twenty-five of the Descendants acting as escorts. The soldiers at the gate summoned their Knight when faced with three Counselors of the One. He questioned them about their party, but their *feli* and gold robes afforded them a large retinue.

"We've had more pilgrims from far northern temples and towns coming in recently than is normal," the Knight mused.

"That's thanks to us, I'm afraid," Tori said. "More will probably be coming. They decided our elevation to Counselor was a sign that they need to do a pilgrimage. I worry about their safety, though."

"Why?" the Knight asked.

Sandy answered him. "Near the turnoff to the town of Stonycreek, a large group was forming. It was mostly Forsaken and Southerners. They were armed and seemed ready to begin a march on Illian."

The Knight exchanged a grim glance with his soldiers. "Could you see how many were in this group?" he asked.

Shane shook his head. "They were camped in the forest as well as on the road. They were trying to conceal their numbers. We put our heads down and left the area as soon as we saw them."

"You were wise to do so—capturing a Counselor to ransom would be a boon to that rabble. They've proven they'll kill even children to get what they want.

We were warned they might organize and march on Illian, with the Voices leaving the city. I thank you for this information. We will be on high alert."

"But will you send someone out to make certain our pilgrims are safe?" Tori asked.

"We don't have the men to do so, Counselor," he said regretfully. "But we don't think they'll bother pilgrims on the road—nothing they could get out of them."

Tori nodded, acting appeased, and they entered the city. Most of the Southern merchant halls were boarded up with graffiti defacing the outside of their shops. No Southerners appeared in the crowds on the street leading to the Temple.

The Descendants in their group melted away into the city to find lodging and wait for Tori's signal.

"Do we go to the Temple of the One first and greet Counselor Elida?" Sandy asked.

Tori shook her head. "We might as well visit the shrines of the deities first and see which acolytes the One wants to convert. Then all the new Counselors can descend on Elida at once."

Shane grinned wickedly. "That's rather cruel," he murmured, but followed her lead.

Voras's shrine was the first doorway in the corridor, and pilgrims parted as the three Counselors swept in.

"I don't expect many acolytes at Voras's shrine to convert to Counselors," Sandy murmured as they marched past soldiers to the altar in the center of the shrine.

Tori put her hands on Voras's altar before the disapproving Knight could accost her.

"Who is called to the One?" she asked out loud. There was a flash of golden light. Two soldiers stared at her in shock, red cloaks bleached to gold. She looked past them as a door opened from the courtyard and three more soldiers, now with gold cloaks, stepped through.

"That's all of you?" she asked.

"There might be more," one former soldier said timidly. "There are many out sparring and on patrol."

Tori nodded, and they followed behind her like chicks as she exited to the hallway. Counselor Elida stood in the doorway to the Temple of the One and raised her eyebrows as she saw Tori.

"Causing trouble, Counselor Tori?" she asked dryly.

Tori grinned mischievously at her. "They're all yours, Counselor Elida," she said, motioning to her followers.

While Elida gathered the new Counselors, Tori, Shane, and Sandy swept into Ivanha's altar.

The Mother Superior objected when she laid her hands on the altar, but the results were instant.

"Oh, yes, yes, yes!" A young man bustled out of the Crone's office, his cloak pure gold. He was carrying a cup of tea. "You have no idea how many years I have waited for this. Here is your tea, you old goat." He poured the cup over the Mother Superior's head, to her gasping horror.

Sandy snickered, but Shane stared as the door to the courtyard opened and women in gold poured through.

"There will be more of us," one woman said practically, "but many are taking care of their children at the rebuilt Children's Home. They won't come until replacements are found."

Sulis had warned Tori during their pledge year that the Templar could *geas* a woman into sleeping with him. Ivanha had a lot of disgruntled pledges from that system of choosing. Fifteen women now followed them to the Temple of the One, and more would be coming.

"This one is mine," Shane said as they entered the shrine of Parasu. He put his hands on his former altar more lovingly than Tori had the other two.

"There is no shame in being called to something higher," he said gently to the watching scholars as gold light glowed around him. "Merely a shift in priorities."

Even so, only about eight left the service of Parasu to follow them.

Sandy pushed ahead in the final shrine and did the calling for Aryn.

"Whiskers," the Cantor said, looking down at his golden cloak. "The Herald and Ranger will be furious. They left me in charge." He shook his head as he realized that his second in charge had also become a Counselor. "I'll need to linger here until we figure out a replacement." Ten others strode to Temple of the One. This time Tori, Sandy, and Shane led them in.

It was quite crowded, with forty new Counselors of the One circled around Elida, who was by the central altar.

"By the One," she said, shaking her head. "Where are we going to sleep all of you?"

Tori laughed at the practicality of that.

"You have ideas, Counselor Tori?" Elida asked acerbically as Tori pushed through to stand by her.

"No, I simply love that a miracle happens—the One chooses dozens of new Counselors—and all you can think is where to house them. You are far more practical than I," she said.

Counselor Elida hugged her absently, while doing a head count. "That is because you are new to this. The One surprises her Counselors so often that we tend toward the practical instead of awe. And we really can only fit a dozen in the Counselors' house, and that's if we stuff beds into all the rooms."

"We can use the attics in Aryn and Voras," one new Counselor ventured. He was bespectacled and pale, probably a former scholar. "They are not being used for pledges this year and already have beds waiting."

Elida frowned. "I suppose that will do for now, though I'd prefer us all together."

"The Cantor is coming as well," Shane told her.

Elida did look shocked at that. "Whiskers. Aryn will not be happy," she said. "I want you three to house with me. I need to know what training we will need for the final battle."

"I'm worried the deities will send their Voices scampering back to Illian after this," Sandy said, looking out over the new Counselors who were chatting excitedly with each other. "They'll want to know what we are up to, stealing their acolytes."

Counselor Elida shook her head. "This will confirm their belief that the One is trying to stop them from going to the Obsidian Temple. They don't know the One wants them to go to the temple. Their arrogance will be their downfall."

CHAPTER 16

Jonas sat atop his placid horse and looked around at
the chaos of Voras's army in shock. He coughed as
acrid smoke wafted his direction and his mare shook
her head uncomfortably.

The Templar had already swung down and was
screaming orders as his Knights gathered around him,
gesturing and attempting to explain. Jonas looked in
the direction they gestured and realized that burned
tarps were covering bodies, dozens of bodies.

"It looks like a battle occurred. Shocking, this close
to the outpost," the Magistrate said to Jonas, looking as
puzzled as he was.

The Herald and Ranger had flipped over a tarp and
were examining the bodies underneath. Jonas climbed
down from his mount, patting her absentmindedly as
he turned her reins over to a waiting aide. He walked
over to the Ranger.

"What has happened here?" he asked.

The Ranger shook her head. "We haven't gotten any sense out of the Templar yet, but it looks like these Knights were assassinated. These aren't battle wounds."

"We've got some bodies from the Tigu tribes over here," the Herald said, coughing as she pulling up another tarp. She'd been coughing most of the trip and the smoke was making it worse.

"How do you know they are Tigus?" Jonas asked.

"They have tribal tattoos, which nontribal Southerners don't," the Herald said. "These bodies don't have wounds, so they were not killed by a weapon. But look at the white around their mouths, foam that has dried. That indicates poisoning."

The Templar huffed up to them, a Knight following behind. "The Forsaken are gone," he said. "Less than a thousand Forsaken remain. Those One-blasted Southerners sent in assassins and killed all the Knights in the cohorts that contained Forsaken. The Forsaken fled north."

"Did your men capture any Tigus for questioning?" Jonas asked.

"They killed themselves," the Templar said. "Took some sort of powder. Blasted cowards."

Jonas rather thought it took courage to kill yourself to protect your territory, but he held his tongue as Parasu stirred in the back of his mind.

"How many men remain?" Jonas asked at Parasu's prompting.

"We don't have an exact count yet," the Templar said. "Between six and seven thousand."

"Can you recover the Forsaken who fled?" the Crone asked, stepping up beside them. "Force the infidels back into service? Or did the Southerners capture them and take them for their army?"

The Templar grimaced. "Most of the tracks lead north. They fled toward Illian, rather than run into the desert. My men believe the Tigus were here only to set the Forsaken free and did not press them into service. It would be costly, both in time and labor, to try and recapture them," he admitted. "We trained those Forsaken to fight. My soldiers report that the released Forsaken took their weapons with them when they fled. They set fire to the camp to distract my troops."

"Were many fighters injured?" the Herald asked.

"We have burns from fighting the flames. Some fighters were wounded trying to keep the Forsaken from fleeing. The greatest loss of life you see in front of you—my most talented Knights, who controlled the Forsaken. This would take an entire tribe to pull off."

The Herald shook her head. "The Tigus here are from different tribes. You can see it in the tattoos."

The Templar examined a couple of bodies as Jonas looked away from the still forms.

"They're savages, little better than the cowardly wild dogs who hang around the edges and harass from afar. They don't cooperate like this," he said in frustration.

Jonas's mouth opened without his volition. "Clearly you've underestimated them, Templar," his voice said in Parasu's flat tones. "There is someone directing these savages now because they have combined into a cohesive whole. We must consider if it is wise to continue this folly and travel farther into the desert."

The Templar stared at Jonas, mouth open slightly. An aide ran over and he turned to the soldier.

"We have a command tent set up for you to get out of the sun," the aide said. "With refreshments for the Voices. We also have cleared an area for the tents of the Voices and their parties."

The Templar nodded and turned to the others. "We will need shelter for several nights, even if the deities decide not to continue the campaign. We should meet again after our parties are settled," he said. "Standing in the sun arguing does us no good. I still need to gather reports about last night's events before I can total our losses."

"I need to find my healers," the Herald said with another cough. "And find the tent they've set up for the wounded."

"We will meet in the command tent at dusk," Parasu said through Jonas. "I will gather my own information throughout the day on these events and report my decision to the other deities this evening."

Jonas turned to the Magistrate and the rest of his party. "We will set up the tents. Parasu wishes to question the perimeter guards, along with those who captured the Southerners before they killed themselves. Once we have set up, you will find them and bring them to my tent for questioning."

Jonas was not permitted to help with setup of his camp, though he would have preferred to do something other than sit under a canvas shelter in the sweltering sun, looking official. His aides were more adept at setting up the large woven monstrosity his rank demanded. He would have been in the way as they sorted poles and ropes.

Most of the sentries had been killed along with the Knights—the Tigus had been thorough. The ones who remained saw nothing as they watched the desert, realizing something was amiss in the camp only when the Forsaken ran past them to escape.

Jonas had settled in his spacious tent, a hand on his *feli*'s head, and was listening to the Magistrate question one of the Knights who had captured the Tigus when Parasu's attention drifted away from the proceedings. Jonas listened, knowing Parasu would sift through his memory later to find what he needed.

Parasu came back with a rush, and Jonas found himself standing before he realized what he was doing.

"Tribune?" the Magistrate queried.

"We will continue this later. Parasu must speak with Voras," Jonas heard his voice say.

The Magistrate and Knight bowed.

"I can lead you to him," the Knight offered, and Jonas inclined his head. As he followed behind the Knight, he asked his deity, *What has happened?*

The One has stolen my people, Parasu said. Jonas could feel his fury. *I had been aware of the One taking acolytes at temples farther out. But he has taken people in Illian, at my altar.*

Jonas entered the command tent in the center of the encampment and found Ivanha and Voras already there, possessing their Voices.

"Twenty of my acolytes," Ivanha screeched at Voras. "You said the One posed no risk, the One was helpless with so few followers. Well now she has plenty, and she stole them from me!"

"We lost eight," Parasu said. "I do not know what the One hopes to gain by making more Counselors."

"The One is trying to stop us!" Voras hissed. "He chose this attack after we abandoned the city, to draw us from our task."

Aryn entered, the Herald's *feli* on her heels. She turned inhuman eyes on the rest of them. "The One stole my Cantor," she growled. "And some of my best acolytes."

Voras chuckled nastily. "You should have chosen your leaders more wisely," he said. "My acolytes were faithful—only five abandoned my shrine."

Aryn bristled, and Parasu stepped between them. "We've all lost acolytes," he said coldly. "The question is why now? And what will we do about it?"

"We continue," Voras said promptly. "This is clearly an attempt to draw us to Illian. To stop our campaign to regain our true selves. We should not let the One force our return."

"If the One wanted us in Illian, why steal our people? Why not try to stop us in the desert?"

"What do you think the attack on the army was about?" Voras waved to the camp outside the tent. "You wanted to know who coordinated the Tigus. Clearly the desert priests have been ordered by the One to stop us. But they do not have the numbers we do, so they sneak in the night before we arrive. In case that doesn't discourage us, the One takes as many of our acolytes as he can, hoping we will abandon our task."

Jonas could feel Parasu mulling this over, looking for flaws in the logic.

"I had a vision," Aryn said suddenly. "Something was being torn away from me—and then I felt a sense of completion, of wholeness. I believe it was a foretelling, come from the ether."

"I felt this, too," Ivanha hissed. Parasu and Voras nodded when the Aryn looked over at them.

"I have felt this as well," Parasu said. "It is the reason I believe we must continue, if we have enough men left in the army to defend us, and fight our way through to this Obsidian Temple. I believe it is a vision of us regaining our powers."

Voras nodded. "My spy who was killed at the Obsidian Temple reported only around three thousand warriors in the South. We have double that number. The Tigus cannot be more than a thousand strong, surviving in the desert without water and resources the way they do."

"But they have the advantage of knowing the terrain," Aryn said. "They know the paths through the desert."

"We have our spies. We have broken and *geased* the Southern caravan guides who can work the spells on the oases. It will not take much to capture the smaller villages along our path. It will demoralize the Southerners to see their men and women fighting against them when they are *geased* into serving us," Voras said.

"What is to stop them from freeing the *geased* men like they just did?" Parasu asked.

"My Voice will hold the *geas*, and he will be well protected. We know their tactics now," Voras said. "With the combined might of our Voices, we can shield our men at night and keep any deserters from escaping."

"Yes," Aryn said, "I agree. We stay to this path. The One is desperate to stop us, is acting out of fear. This tells me we are on the path to regaining what we lost. The time is now, and we must act or we could lose this chance forever."

"The time is now," Ivanha agreed.

"We continue into the Southern Territory," Voras said. "It is agreed."

The other deities set their Voices' bodies down on cushions around the tent. Jonas watched in fascination as divine awareness left their eyes and their bodies collapsed onto the rugs that made up the floor of the tent.

We must be wary, my young Voice, Parasu warned Jonas. *I do not fully understand the One's actions and fear another motive lies behind the taking of our acolytes. I will be with you always, as we continue on this journey.*

Parasu settled into the back of Jonas's mind, brooding over today's events. He opened the tent flap and called the other deities' acolytes to tend their Voices, and then walked to his tent, feeling young and over-whelmed. There was much to think about and plan. He was glad that Parasu would guide each step.

I hate to tell you this, Kadar sent to Sulis after they'd finished catching up. *Especially after hearing about Clay. But I have difficult news about your former masters.*

Kadar had finally reported in on all his doings with the Tigus the day after the Forsaken had been set free from the army. It had been more than a ten-day since he'd last had a chance to contact her, and much had happened to both of them. He was en route with the elders of the tribes to meet up with the warriors of the One, at the very edge of the Sands where the Tigus and warriors of the One would combine forces for the final battle.

What do you mean? Sulis asked, confused. *Which masters?*

Masters Tull and Ursa, Kadar said. *And an energy user named Bento. I learned a ten-day ago they were being re-placed as leaders of the warriors of the One so they could travel to Shpeth. I thought they were taking fighters to pro-tect our cities.*

Sulis's heart sank as he spoke. *What happened to them?* she asked. *Are they dead?*

Yes. They sacrificed themselves. I guess the waymarkers and wards around the oases were set with some sort of blood magic. They were able to reset the protections using their own blood and bones. They died to save the western towns from the deities.

Sulis gasped, opening her eyes, and Ashraf and Alannah looked over at her in concern. She shook her head at them and closed her eyes again.

Ava told Sari how to do the ritual, Sulis said. *She learned from Aryn. Sari must have relayed it to the masters. How horrible. They were strong, intelligent leaders. This will really unhinge her.*

Don't tell her, Kadar sent. *There's no reason for her to know until after the final battle. I don't think many people are being told—only the leaders of each movement.*

Sulis's eyes filled with tears. *They were kind, generous teachers,* she sent.

I'm sorry, sis, Kadar said. *But I thought you'd want to know.*

I wonder if Grandmother and Master Anchee know, Sulis said.

I don't know. Must go now, the sun is rising and we have another day of travel ahead. Hugs and misses.

Hugs and misses. Stay safe, Kadar.

Alannah and Ashraf were watching her when she uncurled from talking to Kadar and pushed Djinn off her lap. She filled them in on the masters' deaths.

"I agree with Kadar," Alannah said. "Don't tell Ava. She will feel responsible."

"I must tell Grandmother and Master Anchee," Sulis said.

But they already knew. Sulis found them huddled with Palou, Sari, and Lasha.

"I felt it when Tull made her sacrifice," Grandmother said. "I did not know what had happened at first. I thought they'd been magically attacked. Sari spoke with Abram. He told us what the masters' plans had been. I felt it when Ursa and Bento completed their sacrifices at other oases."

"You said nothing," Sulis said. But Grandmother had been sadder, more withdrawn since they'd emptied Ivanha's and Voras's statues. Sulis had put it down to exhaustion and age.

"It was best to keep it among ourselves. We cannot let Ava know," Master Anchee said. "Only we and the Tigu elders know, as well as the highest-level warriors of Kabandha. All the others believe they are still on their mission to protect the western cities from the army. Having our greatest energy channelers sacrifice themselves could demoralize our troops. Please do not spread this around to the people from Kabandha who are arriving now."

Sulis gave her promise. Having those wise teachers die saddened her, and she'd known them less than a year. They were her grandmother's colleagues and friends—if she wanted it concealed, Sulis could do nothing else.

Sulis and Ashraf were somber as they ate breakfast. There were new faces at the table from Kabandha and Sulis felt the scrutiny of the newcomers. It was no doubt because she was one of the Chosen, and she hoped she looked up to weaving the deities back into the One.

The Obsidian Temple was once again becoming full. The late summer rains had swept in from the ocean toward the mountains, soaking Frubia and the eastern coast. The rains seldom made it past the high peaks of the Girish Mountains, but the rains in the mountains replenished the chasm's tiny trickle of water to a steady stream.

Sulis had become accustomed to a meditative solitude. Having more people around distracted her, unsettled her. The people sent by Kabandha were not clerics or scholars—they were older warriors of the One who had come to prepare for the final battle. Having fighters sparring behind the dormitories reminded her an entire world existed outside the chasm that did not revolve around the prisons of the deities in the Obsidian Temple. She longed to see the dunes of the desert instead of the black cliffs surrounding her.

She escaped Ashraf's worried eyes after breakfast and was standing, staring at the cliffs behind the dormitories, her heart heavy. She remembered Master Ursa's patient tutelage in scriptures and histories. Her eyes felt hot, though she held back tears, thinking of Master Tull's sharp corrections in unarmed combat.

Master Anchee spoke behind her, startling her. She turned to see Master Anchee and Lasha watching her.

"Are you planning on doing some climbing?" Master Anchee teased. "Clawing your way up that cliff to freedom?"

Sulis sighed and took on his joking tone. "No, I will stay here and be a good Chosen," she said. "This is hard for me. I want to move, not sit in a great crevice. Even in Kabandha, I could escape to the forest behind the city or into the plains. The dormitories are filling up with warriors from Kabandha, and I'm feeling crowded."

"Lasha has mentioned that she, too, needs an excursion. And I believe we may be trying too hard now, to little gain. We have made no further advances on energy flow because we have nothing challenging to do." His eyes gleamed.

"And you've thought of something challenging?" Sulis asked.

He nodded. "The last of the warriors of the One are shutting down Kabandha and arriving here. We can help them release the wards on the path down to the Obsidian Temple. That will give us more practice channeling energy to each other."

"Yes," Sulis said, seeing the sense. "We need a challenge. How do the pilgrims usually handle the wards?"

"Each group is sent with a powerful energy user. But the wards drain them to the point of exhaustion. Sharing energy means we won't be drained."

Sulis grinned at Lasha. "When do we go?"

"When I talk to Amon about it."

They walked toward the temple, where Sulis last saw him.

"Why are they shutting down Kabandha?" Sulis asked.

"Kabandha's entire purpose was to train for the final battle," Master Anchee said. "The teachers and warriors of the One have been preparing their whole lives, and in their lives before, for this. The most able-bodied went with Master Tull and the warriors of the One, north of the Sands, but those who remained are still powerful warriors."

"But scholars and clerics studied at Kabandha," Sulis said.

"They are the last to leave," Anchee said. "Most have some ability to use energy and are setting protections on the old scrolls as they store everything. Those who can channel energy will go to Frubia and the Tigu tribes to shield the Tigus against any hostile energy that could escape."

"What hostile energy?" Lasha asked.

"The energy force that might come from here, in the final battle." He gestured around them. "This was all rainforest. Five hundred years ago, every bit of life energy was drained by the final spell used to capture the deities. In every tribe where a channeler shielded its people, its people survived. The tribes without shields died. All of them. Frubia was a center of energy channelers and they protected the entire city. We have learned from this and each tribe of Tigu will have a channeler; each city will be shielded. After the battle is over, Kabandha will probably be a great learning center for scholars—but it could be many years before the South will be restored. So the resources will be lovingly preserved for our greater future."

Sulis stopped walking, shocked at this assessment. "You think this final battle will destroy the Southern

Territory?" she asked. She'd wondered if she would die in the battle, if the rest of the Chosen would perish in their attempts. It never occurred to her the danger could be so widespread.

Master Anchee grimaced, spreading his hands. "We don't know. During the Great War, the damage was more widespread than we could ever imagine. The Southerners who created the spell expected it to take their lives and those of the living beings in the area around the battle. Instead, it took all life that was not shielded—even the tiniest creatures and plants and fungi in the earth below their feet. This caused the crevice we are in now and the melted stone around the area. But they did not expect it to suck most of the life from the rainforests farther out as well, creating the desert. All humans who were inside the range of the spell died. We cannot know the price of weaving the deities back to the One. But this time we can prepare our people."

Ashraf popped out of the dormitory, feeling her worry through their bond, and she tried to get her feelings under control. She swallowed once. "Yes, let's go practice handling energy some more," she said. "Time to find Amon."

Amon frowned at their request, but nodded reluctantly. "Ava and Sanuri need to remain," he said, looking over at the statues. Ava was standing with Alannah, talking and gesturing to the statue of Ivanha, while Sanuri played with Nuisance. "Ava is making progress with the mandalas that will trap the deities.

I don't want you to distract her. Sanuri helps, in her own way."

Alannah came over to them. "I'm staying here. I can see the energy Ava creates, and it helps her to talk over her ideas with Dani and me. Sanuri says the deities have left Illian. They are traveling with an army. She says they are angry. Things have not gone as they planned."

Master Anchee nodded. "Their path will be slowed as they try to find a guide to get them to the temple. We might have a ten-day yet."

Grandmother and Palou had already borrowed humpbacks from the new arrivals at the stables and were putting supplies on them. Sulis and Ashraf ran to pack some clothes to camp out.

"I think I'm not the only one feeling restless," Sulis murmured as they came out of the dormitories to find Grandmother tapping her foot impatiently.

"There is a strong family resemblance," Ashraf murmured.

They emerged on the campsite above the chasm, past the waymarker, as the sun was setting.

"We'll stay here tonight," Palou said as they made camp and spread their blankets.

Sulis sighed in happiness as the first of the stars appeared above her. "It is nice to see the open sky full of stars," she told Lasha. "The cliffs were shutting me in, obscuring this magnificence."

"It always makes me feel tiny," Lasha said with a shiver as the night temperatures dropped with the sunset. "There are so many stars, and they are so bright."

Sulis was up at dawn. Ashraf sat beside her as they watched the sun rise over the desert. She laid her head on his shoulder.

"Have you ever seen anything so beautiful?" she asked.

He chuckled. "There is nothing to beat sailing in a boat with the sun rising over the ocean, painting the water with golden light," he said.

"That sounds lovely," Sulis said. "I have never been out to sea."

"When this is over, we will go to Frubia, and my family will finally meet the love of my life," Ashraf said wistfully.

Sulis turned to him. "You never got to say goodbye to them, did you?" she said with dawning realization. "You went on a trip to Kabandha and were never permitted to return."

He gave her a sad smile. "They let me write a note," he said. "We exchanged a few letters when I first came to Kabandha. They said they were proud I was serving the One, even as they made my sister heir. I would like to have seen them again, though. I would like to tell them I forgive them—I can create my own life, not dependent on them."

"Then we will visit Frubia first thing when this is all over," Sulis declared. "I will charm your family and you will teach me how to sail."

"I want to learn to sail, too," Lasha said from behind

them. "I've never seen the southern coast or been in a rainforest."

"Then you will come with us," Ashraf decided. "My family would love to meet my Northern friends. There is plenty of room in our domicile. You'd both make excellent sailors."

"That's settled then," Lasha said. "All we need to do is to remake the divine order and then we can nip off south and have some fun."

"Our work here is beginning," Master Anchee said. "I see a caravan heading this direction from the oasis. This will be a good chance to flex our channeling powers. Joisha, is that our first wards teacher Brea leading the caravan?"

"I believe it is," Grandmother said. She stepped forward to hail the caravan when they came closer. She and Master Anchee seemed to know several of the warriors in the group and greeted them fondly.

Brea, a wizened, elderly woman, slapped Master Anchee on the back. "Ah, good to have you youngsters to shoulder this burden. I wasn't certain this old gal still had the energy for this ward. Been decades since I made this trek."

The pilgrims traveling with the warriors were a surprise—four green-cloaked Vrishni from the North who traveled with a handful of Kabandha warriors.

"How did you get here?" Sulis asked, surprised. "I thought the ways through the desert were blocked."

"We were staying in Frubia, in different households," a frail-looking man with a long white beard told her. "We each had a vision to go north. We came upon these travelers and knew our path was with them."

"We are all *farspeakers*," a younger woman said. "We have messages for Alannah and Clay from Counselor Elida."

Sulis shook her head sadly. "You are too late for Clay," she said. "But Alannah can speak with Elida through you."

"I want you to lead the release of the wards, Sulis," Master Anchee said, motioning her over to the waymarker. "It is more complicated than at any other waymarker. Your energy is as strong as your grandmother's, but less developed."

The three Shuttles gathered around, linking to their Guardians. Sulis looked around. "Djinn isn't here," she exclaimed. "I wonder where that devil took himself to."

"Same place Alta is," Lasha said ruefully. "They left after we settled in for the night, probably to do some hunting."

"You can do without your *feli*," Grandmother reproved. "You depend too much on him."

"But it's so much easier with him," Sulis grumbled as she settled into place. She reached her energy out, and Grandmother and Anchee grasped onto it.

"Tell me what I need to do," she told Master Anchee.

As he guided her through the steps, she was merely a voice for the energy that flowed through her. Anytime her energy waned, more flooded into her from the other five linked to her, replenishing her.

She reached the end of the chant and spoke the release word. The wards tried to drain her—but again energy flowed into her.

"Did it work?" she asked, turning to the pilgrims.

She was talking to their backs as they hastened down the steep trail, eager to reach their destination before dark.

"I guess it did," she muttered to his back. "How does everyone feel?"

"I feel like I went for a brisk walk," Lasha said. "A little tired, but still plenty of energy."

"Better than I ever have after working with this ward," Master Anchee said, a big grin on his face. "I'd say this was a complete success."

Grandmother shouldered her pack and gestured to them. "Come, we need to leave now if we want to reach the oasis before the sun cooks us."

Around the campfire that night, Sulis turned to Grandmother and Master Anchee. "Do you really think we can do it?" she asked. "Our ancestors could only trap a small part of the deities, and it cost them everything. How can we succeed?"

"Our ancestors did not have centuries to plan," Grandmother said. "They were desperate, despairing for their lives, and constantly under attack by the followers of the deities. We have honed our skills through these centuries of relative peace. We have greater skill because only those who could work with energy survived that last battle, and we paired up with each other. Our children have been stronger each generation."

"I believe we will succeed as well," Master Anchee said. "This is what we were born for. We will make the One whole again."

"But at what cost?" Ashraf asked softly.

"Whatever the cost, we must be willing to pay it," Palou said. "For our families and for the future of all beings in our world."

"The moon is beautiful tonight," Lasha said, turning the conversation. "A light in the blackest night. I guess that's what we are for each other."

Sulis put an arm around her friend. "I will never regret the journey that brought us together," she said, leaning against Lasha. "No matter where it takes us."

CHAPTER 17

Kadar waited patiently on a bench outside the hall the warriors of the One were using for meetings at this depot, petting Amber, who arched against him. She purred and nipped his hand with little love bites. The warriors of the One had abandoned the Hasifel warehouses to come to this staging area. Most of the warriors were camped out in tents. The Tigus were setting up beside their camp, combining forces with the warriors of the One. Inside the hall, commanders of both the warriors of the One and the Tigus met to decide on who would guide the deities to the Obsidian Temple and how they would get the deities to accept their guide.

"Kadar?" Abram came and sat beside him. Amber transferred her attentions to him, leaving cream fur over his blue robes. "Have they spoken to you yet?"

"Not yet. I think they're debating my plan. It's obvious I'm the one who should be sent. But they're reluctant to block my memory as I've requested."

"Because they might not be able to unblock it." Abram gave a little shiver. "Doesn't that worry you?"

Kadar shook his head. "Grandmother set blocks in my mind years ago that would prevent the acolytes of the deities from finding out secrets. But the deities could easily read my surface feelings and tell that I'm lying when I tell my story to them. Unless I don't believe that I am lying."

"But what if they try to dig more deeply like they did with my father?" Abram asked.

"I hope they will have learned from his death," Kadar said. "I will appeal directly to Parasu. I know his Voice and I think he will be reasonable. I will be careful. I want to come home to my daughter."

"Unlike my father, who will never come home to us," Abram said sadly. "We've already lost so many good people. Who will be left?"

Kadar opened his mouth to respond, but was interrupted by Turo pushing back the door flap and motioning for Kadar to follow him. Kadar squeezed Abram's shoulder once and rose, following Turo into the building. Amber trotted at his heels. She leapt up onto the planning table, causing the people around it to snatch up valuable maps and diagrams. Kadar sighed as the little cat settled on a sheaf of papers and curled up, still purring.

"Kadar, we have discussed your plan at length," Master Gursh said. "The warriors approve, but Master Sandiv wants you to know the full dangers you face."

Master Sandiv's dark face was concerned as she looked at Kadar. "Master Ursa was our prominent mind healer. Her experience and skills far eclipsed mine. We have lost the greatest energy user our generation has known."

"Not lost," a warrior said with a frown. "Her sacrifice will be sung about generations hence. Her sacrifice has saved hundreds of lives."

Master Sandiv dipped her head in acknowledgment. "I can block your memories. I can make you believe that your sister and grandmother were sacrificed at the waymarker to change the wards. I can implant the routes the warriors of the One wish you to take the deities on after we spring our trap for their army. However, I'm not certain I can bring your true memories back."

"But if I see Sulis is alive, that should trigger my real memories to return, shouldn't it?" Kadar asked.

Master Sandiv shook her head. "It might. But you might not believe she is real. It could break your mind. I will do my very best to put in a trigger, but a mind shield thick enough to stop deities could be too great to release. The longer it is in place, the greater the hold will become. If I am still alive, I should be able to release the shield—but my first duty is stopping Voras's army."

Kadar swallowed hard. "I'm willing to take that chance," he said.

Master Sandiv gazed over at Master Gursh, who nodded for her to continue.

"We would also need to block your twin bond with your sister," she said. "The deities would be able to sense through it that Sulis is not dead, and it could break the mind blocks I set. Again—I don't know if the block could ever be removed. Have you spoken with any of the Chosen about this idea? If they have plans for you to aid Chosen Sulis in defeating the deities, this might destroy that choice."

"I need to talk to Sulis," Kadar said grimly. "I had hoped to save her worry so she could remain focused on her tasks. But if you block our bond, she will feel that."

"If you choose to continue, we will leave today and take you directly to the oasis. We will set up a tent, leave a humpback and supplies as you requested. We will block your memories and implant new ones, and you will wake up disoriented and believing your sister and grandmother were sacrificed by the warriors of the One."

"There is barely enough time to set this plan in motion before the army arrives," Master Gursh added. "We will leave you at the oasis alone, so you will not be confused by our presence when you wake. The Voices and the army should arrive soon after."

"If the Chosen do not object, do you have any other objections?" Kadar asked.

Master Sandiv shook her head. "None. If you are willing to take that chance, we will honor your courage. We will seek our midmeal and leave you here to speak with the Chosen."

"And we honor your sacrifice, the risk you are taking," Master Gursh said, slapping him on the back as the others filed out.

Kadar nodded and settled cross-legged on some pillows. Amber "murrped" and stood, stretching her front and then back legs. She leapt from the table to his shoulders, nibbling on his ear.

"Stop that," he grumbled and put her on his lap. He winced as she kneaded his legs through his thin robe. He reached out with his mind.

Sulis, he called.

Kadar, can it wait? We're doing some energy work, Sulis sent, responding to him instantly.

No, Kadar said. *The warriors of the One want a decision from the Chosen about a course of action I've proposed.*

Kadar felt her concern. *I will link to Grandmother and she can speak for the others*, Sulis sent.

When did you learn to do that? Kadar asked.

His grandmother's voice answered him. *We have been training hard. What do you need us for?*

Kadar explained his plan and the possible outcome. He concluded by saying, *They want to know if the Chosen need my skills in the final battle before they put the blocks in.*

There was a moment of silence, and then Sulis burst in.

No! Kadar, you can't do this! It could damage your mind. This is too dangerous.

This is the only way to fool the deities, Sulis. If I do this, I can save lives—possibly even yours. It's a chance I must take.

What would Onyeka say? Sulis asked. *She wouldn't want you to risk your mind. What about Datura?*

Onyeka helped me come up with the plan, Kadar told her.

Sulis sighed. *Bloodthirsty Tigu,* she said.

Grandmother interrupted them. *I have conferred with Master Anchee and Amon. Neither sees a place for you in the final battle. You have found your path and we will not stand in your way. I am so very proud of you, grandson. May the One be by your side. I will see you after the final battle.*

One be with you as well, Grandmother. Please take care of yourself, Kadar answered. He felt pressure on his forehead, as though she'd kissed him, and then she was gone.

Onyeka thought of this plan, Sulis said. *Did she know it might permanently take away your memory?*

No. But she would approve anyway.

But what would your life be like after, if you could not regain it? Sulis persisted.

Onyeka is part of the plan. She will guide us after I separate the deities from the rest of the army. The only people who would be erased are you and Grandmother, Kadar said, regretfully.

So you could still have a family, Sulis said. *You and Datura and Onyeka. Then that's okay, even if you never remember me and have to live away from me so your mind doesn't go crazy. I could live with it, as long as you could still be happy.*

Sis, if something happens, and I don't come back, I need you to look after Datura.

What about Aunt Raella? Sulis asked. *Should I take Datura from her? Raise her as a Hasifel?*

No, but make certain that she is being loved and cared for.

I will, Kadar. But you need to make sure I don't have to. I can't be whole without my twin.

I feel the same about you, sis, Kadar sent, touched. *Stay alive. I want a future where Aunt Sulis, Datura, and Onyeka boss all us hapless men around.*

Love and misses, Kadar.

Love and misses, sis.

Kadar sat for a moment after he'd said goodbye, thinking of his twin bond. He knew there was already a good chance the bond would be severed by one of their deaths. He prayed that neither of them would die and he could regain his connection with Sulis. Kadar knew with certainty that this was his path. He set Amber on his shoulder and rose to find Master Sandiv. It was time for them to take him to the oasis, put the blocks in, and leave him to his destiny.

"I know what you are," the Mother Superior growled at Tori, blocking her in the meal hall as she tried to put her tray away. "I know you are one of those traitorous Descendants of the Prophet. Ivanha knows of your treachery. We are watching you and will remove you if you try to harm our deity."

Aggie shoved the Mother Superior out of Tori's way. Aryn's former riding master sported a gold cloak and a no-nonsense attitude to match Tori's. "Humans harming deities?" she said over her shoulder as she escorted Tori away. "You'd better check what your acolytes are putting in your tea. It's making you more paranoid than usual."

Tori shook her head as Aggie and Shane flanked her. She wasn't surprised by the antipathy the heads of the deity altars held for her, but she was surprised that they were this openly hostile.

"That's your third threat this ten-day, isn't it?" Aggie said as they walked to the Temple of the One.

Tori nodded. "The only altar that hasn't threatened me is Parasu's."

"The Magistrate would consider that unlawful," Shane said. "He might be thinking it, but he would never act on it."

"Act on what?" Counselor Elida asked as they came abreast of her.

"More threats for our leader," Shane said. "This time from Ivanha."

Elida snorted. "I'm surprised it took her so long," she said. "They can't miss the energy we're raising here. It's must be terrifying them."

"I'm not your leader," Tori protested. "Elida is senior to me."

"Seniority doesn't matter," Aggie said. "You and your Northern friends are the ones teaching us how to channel the One's energy into shields to protect the city and the other acolytes from the deities draining their energy. None of us had tried to use it this way."

"It's true, Descendant Tori," Elida said. "We've never had enough Counselors to try this type of energy sharing. And the ability to cut others off from the energy of the deities is not one I've seen before your people came to Illian. In this, you are my leader and I am content to follow."

Tori glanced around the Temple of the One. It was a different place since the One had chosen her new Counselors. It was no longer a dim, quiet meditative spot. Candles lighted every corner as Counselors broke off into small groups to practice raising energy and blocking each other's ability to channel energy from their *feli*. They were working with Descendants who had traveled south with Tori—the best shielders she had. It was bright enough in the Temple with the candles that Tori could see a dozen or so curious eyes of the *feli* watching from the ledges around the dome. There were more *feli* than humans in the Temple, as their chosen *feli* mingled with the unattached ones.

"We need to make certain no Counselor walks alone," Aggie said. "Especially Tori. Threats can easily escalate to violence if the acolytes of the deities think they can get away with it."

"I'd like to see them try," Tori said. "With my training, I can fry them before they get a single blast of energy off."

"But you can't ward off a knife in the back," Aggie said. "And that's what this lot would do. They know you're leading this transformation." She looked over at Tori. "It's funny—you were the quiet one in your pledge group. Sulis was the rabble-rouser."

"Sulis was a great foil," Tori said. "With her attracting all the attention, I never had to hide what I was."

"I wonder what happened to her," Aggie mused as they walked over to one of the small groups.

"This is confidential, so keep it to yourself," Tori murmured, and Aggie bent her head closer. "She's one of the Chosen in the desert," Tori said. "Along with Alannah, Dani, and Lasha from my pledge year. Everything we do here gives them a chance to win the final battle, which will be held in the middle of the desert. If the Chosen fall in that battle, if they fail, everything we worked for is gone."

"Whiskers!" Aggie said, stopping in surprise. "I should have realized. She is a Hasifel, granddaughter to that powerful desert witch."

"Those desert witches may have to sacrifice everything to subdue the deities," Tori said. "When the deities reach for their acolytes' energy to escape the trap the Southern witches have laid, we need to put a shield up between the acolytes and their *feli* so the deities find no energy is available. We also need to make certain the final spell doesn't drain the Northern Territory of life by shielding all living energy."

Aggie nodded. "One guide us all," she said. "We're going to need every blessing she has when the acolytes of the deities realize what we're doing. What group do you want me in today?"

Tori directed her and was about to follow when Elida stopped her.

"Pause a moment. I have had word from the desert," the Counselor said.

"From Sulis? Or Kadar?" Tori asked.

"Neither—from Alannah and the warriors of the One. Vrishni are with them, so we are able to communicate."

"What do they say?" Tori asked.

"Another Descendant of the Prophet, Amon, is directing their efforts now. They have a task for us, a test of our shielding skills."

"Go on?" Tori wasn't certain she wanted to know what cousin Amon was up to.

"The warriors of the One will be manipulating the weather in the desert," Elida said. "They are trying to blow up a small sandstorm to confuse the deities and separate them from their army. The Tigus will augment it with illusion, making the storm seem worse than it is and they will attack the army under the cover of illusion."

"Disrupting weather patterns is dangerous," Tori said. "It seldom goes as planned."

"Which is why they want us on guard. They want us to see if we can shield the North against a disruption of their weather if the casting becomes dangerous."

Tori thought for a moment. "We can't completely shield natural forces like weather currents," she said. "But we could put up a series of partial shields—kind of like breakwaters set out in the ocean to calm the water by coastal towns. Severe weather would hit the breakwaters, and some would spill over until it hit the next breakwater, with the water gradually becoming calmer as it comes across. How soon do they say this will happen?"

"In the next ten-day. They have spies in the army who will tell them when. The sandstorm and illusion will create confusion and terror with the fighters. The warriors of the One and the Tigus will cloak themselves and ride at the back of the storm."

"We'll start setting the breakers now. It will be a good test of our range and our ability to set partial shields," Tori said. "I hope the warriors of the One know what they are doing. If their sending gets out of control, they could kill the people they want to save."

Elida shook her head. "So much is riding on so few people."

Abram stared at the golden horse with suspicion. It glared at him, ears back.

"Kadar wanted you to care for Asfar. If he does not return, she is yours," Kadar's companion, Onyeka, said, handing Abram Asfar's lead rope. The horse snapped at Abram, and Onyeka smacked her muzzle and cursed at her in Tigu. "She will be fine. You must be firm."

Turo slapped Abram on the back, causing Asfar to shy away, as Onyeka turned and threw her leg over her humpback. "Ha! She killed the man who owned her before Kadar. You will have your hands full."

"Delightful," Abram muttered. Turo and Abram were serving as runners for the warriors of the One and the Tigu elders, so Abram had become familiar with the Tigu man's odd sense of humor.

Onyeka's humpback heaved to its feet. A howl startled Abram, and he stepped back as Kadar's cat flung herself at the humpback. Amber caught the saddle halfway up with her claws and climbed the rest of the way onto Onyeka's lap.

"Blasted cat!" she exclaimed, trying to unhook the purring cat's claws from her robes. "Father, take this beast."

Turo backed away. "I caged her in the dormitory," he said. "If the suncat managed to escape, she was meant to be with you."

She glared at the cat, then shrugged. She pressed the back of her hand to her head in farewell, before riding off without a backward glance. Kadar had done the same thing, two days before when he rode to the waymarker with Master Sandiv to have his memories blocked. But Onyeka was traveling south to a camp in the mountains a day east of the Obsidian Temple. Master Sandiv would implant a suggestion in Kadar's mind along with the blocks, directing him to the camp after he'd separated the Voices from the rest of the army.

"My daughter is a fine woman, is she not?" Turo asked. "But, sadly for you, in love with another."

"Onyeka is far too intense for my taste," Abram said as they walked together toward the stables, Asfar following as far back as her rope would allow.

"Just like her mother. Now that woman was all fire! But like you, I prefer a warm bed rather than searing flame," Turo said as he opened the stall door.

It took both of them to convince Asfar the stall was not a cave full of snakes.

"We begin our march through the Sands in two days," Abram said as he bolted the door. "She'll have to stay here. I don't have the time to tame her."

Abram was catching his breath and wiping off his brow when Casia called to him.

"I've been looking for you. With the Tigus here, the masters want to practice coordinating their sandstorm illusion with our weather working," she said. "I'll be with the energy users, raising wind energy."

Turo shook his head. "It is madness, playing with the weather," he said. "Nothing good can come of interfering with the One's natural forces."

Casia glared at him. "We have been experimenting for months. Master Ursa trained and directed us. It is only a small storm. The Tigus will make it seem larger than it is. There is little danger."

She walked away and they trailed after her.

"But Master Ursa is no longer with us," Turo said softly, for Abram's ears only. "And I fear that most of all."

Kadar woke disoriented. His head throbbed like someone had used it as a hammer. He was in a tent, on a bedroll. It was bright and hot in the tent and he was alone. His thoughts were hazy and he tried to get his bearings. He was supposed to remember something, what was it? Something about the warriors of the One, about the deities. Kadar struggled with his thoughts, wondering if he'd hit his head. Then memory surfaced, cleared. He was at the first oasis on the trade route toward Shpeth. His sister was dead. Remembering was like a punch in the gut.

He crawled out of the tent, half-blinded by the full sun. It didn't matter; tears blurred his vision anyway as he knelt by the oasis waymarker that should have responded to his commands, but no longer did. The wards on the waymarker had been changed by Sulis's blood and had been set into her bones. He clutched at the scrap of silk he'd found, a pattern that had been part of her favorite robe. She must have worn it to her death.

Kadar had known when the warriors of the One had sacrificed Sulis. He'd sat straight up when it had happened, waking Onyeka, who slept beside him. She'd held him as he searched for his sister, searched for the bond that was missing.

His mind went to that twin bond and once again, it was gone. She was gone. Kadar wiped his tears away, remembering that he had screamed at the Tigu elders when he'd realized that Sulis was dead. They'd told him that it was Sulis's choice and that Grandmother had sacrificed herself at the next waymarker. His family, gone in an instant. Stupid, heedless sister of his, jumping into death with both feet, as she had always jumped into life. She'd never said goodbye—probably worried he'd talk her out of this stupid sacrifice.

Kadar had grabbed the hardiest humpback and set off to find his sister's body and mourn her death, leaving Onyeka and Amber behind. But he realized it was useless when he arrived. They'd used her blood to change the wards and her bones to anchor the way-stone; no body remained to burn. The Tigu elders had been ashamed of him. They thought Grandmother and Sulis's sacrifice was courageous and fitting. Kadar shook his head. He knew the truth: Sulis and Grand-mother died to protect Datura, who would be in the path of the deities. They died to give Datura a chance to live.

Fury coursed through Kadar. Sulis and his grand-mother were Chosen, so they should have been pro-tected. Instead, the Descendant of the Prophet had convinced the warriors of the One that the Chosen were no longer needed, that he knew all the spells to defeat the deities at the Obsidian Temple. And the war-riors of the One had agreed. They were probably the ones who convinced Sulis to take her own life in this terrible way, to bleed out in the desert. They wanted to protect their precious families by sacrificing his.

Kadar didn't know how long he knelt in the sand. He raised his head when the army approached but still was unable to rise from his kneeling position, so ex-hausted and drained by grief. The dust rose around him, the braying of mules and horses. A smaller party broke off the larger army and approached the oasis. As the party approached, Kadar spied a familiar scholar, perched uncomfortably on his horse. Sulis's old friend, Jonas, looked perplexed as he approached Kadar and the waymarker. Kadar also recognized the Herald, riding beside Jonas, and the Templar. He assumed the dark-haired woman with them was the new Crone.

Kadar rose to his feet as the Voices and their guards dismounted and approached him. The guards seized him, checking him for weapons before forcing him to kneel before the Voices.

"What has happened here?" the Herald asked. "Great power has been used. But for what purpose, I cannot guess."

"Kadar?" Jonas asked, uncertainly. "It is Kadar, isn't it? Sulis's brother? What are you doing here?"

Kadar gestured to the waymarker. "I was Sulis's brother," he said hollowly. "Before they sacrificed her to change the wards."

"Yes," the Herald said. She coughed into her hand, looking ill. "There has been a life sacrificed. That's why I feel such power."

"Free him," Jonas ordered, and the guards let Kadar rise to his feet, staying close enough to restrain him again if ordered.

"They sacrificed Sulis?" Jonas's voice was incredulous. "Why?"

"They knew you had captured Southern guides and *geased* them," Kadar said, gesturing to the men still mounted on their horses. "The warriors of the One wanted to save their families in Shpeth and Tsangia. The wards on all the oases have been changed from here to Shpeth. They took my sister and my grandmother . . ." Kadar broke off, his voice choked, and turned away.

A hand touched his arm and he looked into Jonas's sympathetic eyes. "I am sorry, Kadar. I thought Sulis would be valued here in the desert."

"It was that Descendant of the Prophet," Kadar spat. "He convinced the warriors of the One that the Chosen of the prophecy weren't necessary anymore. The prophecy was declared a sham. And then the most powerful Chosen were sacrificed to change the wards."

The Voices exchanged glances, and Kadar narrowed his eyes, wondering what they knew about the Descendants.

"The warriors of the One probably put a *geas* on Sulis," the new Crone said, her eyes filled with sympathy. "Your sister would not have realized what she was doing until it was too late."

"We don't use *geases* here in the desert," Kadar protested.

The Templar snorted. "All mages use *geases*," he said. "If your warriors decided a death would protect thousands of people—do you truly believe they would hesitate to convince someone to give her life?"

"But why Sulis?" Jonas asked again. "Aren't there more powerful people in the desert?"

"We are ancestors of the Southerner who originally sacrificed her blood and body to create the wards on this oasis," Kadar said softly, remembering what the Tigu elders had told him. "Transferring the wards to someone of the same blood took less power."

"Blood calls to blood," the Herald murmured in agreement.

"Those bastards sacrificed my sister!" Kadar said. "They changed the wards and refused to give me the new ones, exiling me from the rest of my family. I don't even have a body to burn to send my sister to the One."

"We can help you get revenge," the Crone said softly. "If you help us, we can thwart the plans of the warriors of the One to save the lives of other innocent women like your sister."

Kadar felt the coercion in her voice. The spell of her voice settled in his brain. It was less of a *geas* and more of a simple spell of love and understanding. He resisted, and then a voice rose in his subconscious.

Let them believe you've given in, the voice said to him. *You can avenge both Sulis and your uncle Tarik by serving the deities right now. You will know when to resist.*

Kadar shook his head, feeling confused and trying to clear his mind.

The Crone stepped forward and put a hand on his arm, and he looked into her warm brown eyes.

"You won't be alone, Kadar," she said. "I know the desert folk trust in the One, but sometimes the One's plan for us is too obscure to understand our place in it. That's why our deities exist. Ivanha understands how much your family means to you. She can help you return to those you love and bring to justice those who harmed such a strong, loving family. Come with us, guide us, and we will see justice done for your sister and grandmother."

Kadar could feel the Voice's *geas* sink into his mind as he gazed at her face. But some block, probably one his Grandmother set as a child, prevented it from rooting deeply. If he chose, he could brush it aside, like cobwebs in his mind, but he didn't choose to. The *geas* distanced him from the pain of Sulis's death. He and the Voices wanted the same thing right now—to confront the warriors of the One and return Kadar to his remaining family. If he could find a way to exact revenge on the Templar for killing his uncle—all the better.

Kadar reached out and took the Crone's hand. He brought it to his mouth and kissed the back of it.

"You honor me, my lady," he said. "I am touched by your concern and accept your help with gratitude."

She blushed prettily, and took his hand, drawing him over to the other Voices.

"You say you know this gentleman?" the Crone said to Jonas.

He nodded. "Kadar and I took classes together when I was a pledge. His sister, Sulis, shared my pledge class but returned to the desert before she could be chosen by a deity."

Kadar smiled slightly, enjoying Jonas's tact. Sulis had been the troublemaker in that pledge class, and Kadar had been forced to rescue her from the then-Templar, who had nearly killed her during the Pledge Ceremony. Kadar decided to twist their tails a bit.

"I'm also the heir to the Hasifel caravan trade," he told the Voices. "Until this past spring, I ran the caravan routes from Illian through the Sands to Frubia."

Kadar narrowed his eyes as the Voices exchanged

uneasy glances. The Crone put her hand casually around Kadar's arm, as though he were escorting her. She tried to dig her mental claws in more deeply.

"Unfortunately," Kadar said, wondering how much he could stretch the truth before they'd sense he was lying. "I was sent to study with scholars in the south this past spring and have not had any contact with my uncles or friends in Illian since then."

They relaxed a little, except Jonas, who seemed more horrified. Kadar was fascinated to realize none of them could tell it was a lie. Did their deity need to possess them to tell if he lied? Kadar didn't know, but he was willing to take full advantage.

"You have traveled the Sands?" the Crone asked, her eyes wide. "So you have been to the Obsidian Temple?"

The Templar coughed, but Kadar smiled, staring into her eyes, pretending to be entranced by her.

"No," he said. "But I know where the caravan route divides to travel to the temple. My grandmother was a desert priestess and told me how to reveal the way. One path goes to the Obsidian Temple, the other to the next oasis. Only the truly devout are permitted access to the temple."

She laughed softly. "I think the Voices of the deities would be considered devout, don't you?" she asked.

Kadar laughed. "Indeed you would, my lady," he said.

"Then you will travel with us," she said. He was drawn away from the waymarker, as she motioned to her guards. "You will be our leader, our guide in this terrible wilderness we face. You will share a tent and campfire with us."

Kadar laughed again, as a guard brought his humpback to him. He ordered it to kneel and flung a leg over the saddle, leaving his tent.

"It isn't a terrible wilderness, once you know it," he said as his humpback rose. "I think, my lady, you will find a great deal of beauty in the sunsets over the undulating dunes."

"And you're a poet as well," the Crone said, riding close to him. "I do hope it is as you say, and your protection will show us the beauty you speak of. The last oasis was only a half day away. We should be able to reach it before night. Then you can tell us what to expect for the rest of the trip."

Kadar could feel her gently trying to pry into his thoughts, to insert her will more deeply, and he smiled blandly at her as he made his surface thoughts ones of attraction to her and anger for the warriors of the One.

As the Templar shouted orders to his Knights leading the army, Kadar caught Jonas's thoughtful gaze upon him. He looked levelly at the former scholar, until Jonas flushed and looked away.

As they rode away from Sulis's death site, Kadar thought she and his grandmother were spinning in their graves. *I will avenge both of you, and Uncle Tarik,* Kadar silently promised her. *You will be able to rest in peace, knowing that the person who loved you made you proud.*

CHAPTER 18

Jonas watched Kadar as he helped them set up camp for the evening. It had been a shock, seeing him at the oasis. It had been even more of a shock realizing that Sulis was dead. Parasu had read Kadar's surface thoughts, and his grief and pain were real. Kadar was not lying—the desert warriors had sacrificed his sister and grandmother. The Southerners had used death and blood energy, which had been forbidden to acolytes of the deities since the last war, five hundred years before.

This should not surprise you, Parasu said, in the back of his mind. *These Southerners are barbarians. Living out in this wasteland leaves no room for civilized behavior. They do what they can to survive and can be quite ruthless, spending lives to protect what they have.*

Jonas had felt rather sick, watching the Crone sink her claws into Kadar, a man he'd considered a friend in

Illian. The intelligence in the man's face had turned to fawning adoration.

Would you rather that the Templar used his brutal ways upon your friend? Parasu asked. *After what he did to Kadar's uncle? I am rather pleased with this Crone for her alertness. His great pain and the sundering of his twin bond left a gap where she could insert her will. No pain, no blood, and it diminishes his despair. She has done him a great favor. She will prevent him from feeling the sadness of his sister's death.*

Jonas nodded to himself. It was true. Kadar no longer looked like his heart were being torn asunder. He looked peaceful—if a bit silly, following a woman twice his age around like a puppy.

It is strange, though, Jonas said to his deity. *That Kadar doesn't look at the army following behind us. He doesn't seem to see the thousands of men threatening his home.*

Parasu laughed in the back of his mind. *That is the Crone's doing. He doesn't see them, or she prevents him from processing that they follow. That way he is serving only her and her "friends," the other Voices. The same way she is preventing him from thinking about his sister. It is a manipulation of the single-minded fascination that comes with being in love. I've never seen an acolyte wield it so deftly. She is truly worthy of being Ivanha's Voice.*

The Voices met once camp was settled. The Crone left Kadar in her tent, guarded by a couple of Voras's soldiers.

"I don't like this," the Templar growled. "It was too easy. He barely even resisted the Crone meddling with his will."

"Easy for you," the Crone shot back. "It took all my focus and skill to insert my will into his mind. His mind has strong shields. He kept trying to slip away from me. I've got him sleeping right now, but it takes a good deal of focus to keep those bonds strong."

The Herald coughed and grimaced. "The Crone used his intense distress and grief to entrance him," she told the Templar, her voice hoarse from incessant coughing. "She showed a good deal of finesse and skill. More subtle but more effective than your blunter *geas* where the bespelled spends much of his time and energy trying to fight you. This man doesn't even realize he is *geased* and will not fight it."

"I don't like that I cannot see deeper into his mind, past those shields," the Crone said, frowning prettily. "I've pushed any thoughts of his sister to the back of his mind, but I can't see if he has a deeper alliance that would interfere with my *geas*."

"I am certain this is the man who aided the Forsaken when they rose up this spring. We should break his shields," the Templar said.

"No!" the other three Voices protested in unison.

Jonas shook his head. "Breaking those mind shields killed his uncle," he said. "Kadar said his grandmother was a desert priestess. No doubt she inserted the powerful, killing shields in her family. I remember Sulis saying her grandmother helped raise the twins after their parents died."

"You kill this guide and we have no one to replace him," the Herald added. "No one. The other Southern caravan leaders are useless now that the wards to Shpeth are changed. We use this man, or we have to turn back."

"How do we know the wards at the oases in the Sands haven't been changed?" the Templar asked.

"Kadar told me," the Crone said. "They could not find anyone of the same blood or anyone powerful enough to change those wards. He also told me he'd been sent to the South as punishment for helping the Forsaken woman. He has been fairly isolated since, studying with a master teacher of languages. He is easily manipulated by feelings of love."

"That certainly works out well for her," the Herald murmured to Jonas, who hid a smile.

"What do we do with the *geased* Southerners we were using as guides?" the Templar asked. "Should we dispose of them?"

"They will be handy as we get deeper into the desert," the Herald said. "They've been valuable at giving advice on watering the horses and preparing for the dry heat of the desert."

"Kadar mentioned a Descendant of the Prophet here in the desert," Jonas said. "Do we need to worry that they have infiltrated the Obsidian Temple?"

The Templar pursed his lips and looked up, thinking. He grimaced. "I'm not certain. My Knight in Illian has said the only threat up north is a small Forsaken revolt heading for Illian from Stonycreek. The Descendants have not yet shown any power."

"My Mother Superior believes that one of the

turned Counselors is actually a Descendant and may be making the other Counselors heretics," the Crone said.

"I've heard nothing of this," the Herald said with a frown. "I don't see how a deity could miss that a pledge was a heretic during choosing, unless they turned against the deities once pledged and never did energy work again."

"The alleged Descendant is Tori, one of the pledges who circumvented the proper ceremony," the Crone persisted. "She pledged to Parasu before becoming a Counselor."

Jonas opened his mouth, but it was Parasu speaking. "All who have pledged to me have done so wholeheartedly," he said. "It is not the fault of my altar that the One has taken so many."

That silenced the Crone. Jonas knew many of her pledges had been forced into Ivanha's service when a Templar impregnated them.

The Herald sighed. "We can hardly call the Counselors of the One heretics, Crone. They serve the highest power."

"I agree," the Templar said. "Your Mother Superior is imagining things. As for this Descendant in the desert, he has done us a good deed. He has broken up the Chosen of the prophecy, causing several of them to sacrifice their lives. I'd been worried that these Chosen would be guarding the Obsidian Temple against us. The prophecy said they would be very powerful and a match for us."

Jonas nodded. "I am beginning to believe the letter the Descendants sent to us. They truly do seem to wish for the deities to reunite to balance the world once again," Parasu said.

The Crone pursed her lips. "There is one more oasis, and then we reach the final town before the deeper desert the Southerners call the Sands. Kadar suggests we switch as many people to humpbacks as we can. Then it is less than a ten-day's journey to the Obsidian Temple."

"Where will we get humpbacks?" the Templar asked.

"He says stockyards sell them right before the Sands. I hope we can appropriate enough for us and all your mounted troops."

"We'll guard against Tigus while traveling through the Sands region," the Templar said. "Never let your *feli* out of sight. The *feli* can see through their desert magic. The Tigus have lesser numbers, but could destroy everything with assassins directed at us."

Jonas glanced around and realized none of the Voices had their *feli* with them. He glanced over at the Herald, who was realizing the same thing. She shrugged.

"Hopefully the *feli* will be willing to stay beside us," she said.

"If we have to, we'll stick collars on them," the Templar growled.

Parasu stirred and spoke through Jonas. "We deities will speak with your *feli*. They will obey us."

The Templar bowed slightly, and then stared at Jonas. "That's a little frightening, you realize. I never know if I'm speaking to Parasu or speaking to Jonas."

Jonas shook his head. "The acolyte who was Jonas does not really exist anymore," he said. "Parasu is always with his Tribune. Always assume you are speaking to Parasu. Always believe you are hearing his voice."

The ground trembled under Sulis's feet, and she grabbed on to Ashraf's arm for support. They were outside after midmeal and had been walking to the temple for afternoon practice. They clung to each other as the tremor died down.

"What was that?" Ashraf asked, looking at Sulis.

They turned at the sound of people running. Grandmother and Sari dashed past them, heading to the temple at full speed with Anchee and Lasha on their heels. Sulis ran after them.

Sulis gave a cry of dismay when she entered the temple. Ava lay motionless on her back in the center of the circle of the statues, inside the energy mandala she'd been creating. Dani lay on his stomach outside the mandala energy lines. Alannah lay in a heap beside Amon, also outside the mandala. Lasha bent over Dani and Sari ran to Alannah. Grandmother and Anchee stood at the edge of the mandala. Grandmother pressed her hands against an invisible barrier and jerked back again with a curse.

Only Sanuri was awake, staring at them with bright eyes.

"Sanuri," Master Anchee called. "We need you to release the energy from within, so we can tend to Ava. Can you do that?"

Sanuri clucked her tongue. "Too much," she said as she climbed down from the Altar of the One and picked her way carefully off the mandala, not smearing the inner lines. At the far edge, she bent over and made a brushing motion, like she was sweeping invisible sand. Sulis could feel her opening an energy shield that had been closed.

"Careful, Anchee, there's still a lot of energy in here," Grandmother warned, as they carefully picked their way through the mandala to Ava's side.

"Where are you going?" Sulis asked Sanuri as she walked past Anchee to the exit.

"Hungry," the girl said.

Sulis knelt beside Sari as she examined Alannah.

"Is she alive?" Sulis asked.

Sari nodded. "Yes. Her pulse is fine, if a little slow. She doesn't have any visible injuries. But I can't get her or Amon to wake up. What about the rest of them?"

"Same with Ava," Grandmother said.

"Dani won't wake up either," Lasha said. "Where are their *feli*? Usually they're here, working with them. Yaslin should be right by Alannah. She's never absent."

Sulis looked around and realized the *feli* weren't in the Obsidian Temple. Even Nuisance was missing. She reached in her mind for Djinn, but he was nowhere close. "All the *feli* are missing," Sulis said. "Where are they?"

"We'll figure it out after we get these four to the infirmary," Grandmother said. "Sari, do you think it is safe to move them?"

Sari stood. "There isn't anything wrong with them," she said. "They seem to be drained of so much energy, they need time to replenish it so they can wake up."

"There was quite a surge," Grandmother said as Sari went to the doorway to summon help. "I believe Ava has connected to the very stones under us."

"Look at this pattern, Sulis," Anchee urged. He picked Ava up, and he and Grandmother gingerly tip-toed around the lines of the mandala. He handed Ava to a guard arriving at Sari's summons.

Sulis stepped away from Alannah's body, closed her eyes and studied the pattern. It seemed normal, until she got to the unfinished part of the pattern, where Ava's body had lain. She walked around the pattern to feel the energy lines more closely.

"What is that?" She asked, pointing to a strange energy connecting two spaces. "That doesn't relate to a specific chakra."

"No. It is pure elemental earth energy," Anchee said, coming up to stand beside her. "It is a mix of three chakras."

"The line is connecting the smaller mandala of Ivanha with the larger whole mandala," Sulis said, tracing it. "And to the energy of the One."

"If you look closely, Ava has connected this mandala to the very bedrock beneath our feet," Anchee said.

Sulis studied the mandala. It was so complicated she wasn't certain how they would dance it. The four deities each had a complex mandala that linked to the Altar of the One, like four petals of a flower. But each mandala was then connected to the others in an overarching pattern.

"Look." She pointed. "On the other deities' patterns she has left open the same space she was filling in with the earth line on Ivanha's. Does that mean she will have to connect to wind and water and fire as well? What will that do to everyone?"

Anchee sighed and watched as Alannah, Dani, and Amon were carried out. "I don't know," he said. "All I know is that the deities will arrive in less than a tenday, and three of our most important Chosen are unconscious."

"And the *feli* have disappeared," Ashraf said, leaning against Sulis.

"Let's see if we can go to the infirmary and feed them energy to wake them," Sulis said. "It shouldn't be that hard, after all the linking we've done at the wards."

Lasha was already feeding energy to Alannah when they arrived in the infirmary. Sulis put a hand on her back while holding Ashraf's hand, and Alannah stirred, opened her eyes, and blinked.

Alannah tried to sit up, but lay down quickly. She put a hand to her head and winced.

"Ouch," she said. "I've a One-awful headache. What happened?"

"That's what we'd like to know," Sulis said. "You were working in the temple, and then the ground shook. When we ran in, all of you were unconscious."

"Ava!" Alannah said, sitting up all the way to look around. "Is she okay?"

Sulis looked over to the other beds. Dani was sitting up, his head in his hands, as Lasha bent over him. Grandmother, Palou, and Anchee were around Ava's bed, and Sulis could feel the energy they gave her. No one had helped Amon yet, so Sulis went to his bedside and took his hand. Ashraf helped as she sent energy into his body. It didn't take much before his eyes fluttered open.

"What are we doing wasting time here?" he snapped at Sulis, and he tried to sit up. His eyes rolled back, and he passed out again.

"I think he can recover on his own from here," Ashraf said, annoyed.

Sulis was relieved to see Ava stirring in her bed.

"Is she okay?" Sulis asked Grandmother.

"I think so," Grandmother said. "She'll need to rest though. Looks like the energy was simply sucked out of her."

"It was," Alannah confirmed. "She was drawing some sort of combined energy I've never seen before, but she tripped over her own feet and fell onto the line just as it was completed. Even though she and Sanuri were sealed into the mandala, the energy was ripped from me."

"Why would it do that?" Ashraf asked.

Alannah shook her head and winced. "Ouch. I think the *feli* have been shielding us from such things. She's smudged a line or tripped before, but she's always had Nuisance with her, and Dani and I have always had our *feli*. Today none of the *feli* showed up. And then she had this breakthrough with the energy, and Amon was so excited we went ahead with it."

"Why was Amon so excited?" Sulis wondered.

"Because she was connecting Ivanha's statue to the earth," Amon said from his bed, his voice gravelly and weak. "She was tying into the very bedrock of the mountains. That will make the trap irresistible to Ivanha. We didn't know she could tie the mandalas to the elements."

Anchee shook his head. "I wish Clay were here. He would know how to help Ava safely work with elemental energy."

"I think we should wait for our *feli* to come back," Dani said. "I don't ever want to feel like that again. I thought Ava was dying and I couldn't reach her."

Sari nodded. "I think you need to rest for today. You'll stay here, where we can keep an eye on you. The pain you are feeling is backlash from having all that energy disappear at once. Hopefully the *feli* will return tomorrow, and you can figure out how to proceed."

In the morning when Sulis came out of the dormitory to the main courtyard, Djinn was back, looking pleased. He flopped himself down in front of Sulis and wriggled onto his back, asking for a belly rub. Sulis was so glad to see him she scrubbed his fur with both hands, rousing a loud purr from him.

"Oh my goodness," Ashraf murmured and Sulis looked up.

There were *feli* draped on every raised surface of the courtyard, clear up to the Obsidian Temple. There was a mix of the long, lean *feli*, similar to Djinn, and the heavier *feli* of the savannah like Lasha's *feli*, only dun colored.

"By the One, there are hundreds of them!" Sulis exclaimed.

The Kabandha warriors eyed the *feli* warily from windows and the doorways of buildings and kept close to cover rather than practicing sword dances in the courtyard where they usually trained. Sulis could see why as temple master Sari walked to Sulis from the Obsidian Temple. If Sari got too close to the felines, the wild *feli* growled at her. She was remarkably calm, walking among hundreds of snarling felines—but Sulis could see that her breathing was uneven and her face was too still.

"Sulis, can you do something about this?" Sari asked as she came abreast of her and Ashraf. "People are afraid to come out. We have much planning and training to do this ten-day."

"Whiskers!" Lasha exclaimed behind Sulis. "Where did they all come from?"

"Obviously our *feli* found them," Alannah said. Sulis looked at her with concern. Yaslin was by her side, looking as pleased as Djinn.

"Should you be out of the infirmary?" she asked.

"I feel fine," Alannah said. "We need to do something before they start fighting with each other."

"What?" Sulis asked with frustration. "These are wild *feli*, not tame ones. They'll do what they like. They don't follow orders."

"Not much different from our tame ones, then," Lasha said under her breath as Alta bumped her head against Lasha's thigh.

"Well, Sulis, you're the one who used to brag about taming wild *feli* when we were pledges," Alannah said mildly. "You've got the greatest affinity for the big felines. Do your thing."

Sulis looked at Alannah to find a crowd had gathered behind her. All the Chosen were among the crowd. Her grandmother made shooing motions as Ava giggled at Sulis's horrified expression.

"I should have known that would come back to haunt me," Sulis muttered.

"Oh, look," Ava squealed. "There's Nuisance with his siblings!"

She was bowled over by the *feli* cubs, now as tall as the adults.

Sulis spoke to Sari as they watched Ava try to extricate herself from the rough feline tongues. "Where am I supposed to send them? They must have come to assist in some way."

"Maybe you could convince them to go to the ledges behind the temple where the spring splits? It would be cooler there and they would be bothered less."

Sulis walked into the center of the courtyard. She looked around to find all feline eyes upon her. None approached, but at least they weren't snarling at her. Djinn bumped his head against her ribs and she put a hand on his ruff. She closed her eyes and reached out to the energy of the felines around her. She tried to project an image of the ledges behind them, the cool dimness of the little caverns, the access to running water. She opened her eyes. None of the *feli* had moved. Several cleaned themselves to show her what they thought of her suggestion.

"Impressive," Lasha said. "Are you sure you were talking to the cats and not the rocks they're sitting on? I've never seen so many bored *feli* in my life."

Sulis turned to retort but stopped as Amon approached the group. He looked entranced, drawn to the gathering. He pushed his way through the crowd to stand beside Sulis.

"They're here for me," Amon said, a little breathlessly.

Sulis looked at the *feli*. They were intently staring at the Descendant. Several had sat up on their ledges. Amon looked unnerved. He turned to Sulis.

"What am I supposed to do with them?" he asked. "I don't know anything about *feli*."

"Well, getting them out of everyone's way would be a good start," Sulis said, enjoying the man's uncertainty. "I was trying to send them a picture of the ledges and alcoves behind the temple. You may want to try that."

Amon stared at her a moment, then closed his eyes. The *feli* stood. After a few hisses and swipes of claws and teeth, they sorted themselves out and wandered off in different directions, but heading away from the main group of humans. Several *feli* slipped past the guards to enter the Obsidian Temple. Amon opened his eyes.

"That was easy," he said, his voice surprised.

Sari stepped forward. "The show is over, warriors," she said. "You will return to your routines. Please use caution around the new *feli*. They are wild and you should avoid interaction when possible."

The Chosen gathered around Amon as the warriors took formation in the courtyard and sparred.

Alannah slapped Amon on the back. "So you've been chosen by several hundred *feli*?" she asked. "I thought one was bad enough."

"Did anyone get a good count?" Master Anchee wanted to know.

"Over two hundred," Grandmother said. "The shadows hid many."

"You sure showed up Sulis," Lasha said.

Sulis frowned. "I didn't know they were bonded to him. You know how *feli* hate taking orders from anyone but their chosen."

"Do we know why several hundred *feli* just arrived to claim Amon?" Ashraf asked.

Amon nodded slowly. "*Feli* are shielders," he said. "Until yesterday, I had not realized that they were shielding us from energy. But they are also energy enhancers—they are energy. They see through illusions with the clarity the One gives them, but this many *feli* can obscure any energy work we've been doing. They can help strengthen the illusion around the mandala we are setting so that even the deities do not suspect something is hidden in the rock."

Lasha shook her head. "Won't they be a little suspicious about hundreds of *feli* gathered in one place?"

Amon shrugged. "I don't think all the *feli* can fit into the Obsidian Temple. I'm guessing that their presence near the temple will be enough to confuse the deities. That is something we must work with until the final battle arrives. I want everyone at the temple in a sandglass."

Amon strode off toward the temple, leaving the others staring after him.

"I think it's going to be a long day," Palou said. "Clay would tell us to eat a good breakfast."

Lasha sighed. "Amon will be even more intolerable than Sulis about the *feli*, won't he?"

Sulis opened her mouth to retort, stung by the criticism, and then caught the sparkle in the other woman's eyes. She slugged Lasha on the shoulder.

"Ouch, grouchy," Lasha said. "Ashraf, you better get your beloved some *tash* before she wrests control from Amon and sics a hundred *feli* on us."

Jonas dismounted from his horse, and an aide took its reins. He looked around at the abandoned town, the last bit of civilization before the deeper desert took over.

"They must have been warned," the Templar snarled as he peered into an empty shop. "We have spies among us."

The Herald shook her head. "Don't get paranoid. They don't need spies to see thousands of people marching across the desert. We should have realized the towns would scatter when they saw an army coming."

"I thought there wasn't any place to run to," the Crone said. She turned to Kadar. "Where could these people have gone?" she asked.

"There are many smaller domiciles scattered around the area," Kadar said. "Places where people have dug wells or found smaller springs. In an emergency, people could flee to those homes."

"It looks like they cleared out quickly with only what they could carry," the Templar said. "I'll send my men around to gather supplies."

"Most of the humpbacks are gone," Kadar said, frustration in his voice. "They only left injured or sick beasts behind. Let me look through the corrals and see if any are suitable for travel to carry you and your supplies."

The Crone sent him off with a smile and then turned to the others. "We need to make haste. If this village has been warned, they would have sent warning to the desert warriors."

"My Knights are scouting the area. I expected they'd have warriors here to ambush us when we came, but the scouts have reported they've seen no life in the surrounding area."

"So we can expect an ambush once we enter the Sands region?" the Herald asked.

"We will proceed with caution—but that would be unlikely. They don't have enough men to win a full-out battle. In the dunes they cannot find cover to hide and ambush us from. The Tigus can hide themselves, but not with our *feli* present."

"What about an ambush at one of the oases?" Jonas asked.

"We will be the most cautious as we approach oases," the Templar agreed. "Though again, that would create a one-on-one battle. I think the Tigu warriors will try to pick our men off throughout the desert, with small hit-and-run attacks. I believe the attack by the warriors of the One will come when we approach the Obsidian Temple. We will be closest to the mountains at that point. The rocks and cliffs will give them a greater advantage. But we have the greater numbers."

"Simply throwing our fighters at theirs will waste many lives," the Herald said, frowning. "Can we approach from behind?"

"We have only one guide," the Crone said. "We have to follow the route he knows. Who cares how many humans we spend, as long as we win out in the end? Recovering our deities' lost powers is our priority."

Parasu nodded. Kadar ran back to them, not looking happy.

"I think I've found enough humpbacks to mount the Voices and carry some of the supplies," he said. "We'll have to load up your mules and horses as well, and hope enough of them survive until we reach the next oasis."

"We have wagons for supplies," the Crone said, frowning.

"Only if you want to push them every time they sink into the sand," Kadar said. "You'll be lucky if you don't lose most of your horses, with a couple days between oases, anyway. You don't want to lose your supplies as well."

Jonas stared out at the shimmering dunes that lay south of this town. "Is it really possible to make it to the temple?" he asked. "Or should we turn back?"

Kadar grinned. "I can get you there," he assured them. "You might be a little hungry, but I've done this route hundreds of times, in some of the worst conditions you will know. If you are willing, I will find a way."

Parasu stirred in the back of Jonas's mind. "We are willing," Jonas heard himself say. "It is imperative that we visit this temple."

"Then you will visit the temple," Kadar said. "I give you my word."

CHAPTER 19

Kadar waited on his humpback beside the Crone as the Templar sent Knights and soldiers ahead with their *feli*, scouting out the first oasis waymarker. The sun beat down upon their party, broiling them in the early-autumn heat. Kadar knew the Crone's *geas* was supposed to prevent him from seeing the army that followed behind, so he pretended to focus on only the smaller group of Voices and guards. Something deep inside of his brain was guiding his actions, as though he'd been *geased* before he'd met the army and the deities.

The *geas* didn't want him to notice, but surreptitious glances behind showed him the troops were flagging, exhausted from marching through deep sand that sank with every step, requiring twice the effort to move forward. Heatstroke and burns from the sun were common maladies. Kadar didn't know how many fighters the army had lost already in this easiest portion of the journey. The Knights had scoffed when Kadar showed them how to wrap their fair skin and create a desert headscarf. After three days of travel in blinding sun, with blowing sand gritting their eyes and mouths, all the troops now wore some sort of headscarf. Kadar had offered his own beeswax lotion to the Crone, whose lips and hands were so chapped they bled.

The scouts rode back to the Templar. The horses they rode had sunken eyes and walked with their heads down, dehydrated from water restrictions and eating dry feed. Kadar shook his head. Even with watering at this oasis, the beasts wouldn't last the longer distance between this oasis and the next. At last night's camp he'd overheard the Templar talking to soldiers about butchering the horses that had already fallen on the route. The Templar would do better to butcher the rest of the poor animals to feed the humans. But the fighters would struggle to carry their own water and supplies to the Obsidian Temple.

"My *feli* saw nothing," a Knight reported to the Templar. "No Tigus or signs that an army had been to the oasis."

"Could they be waiting behind the wards of the oasis?" the Templar asked Kadar.

Kadar shook his head. "The wards could hide a small party," he said. "But nothing as large as an army."

"Let's get you to the waymarker," the Crone said. "I long to see a bit of blue water in this desolation."

Kadar approached the stone with some dread.

He raised his hands and used the mudras and words of power taught to him by his uncle Aaron. He felt a pang of sadness realizing that Sulis had been here a few months before, had learned these same wards from Grandmother. Now they were both dead.

He finished the chant, placed both hands on the waymarker, and focused his energy, silently sending the last command into the earth. The Crone gasped from beside him.

Kadar looked up to find the way open before them. It was a small oasis, smaller than he remembered, but palm trees and short grasses surrounded the blue water. The troops would drain the water almost to nothing, but the spring would slowly replenish the basin once they'd left. He sagged in relief.

"You were worried, weren't you?" Jonas said from beside him.

Kadar nodded. "I was afraid that the Tigus lied to me," he admitted. "I was afraid a sacrifice had been made here, too, and the wards would no longer open to the old commands."

"I think Parasu would have felt that large a sacrifice," Jonas said. "He felt the sacrifice at the last oasis before we reached it. How many times have you done this, released the wards and made the water appear? It seems most magical when you are as desperately thirsty as our group is."

Kadar grinned. "I've seen it done hundreds of times," he told the other man. "But this is my first time releasing this ward."

He laughed at the consternation on Jonas's face. "I was only taught the wards last summer, when Sulis was injured and I stayed in the desert to help. Before, my teachers were worried our twin bond would give the deities a way of learning what we knew."

He choked as thoughts of Sulis filled his eyes with tears, but the pain quickly subsided, the Crone's *geas* putting a veil between him and his feelings.

"And yet here you are, guiding the deities," Jonas said.

Kadar glanced at him sharply. The man's voice had flattened, his demeanor changing slightly. Sulis had told him Jonas shared his body with his deity, without Parasu taking over completely. Kadar decided that was happening now.

"The warriors of the One should not have killed my family," Kadar told him, letting anger rise up in him at that injustice, letting it cloud his thoughts. "They are not serving the One if they kill innocent people. The Crone has explained your plan to me, how the deities will create balance in the world after regaining their true selves. They will be able to give my family justice and create a more peaceful relationship between the North and the South. It is worth angering my people to create a peaceful, just society."

As Jonas studied him, Kadar let his thoughts drift to the Crone. A peaceful lassitude settled over him, and Jonas looked away.

"Why are you still standing here?" the Templar asked, still on his humpback. "Are the wards down? Is it safe to enter?"

Kadar refocused. "Once you can see the oasis, the wards are down and it is safe to enter. I and the other caravan masters will explain how to water dehydrated beasts. Make certain your men don't cut down the palms or dirty the water with feces, urine, or trash of any kind. No bathing or wading in the aquifer except to draw water for the beasts. This is all the water we will have for three days. Don't let them make it undrinkable," Kadar warned, worried the men would rush to drink and destroy the oasis in the process.

The Templar shouted orders, directing his Knight and soldiers on how to command their fighters. Kadar escorted the Crone to the shade under the palms.

"I will help your men set up your tent, my lady," Kadar told her. "You should stay in the shade to revive yourself."

"You are a gentleman," the Crone said.

As Kadar helped unload the humpback, he overheard the Templar and Herald talking.

"We need to stay here at least a day, possibly more," the Herald said, coughing. "Almost a thousand fighters trail behind and won't arrive until late afternoon, exhausted by the heat and sand, if they survive at all. My healers have left hundreds of bodies behind on the trail—without horses to haul the stricken and water and shade to revive them, my healers can do little."

"The Southerner says this is the easiest section of the journey," the Templar said. "We will have to continue with night marches. I did not want to, because it will be too easy for us to fall into an ambush, but we can't continue in this heat. The troops will have to toughen up. Any unnecessary baggage has to go. We've lost fifty horses, and the rest won't last to the next oasis. The mules are doing better, but I don't know how much farther we can push them."

The Herald coughed again and cleared her throat. "We've already loaded the healing supplies onto the mules," the Herald said. "I'll give orders that any free space must be taken by water pouches and jugs."

"Go rest—have your Ranger give the orders. That cough is getting worse. Heal yourself; Aryn will need you," the Templar said.

"My Ranger will take over as Herald if I fall," the Herald said hoarsely. "That's why every Voice brought a spare. We are expendable."

As Kadar helped set up the Voice's shelters, a line formed at the oasis. Fighters passed buckets down the line to water thirsty beasts and refilled canteens and waterskins.

The Crone put a hand on his arm. "You don't have to sleep out in the open, like you've done the past few nights," she murmured in his ear. "You are welcome in my tent."

Kadar breathed deeply, trying not to resist the *geas* and pull away. He hid how horrified he was at the suggestion he would sleep with someone past his mother's age. He imagined Onyeka laughing at him for his age prejudice and turned to the Crone.

"I am honored, my lady," he murmured as quietly as she had. He showed her the bracelet around his wrist. "But my lover would be quite upset if I shared a tent with another woman. And I quite like sleeping under the stars."

The Crone squeezed his arm, and he could feel her trying to lay her will onto his. He smiled blandly at her. She smiled, a little brittlely.

"I understand," she said. "I would not wish to get in between two lovers."

Kadar gave a small bow and went to help the bucket brigade.

The army stayed at the oasis two nights and a day. The third evening they set out again.

"How do you know what way to turn in the darkness?" the Crone asked, shivering in the night air as they traveled toward the next oasis.

Kadar pointed to the vast, glimmering field of stars. "The star of the Great *Feli* lights the South," he said, pointing to the brightest star. "I learned to navigate by the stars when I first traveled by caravan. It is easier for me than traveling in daylight, though my sister never quite learned the route by starlight. The cairns that mark the way to the first oasis are sometimes covered by sandstorms and we remark them."

"Sandstorms?" the Templar asked. "Do many occur on this route?"

"The autumn rains in the mountains never touch the Sands," Kadar said. "But the winds blow over the desert and create sand funnels and obscure everything. Small sand squalls are common—you have to hunker down and wait them out. Large storms happen only every few years and are often fatal to those who can't find shelter in an oasis or near a large rock."

"Were you ever caught in one?" Jonas asked.

"Yes—near the oasis we are traveling to," Kadar said. "We were fortunate. There was a large outcropping of rocks and a stone of power was among them. My uncle Aaron was able to augment his powers and create a shield over the caravan."

"Stone of power?" the Crone asked.

Kadar nodded. "There are several around the desert. Most are covered by the dunes, but a sandstorm will occasionally reveal a new one or cover an old one."

"What are they?" the Templar asked.

"My uncle said they are connected somehow to the bedrock at the Obsidian Temple," Kadar said. "It pulls the power of a source held in the temple. Occasionally he could even tell who was in the temple when he used the stone."

"How close to the oasis is this rock?" the Templar asked. "Has it been covered over again?"

"My uncle said it was still here last spring," Kadar said. "It's only a quarter day ride from the next oasis. Uncle Aaron always rode to the stone to gain some energy while we were resting at the oasis."

They set up camp in the middle of the desert before the sun rose, their only shelter the tarps and tents set up by their camp. The sun baked them during the day and none of the Voices looked rested when they broke camp in the evening.

A soldier ran up to the Templar. "Fighters in the

ninth and tenth divisions killed horses. They said the horses had succumbed to heat, but the beasts looked fine this morning," he reported. "They were running low on supplies. Should the men be punished?"

The Templar grimaced. "No. Pretend you believe their story. The beasts won't last another day and the men need the meat to keep their strength up."

By the next morning, hundreds more of the troops had fallen behind.

"They're dead on their feet," the Herald reported. "Many are falling asleep as they march."

"We have to keep moving until we reach the next oasis," the Templar said. "We'll spend a few nights there and they can catch up. We are leaving a wide trail for them to follow."

"They won't survive without supplies," the Herald warned.

"We have to continue on. The greater good is what matters. We must get to the oasis."

They did not reach the oasis by the end of the third night, to Kadar's dismay. The humpbacks of a caravan walked longer and did not need to rest like an army of troops did.

"Should we push on?" Jonas asked Kadar. "Even our humpbacks look parched."

The Templar conferred with a scout. "He says a waymarker for the oasis is only a quarter day ahead. We need to push on. The troops need that water."

It was close to midday, the sun blazing overhead, when they reached the oasis. Kadar's own strength flagged as he released the wards on the waymarker and the oasis was revealed.

The Templar screamed orders as the troops behind them surged forward at the sight of water. Knights were stampeded as they tried to hold the troops back. Kadar moved his humpback out of the way of the fighters, looking on with weary frustration. If the fighters reached the oasis, they would foul it for the rest of the people.

A fireball of light and heat hit the front line of the rioting fighters before they could reach the blue water. The smell of ozone and burned flesh made the rest of the stampeding troops recoil, as the stricken men screamed in agony. Kadar blinked away the afterglow of the flare. Dozens of bodies lay on the ground in front of the oasis.

"You will form rank," the Templar screamed, his eyes blazing red with Voras's anger. "You will obey your section leader. Or I will kill every last one of you humans!"

Kadar shivered at the coldness of Voras's voice. The troops muttered, but subsided into order as the Knights directed them around the camp. The Herald's cough was more pronounced as her healers tended to the wounded. Kadar helped drag the dead fighters out into the desert.

Once the Voice's tents were set up, the Templar collapsed, his deity gone from him. The healers carried him to his tent as his second in command directed the watering of the troops.

Jonas stood beside Kadar. "You said that stone of power is by this oasis?" he asked.

Kadar nodded. "Just southeast, a short ride."

"You will take the Voices there," Jonas said. His voice was flat again, and Kadar looked into his eyes and recognized Parasu. "If we deities have a source of power, we can heal and energize our Voices. We use the energy around our Voices to keep them healthy and able to meet our demands. No energy exists in this wasteland for us to draw on. The Herald is ill from lung sickness. The Templar has been drained. The Crone is exhausted from the pain of sunburn. And my Voice needs to regain energy. Be ready to guide us when the sun begins to set over the dunes."

Kadar shook his head. "I will need morning light," he said. "This is not a part of the usual caravan route, so the way to the stone is marked visually, by cairns."

Parasu sighed. "It is probably better in the morning. I do not know that any of the humans will be able to travel without an extended rest."

At first light, before the sun had even risen above the dunes, Kadar was arranging travel with the Voices. The Templar's scouts reported no sign of the Tigu nomads or warriors of the One.

The Templar left his second in command at the camp to maintain order. There was a short debate about whether the seconds of the other Voices needed to come along. In the end, the four Voices, the Mother Superior and the Ranger, and all the Voices' guards rode out. Their *feli* ranged around them, some alongside the humpback, some loping into the distance to scout.

"The advance cohort of warriors and healers is positioned behind the sentinel rocks, a short ride from the oasis," a scout reported to Master Gursh. "Our scouts report a small group of Northerners, led by Kadar Shalendar, has broken off the main army and is traveling east."

Abram stood with Casia behind Master Gursh at the small watering hole they were camped at, a sandglass from Voras's army.

"The separation has gone as planned," Master Gursh said. "Another sandglass and they will have traveled too far to turn back in the face of a sandstorm."

The weather mages, warriors of the One with magical talent, and half the Tigus were at this camp, raising energy under Master Sandiv's command. Once the sandstorm was unleashed, the advance cohort would attack Voras's army. Here at camp, those warriors who were not exhausted by the weather working would form a second attack against the army. The Tigus would continue their illusion, making the sandstorm seem to last half a day. Voras's fighters were expected to surrender when battered by the sandstorm and demoralized by waves of fighters attacking them.

"Abram." Master Gursh gestured him over. "You must coordinate between the Kabandha warriors at the Obsidian Temple and us. I'll need you beside me."

"Casia, you are needed," Master Sandiv said, gesturing for her to join the weather workers.

Abram could feel Casia's pride as she took her place, the youngest among the energy workers, but more powerful than most. Jarol had no energy talent and had already ridden out with the advance force.

Turo came up beside Abram and grinned at him. Abram smiled back nervously and touched the knife by his side.

"Ah, your first battle, right?" the older man said. "Stay to the back and let the fighters do their work. Anyone comes close, stick a knife in him, just as I showed you, yes?"

Turo had found out Abram did not have a weapons teacher and had taken it upon himself to brush up Abram's skills. He had pointed out that the lines of battle often shifted to include noncombatants. Abram was grateful for the man's patient guidance.

"It is time," Master Gursh announced. "Abram, tell the Kabandha warriors we need to unbalance the air currents north and east of our oasis, so the warriors of the One can draw on the energy."

Abram connected with Sari and relayed the orders. Almost immediately he felt a shift in the air currents, a prickling on the skin.

"Enough," Master Sandiv ordered. "Warriors, draw on the energy. Feel the currents as we have practiced."

Abram watched Casia's face. It was focused and her brow puckered as she followed the master's orders. Then it smoothed and she smiled. Abram felt the energy around him rise and the air became thick, hard to breathe.

"It is too much," Turo said, loudly enough for the masters to hear.

Master Sandiv frowned at him. "Do not interrupt," she said harshly.

"You are not a weather worker. It is no more than is necessary. Warriors, focus the energy, begin feeding it into the atmosphere."

Abram glanced behind as the Tigus murmured restively.

"Can all the Tigus feel the energy?" he whispered to Turo.

Turo nodded, his lips pressed tight with worry.

"Now release it," Master Sandiv ordered. "Push the energy east."

Abram informed Sari, *The mages are releasing the energy into the air. They will begin pushing the storm into the deeper desert.*

The feeling of pressure in the air seemed to move away from them. The winds kicked up sand in their path, blowing it eastward toward the targeted oasis. Casia's face was focused, determined as she pushed the winds.

"Maybe it is fine," Turo said in an undertone. "This doesn't seem . . . no!"

The Tigus groaned. Casia's eyes flew open wide in panic. The sand in the distance exploded into the air in a massive wall as winds whipped furiously through Abram's hair.

"Let go of your energy," Turo shouted, and Abram realized he was talking to the mages. "It is rebounding, let it go!"

But it was already too late. Casia screamed in agony, then fell, her eyes wide and blank. The air became choked with sand and Abram was blinded, unable to see more than a length in front of him. All around Abram, warriors were crying out and falling into the sand. Sand slashed Abram's face as he tripped over a body trying to run to Casia. Abram fell to his knees and realized the body was Master Gursh. The master's eyes were open and blood flowed his nose and ears. A strong hand grasped Abram's arm and yanked him up.

"We must get to shelter. Go to the humpbacks by the rocks of our water hole," Turo ordered over the wailing winds.

"I have to get Casia," Abram yelled back, trying to yank away.

The Tigu man was stronger than he looked and he determinedly hauled Abram around, shoving him toward a huddle of bodies already surrounding the water hole.

"She is dead. They are all dead. We must save the living," Turo said as he pushed him into the pile. The men on either side of him linked arms around him. Abram realized he heard a low drone that was not the screaming of the wind. The Tigus were humming. When Abram joined the circle, the wind felt less on his back and the sand did not choke him. Somehow they were using their magic to shield themselves and their water source from the worst of the storm.

Abram felt Sari trying to contact him.

They have all fallen, all the warriors, Abram sent wildly to her, tears streaming down his face. *We are trying to survive.*

Kadar spied the first cairn up a dune shortly after they rode southeast. Up the rise they looked back to see an excellent view of the camp, the oasis, and the empty dunes surrounding the area.

"The desert warriors must be waiting until we approach the Obsidian Temple," the Templar said. "We haven't seen a single Tigu since we began."

The Ranger nodded. "They are probably hoping the desert will reduce the numbers of our troops greatly before they have to fight us."

The Herald bent over her saddle coughing. Her *feli* touched his head to her boot. "They're smarter than us," she said, through gasps. "Letting the heat do their work for them."

"We will still outnumber them, in spite of the desert's toll," the Templar said, but his voice sounded uncertain.

The camp disappeared from sight as they went down the dune, following the stone markers. The black mountains rose in the distance. As they traveled over a smaller dune, the way became rockier, into the foothills of the mountains rather than the endless dunes of the Sands. A warm breeze lifted sand into their faces without cooling them at all.

One of the Knights scouting to the west gave a shout, and Kadar squinted against the harsh wind, blocking sand from his eyes with one hand. A small dark cloud appeared on the horizon, growing rapidly, covering the blue sky. A furious rush of hot, stinging wind blew at his face.

"Sandstorm," Kadar yelled.

"We have to return to the troops!" the Templar bellowed, trying to pull his humpback around. The beast refused to turn to face the wind.

"Too late," Kadar yelled. "We have to make it to those rocks! Hang on."

The humpbacks knew the danger, and once Kadar focused his will on the beasts and pointed them to the eastern rocks, they followed, in spite of their riders' protests.

The wind picked up around them, painful shards of sand flaying any exposed skin. Kadar glanced back once to see the daylight fading as the storm approached and swept everything in its path. He saw the humpback carrying the Mother Superior stumble and fall, but there was no time to go back for her.

They reached the rocks, buffeted by winds, and Kadar ordered the humpbacks to kneel behind the rocks. The *feli* quickly curled themselves into tight balls beside the beasts, tucking their noses under their tails. The Ranger helped the Herald off as the Crone tumbled down from her beast. The Herald's breath was wheezing in her chest as she knelt behind the rocks.

"Our guards are still scouting out there," the Templar shouted above the rising wind. He attempted to make his humpback rise, but Kadar kept the beast under his control.

"Where is my Mother Superior?" the Crone cried. "You must go back for her."

"Get down! You will die if you go out again," he yelled. "They will find shelter elsewhere. Get low to the ground, and cover your face and any exposed skin."

Then the storm was upon them. Kadar motioned for the others to hunker close to the ground between the humpbacks and the rocks. He covered his face with cloth and put it between his arms as he knelt, hunched close to the sand. The whistle of the wind covered all other sounds. The very air had turned against them and Kadar breathed in fine particles of dust and grit even through the cloth covering his face.

The humpbacks panicked as they were scoured by the hot, harsh wind and Kadar clamped down on his control of their minds. His world narrowed to the brutal whistling wind, his clogged breathing, and controlling the beasts that helped shelter them.

The sand heaped around him, piled on his back. He fought his fear of being buried alive, instead finding some relief from the scouring winds by burrowing more deeply in the sand. He kept the area around his face as clear as he could. The humpbacks settled more calmly now that the sand had built around their sides, sheltering them from the burning winds, but the winds raged on around them. Kadar could not remember ever encountering a sandstorm of this length and ferocity. Exhaustion and lack of air took over and he fell into a half doze, barely aware of his surroundings.

"**H**ere comes the energy turbulence from the weather working," Tori told her Counselors in the Temple of the One. "Focus on keeping the partial shields up. Once the energy of the weather they've created hits the shield, you'll feel like you are holding on to a large rock that wants to roll back. People on the first shield, keep your energy centered until I say to let go, then shift to the next shield back."

The Temple of the One was quiet as the Counselors focused. The exits were blocked by numerous *feli*, who spilled into the hallway and did not let the curious peer in to see what they were doing.

The warriors of the One in the desert released energy into the air currents, building tension in waves of wind and gusts. When the energy crested, they released the shields and let it blow out into the desert.

"Too much," Elida murmured, alarmed, when the energy collided with a natural temperature inversion and rebounded.

"Whiskers, that's a killing storm," the former Cantor whispered, horrified.

Tori spoke loudly enough for all the Counselors to hear. "The storm is too large. The mass will go southeast—but the winds will blow storms throughout the desert. If the energy meets the cooler air up here, we could get dangerous storms and funnels. Be ready to shunt it to the desert with the shield."

They spent a tense hour, watching the energy spread out in waves, splitting into dangerous cells as it hit air currents.

"This is it," Elida called.

People groaned as the energy smashed into their shields. She braced the half shield and could feel much of the energy shunting to the desert, as the wilder energy broke over the shield, heading to the next. Wave after wave of energy pushed against the shield as they mentally, energetically shored it up. It died down as the wave hit the second shield.

"Let the first shield go," Tori commanded. She pitied the acolytes at the far southern outpost on the border who were enduring the storms they let through.

The energy waves hit the shields just south of Illian, and their combined shield shunted most of the energy to the desert. The rest broke around them. Tori jumped as lightning struck nearby and thunder rattled the dome.

"Gently release the shield into the earth, as we practiced," Tori directed. She could hear rain lashing the city as more thunder shook the Temple. She could feel the energy of the violent storm, but it was no longer as unstable and would not create wind funnels or killing winds.

Elida raised her hands, quieting the jubilant Counselors. "Excellent work," she said. "Next we will practice full shielding, so no energy can get through at all. Today, go find some food and relax. You have kept Illian and her people from harm."

Kadar came to his senses when the humpback he was hunkered by rose and shook itself free of the sand. Kadar quickly regained mind control so the beast would not flee. The other humpbacks followed their mate. The *feli* were already up and nosing around the stones. The wind had died down, but the sun was still obscured by the grit and fine particles in the air. Kadar clawed out from under a foot of sand covering him and the surrounding area. The Templar was already shaking himself out. Kadar turned to the wriggling lump closest to him and brushed the sand off. The Crone was curled in a fetal ball, and as Kadar uncovered her, she gasped and sat up. She buried her head in her hands and cried with gasping breaths. Kadar didn't know how she had the moisture for tears—his body felt like it would crack and flake apart at the next gust of wind. His eyes were gritty, and blinking hurt as the sharp sand particles scratched under his eyelids.

Kadar watched another sand lump come to life behind her, and helped Jonas clear the sand off his robes and shake out his headscarf. The Tribune seemed dazed as he sat on top of the sand he'd displaced and wiped his face off with a shaking hand.

Kadar was distracted by a cry of dismay behind

him, and he turned to find the Templar, the Ranger, and a guard digging out the Herald. Kadar stumbled over to help the men.

"She's had lung problems this past year," the Ranger said in a hoarse whisper. "This desert air has made it worse."

The Herald did not stir as they dug her out. Kadar looked around for her *feli*, but he wasn't among the felines ranging around their group. They raised her head up to get it out of the sand surrounding her. The Herald's eyes were closed and she wasn't breathing. The Ranger frantically felt for a pulse and then laid his head on her chest, listening as the others watched. He looked up at them, his sand-caked face sporting red-streaked eyes that brimmed with tears. He shook his head.

"You must represent Aryn now," the Templar said. "Herald, we must find out what happened to the others."

Kadar stepped from behind the stones and sank to his knees in uncompressed sand. The landscape was vastly changed; the dunes had shifted and settled in different patterns. A haze still obscured a view of the far distance, but the sun was well overhead and begin-ning to move to the west. The storm had raged sev-eral hours. There was no sign of any life except in their small group.

"It's so different," Jonas said from behind him. "Those high dunes didn't exist before. And the rocks we were traveling toward have disappeared."

Jonas's voice was panicked, but Kadar could not reassure him. "All the cairns will be gone," he said flatly. "Traveling the Sands will be slow until the dunes have settled and compacted slightly."

"What do we do?" the new Herald asked. "How do we get back to camp?"

Kadar looked around the scoured desert. Much of the southeastern foothills had been scoured to the rocks by the winds. It would be a slow slog to walk to them, but they would have certain footing on the rocks.

"I think our best chance of survival is heading for the mountains," Kadar said. "There is a small camp in the foothills the Tigus stay at when hunting in the mountains. It has a spring that comes out of the rocks. I am fairly certain I can return to it."

"No." The Templar pushed forward. "We must return to the army. You said you could navigate by the stars. We will wait until nightfall and return to my men and the oasis."

Kadar hesitated, looking out on the dunes. The gritty dust still hung in the air. "The stars will be obscured for days by this haze," he said. He shook his head and looked at the Templar. "This is the worst sandstorm I have ever encountered. I don't know if the oasis and the army still exist."

"But the oasis had wards," Jonas said in dismay. "Surely the wards would protect it and the people in it."

"We released the wards," Kadar reminded him. "With so many people camped all around, the wards would not have been able to reestablish the shield to protect the oasis from the brunt of the storm. The army had no shelter except their tents, and those would have been buried in the deep sand. Even if we can reach them, I don't know if anyone is left to save."

"You did this," the Templar snarled in fury. "You led us out here. Grab him!"

The three remaining guards seized Kadar's arms.

"He separated us from our men, brought us out here to kill us, and summoned the sandstorm," the Templar growled. "That camp he wants us to travel to is probably full of fighters, waiting to kill us."

"If I had the power to summon a sandstorm, I could have killed you at any time," Kadar said, as he tried to wrench his arms free. "I could have simply ridden off and let you die in the storm. I don't have that kind of power. I'm trying to save all of us."

"You might not have that kind of power, but the Southern sorcerers do," the Templar growled. "When did you start collaborating with them?"

"I'm not. Listen. I promised I would get you to the Obsidian Temple. And I keep my vows. I will still get the Voices to the Obsidian Temple or die trying," Kadar said.

"So witnessed." Parasu's flat tones fell out of Jonas's mouth. "He speaks the truth, Templar. We still have four Voices. We still have a chance of making it to the Temple."

"And how will we fight the warriors of the One when we get to the Temple?" the Templar asked. He waved for the guards to stand down, and they released Kadar.

Parasu frowned. "Through subterfuge. They are expecting an army. We are only a small group of pilgrims. We should be able to disguise our natures and control any who would not allow us to pass. The way of force is past us now—we must now use our intellect and our cunning to survive and triumph."

"We should turn back," the Crone said, fear in her voice. "We can try again another time. We have no one to protect us; we have only the water and food we took on this side trip. I want to go back to Illian. We have to go back to civilization."

Kadar's gaze softened at her distress. "The way is gone, my lady," he said softly, gesturing to dusky sands. The haze glowed red as the afternoon sun hit the particles of sand in the air. It gave their surroundings an eerie feel. "The only way back is to continue forward and find a new route."

Parasu turned to Kadar. "You say you know of a campsite near here?"

Kadar grimaced. "At least a day's travel away," he said. "My Tigu group came to it from a more southern direction, but one of the Tigu women told me what markers to look for, so I could always find my way to the spot, if lost near the mountains."

"How fortunate," the Templar said mockingly.

"You must guide us there," the Crone said, clutching his arm. He could feel her pressing her will upon him.

"We'll check the humpbacks to make certain none

are hurt from the storm," Kadar said. "Drink well, but don't use the water to wash. We still have a long way to go before we reach a spring. I'm hoping we can make the foothills before sunset."

The humpbacks were anxious, not wanting the humans to touch them, but Kadar forced them to settle. None were harmed. Kadar watched Jonas take a tiny sip from his waterskin.

"Drink more," Kadar advised. "I've seen people who died of dehydration with water left in their canteen because they wanted to save it."

The new Herald tenderly covered his predecessor's face with her scarf, and reburied her in the sand.

"I wonder where her *feli* went," Kadar said.

The Herald shook his head. "They simply disappear. Some die with their chosen, but most just leave. I like to think they go back to the wild."

The Herald was the only one who looked back at their sheltering rocks as they mounted their humpbacks and wrapped their faces against the gritty sand still blowing in the wind. Kadar directed his humpback to the rocks at the edge of the sandy dunes and tried not to think of the thousands they left behind.

CHAPTER 20

Sulis sat in the courtyard with the Kabandha warriors, listening as Sari reported Abram's last message. She felt helpless as she watched the energy of the sandstorm roll across the desert, across where she knew Kadar was traveling with the Voices.

"You idiots," Amon exclaimed, standing. "A smaller storm is heading for us! We need to shield this area or the path down will be obscured and the oasis will be obliterated."

"The oasis is protected by the wards," Sari said. "But the path to it and the waymarker could be covered. Can you direct us on how to shield it from the winds?"

"You don't know how to shield?" Amon asked. He glared over at the Chosen. "Link with me and follow my lead. The winds coming this way could funnel into this chasm and tear apart everything we've created."

"Winds!" Ava exclaimed. She and Sanuri had a low conversation, and then clasped hands and ran into the temple.

Sulis reached out and clasped hands with Alannah, beside her.

"What do you think that was about?" she muttered as Amon linked himself into the circle.

"She was worried she'd unsettle the weather if she linked Aryn's mandala to the winds around the chasm, like what happened with linking Ivanha to the bedrock and Parasu to the stream. Oh wow, there are the *feli*."

The tiny stream now gushed like a river behind the temple thanks to Ava's mandala work. Sulis wasn't certain how Amon's *feli* crossed it from the ledges behind—but they suddenly surrounded the group. Amon said they were natural shields, and when they joined the group, a shield snapped into place around the chasm. Amon directed them to expand the shield to the paths around the chasm to the nearest oasis. The first waves of energy bounced off the shields.

"Let a little through, so we don't get a rebound and create more storms," Amon directed. Sulis was surprised to feel drops of wetness on her skin.

"Now let it sink into the earth. The worst is over," Amon said. They did, and Sulis looked up as rain drizzled down upon them.

"We must have shifted air currents and brought rain from the mountains. Hope it doesn't get worse," Ashraf said as they ducked into the temple. "Too much rain could cause rockslides and sudden flooding."

"One disaster after another," Sulis said, pacing by the doorway. "I wish I still had my bond with Kadar. I can't bear to think that he might die in the Sands thinking he was alone."

"He is still alive, as is Abram," Grandmother snapped as she passed by. Her eyes were red and Sulis knew she suppressed tears for all the friends among the warriors she'd just lost. "I would know if they had passed. Let's make certain the weather energy hasn't damaged our work at the mandala. Do something useful rather than sit and worry."

Sulis followed her grandmother. Ava was sitting outside the mandala, roughhousing with Nuisance, but she stood when the rest of the Chosen approached.

"We did it," she said, and then squeaked as Nuisance almost knocked her down. "Aryn is connected both to her winds and to the One. Only one line is not complete."

"Fire," Alannah said, studying the mandala by Voras.

"Palou says some sort of fire comes out of the mountains by the shore," Ava said. "But I don't know how to find it."

"I will help you link to it," Grandmother said. "I've been there."

"Will that make those mountains erupt?" Sulis asked.

Grandmother shrugged. "It might. It is right by the shoreline of the ocean and is too rocky for humans, so an eruption will disturb no one."

"Not today," Ava said with a shiver. "The wind energy was scary. It was really hard to tie down."

Sulis stepped up to the edge of the energy lines of the mandala and closed her eyes. The energy was etched into the very stones of the temple. Every day Ava renewed the energy on the lines with help from Dani and Alannah. Layer upon layer of energy had worn channels of energy into the obsidian floor until the very stones were alive with chakra energy.

"Figured out how to dance it yet?" Master Anchee said lightly from behind her.

Sulis looked over at him. Deep lines of sadness surrounded his eyes. The warriors at Kabandha had been his family. He'd never left after being sent there to train as a boy.

"How many did we lose in the backlash?" Sulis asked him.

Master Anchee looked away. "Your grandmother is no longer linked to any of the warriors of the One who could channel energy," he said, his voice choked.

Lasha put a hand on his arm. "There is a possibility that it somehow severed their connections to your grandmother without killing them."

But it wasn't likely. Sulis knew that was what he was saying. Thousands of men and women, gone in an instant.

"Will the survivors return here?" she asked. "What happens next?"

"Sari said the advance cohort of warriors of the One and the Tigus who were closest to Voras's army were sheltered by rocks and may have survived. They will probably follow the sandstorm into the desert to confront what remains of the army," Master Anchee said. "We have not heard from Abram about the people around him. If any survive, they will probably travel here."

"If the storm is as big as they said, it will be more of a rescue mission than a battle," Ashraf said. "The Tigus won't need to use illusions to conquer Voras's army."

"And what of Kadar, and the Voices?" Sulis asked.

"According to your grandmother, he is alive, and we have to assume he is keeping the Voices alive," Master Anchee said. "We will *farspeak* a general call into the desert, asking anyone who survived where they are and if they need assistance. It is normal rescue procedure after a storm of this magnitude. Hopefully he will respond then. He should continue to the Tigu camp to meet Onyeka as his guide."

"Stay alive, Kadar," Sulis whispered. "Everything depends on you now."

Jonas suppressed a groan as he slipped off his exhausted humpback. Everything hurt and he was wearier than he'd ever been in his life. The adrenaline from surviving the storm had worn off hours ago, and every step of the struggling, plodding beast had hurt his tailbone.

They reached the rocky stability of the mountain foothills after dusk had already fallen. The Voices and guards sat on their humpbacks while Kadar scouted around the rocks, looking for a place to settle and rest.

He returned looking a good deal happier and they followed him to a sheltered spot.

"There is a tiny spring beyond those rocks," Kadar said. "I think it was created by shifting rocks in the storm. Its small enough it'll take hours to refill the canteens, but we have water."

Jonas took a couple more swallows from his waterskin and realized he was starving. The Crone was already chewing on dried meat and nuts. They had packed journey rations to eat at midday, but because of the sandstorm had never gotten them out. He pulled them out of his bag, and then hesitated.

"How much should we save?" he asked Kadar.

Kadar shrugged. "Maybe half?" he said. "There's usually a stash of rations at nomadic camps for stranded travelers—but we can't count on it."

Jonas hesitated, and then ate the dried meat. It didn't matter if he was hungry now or hungry later—he would not be able to continue without food. He offered a bit of dried meat to Pollux, who sniffed it but wasn't interested. The *feli* had less difficulty walking in the deeper sand and had disappeared for a while into the mountains before they'd reached solid ground. He suspected that they'd found some rodents to snack on.

Jonas found himself dozing off as he chewed. He woke enough to use his cloak to soften the rock, as Kadar held a low-voiced conversation with the remaining guards. Then he fell into a deep sleep.

He woke to eerie howling deep in the night, his heart pounding as he sat up. Pollux was sitting, staring into the night, his tail twitching, but unalarmed. The other Voices were dark lumps on the ground, still sleeping soundly—but a standing guard looked his way.

"Go back to sleep, my lord," the guard said. "It's only the scavenger dogs that roam the mountains. They aren't the ones that hunt living creatures."

Jonas lay back and had only enough time to wonder which mountain animals did hunt humans before slipping into sleep.

The heat of daylight woke him, and he sat up to find the camp stirring. The desert was still in a strange sort of dusk, sand particles still creating a haze that partially obscured the sun. As Jonas looked out into the Sands, swirling winds spun a small dust devil into the air, before whipping over some dunes.

I did not want to wake you; your body was so exhausted, Parasu said. *But now that you are awake, I must speak with the other Voices.*

Jonas scrambled to his feet. He was still sore but felt more human now that he was rested and had water.

Kadar was using a waxed canvas bowl to give the humpbacks water, and he nodded as Jonas passed him on his way to where the other three gathered. They were divvying up remaining rations.

"There is extra for you as well, Tribune," the Crone said. "The Templar was carrying some rations for his guards, and four never made it to shelter. We also have the poor Herald's rations."

It looked like the Crone had been able to wash the dried sand off her face, and Jonas glanced around for a basin of water. He looked forward to getting the dry crustiness out of his eyes. He spotted a small basin, with fine silt at the bottom where the others had washed and let the sand settle. Jonas carefully dipped his hands in, gently washing his face and skin without losing too much water.

Kadar joined the group. "If we run out of food completely, we can butcher the extra mount we have. I hate to do it, because we need an extra if one of the humpbacks goes lame on these rocks—but it's better than starving."

"Our *feli* may be able to bring us fresh meat before it comes to that," the Herald said.

The Crone shuddered. "Rodents, lizards—that is what Amia is eating."

"Better than starving," the Herald said.

Jonas accepted the extra food and sat. "Parasu wishes to speak," he said formally, and his deity came to the front of his mind.

"I have been unable to contact the Magistrate," Parasu said. "This tells me he is dead. I cannot see through the eyes of any of the scholars I brought, so I must assume they are dead as well. What has Voras said, Templar?"

The Templar shook his head. "My second, who I left in command, is dead. Any Knight who could channel power died trying to push the storm away or shield the camp with no success. No one left has much magical ability, so he is seeing only flashes of the camp. A quarter of the army remains, but they lack water and have to dig their food out of deep sand. The oasis is filled with sand, but desperate fighters are trying to dig it out."

"Only a dozen of Aryn's healers survived," the Herald said. "All Aryn could see is them digging endlessly, trying to get to buried fighters before they suffocated."

"Ivanha has no one in the camp," the Crone said. "She sees nothing."

"Do we try to return, to help save the remaining fighters in the army?" the Herald asked.

"No," Parasu said. "I have tested the currents of the air. Southerners created that storm. I assume their warriors will follow the storm to make certain our Voices were killed. If we go back, we walk right into their hands."

"Why didn't you sense the storm before it hit?" the Templar asked bitterly. "We might have been able to prepare, to save thousands of lives."

"Weather working is hard to sense, because the energy currents ebb and flow naturally," Parasu said, undisturbed by the accusation. The human Voice was so far below himself that responding in anger would be silly. "The warriors of the One could be at the other end of the desert and disrupt the currents. I am, however, surprised that Aryn did not realize that her element had been corrupted."

The Herald ducked his head. "She, too, is dismayed.

The illness of my predecessor made it difficult for her to sense the air properly."

Parasu considered that, and Jonas felt him accept it. "It is why we still travel to the Obsidian Temple. Once we regain our autonomy, the frailty of humans will not block our senses. We will be whole and powerful once again."

"If you are done talking, I'm anxious to move on," Kadar said. His eyes unfocused suddenly. "Hold on."

Parasu's interest sharpened. *He is a* farspeaker, he told Jonas. *He speaks to another Southerner. I cannot quite hear what they are saying.*

Kadar refocused, looking over at Jonas. "There is a *farspeaker* at the oasis closest to the Obsidian Temple. He is finding the minds of *farspeakers* in the area and asking if they are in need of assistance. The sandstorm was spread throughout the desert, even though the greatest impact was in our direction."

"Do you trust this? They might be looking for us," the Crone said.

"No desert warrior has reached our army," the Templar disagreed. "Even if they had, it would take days of digging to realize we aren't among the dead."

Kadar nodded. "Rescue and guides are sent to anyone stranded after a large storm. If they can provide us a guide through the foothills to that oasis, I can take you to the temple. I'm not certain how to disguise you when a Tigu guide arrives, though."

"Our Voices can darken their skin and change their features to look like Southerners to fool the guide. We will translate their language for our Voices," Parasu said confidently. "It will be harder to hide our guards, though."

Kadar looked surprised. "I've never seen that ability before. Sounds similar to what the Tigus do, blending in with the sand. Let me see who is at the oasis. We can tell the Tigus that the guards are Forsaken you have freed to work in Frubia. Our clothes are ragged enough—at this point we all look like paupers."

He closed his eyes and seemed to focus.

Kadar's eyes opened. "The *farspeaker* gave me better directions to the Tigu camp. We are not far. About a half day's walk. He says a guide is already sheltering there as well as couple of Tigus."

"How does he know this?" the Templar asked. "Ask him."

"I already asked. There is an elderly *farspeaker* at the camp. The guide was taking him to his home, but they delayed to give him rest and became stuck there because of the storm," Kadar said.

"I am ready," the Crone said, standing unsteadily. "I want to get this over with so I can go home."

"Of course," Kadar said, going to her side in an instant. "This must be very difficult for you, my lady. We should walk our beasts through the rocky sections, but if you are too exhausted, you may ride and I will lead you."

She still has her claws sunk deeply into the Southern man, Parasu noted. *He will do everything he can to keep her safe, and us as well because we are with her. I admire her ability to keep the geas strong, even as tired as she is.*

Jonas wearied quickly, both in body and in courage, as they climbed over rocky, unstable footing while their humpbacks resisted and became balky. Kadar calmed the beasts the best he could, but even he was looking weary when they finally came to a flatter space in the rocks and heard voices speaking in the Tigu tongue.

"It can't be," Kadar said, as he hurried forward.

I am disguising you, Parasu said. *Do not be alarmed if you see your reflection. I am also putting a deflecting spell on you, so they will not wish to look too closely.*

Jonas looked down at his arms, which were now brown and more muscular. If he peered closely he could see through the illusion to his pale, thin body. He looked up to find the others had already transformed and were following Kadar. There was a group of Tigus seated around a small fire, on which cooked something that smelled wonderful to Jonas. Two of the people rose and faced them.

"Welcome." An elderly man held out his arms, speaking in the Southern tongue. "It is good to see other survivors of that terrible storm."

Jonas heard a terrible howling. He turned in time to see a small orange-pointed cat leap up onto Kadar's shoulder.

"Kadar?" A tall, lean Tigu woman stood, her eyes wide with shock. "What are you doing here?"

"Onyeka, it *is* you!" Kadar said, his face wreathed in the most genuine smile Jonas had seen since they met him at the oasis. He grabbed the woman in a hug.

"What are you doing here? I did not think I would see you again."

"But, who are these people?" Onyeka asked, frowning.

"I met them at the oasis where my sister . . ." He shook his head. "They were fleeing Illian ahead of Voras's army. They are going home to Frubia after freeing some Forsaken slaves, and I said I would guide them. We had passed the second oasis when the sandstorm hit and I had to get everyone to cover."

The Crone interrupted his excited replay. "Who is this, Kadar?" she asked. To Jonas's ears, she sounded a little jealous.

Kadar turned to them. "My apologies. This is warrior Onyeka," he said. "She is my beloved. And this is my suncat, Amber. It's good fortune Onyeka's here. She knows all the paths and shifting sources of water in these foothills. We'll have no problem find our way back to the route."

CHAPTER 21

Kadar sat at the fire, watching as the other Southerners welcomed the newcomers, and felt confused. Onyeka sat on one side of him, and the Crone, in her new form, sat on the other. Amber, for reasons of her own, had settled on Jonas's lap and was purring as he uncertainly petted her. The Voices' *feli* had disappeared before they reached the camp. He wondered if the Voices had sent them away to allay suspicions.

It was wonderful finding Onyeka when he thought he'd lost her. But when he thought back, he couldn't remember where in the desert they had been when they parted. He didn't think they'd been at Antajale. But if she had been with the Tigu warriors, why was she here, now? The Sepacu tribe was her life. And why did he feel like he should know something more when he looked at her? Something he'd forgotten? Kadar shook his head, knowing his thinking was foggy from the Crone's attempt to *geas* him and his grief over his sister. He distracted himself by listening to the camp talk.

"It did not seem natural," a Tigu woman said. She and her partner, the elderly man and his guide, and Onyeka were the five who had taken shelter at this camp before they'd arrived. "It blew up so suddenly, and after the normal summer winds had died down. Rohir and I were traveling home, so I can give birth, and were lucky to make it behind rocks before the sand hit."

"It was not natural," Onyeka said. "But it got out of control and became too large. I do not know if my father still lives or was killed by this folly."

"What do you mean?" Jonas asked, his voice flat. Kadar could not get used to him like this. He looked like a normal, young Southerner, yet Kadar knew who was under the disguise.

"This was a defense against the invaders," Onyeka said.

"Maybe we should not talk about this," Kadar said, suddenly very aware that Onyeka could give away secrets of the desert to the deities.

She gave him a sidelong glance, and he was confused again. He wanted the deities to go to the Obsidian Temple, didn't he? He wanted revenge on the warriors of the One. But he didn't want to disappoint Onyeka. And he realized that leading the enemy to the temple might, unless he could convince her that it would create more peace in the end.

The Crone put a hand on his arm, sensing his confusion, and he felt calmer. Onyeka raised an eyebrow at the Crone's familiarity, but shrugged.

"It does not matter now," she said. "There is no secret any more. Weather is so hard to control. They wished for a small sandstorm. It was greater than they expected and rebounded on them. So, no Northern army—but no Southern army either. Once again, only we Tigus are left in the desert, because we have the sense not to try to control the winds."

The elderly man shivered. "I felt when it went wrong," he said. "There was too much energy in the air already. Never before has such a sandstorm hit this land. Hopefully never again."

"No one survived?" Kadar choked out.

"Some," Onyeka said. "Those who were close to shelter. Those who did not use energy."

Kadar stood and walked away from the fire, feeling even more conflicted. Onyeka followed him. He turned and hugged her close.

"You are unsettled," she said in the Tigu tongue. "Is it your sister? Were you unable to find her body?"

"It isn't that, Onyeka," Kadar said. "My mind feels confused. I have promised to lead these people, but I no longer know if it is the right thing to do."

"You gave your word?" Onyeka asked.

Kadar nodded.

"Then it is the right thing. We will take them together."

"But, Onyeka, you don't know who . . ."

"Hush . . ." Onyeka put a finger to his lips. "I know more than you think. Do not question what you must do. It is the right path."

Kadar shook his head. "You will be disappointed in me, when you really understand what I do."

"Do you trust me, Kadar?" Onyeka asked.

"Yes."

"Then know that I do understand and could not be more proud of you. Seeing that you survived the desert, that because of you they survived—we will get them to the Obsidian Temple safely."

Kadar stared at her in shock over mention of the temple. "How . . . ?"

She shushed him as the Crone approached. Kadar frowned in irritation, but Onyeka gave her head a small shake and indicated that he should go with the disguised Voice.

"Kadar, I was worried about you," the Crone said. She again put a hand on his arm, reasserting her will.

Kadar rolled his eyes at Onyeka before turning.

"We can't have that," he said, pretending to adjust his robe. "Onyeka was welcoming me back."

"Oh." A blush came to the Crone's cheeks. "I am so sorry to interrupt."

"It is fine. The meat should be about done and we all are hungry," he said. "Onyeka will guide us to the oasis."

"We should rest tonight, water the beasts," Onyeka said. "We will leave at first light. I will search out a water source we will stop at. The day after next, we will reach the splitting of roads that will lead to the caravan path and the oasis. There are dried food stores here we can take, as long as Kadar and I return later to replenish them."

Jonas came to Kadar as he was checking the humpbacks a final time before sleep.

"Do you trust these people?" he asked. "Parasu says every time he tries to read them, he sees nothing."

"It is the Tigu desert magic," Kadar said. "They truly are one with the Sands and can find water anywhere. Onyeka has pledged to help me fulfill my vow."

"But what will she do when she realizes we are traveling to the sacred temple instead of the oasis?" Jonas urged. "What if she tries to stop us?"

"The Tigus do not have sacred places, so she does not feel a sense of protection toward the temple," Kadar assured him, not telling him that Onyeka had spoken of the temple. "Even if she does object, she will step aside when I tell her it is part of my vow. They value honor over everything else. She will not try to stop us."

Onyeka woke them in the predawn light and they walked away from the camp, leading the humpbacks. Amber was perched on Kadar's shoulder, purring madly into his ear. The elderly man was sitting up, watching as they passed, and when Kadar looked at him, he touched the back of his hand to his forehead and mouthed "Suma."

Kadar felt guilty about the trust the man showed to him. Instead of Suma, Kadar would probably soon be known as Darmi or "traitor of the people."

"Stop thinking," Onyeka said, reaching over to prod his ribs. "Leave that to those of us for whom it does not take so much effort."

"Thinking is not hard for me," he growled, trying to grab her hand.

She was too fast for him and giggled as he missed. "The smoke coming out of your ears says otherwise," she teased. "All will be as intended."

Kadar hoped she was right. Onyeka led them to a flatter area, where the hills met the sand. They mounted the humpbacks and rode, skirting the edges of the rocky foothills.

"We found a small spring the sandstorm uncovered when we passed through," Onyeka said. "We will reach it by nightfall."

As they were making camp, a small tremor shook the ground under them. Kadar looked around, wondering if he'd really felt it, but found the Templar gazing raptly to the south.

"Did you feel something?" the Crone asked uncertainly. "It was like the stone shifted under me."

The Templar snapped his gaze away. "A mountain erupted, east of here," he said. "Probably caused by the energy the sandstorm put into the air."

Onyeka looked questioningly at him and he hastened to continue. "I can sense things to do with fire," he said.

"Ah, like we sense the water of the desert," she said. "Do you work at a forge in Frubia?"

"Yes," the Templar lied. "We work with metal craft."

"That explains your fine sword," she said, turning away. "I'd wondered where it was crafted."

Kadar's sleep was restless that night, with endless dreams of his grandmother's and Sulis's disapproval of his actions.

"I'm doing this for you," he whispered. Amber yowled as he rolled over on her, and she flounced off to find a better bed companion.

"Kadar?" Onyeka sat beside him. "Can you not sleep?"

She stretched out beside him and took him in her arms. He fell into a dreamless sleep in her embrace.

They reached the caravan route not long after daybreak the next day and the crossroads early in the morning. Kadar halted his humpback.

"That goes to a big temple," Onyeka said with a shrug. "The oasis is this way."

"We had planned on going to the Obsidian Temple to make an offering before continuing on," the Herald said.

Onyeka frowned, but Kadar could tell she was acting. "I thought only . . . what are they called . . . clerics? Priests? Went to the temple."

"No, sometimes pilgrims who are giving thanks for something go and leave gifts of money and food," Kadar lied. He wasn't sure what her game was, but he was worried that she and the Templar would fight if she did not agree, and he did not know who would be the winner.

"That is fine," Onyeka said. "I have not gone down this path before. Do you know the wards?"

Kadar nodded, and felt another flash of confusion. Somehow he did know the wards, even though he'd never traveled this route.

"Your uncle was a thorough teacher," Onyeka said, before turning her mount down the path.

Kadar shook his head. He must have learned it last summer when Uncle Aaron showed him the other wards for the more traveled oases.

"I was warned that as we travel down this path, you will feel fear and want to turn back," Kadar told the others. "But trust me. That is only a part of the wards."

They rode down the path, but Kadar did not feel a growing fear like Sulis had described to him the first time she'd visited. He didn't feel anything. He worried that he had led them down the wrong trail and they were heading into the mountains when Onyeka made a small noise of surprise.

Kadar looked down the path past her. A tall, pale man stood beside a waymarker. Behind him opened a deep chasm, with a path leading down one side.

"I am Amon, a Descendant of the Prophet," the man said in the Northern tongue. "I felt you coming, just as my ancestors predicted. I greet you with gladness for you have come to bring balance back to our lives."

Kadar watched the Voices exchange glances, hesitating, undecided if the man was a threat.

"How can we trust you?" the Templar asked.

"I have already released the wards hiding the path to the Obsidian Temple as a show of faith," Amon said.

"You could kill me and travel down on your own. But I have told the temple master that friends of mine, scholars, are coming. She will be suspicious if you arrive alone."

The Templar looked around at the other Voices.

"What choice do we have?" the Herald said. "We will be cautious, but after all, we came to the desert on the word of the Descendants."

Amon nodded. "I have a midmeal waiting for you before we head into the chasm. Please dismount. Once you are done we will proceed. We will be at the temple before nightfall."

The party dismounted.

"Who is this man? What is he saying?" Onyeka asked, unable to understand the Northern tongue.

"It is not for you to worry about," Amon told Onyeka in her tongue. "You can eat and return to your people if you wish. We can guide them from here."

"Maybe that would be better," Kadar said, not wanting her to get hurt. "I will meet up with you when I finish here."

"Where you go, I go," she said simply. "Is this part of your promise to them?"

Kadar nodded.

"Then we will eat and go to this temple and see what happens," she said.

While they ate, Amon spoke to the Voices in Northern tongue, leaving Onyeka out of the conversation.

"The statues are in the temple, filled with your

powers," he said. "But I hope you know what to do with them."

"I cannot feel anything in the chasm," Parasu said through Jonas. "It is shielded."

Amon nodded. "Hundreds of *feli* make the chasm their home," he said. "In the fall they travel here and use the temple as a den to raise their young. They are natural shields."

"That must be how the One hid this place for so long," the Templar said. "Will they act against us?"

"They are not bonded with any humans," Amon said. "I have come and gone and they have not harmed me. You will not have to hide your *feli*; they will blend in with the other felines."

"Who is down at the temple?" the Herald asked. "Will we need to fight our way through?"

"The people are scholars and clerics, not fighters, and will not see through your disguises," Amon said. "They burn incense in the temple and chant scriptures. The Southerners sent all their fighters to meet your army. It was a very clever ruse on your part to use the army as a feint as you came in from the foothills. They were not expecting that."

"Neither were we," the Crone muttered to Kadar as she ate another fig.

"They might resist," Amon said. "But we can enthrall them to give you time to gain back your deities' true powers. The Obsidian Guards will be the only real struggle, but Voras easily disabled them this past spring. Your coming heralds a new era of harmony and wholeness the world has needed. When our gods are sundered, nothing can ever be whole. When our gods are whole, the world knows peace and harmony."

"And those supposed 'Chosen people' of the prophecy?" the Templar asked. "Where are they?"

Amon smiled smugly. "They were with the warriors of the One who died. I convinced the warriors of the One that their prophecy was incomplete and they were needed against the army, not here."

Kadar's anger flared. This was the man who convinced his grandmother and Sulis that they were important only for their sacrifices.

"You killed my sister," he said, "and my grandmother with your lies. I should never have led these people here. You are all liars."

He started to rise, and Amon grabbed his arm. His body sat itself down, suddenly devoid of will. He struggled against Amon, but he was too powerful. Kadar's body was not his own.

Onyeka rose, her hand on her sword. "What are you doing?" she snarled.

Amon held up a hand. "He grew upset over his sister's death," he said. "I have simply calmed him."

"Kadar," Onyeka asked in Tigu, "what is wrong? What have they done?"

The three guards put their hands on their hilts, and the Templar and Herald were ready to draw as well. Onyeka was outmatched, and Kadar was trapped and could not help her. He could not bear to see her cut down in front of him as Farrah had been.

"I am fine," he choked out. "They mentioned Sulis and I became upset. There is nothing to worry about."

Onyeka nodded shortly and sat beside him, still glancing worriedly at him.

Kadar realized his body was trapped, but not his mind. He reached out quickly with his mind and found another *farspeaker* below in the chasm.

Beware, he shouted at the other mind. *The Voices are at the top of the chasm, coming down! The Descendant has betrayed you!*

We know, a strange voice replied. *The trap is set. Amon is ours. Do not call again; they will hear you.*

Kadar was utterly confused now. He climbed onto his humpback. Amber chose to ride in front of him, but the *feli* of the Voices flowed down the path in front of them, disappearing quickly out of sight as the humpbacks picked their way down the rocky slope.

"They will meet us in the temple," the Herald said.

As they wound down the side of the chasm, Kadar struggled to understand what was happening, who was the enemy. Kadar expected an attack at any moment on the narrow ridge. He hunched his shoulders, expecting arrows to skewer them as they rode.

The top of a large building came into view as they snaked down the winding gorge, and Kadar realized this must be the Obsidian Temple.

The path ended at the bottom of the great circular

gorge. The floor of the gorge was a pitted black slag of solidified molten rock. In the center of the gorge was the temple, hewn out of the same black rock that surrounded them. Even though it was several hours before dusk, the sunlight made it down to the bottom in only a sliver of light. Kadar's eyes adjusted to the dimness of the courtyard, lighted by torches set up all around. Instead of an army waiting at the bottom, people were seated on benches, casually talking or meditating. No one was alarmed by the group's arrival. No one took up arms to attack them.

A tall woman in elaborately patterned robes walked over and greeted them as they dismounted. Amber escaped his arms and trotted away, disappearing into the temple after the deities' *feli*.

"Greetings, pilgrims. I am Sari, the temple master," she said. "Are these the scholars you've been waiting for, Amon?"

He nodded.

"We have had in influx of visitors. We will stable your beasts tonight, but you are expected to care for them. The meal hall is that long hall behind the temple, and late meal is ready. You are expected to contribute to chores. Make yourselves welcome."

"I wish to show them the temple before the meal is served," Amon said casually, and Sari smiled.

"Of course. I will guide you there," Sari said, gesturing for them to follow. "Your Northern friends will have to stay outside. They can rest on the benches or go find food if you like."

The guards looked uncertainly at the Templar, and he waved them toward the benches by the side of the temple, where they could help if the Voices were attacked.

Two Obsidian Guards stood at attention in the doorway. Sari waved them aside.

"These people have been screened by Amon," she told them. The Obsidian Guards nodded respectfully, and moved into the temple to make way for their party.

The temple was dim and smoky. Kadar could barely make out four statues set around an altar containing an orb of the One that glowed with candlelight from tall candelabra set on either side. Kadar looked down the hall. Two pilgrims knelt in the haze at the altar, wearing dark robes with hoods covering their hair. About a dozen other pilgrims sat cross-legged, meditating back by the walls of the temple. None of them looked up as the Voices walked in. They paused to let their eyes adjust.

"It's so hazy. I can't see anything," the Crone complained with a cough.

"It's partially the incense and candlelight, but mostly all the power contained here," Amon said softly.

Feli lounged everywhere in the spaces that weren't occupied by meditating humans.

The Voices' *feli* rushed up to them, and the hairs on Kadar's arms prickled. He looked over at the Crone, and her eyes were wild and rimmed with red.

"I feel it," Ivanha said, her voice unnatural. "My powers call to me."

Sari turned to them, looking alarmed. Amon touched her and she froze in place. Amon quickly *geased* the two Obsidian Guards. Voras's guards quietly slipped through the doorway to flank the group.

"Quickly now, before anyone realizes what is going on," Amon urged the deities. "I had not expected it to be this easy. Sari was a trusting idiot."

The deities walked swiftly forward, intent on the statues, and Kadar followed. As they approached the altar, Kadar realized that the statues were really larger-than-life human forms: forms of the deities, frozen in time. The deities spread out, drawn to the statues that represented them.

"Hold," Parasu's flat voice stopped the others, who glared at him. "We must use caution. This could be a trap."

"You use caution," Aryn growled. "Nothing can stop us once our powers are regained. The fools have broken themselves on our army and left the door wide open for us."

Voras surged forward, running for his statue, and the others ran as well.

"I see what you do, you will be first to regain your powers and will destroy our statues and trap us forever in this half life!" Ivanha screeched. "You will not keep my powers from me!"

The meditators looked up in alarm at her screech. Voras's guards drew their weapons as the meditators scrambled to their feet. The meditating pilgrims at the altar turned, startled, as the deities rushed toward them. Kadar was shocked to realize that one was Master Anchee. Kadar thought all the Chosen had been killed by the sandstorm rebound. He stumbled and slowed down as the hood fell off the other.

It was Sulis. She was alive. She glared at the deities, and then her brown eyes found his. His world spun and pain flared in his head as she mouthed his name. He collapsed to his knees and fell to the floor.

Tori looked out of the Temple of the One into the hallway as people ran by the door. A strong voice ordered pilgrims visiting the Temple to stand aside.

"What's happening?" she called, as men in red ran through the hallway.

"Forsaken are attacking the main gate," a soldier called. "All fighters and healers are needed."

Tori nodded in satisfaction, watching all the soldiers of Voras and healers of Aryn run through the hallways, rushing to the battle at the northern gate of the city.

She ducked into the Temple of the One. Every Counselor was gathered in the space, seated on meditation cushions while their *feli* reclined beside them. If she reached her senses out she could feel her kinsmen, the Descendants, who gathered in small groups in hostels around the city. Tori knew the fighters among the Descendants would be guarding the shielders as they focused on protecting the city.

"It is time," Counselor Elida said. "Ready yourselves to begin blocking the deities. Quiet your minds and focus. Our greatest moment is at hand."

A *farspeaker* reached to communicate with Tori, and she opened her mind.

The Voices have reached the Obsidian Temple, a Vrishni relayed. *They are entering it right now.*

"They have arrived," Tori told the Counselors as Zara bumped her giant head against her ribs. "The weaving is about to begin. The deities will reach here to find the energy of their followers. We must block each attempt they make to draw energy to escape the trap."

CHAPTER 22

Jonas watched as the other deities rushed their Voices' bodies forward. He could feel the pull of the statue on Parasu. He could feel all the power the statues contained, waiting for them. Something didn't feel right to Jonas, though. So many *feli* in the room confused his senses, but something was wrong. Parasu was firmly in control of Jonas's body, so eager that Jonas could not regain control of his own mind. Jonas could feel how much his deity longed for his sundered powers, wanted to be reunited with them. Parasu's statue was irresistible for him, drawing him as a moth to a flame.

Hold, Jonas screamed at him. *Stop and assess! This could be a trap! It's been too easy, way too easy!*

Parasu heard him and slowed his pace. Jonas could sense how hard it was for the deity to not reach out and reclaim his powers, how much effort it took for Parasu to listen to him and slow down.

You are right. It draws me too much, Parasu said.

"Hold," Parasu's flat voice stopped the others' rush. "We must use caution. This could be a trap."

The other deities mocked Parasu, and then it was a race to see who could get to their statues first. Parasu urgently wanted to reach his statue, to stop the others from destroying his statue if they regained their powers before him. Jonas was barely aware of the pilgrims in the temple shouting as the deities approached. Then the tall sculptured form of Parasu was in front of him, within his grasp. Parasu scanned to see where the other deities were, and a woman standing behind Aryn's statue caught Jonas's attention.

He stopped and stared at Lasha, who looked dismayed to see him. Movement by the Altar of the One caught his eye. It was a man, but beside him was Sulis, who was supposed to be dead. Parasu recoiled, finally realizing that this was a trap and he was surrounded by the Chosen.

Parasu turned away, but a hand grabbed his shoulder. Jonas looked over, into Alannah's eyes. He felt a moment of shocked recognition before she tripped him and shoved him into Parasu's statue, his body hitting the rock hard.

"I'm sorry, Jonas," Alannah said.

Parasu panicked as a whirlpool of energy opened in front of them, sucking Parasu out of Jonas's body. Jonas grabbed for his deity and caught him before he could completely leave the body. His deity clawed his way back, but the statue was linked heavily to Parasu's element of water and Jonas's deity was drowning him, pulling him underwater. Jonas reached his energy out, trying to link to anything that could rescue him and his deity.

A warm, golden energy linked to his, and he tried to drag himself and Parasu from the sucking void.

"You have to let him go, Jonas!" Alannah's voice said roughly. She gasped as Parasu's energy climbed over Jonas's, trying to reach safety. "Remember who you are."

"No, no," Jonas heard a child's voice say. Then Parasu was tossed into the void as something cut through his link to Parasu. Jonas was in his body with a wrench.

He looked up at the statue, now pulsing with Parasu's energy. He reached with his senses to try to bring Parasu out.

"No, no," the girl beside Alannah said. She was holding Kadar's suncat, which stared at him with her piercing blue eyes. "You must not follow."

A wall came between him and his deity. The way to Parasu was blocked. Jonas collapsed beside the statue, his mind battering at the shield.

Sulis watched Kadar crumple to the ground upon seeing her and gasped. Master Anchee grabbed her arm.

"Focus!" he said. "Here they come. Once all the deities are all trapped, we dance."

It went almost as smoothly as planned. The deities were drawn more forcefully to their traps than Sulis believed they would be. Aryn, Ivanha, and Voras reached their statues at about the same time. They did not scream as Clay had—their Voices' bodies simply collapsed, and their malevolent energy filled the void in the mandala. Only Jonas hesitated, seeing Lasha before his deity could become ensnared.

Sulis groaned as Alannah pushed Jonas into the statue and collapsed with him, linked. Sulis would not dance until she knew if Alannah could escape.

"That foolish girl," Master Anchee said softly. "She will ruin everything."

Sanuri ran over to Parasu, and Alannah came back with a gasp. She dragged Jonas away from Parasu's pulsing statue, out of the mandala. Ava redrew the lines of energy that he and the other Voices had thinned and smeared.

The temple had come alive as the Kabandha warriors flooded in. Sari and the Obsidian Guards dropped their pretense of being frozen and quickly subdued Voras's men, holding them captive. Sulis had a hard time focusing in the chaos. Bringing her mind to the dance seemed impossible.

"We must dance," Master Anchee said, gasping as he stepped into the first segment of the mandala. Sulis understood why when she took her position as Sanuri climbed to the top of the Altar of the One, holding Amber. The space was filled with pulling, tearing energy that wanted to escape, wanted to hurt those who held it captive. The personalities of the deities reached out of the statues. The deities were trying to find the energy to escape the trap by sucking their acolytes dry. The soldiers Sari had captured collapsed as Voras drained their energy.

The deities raged when they were blocked from draining the acolytes in the Northern Temples, beating at the shields between them and the energy they needed to escape. The Descendants of the Prophet and the Counselors in the Northern Territory had blocked the deities from drawing that energy.

"Sulis, take heart," Ashraf called to her as he slid a shield between her and the grasping energy of the deities. She looked to find him on his knees, taking the assault for her. Djinn paced the edge of the mandala, clearly wanting to come protect her. Ashraf sent her warm energy of love as Sari ran to give extra energy to him and Djinn settled beside him.

"Dance," Anchee yelled, bringing her mind to the mandala. She stood still a moment, closed her eyes and breathed, finding her center in the middle of this raging storm. She looked inward at the energy around her and danced—starting in warrior pose and shifting her feet as she siphoned the energy through her middle chakra, taming it to throw to Anchee. She didn't have time to see if he sent the energy to her grandmother. The dance was slower than she expected, every move like she was trying to move against a high wind that wanted her to hold still. The energy in the mandala changed when she danced the water energy of Parasu, which attempted to freeze her with cold and ice. She flung herself through Voras's flaming energy, which tried to burn her. Ivanha rooted every step to the earth, taxing her flagging strength, every footstep heavy. Aryn succeeded in blowing Sulis off course—she lost her balance and stumbled, smudging an energy line.

Sulis could feel Aryn surging forward in triumph, but Ava was redrawing the line before Aryn could escape, as Sulis paused and gasped. Sulis could not say if Ava was beside her physically or energetically, but she gathered her courage and danced. Her legs burned and her breath wheezed in her lungs like she was climbing to the summit of a tall mountain. She did not know where she was in the mandala, only that it seemed endless. It would never end and she would die dancing. She gasped as her thigh cramped, but she made her body move smoothly in spite of the pain.

Anchee faltered. His energy, linked to hers, dimmed. She spun on her mandala and made the next pose a gentle yin energy pose she could hold longer. She paused. Her eyes closed, she felt for him. She could not spare energy, but someone bolstered his energy and he echoed her pose. They stood still amid the half-tamed energy, with the deities wailing and beating at their prisons, until he recovered. Then she danced again.

She despaired as her energy flagged and Ashraf could not give her more. She dug deeper and deeper into her own body, trying to keep her movements precise. Then she saw the brilliant space that was the end of the mandala, the completion of the great spell she and Anchee were laying on the deities. She tried not to rush, to complete each space and flow gently—but she was so tired. She pushed the last of her energy to Master Anchee and collapsed, prostrated beside the Altar of the One.

Sulis raised her head wearily. In practice, they had sent energy to Grandmother to keep her dancing, but Sulis had nothing left to give. Her grandmother whirled, spinning the energy and feeding it to Sanuri, who sat above Sulis, humming happily, her hands dancing as she wove a great tapestry of energy. There was so much energy to be spun and woven, and Sulis worried that the ritual could never be completed.

Sulis looked outside the mandala. Palou was focused on Grandmother with his hands raised, feeding energy to her with a *feli* pressed against his side. His hands were slightly translucent as he fed his life force to Grandmother.

He was so focused that he did not see the body of Voras's guardsman beside him. He was so focused that he did not see it come to life and crawl forward, drawing a knife. Sulis cried a warning, but all that came out was a hoarse whisper. The guard plunged the knife in the back of Palou's knee and Palou fell. The guard stabbed him again and again.

Grandmother howled, faltering as her beloved died. The energy began to rebound in on itself, upon all of the Chosen.

Kadar regained consciousness and watched his sister dance some invisible pattern in the stone. His brain saw her as a dancing corpse, as both dead and alive, and he dropped his head into his hands, ignoring the chaos around him. Onyeka knelt beside him.

"You were blocked," she whispered. "It was your idea. Your sister is alive. If you break the block in your mind you will find your twin bond. Your grandmother is alive as well—look, she is dancing."

Kadar looked up as his grandmother whirled past. She was spinning, moving counter-sunwise around the statues. Onlookers formed a loose ring around her path, stepping out of her way if she came close. Ashraf was on his knees, surrounded by people, and Lasha was on the other side of the circle with Ava and Dani by her side. The people around Kadar had their hands raised, shielding, and a man beside Kadar collapsed.

"The warriors of the One around us are helping shield against the deities, who are trying to escape by stealing unguarded energy. He gave too much energy to the shield," Onyeka said. "Kadar, your sister is faltering. You must break through the block so you can feed her energy."

Kadar reached for their twin bond, but it no longer existed. He pushed, but nothing came. He turned inward, as Alannah had taught him in order to mind-speak, and he felt something unnatural. A wall hiding something from him. He pounded on it. The mind shield shattered, and he could remember everything. He sighed in relief and once again looked for his twin bond. There was nothing. His link to her was gone.

"The block is gone," he told Onyeka. "But so is my link to Sulis."

Onyeka frowned, looking past him to Sulis, and opened her mouth. Her eyes widened.

"No," Onyeka breathed and leapt forward.

Kadar watched as she skewered one of Voras's soldiers, kicking his knife away as she pulled him off a man he'd stabbed. She turned the other man over, and Kadar realized it was Palou.

Kadar stood as Grandmother howled. Her spinning faltered and a crushing weight bore down on him. People around Kadar groaned, feeling it as well. Grandmother bared her teeth in a fierce grimace and spun again. She gave a fierce desert war cry and Kadar stepped forward, echoing the cry.

Grandmother reached for his energy, connecting to him through their family bond. He gave willingly, and she sucked the energy out of him. He reached out to other energy and found Onyeka by his side. Grandmother's spinning picked up pace and settled into a rhythm as they fed her energy, gave her new life.

Kadar looked for his sister and found her kneeling by the Altar of the One. She was gazing up at Sanuri, who had Amber on her lap and was radiant with light. All the energy was being fed through Sanuri and she was ablaze with it. She giggled and sang loudly and tunelessly as her hands wove a complicated pattern in front of her, weaving a great tapestry Kadar could not see.

Grandmother circled one more time around the conflagration. She then paused, made a complicated series of mudras with her hands and arms, and collapsed. She stopped pulling energy from Kadar, and he toppled over, surprised by his sudden weakness. He propped himself on his elbow as Alannah stepped up to the altar.

Sulis could feel the braid of energy Sanuri had woven. It connected from the deities to the One. The girl had to keep reweaving it as the deities ripped at the fabric, pulling and tearing themselves away time after time. Sanuri had woven herself into the braid, was as much a part of the fabric as the One and the deities. Sulis was wondering how Sanuri would extricate herself when Alannah stepped up and slapped her hands on the orb. She spoke the first words of the final ritual.

As the words of power spilled over Sulis, she became aware of Amon motioning to her.

"Get up," he insisted. Dully, Sulis obeyed, carefully stepping outside the mandala at his urging. Ashraf staggered up to her and put his arms around her. Nothing had ever felt as good as his body against hers.

"Get out," Amon snapped, pushing both of them toward the door. "Take your beloved and go. Leave the temple before everything collapses. Get everyone out."

Sulis realized that the crowd was fleeing the temple. The wild *feli* were already gone. Djinn nudged Nuisance and they wormed their way through the crowds, following. Sulis looked around for Kadar and stumbled on leaden legs to him. He and a tall Tigu woman had Grandmother's arm, urging her away from Palou's body. Ashraf took Grandmother's other arm and he and Kadar pulled her to the entrance. Sulis helped Lasha and Dani support Anchee, who looked fifty years older.

Alannah spoke the final words of the ritual. The One's orb shone so brightly the entire temple was illuminated. Sulis squinted as she looked back and watched Amon shove Alannah away from the orb and raise his hands, stepping into the mandala, into the maelstrom of woven energy. Alannah sprinted toward them as Amon uttered three words that Sulis had never before heard.

The universe shook. They staggered and fell. Then Alannah was with them. She was urging Jonas forward in front of her, urging all of them forward as the earth shook and groaned. Wind howled through the temple as the walls cracked around them. They dove through the doorway and pushed farther on into the courtyard, into the mass of screaming people. The ground shook so hard they could no longer walk forward. The sides of the chasm collapsed and they could hear people who had gotten too close screaming as the rocks smashed into the dormitories and food hall.

Sulis looked back to the Obsidian Temple. The temple walls had cracked, the roof was collapsing in. A geyser of water shot out of the top of the building before being cut off by the collapse of the side walls. A crack in the earth opened under the temple and half of it collapsed into the hole.

"Sanuri!" Ava screamed. Sulis realized the girl had not come out of the building with them.

"Amon is in the destruction, too. We must go back," Sulis gasped, but Alannah shook her head.

"Sanuri is woven back with the One," she said. "And Amon knew he would be destroyed with the temple. It was his role, his sacrifice as a Descendant. They are gone."

"So this is it?" Sulis said. "I don't feel any different. Did it happen? Did we succeed or was this all for nothing? I thought I'd know."

The earth stilled. Sulis ducked her head down into her hands as heavy dust fell on them from the air above the chasm. She tried not to choke on it as more and more came, burying them. Finally it stopped raining dirt and she pulled herself up. What remained of the chasm was piled with fine silt and the survivors were shrugging it off, standing, and looking around. The last rays of sunlight filtered through the silt in the air, able to enter the chasm because of the collapsed sides. Sulis looked around for Djinn and found him shaking himself off a few feet away beside Yaslin, who was now more brown than white. Sulis helped Jonas and Alannah stand, brushing them off. Kadar was dusting Grandmother off and Sulis stepped forward to help.

Sulis was distracted from her grief by Alannah's hand on her elbow.

"Do you feel it?" Alannah asked. She was caked

with dirt from head to toe, but a smile wreathed her face. "Look at the energy. Do you feel it?"

Sulis closed her eyes and extended her senses. The air around her seemed to radiate. A beautiful light glowed where many different strands of energy had been before. It pulsed with a welcoming light.

"We did it, Sulis," Alannah said, her face ecstatic. "The deities are no longer separate. The One is whole once again!"

Beside Alannah, Jonas dropped to his knees and wept. His *feli* bumped his head on Jonas's shoulder, and Jonas turned and cried into the feline's fur.

"We need to find some torches and get them lighted," Sari called to the survivors. "Night is coming quickly and we need to tend to the wounded."

Abram sighed as he set his pack down by the oasis. It had been a long, hard trek to get here and he wanted to cry with relief. Dusk was falling, but tonight they would have water and a safe place to rest.

"Do not get comfortable," Turo warned. "Something is happening down in the valley of the One."

"At the Obsidian Temple?" Master Yaoni asked. "The weaving has begun, then. Are we too late to help our companions?"

Master Yaoni, master of the archives at Kabandha, had been the only master still alive when the sandstorm had worn itself out—he did not work with energy. He'd had to make the difficult decision to leave the warriors where they'd died and press on to the greater oasis by the Obsidian Temple. They did not know the fate of the healers and the advanced cohort.

The Tigu's water sense had saved them. The desert was unrecognizable—pathways and markers had been obliterated by the storm. But the Tigus knew where to find the water and led them here.

A Tigu woman looked up at the mountains and pointed. They were trembling, as though a giant hand were shaking them. Turo backed away, still looking at the water of the oasis. It had begun to rise.

"The water is coming," Turo said. "We need to run."

They ran back the way they had just traveled. The ground began to shake under them, and Abram stumbled and fell several times. A glance behind showed the water flooding toward him, so he staggered on. They neared the waymarker to the Obsidian Temple and halted. The sides of the gorge were collapsing in—the path down had been sheared away.

"Get down," Master Yaoni said. They huddled together beside large boulders as dirt rained down and the world seemed to shake and collapse around them. Night fell and they still huddled, listening in darkness to water that should not exist, and wondering what would be left when the sun rose again.

The Temple at Illian was in chaos. The acolytes had felt the weaving, had felt their deities dissolve. Tori wasn't certain if they thought their deities had died or if they knew they'd been woven back into the One. Tori could hear running footsteps as acolytes fled their altars, and *feli* now guarded the doorways to the Temple of the One as the Counselors tended their wounded.

Tori flinched as Elida put a hand on the knife wound in her side, making the pain flare before it subsided. Elida sighed tiredly and released the energy, healing the wound.

"That will stop it from bleeding more and start the healing," she told Tori. "But I am too weary to heal it the rest of the way."

"You'd think the One would reward us with energy for making her whole again," Tori said, looking over at the altar, which pulsed with light. "Instead of making us struggle."

"The One is probably as shocked by this as we are," Elida said. "She will have to adjust to this newness of being before she can reach out to help us mortals once again. I don't know how long we will be without her guidance, but we must make do with what we have."

"You are wounded!" Aaron said from the doorway to the Temple.

Tori blinked and realized half the faces in the Temple were now Southerners. More hours had passed than Tori had realized. She'd heard scuffles in the street of guards against Forsaken, but she'd been focused on defending Counselors against fleeing acolytes from altars of the deities. The Forsaken army must have pushed through Voras's soldiers and made it to the Temple. Aaron was standing beside her and she hadn't seen him walk in. She was more tired than she realized.

Tori made a face at Aaron. "The Mother Superior slipped past the guarding *feli* and got me," she told him. "It became messy when the soldiers of Voras realized we were blocking them from saving their deities and came rushing to the Temple."

"They were overpowering us until that point. We were fast on their heels," Aaron said, "But obviously not fast enough."

Tori shrugged. "The war was already over at that point," she said. "We'd blocked the deities. We lost only a few Counselors in the attacks that followed."

Aaron frowned. "We encountered acolytes fleeing the Temple and we let them go," he said. "If I had known they'd fought you, we would have detained them. All the altars of the deities are stripped of anything of value and have been abandoned."

Elida stood. "We know. We watched them leave. I hope they'll simply disperse into the city and try to live normal lives," she said.

"I hope," Tori said with a sigh, but she realized it probably wouldn't be that easy. Tori had felt the weaving and knew the deities were gone—but doubted anyone in the Northern Territory would be willing to accept it. The lives of the common people in the North were based on worshipping the four deities. They would look to anyone who could tell them how to live their lives now. Tori could only hope that good, moral leaders would arise out of that confusion.

"What happened in the streets of Illian?" she asked.

"The viceroy and his heir are dead," Aaron said. "They rode against us and fell when the soldiers abandoned them and the city guard to race back to the Temple. Have you heard anything from Kadar or Sulis in the desert? I still feel the link with my mother, but I don't know if the rest of my family survived."

Tori shook her head. "I can't even communicate with other *farspeakers* in Illian. The intense energy pull of the weaving and the collapse of the energy of the deities has created such interference we may not be able to communicate that far for weeks."

"Who is left to lead the city?" Elida asked sharply.

Aaron bowed to her slightly.

"You are," he said simply. "They will need strong guidance. That is why we came here. The sun is beginning to rise. There are people panicking in the street, waking up and realizing something is wrong. I've got my men keeping them away, but they think the Southern Territory has invaded. The townspeople are beginning to mob the Temple. We need someone to speak to them, calm them. People trust you. Be their voice, now."

Tori grinned as denial turned to resignation on Elida's face.

"What are you grinning at?" she snapped. "I'm designating you my second in command until Alannah comes back. Come on, we need to address our people."

Now it was Tori's turn to feel chagrin as she tiredly followed in Elida's wake. A hand supported her elbow and she realized that Aaron was parting the crowd around her. She mouthed her thanks.

"It is time for the Northern and Southern Territories to become reunited," he said.

Tori fervently hoped that such peace was ahead for their world but feared it would be a long, difficult recovery. She held her head high as she and Elida stepped out to face their people.

CHAPTER 23

Sulis lifted a sack of flour from the pantry they'd dug out of the rubble and handed it to Ashraf, who handed it to the next person down the line. They'd been able to dig out the collapsed structure of the kitchen and meal hall and were lifting out the supplies to see what was still usable.

"Sari sent us as relief. She says to take a break," a man said, and Sulis saluted him and winced as she stood, her back hurting from bending and lifting so long.

Ashraf put an arm around her waist as they walked to the cleared area where food was set up. It was the second morning after the weaving and the sun shone brightly down on them. Sulis looked around at the rockslides that now made up the sides of the chasm. The chasm was more open and the sides were no longer sheer cliffs. Instead it was rock, sharp fields of rock that jutted and sloped upward over many lengths. Sulis sighed.

"Are you well?" Ashraf asked.

"Yes, but I don't know how we will ever escape this pit," she said.

"Sari is sending out people to explore possible routes," Ashraf reminded her. "We'll be on that duty this afternoon. We have food enough to last us for at least a ten-day and a raging river is coming out of the chasm. I am certain people at the oasis will come look for us."

"Did anyone survive?" Sulis asked, despairing. "Only a handful survived down here. And if they did survive—can they come for us? We should be able to see mountains above us, Ashraf. But I see only sky. Our *farspeakers* can't find anyone. What has happened to our world?"

Ashraf stopped and took her into his arms. "Our people are still alive, Sulis. The *farspeakers* can't talk to each other because of the energy disturbance. You know what the healer said—this despair is from being drained so deeply of your energy. I have to believe my family is still alive, as we are."

Sulis wiped her eyes. "I hate this," she said. "I'm not used to feeling so old and sad."

"It has aged us, yes," Ashraf said as he pulled her forward. "But you are not old yet, love."

Sulis had to agree as they came upon Master Anchee, who was being aided by Lasha. He and Grandmother had both been aged terribly by the energy drain. Master Anchee had gone from being a vibrant, active older man to a palsied ancient in the space of an evening. The healer said he'd recover somewhat, but would never be the same healthy man he had been before. Grandmother had recovered better, but grief and exhaustion had made her frail. She did not protest when the healer told her and Master Anchee to rest rather than help with the cleanup.

Kadar was still tending the smoker he and Onyeka had created. The stables had been too close to the side walls of the chasm. All their beasts had been killed and Kadar had been determined to recover as much meat as he could and preserve it. He'd been thrilled that one of the first things they'd discovered in the kitchen was a barrel of salt he could use to preserve the meat they needed to survive. Sulis couldn't help checking inside her mind for him—but their twin bond was gone, probably forever.

Sulis glanced around the chasm. The healer had set up a space for the wounded in the shade of a fallen boulder. A dozen new wounded had been injured by falling rocks or had sprained backs and ankles over the past day. There were some people resting in makeshift tents and others busily tallying supplies. In all, about forty-three people had survived the weaving and the collapse after. They had numbered over a hundred before. Sulis had lighted a candle for Palou, Sanuri, and Amon at their mourning ceremony last night.

"Sulis!" Ava called and ran to hug her. "Midmeal is

served by the rockslide, where it isn't so hot," she said, and she led the way.

Ava and Dani were the only ones among the Chosen who weren't depleted and depressed. Dani was directing the group's scouting efforts, and Ava had taken over meal planning. Grandmother was sitting on a rock beside the cook fire, absently petting Djinn's head. Djinn's eyes were half-lidded with pleasure.

"I'm going to apprentice with Grandmother once we get out of here," Ava said as she spooned stew into dented metal bowls. "She says I don't have to return to the North if I don't want to."

"I think she has earned a spot as my apprentice," Grandmother said, giving Sulis a weary smile. "I could use a helper when we return to Shpeth."

Sulis smiled to hear her grandmother make plans for the future. When they'd dug her out, she had whispered that they should have let her die with Palou. Yesterday Sulis had worried she would will herself to sleep and never wake up. Today her energy was returning, and she had more sparkle in her eyes.

"I'll help you and Sulis," Ava said, making motions for them to eat. They sat on the ground beside Grandmother. "You are coming to Shpeth with us, aren't you, Sulis?"

Grandmother looked at Sulis, who couldn't tell if her grandmother's expression was hopeful or dismissive. Sulis and Ashraf had already spoken about this, talked about what their future would hold.

"I will," Sulis told Ava. "But first, we have to look for

Ashraf's family in Frubia. Once he is certain they are safe and we have a bonding ceremony with them, we will return to Shpeth for good and think about a family."

"And an empire," Ashraf murmured in her ear.

Ava cheered, and a smile pulled around Grandmother's lips.

Sulis addressed Grandmother directly. "I'm not certain I can ever follow in your footsteps and be the leader you have been, but I'm willing to try. I'd like to apprentice to you as well, Grandmother."

Grandmother ducked her head as her eyes filled with tears, and Sulis hugged her.

"I'm only a silly old woman," Grandmother said, waving her off. "But my grandchildren have made me prouder than any woman has the right to be."

"Kadar isn't coming back to Shpeth," Sulis told her. "He plans on settling Datura and himself in Antajale, if it still remains."

"I know," Grandmother said. "I knew when he went to the Tigus, his heart would stay with them."

"He is torn right now between making certain Datura is okay and going with Onyeka to see what happened to the Tigu city of Antajale and her tribe," Ashraf said.

Grandmother nodded. "Kadar worries about his daughter. I believe Tsangia is far enough away from this center of destruction that Datura is safe. Hopefully the energy will settle and we will be able to find people in the surrounding areas to tell us what happened outside this chasm."

"Sulis, Ashraf—just the people I was looking for," Dani called, and Sulis looked over to find him striding toward them, Lasha in tow.

"I think we've found a path up," he said. "It's not an easy route. We won't know if the way is passible unless we take a party out that can hike a couple days. The wild *feli* keep darting up that way, so I think it leads somewhere. I'm getting the more able-bodied to go. Alannah is staying here with Jonas, who isn't up to travel, but Kadar and Onyeka are coming, and I'd like you and Ashraf to come as well, if you're game."

"I want to go!" Ava said.

Dani shook his head. "You're needed here to help Sari organize."

"Can you help with Master Anchee while I'm gone?" Lasha asked hopefully. "It would be a relief knowing someone is looking after him."

"Yes, of course," Ava said. "I'll take care of him and Grandmother. They'll be so energized by the time you get back, you won't know them."

"I can hope," Lasha said, sadly. "I would like that very much."

"Kadar is digging through the recovered tack to find some saddlebags we can use to carry supplies, and I'm trying to locate some rope," Dani said. "I'd like to get going soon after midday, so the edge we're climbing won't be in the searing sun."

Ashraf stood and handed his empty bowl to Ava. "I'll help Kadar pack," he said.

"Have you spoken with Sari yet?" Sulis asked. Dani

shook his head. "I'll talk to her, make certain she's fine with us taking off like this."

They met at the far edge of the chasm and divided up supplies. Sulis grabbed one of the packs, and Ashraf took it from her and handed her a loop of rope and a waterskin.

"You're still recovering," he said. "Are you sure you're up to this?"

Sulis nodded. "I think it's exactly what I need," she told him. "I feel less despairing if I'm doing something. I want to get out of this chasm, see how things have changed."

They wove their way upward. Dani was right—*feli* lounged around the path and darted upward, ducking out of sight as their group passed by. Djinn and the other Chosen *feli* loped ahead and were soon out of sight among the rocks.

Kadar sighed and Sulis glanced over at him.

"Never thought I'd miss that annoying little cat, but my shoulder is too light now," Kadar said sadly. Amber had not made it out of the temple. Alannah suspected that she had rejoined the One with Sanuri.

A layer of dirt had fallen over everything and made the rocks more slippery rather than less. It obscured the edges of the obsidian rocks. Sulis winced as she hit her shin on a black rock. Onyeka sliced her arm on a sharp point of obsidian and cursed roundly in Tigu as Kadar laughed at her language and wrapped the cut.

They created their own path, weaving between rocks. Dani planted colorful strips of torn cloths between rocks, marking the path back. They helped each other over large rocks, continuing to spiral upward.

Dani found a place among the rocks to camp for the evening and they chewed on dried humpback strips without a fire. They'd gone far enough up that the rocks were no longer the black obsidian, and were less sharp to lie on.

Lasha sat silently. She hadn't spoken much on the hike, only responding to Dani's commands with one-word answers. Sulis sat beside her and nudged her.

"You're so quiet," Sulis said. "That isn't like you. Are you ill?"

Lasha glanced over at her and Sulis could barely make out her silhouette in the falling darkness.

"Alannah plans on going to Illian and taking Jonas with her. They'll be staying with the Temple," Lasha said.

"If anything remains of the Temple," Sulis said.

"She wants me to go with her but, Sulis, I don't really want to return," she said softly. "I don't know where I belong."

"You've always wanted to see the world," Sulis said. "Come with Ashraf and me when we go to Frubia," Sulis said. "Maybe you'll decide you want to go back north, or maybe you'll find something to keep you here."

Lasha looked over at her, and Sulis could see her indecision.

"It will be dangerous," Sulis warned. "We don't know if the oases still exist or what we will find as we travel. But if you decide you love to travel, you can always hire on with our caravan. Ashraf plans on rebuilding the routes."

Lasha nodded. "Maybe I will travel with you, if I won't be considered a pest," she said. "You're right, I have some thinking to do."

"Ashraf thinks we'll have several people with us, wanting to return to Frubia to see if their families are safe, so don't worry about disturbing us," Sulis said.

Onyeka spoke up from Lasha's other side. "And if you are not happy in Frubia, you should come to join the Tigus. You have a fierce heart, yes? You would be welcome with us."

Lasha grinned at that. "Can you picture me riding to visit my parents in Illian, armed with a curved sword and Tigu tattoos on my arms?"

They laughed at the image and turned in.

Dani woke them at first light, and the way became steeper. The *feli* they followed could scramble up easily onto rock ledges that they had to carefully find footholds and handholds to climb. They rested often as their already drained energy flagged.

"Is it getting dark already?" Onyeka asked, puzzled.

"It's getting cloudy," Kadar said, glancing up. He looked at Sulis in wonder. "Those look like rainclouds."

Late in the day they reached a rocky outcropping. Dani scouted around it, looking for handholds or something to grapple with the rope and hook. He growled in frustration.

"Where are the *feli* when you need them to find you

a path?" he asked. "We may need to double back and find a way around this."

Sulis realized it was true—the *feli* had disappeared for most of the afternoon. She'd assumed it was because they were resting in the heat of the day, but maybe their party had taken the wrong route.

"Hush," Onyeka said, suddenly drawing her dagger. "I hear something."

They quieted. The group stared around at each other, listening. All was silent, not even a breeze stirring against the rocks. Then they heard it—distant voices, above them and farther south along the chasm. Kadar's face split in a grin and they all cheered.

"Hello!" Kadar yelled as loudly as he could. "Who is up there?"

No one responded, and the voices receded slightly.

Onyeka gave a great desert war whoop, and Kadar, Ashraf, and Sulis joined in until the chasm echoed with the sound. Dani and Lasha grinned.

There was a pause, and then a war whoop came down to them.

They played a game of call and response, climbing over rocks under the rock shelf, to get closer to the people above them.

There was never a break in the outcropping above them as they walked, but they reached a point where the other group was right above them.

A dark face poked over the cliff, the man lying flat on the rock to look over at them. It was their cousin, Abram.

"It's Kadar and Sulis," he called excitedly behind him. "Are you all well? We are tying off a rope. Can you make it up to us, or should we come down?"

"We'll come up," Sulis called. It wasn't that high, only lacking in handholds they could climb. "I want out of this place," she told the others, who nodded in agreement.

Sulis was next to last as they used the rope to climb the rocky face. Abram pulled her up onto the shelf and embraced her enthusiastically at the top.

"I knew you were alive," he said. "Even when we found the path down collapsed and they told me no one could have survived that energy blast."

"You must have inherited Grandmother's energy linking talent," Sulis said as he helped Ashraf onto the shelf and ushered both of them to his group. Half the rescue party were Tigus, and Onyeka was hugging a tall older Tigu man.

"That's her father, Turo," Kadar told her. "Abram says we are close to the surface. They'd just found a path down and hiked a ways when they reached this outcropping."

Sulis eagerly followed the group, looking around at the changed landscape. Though they were close to the surface, she did not see the craggy mountains looming overhead. They reached a final ledge and Ashraf heaved himself up, then turned and gave Sulis his hand, helping her crawl out.

"By the One," Kadar said softly, and she stood and looked around.

The tall cliffs of the mountains were gone. It looked like a giant hand had knocked them over, leaving jagged hills behind. Rocks were strewn on vast fields to the south of the black hills. Off in the distance, Sulis could see a golden light and smoke at the top of one of the taller hills, molten rock pouring down the side.

"Our city," Onyeka breathed, turning to her father. "Was it destroyed?"

"We don't know," Turo said. "The warriors of the One sent their energy channelers to the city before the weaving. We pray to the One they were able to protect our tribes. Look how all the rocks settled on the south side. We think that was from the shielding they set up."

"Sulis," Ashraf said. "Turn around."

Sulis tore her eyes from the decimated mountain and turned.

"What?" she murmured, and moved around a large rock in her way.

There was a great lake spreading down the valley, clear off into the distance. Sulis could see the way-marker to the path they were on sticking out of the shallows closest to them. A large camp was set up a short way from them, spreading around the edges of the lake.

Abram stepped up beside her. "Our group had barely made it to the oasis when the weaving began. When we felt energy being drawn, and the ground shook as the mountains collapsed, suddenly water spewed out of the earth, like it was pulled to the surface by a great force," he said. "We grabbed what supplies we could and ran, but some people were too slow and drowned. We ran clear to the waymarker and could still hear water rushing in the dark. When the sun came up, we saw the lake. We don't know how far it goes."

"Any other surprises?" Sulis asked.

Abram shrugged. "We don't know. We still haven't been able to communicate with people far away," he said. "The energy is too unstable. We don't know what happened to our healers and the warriors of the One who were closer to the deities' army during the sandstorm. We've sent out runners in each direction. Until they return or we can *farspeak* again, we don't know how much our world has changed. Come, Master Yaoni will want to see you and hear that some of his friends survived. You must have quite a tale to tell."

"We certainly do," Sulis murmured to Ashraf as they walked toward the camp. "How are we going to get around this lake to go to Frubia?"

"We'll manage," he said with a grin. "It will be a new adventure, exploring this changed world.

"A new adventure indeed," Lasha said, stepping up beside them. "We must be completely crazy."

Sulis glanced between them and grinned. "I can't imagine better people to go exploring with," she said.

They paused and looked up as large raindrops began falling on them. Ashraf grabbed her hand and she grabbed Lasha's and they ran laughing to the tents and people waiting below.

EPILOGUE

Djinn watched his people run to the human-made shelters, his tail lashing at the indignity as he considered the rain. Alta swatted at his twitching tail and dashed ahead, plunging into the waters of the lake for a swim. Pax joined her and they splashed in the shallow waters together.

Danger had passed. The One had given all his most faithful companions a choice—go back to the wild and live free, or stay with their humans. The *feli*'s vow to protect the humans from the deities was fulfilled. They were free. Djinn knew that many *feli* had returned to the wilds around them, especially those who resided in the stinky, closed-in city.

But Djinn knew his people would be lost without him. They were so clumsy, these gawky two-leggers, so much like the *feli* cubs before they gained their first growth. And Djinn did like his chin scratches and belly rubs. Humans could be terribly useful. He would be lonely without his Sulis, and her mate was respectful enough to him. And they did odd things that somewhat baffled him, but also kept things interesting.

The other *feli* of the Chosen agreed with him. They were lucky to have interesting humans to bond with. They would see what these interesting humans did in this new world.

Djinn's ears pricked forward as he saw movement in the rock. An unwary hare peered out at him and he gave chase, finally stretching cramped legs as he overtook the creature.

A successful hunt, water to play in with his *feli* companions, and a human to squeal in protest as he lay his wet body down against hers in the night. Such silliness to worry about the future when now was here. Djinn gave a great sigh, laid his head on Sulis's chest, and purred as she stroked him behind the ears.

ACKNOWLEDGMENTS

Wow, the Desert Rising series is completed! I could not have done it without the guidance of my wonderful editor Rebecca Lucash and the entire staff of Harper Voyager who brought Sulis, Kadar, and Djinn to life. And, of course, thanks to my first reader Janice Berry Paganini who led me in the right direction once again.

I'd like to thank all my friends in my yoga community for keeping me centered and sane. A special thanks to Rebekah Walters for bringing Djinn to life in fused glass, to Judy Lensing and Rose Beach for being number one fans, and Emily Baxter for creating new fans through her book club. Thanks to Jim Gill with the Dover Public Library and Glen Welsh with The Book Loft of German Village for hosting me, and all the fans and friends who came out to show their support. Huge thanks to all my readers—there would be no Djinn without your love and encouragement.

Much thanks to my family for their love and support through the publishing process. And all my love to Brian for being my support and for driving, coaxing, and loving me through this whole crazy business.

ABOUT THE AUTHOR

KELLEY GRANT grew up in the hills of Ohio's
Amish country. Her best friends were the books she
read, stories she created, and the forest and fields that
inspired her. She and her husband live on a wooded
hilltop and are owned by five cats, a dog, and numerous uninvited critters. Besides writing, Kelley teaches
yoga and meditation, sings kirtan with her husband,
and designs brochures and media.

www.kelleygrantbooks.com

Discover great authors, exclusive offers, and more at
hc.com.